THE
FAMILY
GUEST

BOOKS BY NELLE LAMARR

Jane Deyre

Butterfly

Remember Me

Undying Love

Endless Love

Golden Rules

Golden Vows

That Man Trilogy

That Man: The Wedding Story

That Man: Matrimonial Misadventures

Sex, Lies & Lingerie

Sex, Lust & Lingerie

Sex, Love & Lingerie

Unforgettable

Baby Daddy

THE FAMILY GUEST

NELLE LAMARR

Bookouture

Published by Bookouture in 2023

An imprint of Storyfire Ltd.
Carmelite House
50 Victoria Embankment
London EC4Y 0DZ

www.bookouture.com

ISBN: 978-1-83790-687-1
eBook ISBN: 978-1-83790-686-4

For my family.

PROLOGUE

I didn't mean for them to die.

They were accidents.

At least that's what I told the police.

And that's what I've told myself.

But don't believe a thing.

I've been trapped in a web of secrets and lies.

And can't live with it anymore.

It has to end.

Today, I'm finally going to confess.

To everything.

Every.

Last.

Sin.

And then get down on my knees and beg for forgiveness.

ONE

PAIGE

"There she is!" My mother pointed to a statuesque girl wearing a pink baseball cap standing outside arrivals at LAX's international terminal. Stylishly clad in all white—linen capris, an oversized sweater, and designer mules—she hopped out of the car, taking with her a large homemade sign with lots of red marker hearts that said: *Welcome to LA, Tanya!* It was so tacky I could puke.

Holding it up high with both hands, my mom shouted out Tanya's name at the top of her lungs to get her attention while my dad turned the car off and followed her. Listlessly, I cranked the back passenger door open and joined my parents on the curb. The airport was jam-packed with vehicles and travelers, but we'd managed to score a parking spot close to the terminal. For all I cared, it could have been a mile away. Make that ten. I wasn't looking forward to meeting our exchange student.

My gaze stayed on the girl as she caught sight of us. With a wave and a bright smile, she made her way through the crowd to our car, which we couldn't leave unattended. In the photo my mom had shown me, her hair was shorter, more of a dirty blonde, and she was a bit heavier. But this girl was whippet thin, had long platinum-blonde hair, and was trendily dressed in skinny jeans, a hoodie, and bright white sneakers. Despite being laden with a backpack and a humongous wheelie bag, she had the gait of a supermodel, her stride long and bouncy. From a distance, I thought she looked a bit like my sister, Anabel, except taller, lankier, and blonder. Though to me all blondes looked alike, especially here in Southern California; it was kind of creepy.

Maybe, subconsciously, my mother had been seeking a replacement when she chose to host this exchange student. Trauma, said our family therapist, could have weird lasting effects on us. Us, by the way, consisted of me, my mother, my father, and my little brother, Will, who was away at some interstate robotics conference he couldn't miss. Twelve-year-old Will was a nerd. Our in-house Geek Squad, party of one.

I had pressing things to do too, like seeing my best friend, Jordan, who was leaving for Berkeley tomorrow, and hooking up with my boyfriend, Lance, who'd been away all summer, but my mom had insisted I come to the airport. She was excited for me to meet our exchange student. She was so clueless. I had no interest in another family member, not even a temporary one.

Fifteen months older than me, my sister Anabel had died over two years ago, and I was content being the only daughter. My sister and I were never close. She was my mother's favorite and I didn't hold a candle to her. Not even a close second. "This is my daughter, Anabel," my mom used to say. "And this is my *other* daughter, Paige." I was always the *other* daughter, and still was.

At least for my brother I had always been number one. I loved Will and never wanted to lose him. If something terrible happened to him, I would totally freak.

Weaving through the pack of weary-looking people returning to LA or visiting our City of Angels, which I thought was a ridiculous nickname for this crime-ridden place, Tanya picked up her pace, her wheelie bag beside her. It was one of those sleek, hard-shelled ones. Burgundy red and shiny.

Tanya was at last within breathing distance of us. Placing the sign by her feet, my exuberant mother welcomed her with arms wide open. Letting go of the suitcase handle, our family guest fell right into them. They held each other tightly as if they were two close friends who hadn't seen each other in years. Finally, she broke free.

"I'm so excited to be here, Mrs. Merritt."

"Have you been waiting long? I'm sorry we're late."

"No worries. It's not your fault. Our plane got in a half hour early. And I breezed through customs. I flashed a big smile with a cheery 'hello' and the agent let me right through." She had a charming British accent that sounded a lot like Emma Watson's and a smile that was movie star dazzling. Cheek-to-cheek, with a set of perfect pearly-white teeth. Well, except for a small gap between the two front ones.

Her smile met her eyes. Expecting them to be a greenish-blue like my sister's, I was surprised to discover they were as brown as my dad's. Combined with her thick licorice-black brows, which also resembled his, it made me wonder if she was a natural blonde. Either way, with her willowy body and exotic looks, she was, in a word: beautiful.

"How was your flight, dear?" asked my mom, her eyes still riveted on her. "Oh, and please call me Natalie."

At least she didn't say "Mom." Or Nat, which was reserved for my father, who hadn't said a word yet.

"It was fine, but really long, Mrs. Merritt." She caught herself and giggled. "I mean, Natalie. And by the way, you are *so* pretty! Even prettier in person!"

Freaking kiss-up.

"Oh, please. You're too kind!" My size-four, blonde, blue-eyed mother, a former model, blushed. It was as if, in that second, she and Tanya bonded for life.

I forced myself to say hi, trying to diffuse the attention my mom was lavishing on her.

Our exchange student looked at me and grinned. "You must be Paige. Your mum's told me so much about you."

Inwardly, I cringed. *Like what? She prefers flea market finds to designers and wears Birkenstocks with socks. She eats weird things and needs to lose ten pounds. Oh, and I think she's still a virgin.*

"That's nice." I managed a polite smile. Fake was more like it.

I'm sure my mom had sent her pictures of me, but I didn't hear her telling me *I* was much prettier in person. Probably because I wasn't. I hadn't inherited one bit of my mother's slender beauty. Well, except for her wide-set sapphire-blue eyes. With my riotous auburn hair, square jaw, and big bones, I looked a lot like my father. While he was impossibly handsome, his classic features hadn't translated well on me. *Lost in translation.* Some girls are just lucky and born beautiful. I felt a pinprick of envy as Tanya's chirpy voice cut into my thoughts.

"I can't wait to hang out with you. Maybe we can go shopping together."

The latter was more of a statement than a question.

Sparing me from responding, my mother introduced my father, Matt. Yup, meet my parents. Matt and Nat. I often thought they should open a deli—Matt 'n Nat's. A dry cleaner would work too.

My dad, the successful businessman he was, extended one of his broad, long-fingered hands. (Well, at least I'd inherited those, along with his athleticism, which helped make me a star player on my school's girls' basketball team.) Miss Kiss-Up took it graciously and offered another saccharine smile.

"So nice to meet you, Mr. Merritt."

"Welcome to Los Angeles, Tanya." He kept his gaze on her longer than necessary. I'm sure he was noticing the vague similarity between her and Anabel. As well as the size of her boobs. They were impossible to miss.

"We're looking forward to having you spend your senior year with us."

Speak for yourself, Dad. Tanya was not my idea. Things were just returning to normal (whatever that was) and now there was a new addition offsetting the equation of our family. An unknown variable.

Tanya thanked my father and added, "It's my first time in Los Angeles."

Being the daughter of a diplomat, she must be well-traveled. Yet, oddly, there wasn't a dent on her suitcase. Not even a nick. Maybe it was brand new, and she'd had it plastic-wrapped at Heathrow although I didn't see any baggage tags. Maybe she'd pulled them off, something I always did.

Whatever. My dad responded, "I'm sure both my wife and Paige will love showing you around."

"I can't wait to go to Urban Outfitters!"

Mentally, I rolled my eyes. Given the wealth of attractions LA had to offer, from world-class museums to Hollywood memorabilia, not to mention nearby Disneyland as well as the breathtaking coastline, some retail emporium you could shop at online and could probably find in London wouldn't be high on my list of priorities. Her interests were obviously different from mine.

My father craned his neck to check on our car. It was still parked where we'd left it. But not far behind it was an airport police patrol car. "We'd better get going before I get a ticket. The airport police are very strict about how long you can remain parked curbside."

He offered to take Tanya's suitcase, but she told him she could manage it. Together, we hurried back to the car and got there just before we got ticketed. I watched as my dad pushed down the handle of the bag and then loaded it into the trunk of his shiny black BMW 750i.

I was surprised by how effortlessly he lifted the big red suitcase. My six-foot-two father ran, swam, and worked out with weights regularly, but it was almost as if the bag was weightless. Then, he helped Tanya remove her backpack and groaned like he'd pulled a muscle.

"Jeez. What's in this bag? It weighs a ton."

"Oh, just my laptop, some makeup, and my personal stuff."

With that and a grin, she followed me as I slid into the car. As my father pulled away, I wondered: Why did I have a bad feeling about this girl?

TWO

NATALIE

"Oh my gosh! Your house is *so* beautiful. It looks just like one of those mansions you see in fancy design magazines."

I smiled at Tanya's gushing words as we pulled into the driveway. It *was* a beautiful house. An almost six-thousand-square-foot Italianate that dated to 1926 and was located on one of the best streets in Hancock Park. While it wasn't one of those Beverly Hills McMansions favored by the Hollywood elite and "new money" crowd, it was the five-bedroom house of my dreams with its soaring ceilings, grand entryway, and sweeping marble staircase. Many of the fixtures inside the house were the originals, and I'd painstakingly furnished it with Art Deco finds, some reproductions but all true to the period. After I'd recovered from my breakdown, I'd painted the exterior with a fresh coat of Mediterranean-pink paint and replenished the expansive front yard with rows of English roses so it looked more majestic than ever. Our mini LA palace.

As Matt parked the car, I glanced in the rearview mirror at our exchange student. Now wearing her baseball cap backward, I could better see her face. Her long-lashed dark eyes, full, slightly parted lips, high cheekbones, and strong dimpled chin.

Her wide-eyed expression reminded me of Anabel, whose *joie de vivre* had been such a marked contrast to her violent death. With a hard blink, I shoved the horrific memory to the back of my mind.

Beautiful, spirited Tanya was going to breathe some much-needed new life into this house. I was sure of it.

In unison, we undid our seat belts. Well, except for Paige, who sat cross-legged, reading a thick book on Renaissance sculptors. While Tanya and I had animatedly talked about all the things to see and do in Los Angeles as well as the best places to shop on the way back to our house, Paige had kept her nose in her book for the duration of the ride. She'd always been closed off, but had grown more so since her sister's death, something she never talked about. At least to me, that is. Though in all fairness, perhaps I'd never given her the opportunity when she needed it most.

I craned my neck and looked back at my daughter. "Paige, we're home. Please put your book away and unbuckle your seat belt."

Without so much as glancing up at me, she told me she wanted to finish her book and go with her father to pick up Will.

"Fine." I pinched my lips together, not wanting to create a scene in front of Tanya, especially on her first day here. And besides, it would give me some one-on-one time to get to know our new houseguest better.

Matt hopped out of the car first, and with me and Tanya behind him, he brought her two bags to the front door. My eyes stayed trained on my husband's trim physique. Even with his back to me, he cut a beautiful picture in his designer jeans and slim-fitting shirt. Tall, athletically built with broad shoulders, a tapered torso, and long muscular legs, his body was his temple and he worked out religiously. Face-wise, he was movie star handsome with strong chiseled features, thick enviable brows,

and wavy reddish-brown hair that had just started to show signs
of graying, which only added to his allure.

And he was rich. Not billionaire rich, but rich enough to
buy this five-million-dollar house, indulge in luxury cars,
designer clothes, and first-class travel. He put all our kids in
elite private schools and afforded me the lifestyle of a Beverly
Hills housewife—a daily regimen of Soul Cycle or Pilates, shopping on Rodeo, lunch with a friend, a touch-up here and there,
and whatever philanthropic activity fell on that particular day.
My gal pals teased me that they would kill to be married to a
man like Matt. The perfect husband.

Not really. Nor was I the perfect wife. If he knew my
secrets, I'm sure I'd lose him.

But instead, I'd lost Anabel.

I pushed those dark thoughts away as we stepped inside the
house.

Tanya squealed. "It's as pretty inside as it is outside. I love
it! I feel like I can live here forever!"

I did too, I thought, as Matt returned to the black sedan and
backed it up onto the street. Closing the front door, I glimpsed
Paige sitting in the back seat, her nose still buried in her book.
Not once did she make eye contact with me.

Sometimes I thought she hated me.

Only not as much as I sometimes hated myself.

A loud bark followed by the skitter of claws across the
smooth hardwood floor put an end to that thought.

Barreling our way was a huge furry beast. He beelined
straight for Tanya, getting on his hind legs and pawing at her,
yelping madly and almost knocking her down.

Fighting for her balance, Tanya shrieked, her eyes wide
with panic.

Though I knew his barking was innocuous, just his excited
way of greeting any visitor, I'd be freaking out too if I was her.
Our big brown dog looked menacing.

Tanya grew more panicked, her face paling. "Get him off me! I'm afraid of dogs."

"Don't worry. He's really sweet!"

"Please!" A desperate shuddery plea.

I immediately grabbed his red leather collar and tried to pull him off. Well over one hundred pounds and coming up to Tanya's shoulders, he was a force to be reckoned with, even at the age of nine.

"Bear, *off!*" I commanded and instantly he acquiesced. "Good boy!"

"Thank you..." stammered Tanya, clearly still shaken.

I felt terrible. Our exchange student's first minutes inside our house and this happened. I'd asked the kids to put him in the backyard, but maybe they hadn't. Or maybe, our longtime housekeeper, Blanca, had let him in. She had a soft spot for our loveable dog and had done that before.

Hunched over, gripping his collar, I apologized and introduced Bear to Tanya. "Please don't worry, dear. He's really harmless. More like a big sweet teddy bear."

The kids, except for Anabel—who'd wanted nothing to do with walking a dog or cleaning up after him—had begged for a dog. Matt hadn't been keen on the idea either, but when a string of burglaries had erupted in our neighborhood, he'd changed his mind and said we could get one as long as it was a guard dog. So, we'd all gone to the pound and found the biggest dog we could. He also happened to be the cutest. One look at him, with those big brown take-me-home eyes, and he was ours. Enamored four-year-old Will had named him. "Mama, he looks like a big bear." And hence his name... Bear. I'll never forget my little boy hugging our new dog, Bear sitting and giving him wet slobbering kisses all over his face.

Matt had looked the other way, not wanting to upset our son. Later that day, to my horror, he bought a handgun. *Real* protection. He kept it locked in our safe. Loaded, no less. I hoped we'd never have to use it.

Tanya, still looking frightened, didn't buy into my words. "Natalie, can you please get him away from me?"

"Of course. I'll put him outside." Fortunately, our dog enjoyed romping in our big yard, and the weather was nice. He also had a doghouse to hang out in.

When I returned, Tanya was gone.

I assumed she'd wandered into the kitchen, perhaps to make herself some tea.

Wrong. I found her in the living room. Helping herself to an expensive bottle of cabernet from our bar.

"Dear, what are you doing?" I asked as she generously poured the blood-red liquid into a crystal goblet, filling it to the brim.

"I hope you don't mind. I needed to chill after Bear." She put the wineglass to her lips and took a long sip. "Can I pour you some too?"

I held back the urge to reprimand her. *And* the urge to say yes. "Your father lets you drink?" *And this early in the afternoon?* It wasn't even three o'clock.

Another swig. "It's allowed in the UK to drink with a parent when you're seventeen."

"Hmm. I didn't know that."

A frisson of guilt rippled through me. Sometimes, I used to share a little wine with Anabel. In hindsight, I wish I hadn't. Maybe she'd still be here with us.

"Tanya, I'd still like you to put the glass down and the bottle away." With a slight frown, she obliged. "Now, let me show you to your room."

Tanya's face brightened. "I can't wait to see it!"

My stomach twisted. Now, I wished I'd had that wine. I hadn't been in *that* room for over two years. Well, at least in the daytime. Bracing myself with a fortifying breath, I led our exchange student up the winding flight of marble steps.

"Be careful." I heard the tremor in my voice as I looked over my shoulder to check on her. My new ward was wearing her heavy backpack and had insisted on carrying up her large piece of luggage. By the effortless way she mounted the curved stairs, she seemed to be in good shape, but it still made me anxious. "Hold onto the banister. I don't want you falling down your first day here." At that thought, a cold shiver zipped through me.

"Don't worry, Mrs. Merritt. Whoops! I mean Natalie. I've got it."

To my relief, she gripped the intricate ironwork railing, also original to the house, with her free hand. I let out a breath when we both reached the landing.

Tanya's eyes darted left and right.

"Which way is my room?"

"To the right."

I followed her as she wheeled her suitcase across the long hallway. It moved smoothly along the polished dark oak floor. I couldn't help but notice how gracefully the slender, long-legged young woman moved. Like a gazelle.

"Tell me when to stop," she called out.

We passed Will's room, his bathroom, Paige's room, and another bathroom. When we got to the last door at the end, I said, "Stop!" I made my way in front of her and turned the brass knob. I pushed the door open and was hit by an explosion of shocking pink and sunlight. I felt dizzy. A little nauseous.

"Are you okay?" asked Tanya, sensing my distress.

"Y-yes. I'm just a little winded from climbing those stairs," I lied. Thanks to my Pilates and Soul Cycling, I was in the best shape of my life.

Catching my breath, I let Tanya enter first.

Her eyes wide, she gasped. "Oh my gosh, I *love* it! It's like a princess's room."

Indeed it was. Not a thing had changed since I'd last been inside it. I'd instructed Blanca to maintain the room exactly as she had when Anabel was alive. My eyes swept across it, taking in the frilly canopy bed with all her precious stuffed animals, the matching cottage-white furniture, the Justin Bieber posters, her cheerleading trophies, and all the framed photos chronicling her short life. Not a thing was amiss. It was like Anabel could walk in at any moment.

Dropping her bags on the pink shag carpet, Tanya headed straight to the bed and splayed herself on the duvet like a starfish. She gazed up at the canopy and let out a long, contented sigh.

"I could sleep in this bed forever. It's so yummy!" She randomly cuddled one of Anabel's stuffed animals against her chest. For a moment, my mind played a trick on me. I was seeing Anabel instead of Tanya. I blinked the mirage away at the sound of her accented voice.

"I can't believe you designed this room especially for me. With everything I could possibly ever want."

My chest tightened. I chewed on my bottom lip. "Actually, it belonged to my other daughter." A painful pause. "Anabel."

Our new family guest sat up, her long legs dangling over the side of the bed. Clutching the stuffed animal, an adorable koala, she looked at me, surprised.

"I didn't know you have another daughter."

"*Had*," I corrected, tears stinging the backs of my eyes. "She died a couple of years ago."

"Oh, I'm so sorry!"

"I should have told you..."

"How old was she?"

"Sixteen." *Sweet Sixteen.*

Tanya clasped a hand to her mouth. "Oh my goodness! That's so young. Is it okay if I ask how she died?"

My heart stuttered in my chest. "I'd rather not talk about it."

"I understand. It still must be really hard for you."

Appreciative of her sensitivity, I willed the horrific memory away and refocused on our new resident. "Dear, I want you to make yourself at home here."

Tossing the koala onto the bed, Tanya jumped off it and surveyed the room. "Can I change things around a little? You know, like add a few things of my own?"

In hindsight, I should have put away Anabel's personal things. Her photos and posters as well as her treasured plush animals. The latter held bittersweet memories for me; each year, I'd given her one on her birthday. Sadly, the koala was the last.

"Yes," I replied, "as long as you don't move the furniture around. You can put some of your clothes in her set of drawers; they're empty. And the rest of them in her closet. I hope you don't mind that many of her clothes are still stored in it, but there should be room for yours."

"No worries. I didn't bring much. Would it be okay if I borrowed some?"

I hesitated, then said yes. I didn't want our exchange student to think I was an obsessed nutjob. *Truth: I was.* "You're probably the same size. Just take good care of them."

"Of course." She shed her baseball cap and raked her slender fingers through her long platinum locks. "Natalie, maybe you could take me shopping later this week. I could really use an LA wardrobe."

I smiled. "I'd love to do that. Why don't we say tomorrow after school?"

"Cool! Thank you. Oh, and, Natalie, one more thing... I really need to use the loo." She giggled. "I mean, *bathroom.* Could you tell me where it is?"

I pointed to another door. "It's right through there. It connects to Paige's room."

She scrunched her face, her jet-black brows knitting together. "What! Seriously? I have to share it with *her*?"

The tone of her voice was slightly disarming, but maybe she was just tired and needed some reassurance. "Yes, dear. But don't worry. There are double sinks. And Paige is very neat. I'm sure the two of you will work things out."

"I suppose." Her face relaxed, but without a smile.

Anabel had never been good about sharing the bathroom with Paige. Most of the time, she'd hogged it. I hoped things would be different with Tanya.

"Why don't I let you settle in? Take a shower and a nap if you need to, but please join us for dinner in the dining room at six thirty."

"Perfect!" The smile returned. "I can't wait."

She strode over to me and gave me a hug. "Thank you again, Natalie, for giving me this incredible opportunity. I want to be..." She stopped mid-sentence. "Like part of your family while I'm here. The perfect houseguest."

Her words touched me. And the warmth of her arms around me was comforting. I felt a ping of optimism. It would be good for me to have another teenage girl in the house.

As she squeezed me tighter, my chest constricted and I felt myself shiver.

Would the ghost of Anabel come back to haunt me?

THREE

PAIGE

During the car ride to pick up my brother, I'd decided to give Tanya a chance. She seemed a little shallow, but nice enough. Not stuck-up like my sister. Or as vain. The least I could do was try... but *this*?

"What are you doing in my room?" I asked, forcing my voice to be as level as possible.

"Oh, hi!" she said brightly without looking up at me.

Our new exchange student was curled up on my bed, painting her toenails. Okay, I got that I had to share the bathroom with her, but this was not acceptable. Especially without consulting with me. I tried to maintain my cool, but it wasn't easy.

She had her own room—my sister's—on the other side of the bathroom. It was called a Jack and Jill suite, one of the so-called charming features that had sold my mother on this house. She'd thought it would help me and my sister bond. When we'd moved here, Anabel was thirteen, already long and lean with a peaches-and-cream complexion; I was twelve, stuck with baby fat, braces, and pimples. Our hormones raging, I hated her and she hated me. My mother was wrong. So wrong.

The last thing I'd wanted to do was share a bathroom with my sister, who spent more time in front of a mirror than any girl I knew. And she took long baths and showers that seemed to go on to the next day. I used to feel like I had to make an appointment to pee, poop, or shower in private.

Sometimes I'd wanted to strangle her and had told her that to her face. Though I never *really* wished for my sister to die, I had to admit it was nice having the bathroom to myself with her gone. I had urged my mom to give our exchange student the spare bedroom she used as her office, but she absolutely refused, stating she needed her personal space, "a room of her own," with gala season just around the corner. My mom was on the board of numerous cultural institutions and philanthropic foundations and was always heading up some committee that organized fundraising benefits. Unlike me, who was somewhat of a loner, she was a social animal. Much like my sister had been.

My arms folded across my chest, I waited for an answer. "Well?" I asked, my voice rising.

Laser-focused on her toes, she still didn't make eye contact with me as she chewed her gum. "What does it look like? I'm painting my toenails. Do you like the color? I found the bottle in my bedroom."

My bedroom. Her use of that possessive adjective jabbed me like a dart. It wasn't her bedroom. It belonged to my sister. In fact, nothing in this house was hers. I hadn't spent more than an hour with this girl, and the chance of me liking her was diminishing by the second.

"Get. Off. My. Bed."

"Wow! Someone needs a chill pill." She blew a bubble and popped it loudly. "I thought it would be fun to hang out. Get to know each other. But no worries; I'm almost done."

Simmering (honestly, I did need to chill), I watched as she moved from toe to toe. I couldn't help noticing how slender and arched her feet were, how dainty her toes were. The metallic-red nail polish made her toenails look like little gems and reminded me of both my sister's and mother's. Like everything else, I had inherited my father's flat feet, and my toes were stubby. And from playing basketball and all the training, my toenails were a mess. Jagged and broken. A few ingrown. My mother was always on at me to take better care of my feet, to come with her to have a mani-pedi, something she used to do weekly with Anabel.

No, thank you.

Rage surged inside me while Tanya took her time, carefully applying the nail varnish. I had the burning urge to pull my comforter out from under her and fisted my hands by my sides so I wouldn't. Anger management was definitely not my strong suit. It was a trait I'd inherited from my temperamental father. So I thought.

Still stroking her nails with the wand, she brushed a strand of her suspect blonde hair off her face with her free hand. "I spent some quality time with your mum. Before she showed me to my room, I had some wine with her. A delicious California cab—"

I cut her off. "My mom let you have alcohol? You're not twenty-one, are you?"

She blew another bubble and popped it. "I'm seventeen, but in the UK you're allowed to drink at home with an adult. Papa and I love to share a drink whenever he's in town."

My parents would ground me for life if they caught me drinking—with them or without them. Or invading the liquor cabinet like one of those spoiled *Gossip Girls*. I'd always wondered if they knew Anabel was sneaking Stoli and Jack Daniel's from my father's bar at the tender age of thirteen. And, if so, why had they let her get away with it?

Tanya cut into my thoughts. "Anyway, your mum told me so much about you guys."

I didn't want to know. The perfect family. The perfect lies.

Wine did that to my mother. Let her escape. Along with her Xanax and all the carefully planned activities that filled every minute of her vapid life.

"What exactly does your father do?" she asked.

"He's a money manager."

I actually didn't really understand what my father did. He said he invested other people's money, his roster of clients star-studded with celebrities and moguls. It was a win-win. They made money; he made money. And we got to live in this big house, go on fancy vacations, and do all kinds of other stuff only rich people did. All the money in the world, however, could not bring back my sister. Tomorrow, I'd learned, isn't promised to anyone.

"What about your father?" I asked Tanya, pretending I didn't know.

"Didn't your mum tell you?"

"No," I lied. "I honestly don't know much about you." That at least was true.

She didn't look up from her feet. "Papa's a diplomat. He travels all over the world. That's why he put me in boarding school."

"What about your mother?"

She shrugged. "Oh, she's dead. She died in labor, giving birth to me."

"I'm sorry." Those were the only words that came to mind. The barest nicety.

"Don't be. I never knew her." A beat. "It's nothing like you losing your sister. That must have been awful."

"How do you know about that?"

"Your mum told me."

My blood curdled. What pack of lies had she shared? Even I didn't know the truth behind my sister's death. "What did she tell you?"

Tanya examined her toes; one foot was done. "She didn't

want to talk about it."

Good, because I didn't want to talk about it either. Had my sister lived, she would have likely been a quadriplegic, paralyzed from the neck down. Confined to a wheelchair and dependent on others. Being the free-spirited, social animal she was, for her that would have been worse than death. So maybe it was a blessing she'd died. A blessing in disguise.

Thankfully, Tanya stopped me from flashing back to that fatal day and changed the subject. "I'm looking forward to meeting your brother, Will."

"He's annoying," I responded, not wanting to share him with her. Not one teensy bit.

With a flourish, she splashed a dot of the polish on her left pinky toe. "It's going to be so nice to be part of a family. And to have a mother for the first time in my life."

She's *not* your mother, I wanted to tell her, but kept my mouth shut, happy she was done.

"Do you want me to do your nails?" she asked sweetly.

"Thanks, but no thanks."

"No worries. Maybe another time."

Setting the nail polish on my night table, she carefully climbed off my bed and stood on her heels, her painted toes pointing to the ceiling.

"Hey, do you have some flip-flops I can borrow? I don't want to mess up my nails."

I'm sure I had a pair hiding somewhere, but I didn't want to share anything more with this girl. I said no.

"No biggie. I'll add a pair to my shopping list." I watched as she headed to the door to the bathroom that connected our rooms, walking stiffly on her flexed feet.

"I'm going to take a nap. I don't want jet lag to get in the way of dinner. My first family meal in ages!" She waved to me with a flutter of her fingers. "Ta-ta. See you later."

As soon as she disappeared, I ran over to the bathroom door

and locked it. *Click.* I didn't want her wandering back into my room. Then, I darted to the other door and attempted to lock it too. But the damn lock, which was probably as old as this house, was jammed. My brother, Will, could fix it. He could fix anything. I bet he could even install a new doorknob that allowed me to also lock the door from the outside. A trip to the hardware store in nearby Larchmont Village couldn't come soon enough.

And a new doorknob wasn't the only thing I'd be buying.

A wicked smile curled on my lips.

FOUR

NATALIE

For the first time since Anabel's death, I savored our nightly meal. While most families these days ate dinner in the kitchen, I preferred to eat it in our formal dining room. We had one, so we might as well use it. Due to everyone's busy, conflicting schedules, it was the only meal our family ate together, though both Paige and Will would have much preferred eating dinner in their rooms. Not happening. There were no ifs or buts about it, and I had my husband's support.

I religiously made dinner. My meals were planned ahead, and I was always home by five to get things going. It was another form of relaxation, and I enjoyed trying out new recipes while I drank a glass of wine. I once read that a home-cooked meal shows your family you love them. My mother, who could care less about me, had never cooked a day in her life, so I had to believe that was true.

What I was unsure about was whether my family's feelings were reciprocal. They never complimented me on anything I made, no matter how much effort I put into it. Paige and Will only spoke when spoken to, answering questions with the fewest words possible, often just one.

"How was your day?"

Okay.

"What did you do?"

Stuff.

"Anything special?"

Uh-uh.

When Anabel was alive, I looked forward to dinner because, even if Paige was combative and Will was close-mouthed, there was positive energy. Outgoing Anabel loved sharing her day and hearing about mine. Even able to engage my workaholic husband, she let her sister's snarky remarks roll off her back. Since her death, conversation around the dinner table had died too.

But tonight was different. More like old times. Tanya was excited and animated. And she devoured my grilled, rosemary-and-garlic lamb chops as if she hadn't eaten a decent meal in ages. Maybe she hadn't. She was rather thin. Maybe her boarding school food wasn't very good.

"Mrs. Merritt—I mean *Natalie*—these are delicious!" With a wide smile, she forked another piece of the tender, medium-rare meat.

"Thank you. I'm thrilled you're enjoying them. I bought them at the Original Farmers Market from my butcher. It's a nearby Los Angeles landmark dating to the thirties, adjacent to The Grove, one of my favorite outdoor shopping malls. It has a Nordstrom and a Sephora. Plus so many other wonderful stores and restaurants. I can't wait to take you there."

Tanya's eyes twinkled with excitement. "And I can't wait to go! It all sounds so amazing."

Delighted, I took another sip of my pinot noir and noticed Paige hadn't touched the chops. Hesitantly, she was eating only the cucumber salad, string beans almondine, and the rice pilaf. I turned my attention to her.

"Paige, what's wrong? You don't like the lamb chops?"

She answered my question with a question. "Are these beans and rice made with butter?"

"Of course. It makes them tastier."

Making a horrified face, she spat out a mouthful of the rice. "Eww! I've told you a *hundred* times. I've gone vegan. I'm no longer eating any animal products."

"Wow! That's so noble of you," commented Tanya, cutting into one of her chops. "That would be really hard for me to do."

Paige narrowed her eyes at Tanya and then eyed us all. "You're all just a bunch of cannibals. You'd probably eat each other if you could."

I shot her a stern look. "That's enough, Paige. Eat what you want, but please don't make judgments. Or tell me you're hungry later."

Without another word, she went back to picking at her greens. I hoped she wasn't developing an eating disorder.

To my relief, Tanya changed the subject. "Mr. Merritt—"

"Matt," he corrected.

She smiled as a blush fell over her cheeks. Such lovely cheekbones. Though not quite as high as Anabel's or mine.

"Matt..." His name was soft on her lips. "Paige told me you're a money manager. That sounds fascinating."

Pleased to be the center of attention, my husband's face lit up. Over the course of the next twenty minutes, he and Tanya went back and forth with questions and answers, and I learned things about my husband's job I'd never known. I moved on to my second glass of wine as they continued to banter. Wide-eyed, Tanya seemed to hang onto his every word. Like each one was gospel.

"Where did you go to college?" she asked.

"Stanford undergrad, and then the business school."

"Seriously? That's where I want to go!"

Paige's ears perked up while my husband wiped his mouth with his napkin.

"It's a wonderful school. One of the best in the country. We're having Paige apply there early decision."

My daughter shot eye daggers at her father. "You know I don't want to go to Stanford. I want to go to RISD."

Riz-Dee. The Rhode Island School of Design. The school I once dreamed of attending to become an illustrator. That never happened.

Furrowing his dense brows, Matt deflected the daggers. "There's no discussion. No daughter—or son—of mine is going to some artsy-fartsy design school. You need a real education to get ahead in this world. Tanya, here, seems to understand that."

At the mention of her name, our guest lit up like a lantern. She looked at my husband like he was God.

Matt's eyes were dark, narrow, and cold and stayed fixed on our defiant daughter. He set down his utensils with a bang, but I was thankful he didn't stab his fork or knife into our rare satin-wood table. His temper had gotten worse over time. "Paige, you're applying to Stanford, so you better get cracking on those essays, which are due soon. End of discussion."

"Matt, what's early decision?" asked Tanya, cocking her head while Paige pouted. "I'm not that familiar with the American college application process."

Matt turned to her. "It's when you apply to only one school and if they accept you right away, you must commit to going there." He took another hearty bite of his chops. "Tanya, if you really want to go to Stanford, you should do that. Paige can help you download an application, and if she doesn't, I'll be glad to. Or you can ask my son, Will. He's a computer whiz."

Will ran a hand through his cluster of auburn curls and rolled his hazel-green eyes. "Sheesh. It's not hard. Even a dumb girl can do it."

It was the most words he'd uttered around the dinner table in ages. I caught Paige smirking. Tanya looked affronted, but I couldn't blame her. I was happy she let the dig go. I wasn't in the mood for a fight around the table.

"Talking about school, who's excited about their first day tomorrow?"

Both Will and Paige looked at me as if I'd asked them to clean the toilet or pick up dog poop. Almost on cue, barking sounded.

Will looked up from his plate, his expression perplexed. "What's Bear still doing in the backyard?"

"Sweetheart, Tanya is afraid of him. We're going to have to keep him outside whenever she's not upstairs in her room."

My son frowned. "That's so not fair!"

"Totally!" concurred Paige. She always stuck up for her brother, no matter what. "He's part of the family and should be inside with us. Why can't Will keep him in his room when she's around?"

"I suppose that would work." I looked at Tanya. "Would that be okay with you, dear?"

"Fine." I detected resentment in her voice. Fortunately, no one made another comment. Issue resolved, I clapped my hands together. "Now, will someone please answer my question? Who's excited about starting school tomorrow?"

Paige and Will went back to their meals and their normal silence around the dinner table. Sometimes I wanted to shake them.

"I am!" chimed in Tanya. "Coldwater Academy sounds awesome."

With an approving nod, Matt gave her a thumbs-up. "It's the top private school in all of Los Angeles. Maybe in all of California. You'd think my two children would be grateful to get such a stellar education, but they're not. Sometimes, I think we should pull them out and put them in public school. Let them get a taste of the real world."

"Matt, stop!" I begged. "I'm sure they appreciate everything we give them."

"Can I please be excused?" asked Paige.

"Me too," added Will. "I'm bringing Bear up to my room."

Without waiting for permission, the two of them bolted from their chairs and marched out of the dining room. They were like an army of two. Sometimes, I thought if they possessed a gun, they'd use it on me and their father. I'd read horror stories of parents being shot by their kids, which only fueled my ongoing battle with Matt to get rid of the gun he'd bought. A battle I knew I was never going to win.

"Natalie," said Tanya, pulling me out of my thoughts, "that was the best meal I've ever had. Can I help you clear the table?"

I was pleasantly taken aback. Neither Paige nor her brother ever offered. Nor did my workaholic husband, who always headed straight to his office after dinner for an hour or two. I smiled warmly at her.

"Darling, that's so sweet of you to offer, but there's really no need."

"You're sure?"

"Positive. Why don't you go upstairs and hang with the kids? Or relax in your room. You have a big day ahead of you tomorrow."

She returned my smile, and said a polite goodnight to me and Matt, thanking us profusely for our hospitality before she departed.

"What a fine girl," my husband commented. "Maybe her gratitude and common sense will rub off on Paige."

I chortled. As I got up to clear the table, I thought about Tanya.

I was already beginning to love her like one of my own.

FIVE

PAIGE

The alarm of my cell phone trilled in my ears. My eyes fluttered open and consciousness flooded me. It was the first day of school. My last year in high school. Thank God. I was ready to move on. Find my people, and leave all the haters behind. Groggily, I sat up and then staggered to the bathroom.

I unlocked the door and swung it open. As a blast of heat assaulted me, my sleepy eyes bugged out. The steamed-up bathroom was a freaking mess. A puddle of water spread on the white tile floor next to a pile of damp, crumpled towels. The toilet was clogged with God knows what, and my blow-dryer, still hot to the touch, was dangling dangerously above it. Every one of my personal hygiene and self-care products had been used. From my toothpaste and deodorant to my moisturizer and hair balm. Not a single thing had been put away. She'd even used my sink, now gooped up and strewn with long golden hairs. Ugh! And as if this wasn't enough to make me want to scream or strangle her, every square inch of the mint mouthwash-stained counter was covered with her beauty supplies and makeup. Mascara. Eyeliner. Lip gloss and more. So much more.

The room looked like the inside of a CVS drugstore after a 6.0 earthquake. A total disaster.

Frigging Tanya!

Fury filled me and I cursed out loud. Fuming, I twisted the knob of the door to her bedroom and flung it open so forcefully I almost tumbled inside. *Screw Jack and Jill.* The tumbling-down-the-hill siblings or whatever they were could rot in hell for all I cared. And I still didn't understand why they named these adjoining bedroom suites after some stupid nursery rhyme.

"Good morning!" chirped Tanya as I caught my balance. Her voice was as bright as a sunbeam, mine as dark as a storm cloud.

"How *dare* you leave the bathroom like that!"

While I was by no means a neat freak, I kept things clean and tidy. So had my narcissistic sister. The state of the bathroom this morning was like nothing I'd ever seen. And I felt totally violated by her using all my things. She was even wearing my navy velour robe! And styling her blow-dried hair with my detangling brush. Now, as far as I was concerned, it had cooties.

"Paige, I'm sorry. I meant to clean it up afterward, but you didn't give me a chance. I didn't think you'd wake up as early as me."

"Clean it up now!" I ordered, wishing I'd taken a photo of the mess with my phone. "And put *my* hairbrush away!" Actually it didn't matter because I was going to have to buy a new one.

"No prob." She sashayed into the bathroom and I followed her to my room, slamming the connecting door shut behind me. She began singing one of my sister's favorite songs, Britney Spears's "Oops!... I Did It Again." Totally off key. And then I heard the toilet flush. I loathed the idea of having to share the toilet seat with her. For all I knew, she had some kind of STD.

I wished I could stuff her mouth with toilet paper and flush her away.

A half hour later, I was ready for my first day back at school. While not making it perfect, Tanya had done a pretty good job cleaning up the bathroom, and the hot shower had washed away a lot of my anger. I took a final look at myself in my dresser mirror, pleased with what I saw. I was wearing just the right amount of makeup, my hair didn't look too bushy, and my cut-off jeans and tie-dyed T-shirt (both Goodwill finds) flattered my athletic figure. Grabbing my backpack, I headed to my bedroom door, and as I stepped foot in the hallway, I got my second shock of the morning. This time my heart stopped.

"What are you doing in my sister's clothes?" I spat out once my heart went back to beating.

Tanya was wearing Anabel's white ruffled miniskirt that showed off her long bronzed legs, and a coral halter top that showed off her matching toned arms and significant cleavage. She was even wearing my sister's silver charm bracelet—the one my mom had given her for Christmas. Though I'd not been in my sister's room since her death, I knew my mom hadn't changed a thing or given a stitch of her clothing away. She kept the princess-pink room with its canopy bed intact like a shrine. Sometimes, late at night, I could hear her in there crying. Praying for forgiveness.

Adjusting her backpack, Tanya shot me a perplexed look. "You look as if you just saw a ghost."

It was almost as if I had. For a split second, I thought I'd seen my sister. Like she'd risen from the dead. I think it was the long blonde hair and her lean athletic body. Though it was only a passing resemblance, I was more convinced than ever my bereaved mother had sought Tanya out as a replacement. Rebellious, sassy, frizzy-hair me was no replacement for the beautiful fair-haired daughter she'd fawned all over. And mourned to the point of a mental breakdown.

I meant nothing to her.

Inhaling a breath, I calmed myself. "I'm just shocked to see you in my sister's clothes."

She smiled sweetly. "Your mum said I could borrow them until we went shopping."

"What about all the clothes in that big red suitcase of yours?"

She dismissively flicked a hand. "Oh, there's hardly anything inside it. I left most of my clothes back home. Icky school uniforms and nothing suitable for LA. Just a bunch of cold London-weather stuff. And *so* boring. A diplomat's daughter can't be caught in anything too risqué. It would be all over the tabloids."

As she spoke, I recalled how effortlessly my father had hauled her suitcase into his car trunk. She must be telling the truth.

"Papa, however, said I could get a new LA wardrobe and bought me a suitcase to fill with all my new clothes."

I guess that's why it looked brand new. Not seeing the point in being combative, I told her we should head downstairs. "Will's probably already down there. I don't want to be late for school."

And then I got my third shock. Not poor Bear, who was already in the backyard, whining and scratching at the French doors. Mingling with my parents and my brother in the kitchen was one other person...

My boyfriend, Lance.

I stopped dead in my tracks. Our eyes locked.

"Hey!" he called out.

"Hey!" I parroted, studying him.

I hadn't seen him all summer. He'd gone on some anthropological dig in the Galápagos Islands and had gotten back yesterday. He looked different. Taller. Tanner. More filled out. His sandy hair blonder and longer. He looked beautiful—all man—

and at the sight of him, I felt my body heat and my heartbeat quicken. Unable to take my eyes off him, I wanted to kiss him so badly my jaw ached. I, however, never engaged in public displays of affection. Especially in front of my parents.

We'd texted each other, and while he'd posted photos and videos on Instagram, most of them were of the exotic locations he'd excavated and the wildlife he'd encountered. My phone was filled with images of him being the socially conscious explorer. He'd read that colleges looked at applicants' social media and felt that posting pics showing his commitment to the environment and global warming would help him get into Brown early decision. Another reason I had my heart set on RISD was that it was also in Providence, Rhode Island, a five-minute walk away.

Tongue-tied and tingling all over, I looked at him longingly. I wanted him to say, "you look great" or "I missed you," but his eyes were no longer focused on me. They were on Tanya.

"Hey, who's your new friend?"

In my enraptured stupor, I'd totally forgotten about her. Now, I wished I could make the miniskirted beauty evaporate like water.

"Oh, Lance," chirped my mom, sparing me from introducing her, "this is Tanya Blackstone. Our exchange student. She'll be a guest at our house all year... well, at least until school ends."

"Hi," he said, with a sheepish grin. There was a glimmer in his amber eyes that wasn't there before. "Paige mentioned you to me."

Yeah. Like how pissed I was with my mother for inviting her to stay with us.

Tanya smiled. It was the same coy smile I'd seen last night at dinner. "Hi. Are you Paige's boyfriend?"

Lance blushed. "Kinda."

What!? He *was* my boyfriend. Okay, so maybe I hadn't

slept with him yet, but kids at school knew we were a thing. I fiddled with the necklace he'd given me before his trip. The small, dangling gold heart felt cold between my fingers.

His eyes stayed riveted on her. "Are you British?"

Her gap-toothed smile widened. "Yes, I am."

"Cool. Welcome to LA. Have you seen much?"

She shook her head. "No. I just got here yesterday."

"Then, I'll have to show you around."

Um... over my dead body!

"Great! I'd love that." She flung back her head and raked her hand through her lustrous hair. She looked as if she was about to audition for a L'Oréal commercial. Or audition for him.

Before this conversation went any further, or I seized the kitchen shears and lopped off her locks, I cut it short. No pun intended.

"We should go. We're going to be late." I grabbed a granola bar off the island counter. Tanya followed suit.

"What about lunch?" asked my mom.

"We'll get something off the food truck." I unwrapped the bar and, after taking a bite, offered to pull out my car.

Actually, it was my sister's car. A high-end Jeep Cherokee she'd barely had the chance to use, and to be honest, I was glad it was now mine. I kept it in the detached three-car garage, always immaculate. I wasn't looking forward to having Tanya contaminate it.

"Don't bother," said Lance. "My father let me borrow his Escalade. We can all fit in."

Five minutes later, Will and I were strapped into the back passenger seats. Tanya had beat me to the front seat and was chatting Lance's ears off. This already wasn't a good first day of school.

I wanted to throttle her.

And I knew things were only going to get worse.

SIX

NATALIE

Mondays were always busy for me. Today, I had my private Pilates instruction at nine, my weekly blowout at my hairdresser's, followed by a board meeting at the Getty Center, and a late lunch with Gloria Zander, the CEO of Gloria's Secret, the lingerie conglomerate, and founder of Girls Like Us, a small nonprofit that helped abused girls. She was interested in working with me to help grow GLU.

Our two-hour lunch was fantastic. I admired Gloria, a stunning woman who'd risen from challenging beginnings like my own. She offered me a job, and I told her I'd think about it. I frankly wasn't sure Matt would approve.

The lunch went on for longer than I anticipated, but I had just enough time to pick up Tanya after school to take her shopping. I'd texted Paige to meet us, but she already had some after-school activity, as did Will. As I drove over Coldwater Canyon, I wondered how our exchange student's first day at Coldwater Academy had gone. Starting a new school, let alone in a new country, couldn't be easy. Especially high school. Thankfully, she had Paige to show her the ropes. And maybe Lance had too.

I was excited to hear about her day and equally excited to

take her shopping. It had been so long since I'd gone on a mother-daughter shopping spree as Paige preferred to buy everything online or haunt thrift stores and flea markets that repulsed me. Goodwill was a thing of my past that I cared not to revisit.

Only one worry crept into my head as I drove to the school. That I might run into Alexa Roth, the mother of one of Paige's classmates. To say we'd had a falling-out would be a euphemism; she had very nearly ruined my life.

My dread dissipated as I pulled into the Coldwater parking lot and found a spot. Alexa and her showy red Bentley were nowhere in sight. A smile crossed my face as I searched for Tanya. She wasn't my daughter, but I'd felt an instant connection and already loved spending time with her. She was a breath of fresh air. Despite the horde of kids pouring out of the school at the sound of the dismissal bell, I spotted her immediately. With her tall lanky golden beauty, she stood out in the crowd. I honked my horn and called out her name. And waved. Upon catching sight of me, she broke into a smile and sprinted my way.

"Hi," she said brightly as she clicked open the passenger door. She settled into her seat and placed her backpack and laptop bag on the floor mat between her feet. "Oh my gosh! I love your car. You didn't tell me it was a convertible. This is my first time in one."

In total awe, she examined the deluxe features and rubbed her hand over the cream-color leather armrest. "This car is amazing! I thought for sure you'd have one of those monster mom cars."

I laughed. "I used to, but once Anabel got her driver's license and a car, I no longer felt the need for one."

I had actually hated driving my Range Rover, even though it was the Rolls-Royce of SUVs. It made me feel old and frumpy, and parking the monstrosity was a nightmare. The day after Anabel turned sixteen, I traded it in for the car of my dreams. This gorgeous two-seater Mercedes SL Roadster, the exterior a dark metallic blue that matched the color of my eyes. Sadly, it had sat dormant in my garage for almost a year after she died, on account of my breakdown. Finally, when I'd recovered, I got behind the wheel again. And now, every time I drove it with the top down, the wind blowing against my face, I felt transported. Like I was Grace Kelly in *To Catch a Thief* driving through the winding roads of the Côte D'Azur.

"I feel like a movie star in this car," gushed Tanya, buckling up. "I'm so excited to take a drive in it."

"You're going to love it." I let her know there was a pair of sunglasses in the glove compartment. Adjusting her seat belt, she opened the box and put them on. The Ralph Lauren aviators looked great on her, and I told her so.

"How did your first day at Coldwater go?" I asked as we pulled out of the parking lot and headed down the canyon toward Ventura Boulevard.

"It was fantastic. I'm in lots of the same classes as Paige. And a few with Lance. Lance was like a big brother and showed me all around. He also introduced me to some of his cute friends, though he's pretty cute himself."

"He really grew up a lot this summer," I said, reflecting on how surprised I was to see him this morning. I almost didn't recognize him. Tan and filled out, he was a good-looking young man. I didn't like to admit it, but what he saw in Paige bewildered me. But maybe he saw something in her I didn't. It pained me to realize I hardly knew my second daughter. Another thing I wasn't proud of.

"How long have he and Paige been together?"

"Almost two years. They hooked up the beginning of sophomore year. He had just transferred to Coldwater from another private school." I paused. "And she had just lost her sister... the May before."

"That must have been terrible. I mean, your daughter dying."

"Yes, it was." I needed to change the subject. With the wind blowing in my face and in such good company, I was in a happy place. And wanted to stay there.

"So, are you excited about going shopping?"

"*Super* excited! I've never had a mum to go shopping with."

At her words, my heart pinched. I knew how hard it was to grow up without a mother. Mine might as well have been dead.

The honk of a horn behind me jolted me out of my thoughts. The red light we'd stopped at had turned green and I hadn't moved. The guy behind me honked again.

"Bug off, asshole!" I yelled.

"Yeah, bug off, *arsehole!*" Tanya mimicked in her charming British accent.

In unison, we flipped him off as he zipped around us, and shared a good laugh before turning onto Ventura. As we drove toward Hollywood, I pointed out a few sights. The Hollywood Bowl, which we passed, and the famous Hollywood sign in the distance. Tanya, not impressed, thought it would be bigger.

Urban Outfitters was located on trendy Melrose Avenue, five minutes away from our house. I readily found nearby parking on a side street and, arm in arm, we skipped to the popular store. I felt like Dorothy in *The Wizard of Oz*.

There was a Starbucks across the street. "Do you want to get a coffee first?"

"No, I'm good. I really can't wait to go shopping."

"What do you need?"

"Everything!"

I laughed. While I assumed that she had a debit card and that her father the diplomat had given her spending money, I was going to treat her to her new wardrobe. We wouldn't miss the money, and it would give me enormous pleasure.

One hour later we were shopped out. Each of us was

carrying two big bags full of clothes and accessories. Plus some sexy lingerie that Tanya insisted I buy when she saw me eyeing the lacy garments. "I bet Matt will really like them," she'd whispered in my ear.

The passionate sex Matt and I had once enjoyed had died the same day as Anabel. And now our sex life was non-existent.

But maybe this free-spirited girl was right.

It was time to reignite his fire.

SEVEN

PAIGE

For the fourth time today, my eyes bugged out. Setting my heavy book-filled backpack on the floor in the entryway, I looked up and saw Tanya bounding down the staircase. Wearing the khaki overalls, white T-shirt, and Doc Martens I'd ordered online from Urban Outfitters. A few back-to-school basics. The package wasn't supposed to come until the end of the week. It must have come early. And she'd opened it! The nerve of her!

"Hi," she said cheerfully, fixing her hair into a messy bun. "How was your Chess Club meet—"

I cut her off. "How dare you open a package that was addressed to me!"

She gave me a perplexed look. "What are you talking about?"

I pointed my finger at her. "Those overalls! They're mine! I bought them online from Urban Outfitters."

"Chill. They're mine. Your mum bought them for me at Urban. We went shopping together this afternoon. It was so much fun!" She breezed by me. "Maybe we could both wear them to school, and we'll be like twins."

I gritted my teeth. *No freaking way.* The overalls made her look like a *Seventeen* magazine cover girl. They'd probably make me look fat and washed-out. My blood roiling, I picked up my backpack and humped it up the stairs, taking two steps at a time. Tanya called out to me from below.

"Do you want to see what else your mum bought me? I can put on a fashion show."

No, thank you! It wouldn't surprise me if she'd sneaked into my room this morning while I was in the shower, somehow accessed my account, and copied everything I'd purchased just to piss me off. When I reached the second-floor landing, I pulled out my phone from my backpack and managed to cancel the order before it shipped.

"I'm going to help your mum make dinner," I heard her say as I put my phone away, something I now had to guard carefully along with my laptop. "Will you help me with my calculus homework after we eat?"

Not answering her, I stomped to my room and locked the door behind me as well as the door to the bathroom we shared. More urgently than ever, I needed to get a new knob for the hallway door, one that enabled me to also lock it from the outside. Maybe tomorrow I'd do that. Or have Will bike over to the hardware store to pick one up for me. He'd know exactly what to buy.

At least right now I was safe from her. She couldn't get into my room. I should start my homework, but I couldn't concentrate on it if I tried. She was on my mind. Consuming every thought. I hated the way she was sucking up to my mother, my father, *and* my boyfriend. Lance showing her around school today was bad enough, but sharing his tuna sandwich with her at lunch had almost made me barf.

Kicking off my Birks, I plunked down on my bed. My father always said to succeed in business, you need to know your enemies. Plain and simple. Tanya might act all nice and sweet around me, but she *was* my enemy.

What did I know about her?

The truth is... hardly anything. All I knew was that she was British. Born in London, and an only child. Her father was a diplomat who traveled a lot. And her mother had died in childbirth. Oh, and she was seventeen and went to some fancy-schmancy boarding school. Oddly, I'd not found her on social media when I'd checked during free period. Not Facebook, Instagram, Snapchat, or TikTok. Every teenage girl I knew, even me, was at least on IG. Why wasn't she? Maybe her diplomat father forbade her.

I pulled out my laptop from my backpack along with a spiral notebook and lead pencil. My mother had gone online and ordered a boatload of school supplies for me and Will as well as Tanya so we wouldn't have to go to Staples and fight the crowd of back-to-schoolers. Except for the time she was incubated in her room after Anabel's death, she always thought ahead. And was always thorough and methodical. It was time for me to be more like her. Think ahead. Be thorough and methodical.

Know your enemy.

Opening my notebook to the first page, I jotted down the following:

- *Father's Full Name*
- *Mother's Name*
- *Name of Boarding School and Contact Info*
- *Double-Check Social Media*
- *Investigate TB's Personal Possessions*
- *Locate TB's Passport. Student Visa. Driver's License?*
- *Locate TB's British Airways Roundtrip Ticket/Boarding Pass*

- *Access TB's Cell Phone*
- *Access TB's Computer*

The last two items were going to be the hardest because they were probably password-protected. Maybe Will could help me. He was a tech whiz and could likely hack into anyone's accounts.

I thought about sneaking into her room, but didn't think there'd be enough time. And I sure as hell didn't want her to catch me snooping around. I'd have to figure out a way to get her out of the house for a few hours. And maybe I'd have Will join me as my partner in crime.

With that in mind, I embarked on my investigation and googled *Blackstone English Diplomat*. There were a lot of entries for some private equity company (whatever that was) called Blackstone, but nothing fitting my description. After scrolling for a minute, a possibility came up: *Sir Warren Blackstone*. Excitedly, I clicked on it. I read the brief description of his diplomatic career. Most significantly, he was dead. He had died in a private plane crash five years ago. It did not list any next of kin or survivors. Weird.

I heard my dad's car pull into the driveway and glanced at the time. Like clockwork, he was home at six o'clock. He'd wash up and unwind with a Scotch for a half hour and then, at six thirty sharp, we'd all sit down for dinner.

I had a little time to do more research. I decided to double-check Tanya's social media presence. Once again, nothing on Facebook, Snapchat, or TikTok, but to my surprise, she now had an Instagram account. Her handle: @TanyaBDreamer. She'd posted a dozen photos of my sister's room with the hashtags #thinkpink, #homesweethome, and #princessliveshere... numerous selfies posing in her new outfits with the hashtags #supermodel, #urbangirl, and #LAgirl... several with my mother on their shopping outing with the hashtags #shopaholics, #fashionistas, and #likemotheranddaughter... and finally one last photo... of Lance with the hashtags #hottie, #boyfriendmaterial, and #ColdwaterAcademy, which would likely draw the attention of every student. Classmates were already posting obnoxious comments like *Go for him! You'd look hot together! Take down his rude prude!* And God knows what they would say to my face tomorrow. The audacity of her! And to top things off, Lance was following her! Yet another one of her fast-growing army of hundreds.

"Dinner's ready!" I heard my mother call out.

So furious, I had no appetite.

On top of that, my mind was spinning with the question: Why hadn't Tanya ever posted on Instagram before today?

EIGHT

NATALIE

I was looking forward to another family dinner.

Tonight I'd made herb-crusted salmon, following a simple recipe from my favorite cookbook, *The Barefoot Contessa*. I'd also made a lovely lemon-vinaigrette salad with hearts of palm, strawberries, and bib lettuce, as well as a big batch of pasta with fresh chopped tomatoes, basil, and olive oil. I was being mindful of Paige's new diet—had even bought a few vegan cookbooks online—and although she'd likely pooh-pooh the salmon (thank God it wasn't a whole fish that had eyes), she could indulge in the salad and pasta. It had been so much fun to have Tanya in the kitchen as my helper, and she had a knack for making everything we plated look so pretty. Like both my daughters and myself, she had an artistic flair.

Matt, for the first time in ages, complimented my meal and I told him Tanya had helped me prepare it, omitting the fact we'd downed an entire bottle of sauvignon blanc in the process. With a nod of approval, Matt asked our family guest about her first day at Coldwater. She animatedly told him all about it, not leaving out a detail. He was pleased it had gone well. When he asked Paige and Will about their day, they replied in unison with three monotone words. "It was okay."

Paige's head stayed bowed as she picked at her salad and twirled her pasta with her fork.

"Paige, is everything okay?"

"I'm not hungry."

"I don't think you're eating enough."

"She's missing out," piped in Tanya, helping herself to seconds. "Can someone please pass me the pasta?"

Matt obliged and commented on how cute Tanya's outfit was. Paige crinkled her nose while our exchange student beamed, her eyes twinkling.

"Thanks, Mr. Merritt... I mean Matt. Natalie took me to Urban Outfitters after school. We had so much fun shopping. She even bought you a present."

Matt's brows shot up. "Oh really? What?"

Tanya winked. "You'll have to find out for yourself."

My husband's eyes met mine, and for the first time in ages, I felt a spark of excitement. Wearing the sexy lace lingerie I'd purchased today, I squeezed my legs together under the table to quell the tingly sensation. God, it felt good! Made me think of all the good times, and the first time we met.

As if Tanya had been reading my mind, she asked, "How did the two of you meet?"

My breath hitched in my throat. I took a long sip of my wine, and so did Matt. His eyes glinted with a hint of desire and he twitched a wry smile. I think he was reminiscing about our very first encounter.

"Come on!" coaxed Tanya. "Tell. I really want to know. I bet it was really romantic."

Paige and Will exchanged eye rolls. "Do we seriously have to hear this story again?" asked Paige.

We'd told it countless times. At holiday gatherings. Dinner

parties. Family picnics. Anabel, the romantic, could never get enough of it. Paige, the cynic, had grown sick of it. Will quite frankly didn't care one way or the other.

"It was love at first sight," my husband began, setting down his wineglass and ignoring Paige's protest.

"Really?" asked Tanya, all starry-eyed.

"Yes," I replied. Lust was more like it.

"Where did you meet?"

Matt answered. "Here, in Los Angeles. At a... um... toy expo."

Thank God he didn't say it was an erotica fest. Filled with sex toy exhibitors.

"Is LA where you're both from?"

"No," said Matt. "I'm from San Francisco... Nob Hill."

Snob Hill, I mused as he continued.

"My parents still live there. And Nat's from Palm Springs."

Well, that's what I'd told him. And the kids. It was close enough.

"How did the two of you meet?"

"Nat was assisting the company that I was thinking of investing in at the trade show. Demonstrating the breakthrough product they'd developed. I was in VC at that time."

"Venture capitalism," said our exchange student, proudly.

Matt looked impressed. "You're a smart girl, Tanya. I'm sure neither Will nor Paige would have known that."

Sitting side by side, Paige and Will exchanged a look as if they were silently communicating with one another. To my frustration, they did this often. Oblivious to them, Tanya carried on.

"I saw that on your LinkedIn profile and looked it up."

I found it a tad uncomfortable that Tanya had researched us, but I suppose any bright exchange student would want to know about the couple she was going to spend a year abroad with. I bet she'd googled me too. At most, she'd learn about my philanthropic activities and see the myriad photos of me and Matt at the many five-hundred-dollar-a-plate benefits I'd hosted. Thankfully, she'd never be able to find anything about me prior to our marriage. I'd successfully buried my past under layers of lies. Had Matt known about it, I'd never be where I am. Who knows how my life would have turned out? Happily ever after is not promised to those who come through the school of hard knocks, especially someone like me.

"I was a trade show model," I interjected, getting back to the story. Sometimes, I used to do "adult" stuff, the bucks too great to pass up, though I'd hated every minute. The money had allowed me to transform myself. Straighten my teeth. Lighten my hair. Buy some decent clothes. Get a place of my own far away from where I grew up.

Matt had no clue.

Tanya's eyes widened. "Wow! You were a model? Because when I went online, I didn't see you in any runway shows or fashion magazines."

I let out a nervous laugh. "Why would I lie?" The hypocrisy of my words ate at me. I was a twenty-four-seven living lie.

Tanya persevered. "Did you model under your maiden name?"

"Yes. Natalie Taylor." *Another lie.* Thankfully, Natalie Taylor had no online presence. Well, at least, *that* Natalie Taylor. Now, some TikTok singing sensation shared my name.

Matt went on, and I must say that having him talking about me—about us—was kindling a flame of desire inside me. Reliving every vivid second, I squirmed in my seat as he told Tanya more about our first encounter, leaving out the graphic details about how I'd demonstrated the "toy."

How animated I was.

How convincing I was.

How seductive I was.

I'd sold him not only on the company but also on me. He asked me out for dinner, and after dinner, invited me for a nightcap in his hotel room and the rest was history. After a whirlwind romance, he married me. Eloping to Vegas to spite his estranged, controlling mother. Nine months later I gave birth to Anabel.

For the first time in years, before they excused themselves, Matt told the children they could go upstairs. Paige and Will readily complied, but Tanya insisted on helping me with the dishes.

"No need, Tanya," said Matt. "It's *my* turn to help my wife out tonight."

With a coy smile, she slunk away. Matt and I remained seated, facing each other. After a few awkward, silent moments, I stood up and began to clear the table.

"Stop," Matt commanded. I couldn't remember the last time I'd heard that tone of voice. He was back to being the assertive alpha I'd married. "Let's go to my office."

Five short minutes later, we were in his small office, the door locked. The lights dimmed.

"Take off your clothes." Wordlessly, I did as he asked, leaving on my new, skimpy black lace underwear. My skin tingled with goose bumps as he studied me.

"Damn. You're still so hot, Nat. Lace becomes you."

Five long, heated minutes later, we were panting, coming down from our euphoric highs. He'd taken me over his desk. Over the edge. He hadn't done this in ages. Nor had I felt this way in forever. Totally consumed. Totally his.

For the first time since the night Anabel died, our marriage was back on track and alive again.

Zipping up his fly, my husband kissed me. His lips lingered on mine.

"I love you, baby," he whispered.

"I love you too."

Later we continued what we'd started upstairs and fell asleep, drenched and spent, in each other's arms. It was the best night with my husband in years.

Tanya had been so right. All I'd had to do was reignite his fire.

NINE

PAIGE

I knocked on Will's bedroom door, the affixed sign in my face.
STAY OUT! Beneath the words was one of those skull-and-crossbones configurations.

Will liked privacy and I respected that. The feeling was mutual.

I rapped again on the hard slab of wood. "Willster, it's me. Can I come in?"

"Enter."

I turned the doorknob, surprised it wasn't locked, and pushed the door open.

Will was sitting cross-legged on the top of his bunk bed, his computer on his lap. Actually, it was more than a bed. It was a massive blond-wood unit that featured sleeping quarters on the top level and a desk and shelves below filled with boxes of Legos, his collection of Harry Potter books, Star Wars toys, and various-size robots he'd built. Steps led up to the bed. It was kind of his retreat. His geek throne, as I called it. My genius brother had put it together himself. Beneath it, Bear was curled up on the colorful space-themed rug, next to my brother's latest robotic creation. Thank goodness Will had figured out a way to keep him in the house away from Tanya. Bear didn't seem to mind being holed up in my brother's room. Our family dog was super-attached to him and faithfully slept in his room every night. At least that hadn't changed.

My brother looked down. "What's up, Pudge?"

Pudge was his nickname for me. It's what he called me when he was a toddler and it had stuck. If anyone else called me that, I'd smack them. From Will, the nickname was endearing. I met his eyes. "Do you have some time?"

He snapped his laptop shut. "Yeah, sure."

A few moments later, I was seated on his bed facing him. On the wall above us hung a *Star Wars* poster.

"What do you think of Tanya?"

Will shrugged. "I dunno. She's okay, I guess."

It was easier extracting a splinter out of a finger than extracting an opinion out of Will. Twelve-year-old boys were like that. The nerdier, the tougher. But I had to say that Will was adorable with his curly auburn hair, button nose, and sprinkle of freckles. We looked a lot alike and I was confident he was going to grow up and be as handsome as our father. A total babe magnet, though right now he had little interest in girls. *Obviously*.

"Doesn't it irk you she hates Bear?"

"As long as he can hang out with me, I don't care."

"Don't you think there's something weird about her?"

"All girls are weird."

"I'm not weird, am I?" I made a funny contorted face that made my usually serious brother laugh.

"You're pretty cool for a girl."

"Thanks." I gave him a noogie. Will and I had always been close in our own coded way. And we'd grown closer after Anabel's death. I'll never forget holding his hand as we stoically watched my sister's casket being lowered into the earth. Both of us clad in black, me in a hideous knee-length dress my mother had forced me to wear, and my ten-year-old brother in a black suit that was two sizes too big for him. While my mother had sobbed nonstop, neither of us had shed a tear. He'd never been close to Anabel, who, with her busy social life, had no interest in little-boy stuff. Legos, video games, and robotics had no place in her self-centered world. For her, Will had simply been a nuisance.

I, on the other hand, loved to help my brother build things with his Legos—from Lego dogs and Mindstorms robots to elaborate neighborhoods and space stations—maybe because it wasn't that different from sculpting. Sculpture was my passion, and another reason I wanted to go to RISD is that they had one of the best fine arts programs in the country. Lucky for me, I had a studio set up in the backyard. My happy place. Thank every scrap of clay my mother hadn't asked me to give it up to house our exchange student.

Knowing my time with my brother was limited, I asked him, "Does Tanya remind you of someone?"

"Yeah, a little bit of Anabel."

"A *big* bit," I corrected. You didn't have to be Sigmund Freud to figure out that my mother was seeking a replacement. And that Tanya had literally stepped into my sister's shoes. "Didn't you find it cringey that she wore Anabel's clothes yesterday?"

"She did?"

Boys. I mentally rolled my eyes. It was time to cut to the chase.

"Willster, I've got a bad vibe about her."

"Like what?"

"I'm not sure she is who she says she is."

Will cocked his head. "What makes you say that?"

"Well, for starters, she told me her father is a British diplomat and I can't find him anywhere on the Internet. The only dude I found that was close is dead."

"That's weird..."

"Totally weird. And up until today, she wasn't on social media. I don't know one high school girl, including myself, who isn't on Instagram. Now all of a sudden, she has an IG account. I'll show you."

Slipping out my phone from a pocket, I quickly accessed Tanya's new IG account and showed him the photos she'd posted. She now, amazingly, had over a thousand followers. One thousand and seventy-five to be exact.

Will's eyes grew wide as I scrolled. "What's a photo of Lance doing there?"

"Yeah, that really pissed me off. And she's making it out like he's *her* boyfriend."

"That sucks."

"Big-time."

Will took the phone from me, scrolling further, and then made a horrified face. "*Eww!*"

"What?"

His freckles almost jumping off his face, he handed the phone back to me, and I saw what had grossed him out.

"Oh my God!" It was photo after photo of Tanya posing in the skimpiest of bikinis and showing off her to-die-for body. While I was sitting here with Will, she was in my sister's room taking half-naked selfies. Already boys from my school were posting comments like *Freakin' hot! I'm in love with you! You rock!* with heart-eye and flaming-fire emojis. Panic swelled inside me. What if Lance saw them? It took all my self-restraint not to freak out in front of my brother.

"Should I show them to Mom and Dad?"

Will, the thinker, pondered my question. "Nah."

"Why not?"

"Best-case scenario: They'll probably just lecture her. Maybe confiscate her phone for a few days. Worst-case scenario: She'll make her IG account private."

I weighed Will's words. He was right. I couldn't afford to lose access to her Insta. What she posted might be revealing. And God knows how else she would retaliate. For all I knew, she'd figure out a way to screw Lance right before my eyes.

"Okay, Einstein. What should I do?"

"You need to follow her."

"Well, I can't exactly shadow her every minute of the day."

"No, dodo. I mean, on Instagram."

"Then she'll think I'm spying on her."

He rolled his eyes back. "Just create a new account with a fake ID. She'll have no clue."

God, I loved my little brother. Our family brainiac. He'd even skipped a grade and was going into high school next year.

"Great idea!" I said, logging out of Instagram.

His face split into a grin. "You could have thought of that, but then again, you're a dumb girl."

I knew he didn't mean that and was just needling me. But I decided to play into it.

"I *am* a doofbrain, and that's why I need your help. The thing is, we have this strange, obnoxious girl living in our house. And we virtually don't know a thing about her. I want to find out everything there is, even if it means hacking into her computer."

Will's face lit up. "I could do that." He snapped his fingers like he was a magician about to make a rabbit appear. "Easy-peasy."

"We just have to get access to it."

"There's gotta be a way."

I smiled. I'd always told him, "Where there's a Will, there's a way."

I now officially had a partner in crime. And our secret mission had a name: *Operation Tanya.*

"One last thing. I'm going to need your help to install a new doorknob—one that locks from both the inside and outside. I don't want her to have access to my room. It's bad enough I have to share a bathroom with her. And FYI, she's a total pig!"

Will snorted. I cracked up, laughing hard.

Five minutes later, I was back in my room.

And @TanyaBDreamer had one more Instagram follower. I stared proudly at the avatar I'd created. She was clad in a superhero outfit, masked and caped. Inspired by my kick-ass childhood heroine.

@SpyGirl2.

TEN

NATALIE

"Natalie, what are you doing?"

The voice, though I recognized it, startled me. Tanya. I flinched, almost knocking over my glass of wine. I looked up and met her gaze.

"Oh, hi, honey. I didn't expect you to be home from school so soon."

Still armed with her backpack and laptop bag, she waltzed over to me and observed the numerous round coasters scattered on the dining room table.

"What are you doing?"

"I'm planning the seating arrangement for a gala I'm hosting at the end of October. It's a benefit for FAFAK."

She looked at me quizzically. "FAFAK?"

"Free Arts For Abused Kids. It's a nonprofit organization that's close to my heart. I'm on the board of directors and I chair the annual gala that raises hundreds of thousands of dollars."

"Cool. Can I help?"

"Sure. Put down your bags and have a seat." Lowering them to the vintage Chinese rug, she gracefully settled into the chair next to mine; they were both middle seats affording us wide access to the eight-foot-long table.

Her eyes dropped to my half-empty wineglass.

"Natalie, can I possibly have a glass of wine?"

Though we'd secretly shared some yesterday, I was now hesitant about letting her have any on a school night.

"I don't think that's a good idea. I don't want anyone seeing you drinking." *Especially Paige.* "What about a lovely cup of tea?"

She scrunched her face in disgust. "Seriously?"

I found her reaction strange. All Brits loved tea, didn't they? They were practically born drinking it.

Absently, she played with a coaster, making circles. "I have an idea. You can pour some wine in one of those ceramic mugs I saw in your cupboard. The tribal-looking ones. That way no one will know what I'm drinking."

Though she said she was of drinking age in England, I still had mixed feelings about it, but didn't want to come across as uptight. Plus, I was sure half the kids in Paige's class already drank with or without their parents' knowledge.

"Okay, just a little," I compromised and headed to the kitchen. A minute later I returned with a half-full mug of sauvignon blanc.

"This mug is so amusing," Tanya said as I handed it to her, happy she was content with the small amount of wine.

I twitched a smile. "I know. Matt found the set while we were vacationing in Hawaii. He loved that they looked like tikis and came in assorted colors. Like everything else in our life, he couldn't live without them. We have so much stuff we don't need. And have never used. We could literally open a gift store."

Taking a sip of her wine, Tanya giggled. I loved that she shared my sense of humor. Anabel had, too, but Paige usually rolled her eyes at my little jokes.

She imbibed more of her wine. "That's so awesome you guys went to Hawaii. I've never been there."

"We may go back this Christmas. This time to Maui instead of the Big Island."

"I'd *love* to go with you!"

I was more surprised than delighted. "Honey, don't you want to go home to your family in England over the holidays?"

Tanya shrugged. "Not really. Papa is never around at Christmas and it's usually so cold in London." A cloud of sadness fell over her. "And lonely."

The poor girl! My heart ached at the thought of her spending Christmas alone. "Then, of course you can come with us."

"Oh my goodness! Really?" Her face lit up like a Christmas tree.

"Absolutely. You're not just a houseguest. You're part of the family now... but right now, let's focus on the gala. I only have an hour before I need to start making dinner."

"Sure." She glanced down at the coaster-covered table. "Where is it taking place?"

"In our backyard. It's the first time I'm hosting a gala there. I did a financial analysis, *without* Matt's help I should add. By not spending money on a ridiculously expensive hotel ballroom, we'll be able to raise so much more money for all the poor abused children who need art to enhance their lives."

"That's brilliant." Then a pause. "Natalie, what kind of childhood did you have?"

I was so taken aback by her question, at first I didn't answer. I took a sip of my wine and tried to slow the words racing around my head. *Choose one.* "Ordinary."

She looked surprised. "I thought for sure you grew up in a big, beautiful house and had a fairy-tale childhood."

"Hardly." To stop myself from going further—I'd already

said too much—I gulped down more of my wine. "Tanya, dear, let's change the subject."

"No problem." She returned to her wine.

I was grateful she didn't prod further. I had too much at stake. Matt had no idea what I'd gone through. Nor did his snooty Nob Hill parents. If they knew, God only knows how differently my life would have turned out.

Tanya set down her mug. "So, where do all these abused kids live?"

"All over. Many are in foster care, having been taken away from their abusive parents or abandoned by them."

"That's so sad." She bit her lip. "You know, sometimes I feel like I've been abandoned."

I looked at her pointedly. "How so?"

"Well, you know, my mother died. And my father travels for work all the time. Poor me *never* gets to see him. I wish Papa could be more of a stay-at-home dad like Matt. And I wish I had a mum in my life like you." Tears began to fill her eyes. "Sometimes I've felt so alone and neglected I could die."

Her words sucker-punched me. How often had I felt that way in my life! Especially in my youth.

"You poor thing. Here, let me give you a hug." I shifted and wrapped her thin body in my arms. She sniffled and reciprocally looped her arms around me.

"You and Matt have already given me so much. For the first time in my life, I feel like I *do* have a family. Will and Paige are so lucky to have you as parents."

They are, I thought to myself. But, by the way they often behaved, you'd never think they knew that.

"Natalie, can I tell you something else?" She paused. "And you promise you won't be mad at me?"

Hesitantly, I said yes.

"Sometimes I think my father should go to prison."

A brow lifted. "Why do you say that?"

"Because abandoning a child is a crime," she said to my face and then quickly added, "At least in England."

A chill ran through me. "Yes, it is here too." I took a glug of my wine. "Honey, I know you don't really mean that. C'mon, let's get back to work."

"Thanks for understanding, Natalie." To my relief, she instantly went back to being her cheerful, eager-to-please self. "What do you want me to do?"

Still a bit unnerved by her words, I handed her a black Sharpie. "Why don't you number the tables—I mean, the coasters—while I work on the seating arrangement."

I reached down for the printout, sitting on the chair next to me, that listed all the guests that were coming. Three hundred in total. That meant thirty tables with ten settings each. Deciding who to put with whom was always the biggest challenge of organizing these events. While some had purchased a ten-thousand-dollar table to share with their friends, many had bought individual tickets, and trust me, not everyone liked each other or shared the same views. I had to be particularly mindful of keeping like-minded people together in this politically polarized world.

"Is there a theme?" asked Tanya as she lithely moved around the table, numbering the coasters.

"Just a color theme. This year it's blue and white. I still haven't figured out what kind of flowers to put on the tables."

Tanya looked my way. "What about forget-me-nots? The blue flowers, a reminder of all the abused and abandoned children in this world."

"How fitting! Thank you, my dear."

"You're welcome." She smiled and then handed me the marker. "I'm all done."

I scanned the numbered coasters. Perfection.

"C'mon, sit down. Enough work for today. I really appreciate your help." In my head, I heard a little voice reminding me that Paige had never helped me with one of my galas. I tuned it out and said to Tanya, "Let's finish our wine."

Joining me, we chatted about her second day at school. It sounded like she was really fitting in and enjoying her coursework.

"Good for you! I had no doubts about you."

"Thanks! So, how did it go last night with Matt?"

At her unexpected question, I felt myself blush. Our epic sex had left a tingly warmth in my body that I'd felt all day.

"Um, er, we had a wonderful evening."

"I thought so. You're gorgeous, Natalie, but today you look positively radiant."

"Thank you." I put my hand to my heart. The heart that was again beating with love for my husband.

"By the way, what are you going to wear to the gala?"

"I'm not sure yet. But it has to be blue."

"What about that gown you wore to that mental health extravaganza last May? It was divine."

She was referring to one of my Dior gowns. Wondering how she'd seen me in it, I asked, "How do you know about that gown?"

"I saw a photo of you in it online. You looked absolutely stunning!"

"Oh. Thank you," I said, recalling how many paparazzi had been at that well-heeled event. "I'll think about it."

Reaching for her bags, Tanya stood up. "Well, I'm going to head upstairs and get started on my homework. And try to download that Stanford application."

"Let us know if you need any help with that."

She padded toward the grand entrance. The staircase. "See you at dinner."

"Thanks again, my darling, for all your help."

For everything.

ELEVEN

PAIGE

My investigation into Tanya's past didn't progress much over the course of the next few weeks and I was completely frustrated. A snail moved faster.

At Will's suggestion, I asked my mom, not Tanya, for the name of the school she went to in England. He'd told me that asking our exchange student might arouse suspicion and I agreed. The name of the school was Briarwood. Googling it, I learned it was a fancy private girls' school located in the English countryside just outside of London. I shot them an email inquiring if they had a student named Tanya Blackstone, under the pretense we'd become best friends over the summer in London and I wanted to send her a birthday present. Apparently the school of choice for many English aristocrats and diplomats, their response was they never gave out any student information and the best thing to do was to courier the item to the school, care of the headmistress. Whether Tanya was a student there or not remained ambiguous.

I also asked my mom if Tanya was going back to England over the holidays with the hope of seeing her plane ticket, or her passport. Not to mention with the hope of having a reprieve from her. Imagine my shock and dismay when I learned that she was going to spend Christmas with us as her supposed diplomat father wouldn't be around. Was he *ever* around?

I then inquired about her return to England when school ended. My mother said it was up in the air. Tanya had told her she might want to visit another US city like New York or Miami before going back home, so she hadn't yet purchased a return ticket. Knowing my mom's passcode, I managed to access her iPhone, hoping to find an email or text from our exchange student with her British Airways ticket info. To my disappointment, I found nothing. Maybe my mom had deleted it and written down the information elsewhere. Though we'd met Tanya in front of LAX's international terminal, there was still no proof she'd boarded a flight from London to Los Angeles. And I knew the airline would never divulge passenger information.

When it came to finding out the first name of Tanya's mother, I asked her directly on the way to school one morning. Slightly put off, she prefaced her response, "Why is it important for you to know that?"

"Oh, I was just curious."

"What does it matter? She's dead." And then she shut me out and returned to her phone. From the corner of my eye, I watched as she took yet another pursed-lips selfie and posted it alongside the hundreds already on Instagram. Her following was approaching five thousand.

After her living with us for close to a month, I still didn't know much more about Tanya Blackstone. Except that Insta-Queen had a tongue whose length rivaled Miley Cyrus's. To my frustration, neither Will nor I had been able to gain access to her room. She was always in it whenever we were home. And she guarded her laptop and phone with her life. It was like they were appendages.

Overnight, she had become the most popular girl in my

class. Every girl wanted to be her. Every boy wanted to have her. They were in awe of her lithe, long-legged, carefree beauty, loved her style, and fawned over her English accent.

Academically, she wasn't the brightest bulb in the pack. She struggled with her schoolwork and oddly had no familiarity with classic British authors. When I asked her if she liked George Eliot, she told me *he* was one of her favorite British singers and broke into the song "Wake Me Up Before You Go-Go." Yup, Stanford material.

But despite her academic limitations, our quote, unquote "English" exchange student was clever. She had an enviable knack for getting away with things, and whatever assignments she couldn't handle, she charmed others to help her. She got by. Male teachers were particularly forgiving, and it made me want to puke.

Worst of all, I couldn't escape her. On top of being in every class I took, except for AP Chemistry and Advanced Sculpture, she decided to try out for the girls' basketball team. I urged her to try out for soccer, a sport she called football and claimed to play back home, but she was insistent on trying something new. With her height and agility, she was a natural. *She shoots, she scores.* With my best friend and teammate, Jordan, having gone off to Berkeley, there was an opening for a forward on the team; Tanya landed the spot.

Throughout the month of September, we had practice every day after school in preparation for our first game with our rival Huntley Hall, an equally prestigious private school located not far from Coldwater. Hence, I was tasked with driving her home from practice. She was always chatty, wanting to know things about my parents and especially my boyfriend, Lance. I was close-mouthed, and finally told her to bug off and stop asking me questions about my personal life. It was none of her business. She simply shrugged and muttered, "Whatever," and occupied herself with her phone until we got back to the house.

With each passing day, I missed my best friend, Jordan, more and more. Her full name was Jordan Jackson, but everyone on the team called her Air Jordan, a nod to the legendary Chicago Bulls player Michael Jordan. My nickname for her was Fly because in addition to having wings on her feet, she was stylish and attractive, as well as fiercely unique. A Face-Time call with her was long overdue. I badly wanted to catch up with her and vent about Tanya, but I knew she was adjusting to college life and didn't want to burden her with my problems.

Despite all the angst in my life, and the fact that Tanya was in it, like a tick burrowed under my skin, the month of September flew by. On the first Monday of October, basketball season officially kicked off. We had our first game with the Huntley team. No matter how many times I had experienced this day, I was a jittery mess. My stomach twisted with nerves, and my chin had broken out with zits—those painful, below-the-skin cystic ones that lasted forever. And to make things worse, Tanya—the thorn in my side—wanted to ride over with me to their campus for the game.

"Why can't you hitch a ride with someone else?" I asked, the irritation in my voice obvious, wishing Fly was with me instead. With her recently lightened blonde hair swept up in a high ponytail, Tanya was already wearing our team uniform—maroon-and-white basketball shorts and a matching sleeveless jersey—and I couldn't help noticing how toned her long tanned legs and arms had become since joining the team. They were eye-turning to begin with; now they were even more spectacular. She belonged on the cover of *Sports Illustrated*.

She stood outside my Jeep, holding the passenger door open. "It's not like I really want to ride with you, Paige, and put up with your repugnant hairy armpit odor, but it's more convenient. I can leave all my stuff in your car and go home with you. All my friends on the team—or coming to the game—live in Beverly Hills or Sherman Oaks, and it would be so inconvenient for them to drive me home. And if we lose, that would be really inconsiderate when they probably want to get home as fast as possible and drown their sorrows."

Though I had the sudden urge to drive off and leave her behind, I gave in, her very presence grating on me. Wearing on my nerves.

"Fine. Get in. Just don't talk to me. I need to concentrate on my driving. And the game." With a cheeky grin, she hopped into my Jeep.

"I just know we're going to win," she cooed, buckling her seat belt. "Oh, and by the way, what's that ugly thing on your chin?"

Looking in the rearview mirror as I pulled out of my parking spot, I caught sight of the monster zit that I'd picked at and turned into a fiery red mess. I scrunched up my face and grimaced.

"Did Lancey bite it and suck out the pus?"

"Shut. Up."

"Aren't we a *narky* one?" Without another word, she reached into her backpack and withdrew an open pack of gum. It was her favorite... Trident original. She plucked two sticks from the blue pack, peeled them open, stuck the wads in her mouth, and tossed the wrappers on the floor mat. To make things worse, she began chewing the gum like a cow. It was annoying, but better than having her chew my ears off.

The short drive to Huntley felt like an eternity. The only thing that got me out of my foul mood was a text from Jordan. *Break a leg, Merritt!* It's what she always told me before our first game, with a high five. It had always brought both of us good luck. As we pulled into Huntley's visitor parking lot, I texted her back. *Thanks! Miss you! Love you!* And added a kissy-face emoji. She signed off with F.L.Y. It stood for Freaking Love You. With a smug smile, I turned to Tanya.

"Break a leg, Blackstone."

The dumb blonde grinned. "Thanks."

Except I really meant it.

———

The Huntley gymnasium was packed, the bleachers lined with students along with some parents. My parents, as usual, weren't in attendance. My mom was in an all-day meeting, planning her upcoming gala, and my dad was on a plane, flying home from a client meeting in Dallas. Lance wasn't there either, unable to make it because he had track practice. He was on the cross-country team and generally ran several miles every day after school in preparation for his upcoming meets.

Despite Lance's absence, it didn't stop his friends from coming. I'd never seen such a big boy turnout for one of our games. There could only be one reason: The team now had hotness embodied in long, lean, beautiful player number twelve —Tanya Blackstone. Trust me, none of them was here to watch her bounce a ball; watching her big boobs bounce as she dribbled one was more like it. For someone so skinny, she was incredibly stacked. I wondered if she'd had implants.

Coldwater and Huntley were longtime rivals. Last season the Huntley girls' team had been mediocre and we'd easily defeated them, but they'd since upped their game. The ball passed between teams, from court to court, the dribbling action so fast it was almost a blur. I was breathless and sweaty. We were now in the last quarter and the score was tied at 45–45. Tanya and I had been the high scorers, her score exceeding mine by three points. I had to say her beginner skills were extraordinary and I couldn't help noticing how loudly the Coldwater crowd cheered each time she made a basket.

Five make-or-break minutes remained in the game. The ball was in our court. With a jut of my chin, I signaled to the player who had control of it to pass it to me. Though about twenty feet away from the basket, I was confident I could make the long shot. A very focused Tanya, her knees bent and arms outstretched, was breathing down my neck.

"Get back!" I yelled at her as my teammate Claire tossed the ball. "This shot is mine. I've got it!"

"*No!* It's mine! Get out of *my* way, you fat cow!"

There was no time to spare. The burnt-orange ball flew high overhead and both of us scrambled for it. She darted in front of me, and as her arms reached into the air, I gave her a hard shove. As the ball soared past me, she tumbled onto the laminated floor. The referee blew his whistle and called for a timeout. Everything came to a halt as the Coldwater crowd booed and both team coaches ran onto the court. I looked down at Tanya. She was clasping her right ankle.

"You deliberately pushed me!" she cried out, venom mixing with the tears in her eyes.

"Tanya, are you okay?" asked our concerned coach, Mr. Whitney, a very handsome and popular English lit teacher. He crouched down and cupped her shoulders, a little too tenderly. It was obvious he had eyes for her. As did every Tom, Dick, and Harry.

"Can you walk?" asked the Huntley coach, an equally smitten parent volunteer. *Creep!*

Tanya grimaced. "I don't know."

I watched as they helped her up. Her ankle buckled. She made a pained face and winced.

"Hold onto us," said Coach Whitney, practically salivating.

"Oh, thanks," she purred, batting her long eyelashes.

The actress. I bet she was faking.

Wrapping her arms around the two coaches, she hopped off the court on one foot. Along with the enamored crowd, my teammates cheered and applauded our high scorer. Tanya theatrically blew them a kiss. Rising to a standing ovation, the fans on the bleachers chanted her name over and over, louder and louder. *Tan-ya. Tan-ya.* It was like a stampede of fawning rock star fans. I wanted to vomit.

To make things worse, we lost the game by just two points. And everyone blamed me for having hogged the ball. My heart heavy, I drove home alone, Tanya nowhere in sight.

I'd wanted her to break a leg. Regretfully, I should have remembered my beloved grandma's words of wisdom, because she was never wrong.

Be careful what you wish for.

TWELVE

PAIGE

All the lights were on when I got home. After parking my Jeep in the garage next to my parents' cars, I slumped inside our house via the side door. I wondered if Tanya was back and had told my parents about the incident. Was it too much to hope she'd been taken to the emergency room and gotten hit by a truck on her way there? Too much to wish for?

Not stopping in the kitchen for a snack or a much-needed glass of water, I trudged upstairs to my room and made my way to the bathroom. I didn't know if I needed to pee, poop, or puke when, suddenly, I heard voices coming from Tanya's room. Noticing her bathroom door was unlocked, I flung it open. My eyes went wide, my jaw slack, and it took me a long moment to recover.

"Lance, what are you doing here?" I asked, standing between the doorjambs so stiffly I thought I had rigor mortis. Clad in his tracksuit, he was sitting on the edge of Tanya's bed, her foot resting on his muscular thighs. He was holding an ice pack to her bandaged ankle.

"Oh... hi, Paige."

"Answer my question."

"I got out of track practice early and came by to see your game. When I saw Tanya standing outside, her ankle bandaged and obviously in pain, waiting for your mom to pick her up, I offered her a ride home in my car. It was the least I could do."

"Oh, and did you carry her into the house and up the stairs, *Sir Lancelot*?" The image of her in his arms made me feel more nauseous than I already felt. If I was going to vomit, it better be the projectile type that splattered all over their pretty faces.

"Oh yes, he did," replied Tanya dreamily, giving Lance a warm smile. From where I was standing, it looked more flirtatious than grateful.

I wanted to rip it off her face like a Band-Aid. Then stick it to him. Before I could do or say something I'd regret, her bedroom door swung open, and my mom walked in, holding a pair of crutches. I don't think she knew I was there, as her compassionate gaze went straight to Tanya.

"My poor darling. I found these in our crawl space. These are the crutches Anabel had to use when she tore her ACL while skiing in Aspen. I think you're about the same height, so they should fit you."

Remaining invisible, I watched as Tanya stood up and put them under her armpits. Hesitantly, with her bandaged foot raised, she took a step. Then another.

My mother beamed. "Tanya, you've got a wonderful handle on them. It took Anabel a week to get used to them." She cast her eyes at Lance. "Lance, dear, I don't want her going down our stairs on crutches. That's far too dangerous."

A veil of worry fell over her. She must have been thinking about Anabel's fatal accident. As evil as it sounded, I wished the same for Tanya. *Ta-ta!*

My mother cut my mental ramblings short. "Lance, you're a strong, handsome young man. Do you think you can carry Tanya down the stairs? And of course, we'd love you to stay for dinner."

"Of course, Mrs. Merritt," my oh-so-gallant boyfriend replied, effortlessly gathering Tanya up in his brawny arms. With a smirk directed at me, Tanya wrapped her arms around Lance's shoulders.

My hands were balled up into fists as I followed them down the stairs.

How hard would it be to give them a little shove?

I wanted her out of my life.

Whatever it took.

THIRTEEN

PAIGE

The next couple of days were a living hell. Everyone fawned over Tanya, who was hobbling around with the aid of her crutches. I swear if aliens descended upon us, they would have doted on her too.

There was one exception—yours truly, who resented having to do the littlest thing for her, just because she was incapacitated. Lance might as well have moved into our house because my parents needed him to carry her up the stairs in the evenings and down them in the mornings. Sometimes, he carried her in his arms, other times piggyback or caveman-style over his shoulder, the two of them forever giggling. More than once, I wanted to push them both down the long windy marble stairs. While my father could have likely schlepped her up and down, my mother feared he'd hurt his back, which flared up from time to time from an old tennis injury. Lance was more than happy to help out. A little *too* happy, if you asked me.

The physical closeness between Lance and Tanya gnawed at me like a flesh-eating wound. And it wasn't limited to him helping her up and down our stairs. He drove her to school every morning and then back home, carried her books from class to class and, most disturbingly, hung out in her room to help her with her homework when I knew for a fact that he could barely do his own.

With both doors to her bedroom locked, I wondered what they were *really* doing. I often heard giggles if I put my ear to her bathroom door, other times music. I was setting myself up for doom. The inevitable. At some point, I expected to hear moans and groans that escalated into shrieks and grunts. There was a name for someone like me that I'd learned in my psych class: I was a masochist.

My only solace was my brother, Will. Hanging out with him on his geek throne, on Day Three of this madness, I told him my deepest, darkest fear: I was losing Lance to our manipulative exchange student.

"Have you confronted him?" Will asked.

"Yeah, I have. He thinks I'm acting jealous. Maybe paranoid."

"Do you *really* want to know what's going on behind closed doors?"

I pondered his question for a few seconds. Did I? Could I face the consequences of discovering my boyfriend was cheating on me with Tanya? I'd saved myself for Lance, but maybe she'd already beaten me to being his first. I felt a stab of pain in the pit of my stomach as I answered my brother's question.

"Yes."

Will flashed me his goofy I-can-solve-anything grin. He'd already replaced my doorknob with a new one that automatically locked from the outside when I closed my bedroom door. I needed a key to get back in, but the small inconvenience was worth it to keep Tanya out. I watched as he snapped his laptop open and began to press the keys. His dexterous fingers glided across the keyboard like a pianist's. He flipped the computer around so the screen was facing me. I studied the image on the screen.

"What's this?"

"A spy cam. I can order it online and have it here by tomorrow morning. We'll ditch school early and I'll install it. We can set up an app on both your phone and laptop and then, in the afternoon you can watch *The Lance and Tanya Show*." He added air quotes.

I couldn't help but laugh. He made it sound like some tacky talk show. Or another bad reality series.

"Aren't you going to watch with me?"

My little brother pulled a face. "No way. Gross!"

I laughed again, my brother's expression turning serious.

"Here's the deal: If you see something you wish you hadn't seen, you can't go all emo on me. If you do, I'm done with *Operation Tanya*. End of." He theatrically mimed wiping his hands clean.

"Deal!" I raised my hand to high-five him. His palm met mine with a stinging slap.

"Deal!"

Afterward, I thought about the consequences. On the one hand, I had nothing to lose.

On the other, I had everything to lose.

———

The following day, Will and I ditched school before last period, but things didn't go according to plan. There was major construction on the way home, delaying us by forty-five minutes, so we had little time to install the spy cam, which was waiting for us in our driveway. Will hopped out of the car to retrieve the package before I pulled my Jeep into the garage. Neither my mother nor father was home.

I had been hoping to snoop around Tanya's room, which

was surprisingly very tidy, but there wasn't enough time. Will worked quickly to install the minuscule camera, placing it on the ceiling in a corner. It had a tiny roving lens that could capture various angles of the room—from her desk to her bed and beyond. Because it was white, it inconspicuously blended in and looked more like a smoke detector. Chances were the wrapped-up-in-herself Insta-Queen would never notice it.

As Will worked away, I heard a set of footsteps and giggly chatter nearing us in the hallway. *Them.* Just in the nick of time, the installation was complete. We narrowly escaped being discovered via the bathroom connecting to my room, with Will scurrying to his own room when the coast was clear.

Showtime. The first episode of *The Lance and Tanya Show*. Sitting cross-legged on my bed with my laptop, I was bubbling with nerves. A big part of me wanted to slam the computer shut. More wise words from my grandma floated into my head —*Ignorance is bliss*—but I ignored them.

With my heart in my throat, my eyes fixed on the screen as Tanya's door opened. She hobbled inside the cotton candy-pink room with Lance behind her. He kicked the door shut with his heel while Tanya clicked a remote and turned on some music. A slow dance remix of Britney Spears's "I've Just Begun Having My Fun" began to play.

My eyes almost popped out of their sockets when Tanya tossed her crutches onto the bed and began to dance in the arms of my boyfriend. There was *nothing* wrong with her ankle! Unable to blink, my eyes stayed pinned to the screen as they swayed to the song in perfect sync. Tanya's head resting on his chest, her eyes blissfully closed, Lance smiling dreamily, his arms looped around her tiny waist.

A fireball of rage shot through my veins, making me think I was going to combust. I vaulted out of my bed and, in my haste, stupidly tripped over my charger cord, falling hard to the floor. A sharp pain shot up my right ankle. Maybe I was the one who was now going to need the crutches if they didn't become part of a crime scene investigation.

Adrenaline flowing, I stood up and stormed out of my room as fast as I could, ignoring the searing pain in my foot. Half sprinting, half limping, I charged to Tanya's room and wrenched her door open. My face was so heated I could feel my cheeks flaming. About to implode, I stood at the doorway.

"Studying much?"

Both Tanya and Lance stopped dead in their tracks. Tanya smirked at me while Lance turned fire engine red.

"Paige, it's not what you think!" he stammered, throwing his hands up in surrender.

"I have *eyes*." I limped over to the crutches and shoved them under my armpits. Scrunching my face, I glowered at Tanya.

"Still need these?"

"Oh, my foot's much better now." With a vapid smile, she glanced down at her still bandaged ankle and wiggled it. "And just for *your* information, I was teaching your boyfriend how to slow-dance in time for your mum's upcoming gala which she wants us to go to. Something Miss Clodhopper couldn't *possibly* do." A beat. "You're welcome."

Lance gazed at me, his face more relaxed. "That's the honest truth, Paige. Tanya's been teaching me to dance in exchange for helping her with her calculus."

"Since *you* won't," added Tanya.

I took several breaths in and out of my nose. "I think you should go home, Lance."

Without another word, he grabbed his backpack and scurried out of the room.

Taking the crutches with me, I hobbled back to my bedroom. I didn't really need them, but they'd make a good weapon if I ever needed to defend myself against her.

Giving him the benefit of the doubt, I decided to believe Lance. But there was no way in hell I could trust Tanya.

The spy cam was going to stay put. And every day after school I was going to tune into *The Tanya Show* and watch her every move.

In time, something would give.

And I'd have something on her.

FOURTEEN

NATALIE

On Friday, I had an unexpected guest.

My mother-in-law, Marjorie Merritt. One half of the couple Matt and I jokingly referred to as the M&M's. Martin, her husband, was in La Jolla, getting ready for a weekend golf tournament, and Marjorie had spontaneously decided to stop off in Los Angeles to see Paige and Will, her only grandchildren, if you didn't count Anabel. The sad truth was maybe Anabel *didn't* count. Marjorie had never cared for her, and had made no secret about it when she had been alive.

My relationship with my mother-in-law had improved over the years. At first, she was icy cold toward me. Borderline vindictive. She was convinced it was my idea to elope with Matt, though it was his, and faulted me for not giving her the opportunity to plan an elaborate wedding. She initially didn't trust me—or respect me—and thought I was a gold digger who had trapped her son by getting pregnant. But, over time, I'd proved to her I wasn't. She was impressed by my many philanthropic endeavors as well as by my good taste and family values. She was a woman from the "old school," who believed a woman's place was at home. To make a nice house and attend to the needs of her husband and children, and to use any spare time to make the world a better place. She was also of the belief that if your husband's eyes wandered, look the other way. Maybe I should have.

Though I still wouldn't describe my relationship with my mother-in-law as close, it was at least cordial. Maintaining her distance, she was staying at the nearby Four Seasons and would be heading down the coast in the morning to meet her husband.

"You look well, Natalie," she said as we shared some gin and tonics in the living room, seated across from each other on the twin damask couches. A G&T with a slice of lime was her choice of drink, and though I much preferred a glass of wine, I decided to go with the flow. She took a sip of the ice-filled cocktail. "How's everything between you and Matthew?"

Marjorie only called her middle child by his full name and never once called me Nat.

"Everything's wonderful," I said, setting my tall glass down on the coffee table between us. Marjorie had seen me at my lowest following the death of Anabel, and had come to stay at the house to take care of the kids while I lay in my bed like a decaying vegetable. She had no idea of what had really happened. Anabel's tragic accident was only part of it.

"And how are the children?"

Marjorie adored Will and Paige, and for that I was grateful. Loving grandparents were something I never had and, along with Matt's two other siblings, they gave the kids a sense of family, which was important to me.

"They're well. Paige is in the process of applying to college and Will is immersed in all kinds of cyber stuff I don't understand."

"Where is Paige considering applying?" My mother-in-law had a special fondness for Paige. Maybe because they resembled each other, though her hair was now silver gray and styled in a short chic bob. They also shared many of the same interests, the top one being their passion for art.

"As I'm sure you know, she really wants to go to the Rhode Island School of Design, but Matt's insistent that she apply to Stanford early decision."

My mother-in-law made a dismissive face. "Not everyone needs to go to Stanford like Matthew and his father to make their mark on the world. Paige should go wherever she pleases; success is a by-product of happiness. And she's young. Before I leave for La Jolla in the morning, I'm going to have a word with Matthew."

I flashed her a small grateful smile. "I'd appreciate that. Maybe he'll listen to you."

Just as I was about to change the subject, a charming voice entered the room.

"Hi, Natalie. I didn't see you in the kitchen and thought I heard voices coming from here."

Tanya. Marjorie's eyes following mine, I gazed in her direction.

"Oh, hello, dear!" Seeing her always brightened my day and I was pleased her sprained ankle had healed quickly. Over the week we'd grown closer, and she'd continued to be such an asset in helping me put together the gala, now only a few weeks away. With the event so close, I was glad Marjorie was going back to her hotel after dinner. I had too much to do and my opinionated mother-in-law would only get in the way.

Her lips pursing, Marjorie scrutinized Tanya. "Natalie, might this be the British exchange student from London you've been telling me about? I was hoping to meet her."

"Yes, it is." Smiling, I motioned her to join us. "Tanya, come here. I'd like to introduce you to my mother-in-law, Marjorie Merritt... Paige and Will's grandma," I added as she strutted our way. "Marjorie, this is Tanya Blackstone."

Tanya extended her hand and my mother-in-law stood to

shake it. "Hello." The frost in her voice could make someone shiver. And freeze over the space between them.

"Should I be giving you a hug?" asked Tanya.

"A handshake will suffice."

As if our exchange student had the plague, Marjorie broke free of Tanya's grip and sat back down. Smoothing her gray flannel slacks, she crossed one ankle over the other, drawing attention to the classic Ferragamo flats she always wore. She must have had a pair in every color.

"Come. Please join us," I told Tanya, patting the plump cushion to my left.

"I'd love to," she said, plonking down next to me and dropping her backpack by her feet. She eyed the tall glasses in our hands. "What are you drinking?"

"Gin and tonics." *And no, you can't have one.*

Thankfully, she didn't ask me to make her a drink or get her a glass of wine in front of my hypercritical mother-in-law, and instead studied her.

"Marjorie—"

"It's Mrs. Merritt to you." My mother-in-law's haughtiness made me bristle, but Tanya seemed unperturbed and obliged.

"Of course, Mrs. Merritt. I just want to say I love the color of your sweater. And your pearls are stunning."

Marjorie glanced down at her salmon cashmere crewneck, which was offset by a strand of South Sea pearls, a diamond-clasped family heirloom that was worth over a hundred thousand dollars. One day, she wanted Paige to have them.

"Thank you," she said, her focus returning to Tanya. "So, Tanya, where do you live in London? My husband and I have spent a great deal of time there. It's one of my favorite cities in the world."

"Mine too! Papa and I live in Belgravia."

Marjorie nodded. "A lovely area. Do you live near the park?"

"Not far."

"Which one?" she asked, her tone sounding more and more like an interrogation. "There are so many."

"Kingsington Park." Gathering her backpack, Tanya hastily stood up. "So nice to meet you, Mrs. Merritt. If you'll excuse me, I have a lot of homework to do."

"Of course. I look forward to seeing you at dinner."

"Same." Smiling brightly, she pivoted and swanned out of the room.

Once she was gone, I took another sip of my G&T. "She's lovely, isn't she, Marjorie? She's been a joy to have around."

Marjorie stirred the ice cubes in her drink and then looked at me pointedly. "How did you find this girl?"

"Through an accredited exchange student program."

"How much do you know about her?"

"Well, her mother died in childbirth. Her father's a diplomat, and she goes to a posh private school outside of London."

"Hmm." Marjorie frowned. "Though she appears to come from an educated upper-class family, her English accent is not right."

I cocked my head. "What do you mean?"

"Individuals who come from backgrounds like hers speak Queen's English. Her accent is off. In fact, I can't even place it."

"Maybe being around American kids has messed with her accent," I countered.

"That's not all. She mispronounced the area of London where she lives. It's Bel-gray-via, not Bel-grah-via. And there is no such place as Kingsington Park. It's Kensington... Gardens. I find these faux pas very odd and somewhat disconcerting. Oh... and she also referred to my top as a sweater when every Brit I know calls it a *jumper*."

"She was probably just nervous meeting you." I sometimes joked with Matt that I should call his mother "Your Majesty." He didn't disagree.

Marjorie finished her drink. "I'm just saying you can't always judge a book by its cover." Standing up with her glass in her hand, she offered to help me make dinner.

As much as I appreciated her offer, I would have much rather had Tanya in the kitchen with me. We'd secretly share a glass of wine and laugh. And I could tell her anything without fear of being judged. Well, almost everything. My secrets were mine. Mine alone to bear.

My mother-in-law took the prize for being The. Most. Judgmental. Woman. In. The. World. If she knew my secrets, I'd be extricated from this family.

And that's not all.

FIFTEEN

NATALIE

Dinner was livelier than usual as both Paige and Will were thrilled to see their grandmother. While Marjorie and Martin didn't live that far away from us—San Francisco was a six-hour drive and only a little over an hour by plane—we no longer saw them frequently. Maybe three or four times a year for Thanksgiving, their birthdays, and occasionally for Christmas. Less and less since Anabel's death as the kids' busy school schedules and extracurricular activities took precedence. So, it was a bonus for them to have this unexpected visit.

With his controlling mother at the table, Matt was unable to dominate the conversation and talk about work or politics. Marjorie took the lead instead, focusing on the kids. She was delighted to hear that Will's robotics team had won first prize and was advancing to the interscholastic state finals, and she was surprised by how much he'd grown. "You're going to outdo your father and be *far* more handsome."

Will beamed, proud of his achievements. I had the feeling that he was going to go to MIT one day and become an engineer. Break away from the family tradition of men going into finance.

Marjorie turned her attention to Paige. "Dear, you look like you've lost weight." She wasn't saying it as a compliment.

"A little," replied my daughter, picking at her salad. With my mother-in-law's help, we'd made a meal that Paige could eat without taking offense—penne with a pesto sauce, a kale salad with quinoa, and garlic-roasted asparagus.

"Are you feeling okay?" she asked, concern in her voice.

"She's gone vegan!" jumped in Tanya, whom Marjorie had so far ignored.

My mother-in-law shot Tanya a scathing look. "Excuse me, young lady. I wasn't talking to you." I felt myself bristle as she redirected her gaze at my daughter.

"Yes, Grandma. I've gone on a vegan diet."

"Tell me about it."

Paige explained her newfound aversion to eating any food that was an animal or animal product. To my surprise, my mother-in-law approved, telling Paige about her recent involvement with animal rights organizations and global warming. "We need more kids like you to save our planet."

She took a sip of her wine. Tonight, a lovely pinot grigio.

"And how are things going with your boyfriend? Lance, isn't it?"

"Yes, it is. You have a great memory, Grandma." My daughter gave Tanya a sideways glance before continuing. "Everything's good."

Her voice sounded tentative. I'd noticed how much time Lance and Tanya were spending together. I made a mental note to talk to Paige about it, not certain she would open up to me. The banter between my mother-in-law and daughter continued, the subject changing.

"So, my dearest, your mother told me you're applying to colleges. That you're interested in the Rhode Island—"

Matt cut his mother off. "She's applying early decision to Stanford. You'll be able to see her all the time. Palo Alto is only a half hour drive from San Francisco." His gaze shifted to Paige. "So, how's the application coming along?"

Paige looked him hard in the eye. "It's *not!*"

"What do you mean?" asked my husband, anger rising in his voice.

"For God's sake, Matthew," snapped Marjorie. "Leave her alone. She should go wherever she wants."

"*I'm* applying to Stanford!" Tanya blurted proudly.

My mother-in-law turned to her. Her face glacial. "Frankly, my dear, I couldn't care less. You're *not* my granddaughter."

"Marjorie!" I bit out, wishing I could ask her to apologize for her rude remark. But I couldn't. It would lead to an ugly showdown, and one that I would never win. Her Majesty was a force to be reckoned with and felt she could say whatever she pleased. Whenever she pleased. She liked to wield her power.

Feeling bad for our exchange student, I almost got up to give her a hug. To my great relief, she opened her mouth for a second, but then snapped it closed and went back to eating her dinner. In a way, by not responding, she had triumphed over my patronizing mother-in-law, whose attention was now diverted by her son.

"Listen to this. My new client, who's a big shot sportscaster, gave me a pair of Lakers tickets. VIP seats on the floor."

Paige's eyes lit up. She loved the Lakers, LA's popular basketball team, and loved going to their games, despite sitting in the nosebleed stadium seats we had. She was devastated when her sports idol Kobe Bryant and his teenage daughter perished in a helicopter crash. She cried for days, and even made a lifelike sculpture of him, which she kept in her studio as a remembrance.

"Oh, Dad! That's *so* exciting! When are the tickets for?"

"The last Saturday in October. But I want to take Tanya."

Paige's jaw fell to the floor. Her face crumpled. "What!?"

"Relax, Paige. There will be other tickets. I just thought I should give Tanya a unique American experience while she's here. One she'll never forget."

"Oh my God! I'm so excited!" squealed Tanya as tears gathered in my daughter's eyes. She was crushed.

Holding them back, she bravely stood up and excused herself from the table to do her homework. She gave her grandmother a hug. "I love you, Grandma. Have a safe trip to La Jolla and give Grandpa my love. I can't wait to see you both over Thanksgiving."

After giving her father a glaring look, she fled. Will followed her.

"Did I say something wrong?" asked Matt with more bewilderment than guilt.

"Honey, why don't you go to your office? I'm going to clean up."

"Fine." Rising from his chair, he wasted no time disappearing.

Only three of us were left. Me, my mother-in-law, and Tanya.

"Natalie, can I help you tidy up?" asked our exchange student.

Marjorie answered before I could, her voice icy. "Tanya, I'd like to spend some more time with Natalie... *alone*. So, why don't you please join the children upstairs?"

Tanya looked miffed, then flashed a smile. "I understand. Have a nice time in La Jolla, and I can't wait to see you again."

My mother-in-law watched as she slid out of the room. Her face impassive.

No kisses.

No hugs.

The last of the dishes were loaded in the dishwasher.

"Do you want a nightcap before you head back to the hotel?" I asked my mother-in-law.

"Just some coffee. Decaf if you have it."

I made the coffee quickly with our Keurig. Bringing the two steaming mugs to the kitchen island, I set them down, and we each added a splash of half-and-half from a small bone china pitcher. The way we both liked our coffee was one of the few things we had in common. We took sips of our piping hot brews and then Marjorie spoke first.

"I'm concerned."

My brows lifted. "About what?"

"About Paige. She seems unhappy."

I took another sip. "Senior year is difficult. With college apps and the unknown ahead. It's very stressful. So much pressure."

"Yes, I agree, but it's more than that."

Sitting opposite her, I met her eyes. "What do you mean?"

"I sense there's a great deal of friction between Paige and that exchange student of yours."

"I can't blame her for being disappointed that Matt's taking Tanya to the Lakers game instead of her."

"She looked totally crestfallen. I'm adding that to the list of things I plan to talk to him about."

"Good luck. You know Matt. Once he makes his mind up, it's impossible to change it."

"He's stubborn. Just like his father." She took another sip of her coffee. "Do they get along?"

"Who? Matt and Paige?"

She gave me a sharp look. "No. Paige and your exchange student."

I hesitated for a moment. "Yes, more or less. It's not a perfect relationship. You know how girls are. You know what it was like with Anabel."

"I hate to say this, but let's be honest: We both know Anabel was somewhat of a spoiled child."

Her words stung. But they were true. Yes, I'd spoiled Anabel but out of need. Guilt. I bit down on my bottom lip to refrain from saying something I would regret. With all her faults, I'd loved Anabel with all my heart. And still did.

Marjorie saw the hurt on my face. "I'm sorry, Natalie. I didn't mean that. Martin and I loved Anabel as much as we love Paige and Will. It's just that we never seemed to be able to please her."

I thought back to an early Christmas when they'd bought her a beautiful tricycle and she'd had a temper tantrum because it was red, not pink. And her thirteenth birthday when they'd given her a new laptop, which she'd handed back to them because it was a MacBook Air and not a MacBook Pro. I suppose it was my fault she was so difficult because from the minute she was born, I had vowed to give her everything I never had. Everything she wanted. And Matt was an enabler.

Looking back at the past, I felt a bubble of remorse rise inside me. "Anabel was a demanding child. I think she was born that way." I wasn't going to admit I'd made her that way while my mother-in-law scrutinized me.

"I don't believe children are born any which way. They are what you *make* them. Products of their environments."

The truth is, I believed some children *were* born evil. The bad seeds that grow up to be rapists, murderers, and serial killers. No matter what parents did to help them, it was in their genetic makeup. I didn't want to debate this with her, so I was happy when Marjorie checked her watch and said she should get going.

My eyes followed her as she stood and spilled the remains of her coffee into the sink. She opened the dishwasher and placed the empty mug inside it. Then turned to face me, her eyes locking on mine.

"Natalie, I know we've had our differences, but you must spend more time with Paige. That questionable exchange student is taking up too much of your time. Your daughter comes first."

With that, she called for an Uber, and when it came time to say goodnight, she pecked me on the cheek as if I tasted like poison.

I watched outside as the car disappeared down the street. Inhaling the crisp fall air, I folded my arms around my chest and thought about her words.

Your daughter comes first.

In the distance, a coyote howled. A fierce chill gripped me.

Maybe I'd failed my daughters as a mother. One had died and the other had shut me out.

I hugged myself tighter to ward off a shiver. Paige was a precious gift. I'd lost one daughter. I couldn't bear to lose another.

Hadn't I been punished enough for my sins?

SIXTEEN

PAIGE

I was dreading tonight. My mom's black-tie gala.

While I'd heard about this event *ad nauseam* over the past few months, nothing had prepared me for the spectacle that awaited me.

The yard was dazzling. The trees and shrubs were glittering with fairy lights and surrounded by candlelit tables with shimmery white linens and tall crystal vases overflowing with beautiful blue flowers. Forget-me-nots, I'd been told. The money raised from tonight's event would go to giving an arts education to abused children. Not every child was as lucky and privileged as me to have wealthy parents who could afford to put them in a private school where art and music were part of the curriculum; I even had my own sculpting studio. I felt a connection to this organization and was proud my mom supported it. A prickle of guilt gave me pause. I should have helped her with the gala. It was for a good cause, after all.

While a harpist played Vivaldi's *The Four Seasons*, I worked myself into the crowd, the men all in tuxes and blue bow ties, and the women dripping in diamonds and dressed in shimmering gowns in either chiffon white or blue jewel tones. I suddenly felt a little underdressed in my simple navy sheath, and I wasn't wearing any jewelry except for Lance's gold heart necklace and a pair of sapphire stud earrings, a birthday present from my grandma. The earrings were beautiful, and they used to be hers.

Having lost Will to his one friend who was here to keep him occupied, I looked for Lance and found him standing near the pool, which was lit with floating tea candles and water lilies, with his back to me.

"Hey," I said, tapping him on the shoulder.

With a start, he spun around.

"Hey!" He gave me a quick once-over with the smallest of smiles. "You look nice."

My heart sank a bit. Scratch that, it sank like the *Titanic*. Is that all he could say to me? *Nice?* To please my mother, I'd worked hard to make myself look attractive. Fixed my wild hair into a neat bun. Cleaned the clay out of my fingernails and buffed them. And honestly, my toned, svelte body looked hot in my slinky gown. Before I could say a word, a tart voice pierced my ears.

"Well, well, if it isn't the Devil Wears Target."

Tanya. Drop-dead-beautiful Tanya! Made up to perfection with her blonder-than-ever hair swept up, she looked movie star stunning in a strapless, body-hugging turquoise gown, strappy silver stilettos, and glittery diamond teardrop earrings that looked familiar. In one hand was a half-filled flute of champagne.

"Wow! You look *amazing*," gushed Lance. Looking her up and down, he couldn't take his eyes off her. It was as if he'd just discovered Cinderella at the ball.

She shot him a seductive smile. "Thanks. You clean up well yourself, Lance-man." Pursing her frosted pink lips, she gave me a once-over. "Paige, on second thought, did you find that rag in a thrift store?"

I wanted to slap her. "Actually, it's a Marc Jacobs original."
Truth, it was some unknown designer dress I'd found on a recy-
cled clothing site for practically nothing.

"Could have fooled me." She took a swig of her champagne.
"Did you notice my earrings?" As if I hadn't, she flicked one of
the dangling diamonds with a finger. "Your mother gave them
to me."

"That was nice of her to lend them to you."

A smug smile snaked across her face. "Actually, Paige, she's
letting me *keep* them. A little thank-you present for helping her
out with the gala."

Her limited-edition Tiffany treasures? An anniversary gift
from my dad! I was so fuming mad I wanted to rip off the
earrings from her lobes and throw them as far as I could. Now, I
was *really* sorry I hadn't helped my mom out.

Tanya batted her long, mascara-laced eyelashes. "C'mon,
Lancey. Let's get something to drink. I could use a refill."

I watched as she grabbed his hand and tugged him away.
She may have gotten my mother's earrings, but there was no
way she was getting my boyfriend. Exploding with bubbling,
red-hot rage, I stuck out my foot.

The next thing I heard was a shriek and she was flying into
the pool.

The deep end.

SEVENTEEN

NATALIE

The night could not have been more perfect. The unseasonably balmy weather was divine. The backyard looked spectacular. The turnout was incredible, with everyone complimenting me on both the glittering fairy-tale décor and my teal-blue Dior gown, the one Tanya had urged me to wear.

Thankfully, the woman who used to co-chair this event with me wasn't here. Alexa Roth. The woman who had almost destroyed my marriage, my family, *and* my life. So I could relax, and enjoy all my hard work.

The party in full swing, I was about to announce dinner when panicked screams blared in my ears. A woman's cries, a voice I didn't recognize.

"Somebody help me! I can't swim!"

My heart raced. Oh my God. It was coming from the pool. Had one of my guests fallen in?

"Help!" the voice cried out again.

Standing next to my debonair husband, I squeezed his arm. "Matt, I think someone's drowning!"

"Jesus." Breaking away from me, he sprinted over to the pool, with me trailing behind him, running as fast as I could in my six-inch-high Louboutins, hoping I wouldn't trip and break my neck. Under my breath I cursed and wished I'd trusted my gut and not listened to the event planner about keeping the pool exposed. What if someone died at my gala? A horrific mixture of remorse and fear coursed through me, and I prayed to God we'd get to the pool in time to save whoever had fallen in.

Breathless, I got to the pool and gasped. Floundering in the deep end was our exchange student, Tanya. Her arms were flailing, and she was coughing and shrieking, barely managing to stay afloat. Paige's boyfriend, Lance, was already in the pool trying to reel her in, and I watched with my heart in my throat as Matt dove in and joined him. Together, they pulled her to safety and hauled her out. Flat on her back, she sputtered and hacked. A small crowd of voyeurs had gathered around us. I reached for Matt's jacket, which he'd shrugged off before diving in, then crouched down beside her and covered her shaking, soaking wet body.

"Tanya, darling! Are you okay?"

"She pushed me in!" she rasped, her voice sounding nothing like the British one I was accustomed to.

"Who did?"

She weakly lifted a hand and pointed a finger.

"Her!" she choked out.

Craning my neck, I followed the direction of her finger and gasped again. She was pointing directly at Paige.

My heart still beating double time, I tried to take hold of my emotions. They were all over the place. The one that won out was shock.

"Paige, is that true? Did you push Tanya into the pool?" I tried to keep my voice level.

My daughter looked me straight in the eye. "I didn't touch her. Ask Lance. He was with us."

Dripping with water, Lance confirmed she hadn't. "Mrs.

Merritt, I think Tanya tripped in those high heels she's wearing."

Paige twitched a smile. "Exactly. Plus, she was a little tipsy."

With a struggle, Tanya sat up and glared at Paige. Darts shot out of her waterlogged eyes. "I only had one glass of champagne, you liar. Not even!" The accent was back, but I couldn't believe how vitriolic her tone was.

"Whatever," retorted Paige, mimicking her British accent. And then in her normal voice, "I'm surprised you can't swim, especially since your fancy boarding school in England has an Olympic-size indoor pool."

"I never learned how. And that's none of your business."

"Enough, girls!" And I meant it. I was eager to get back to my gala and not let this unfortunate incident get in the way of its success. I looked at the growing crowd of spectators. Everyone loved a little drama. That's why cars slowed on the freeway when they passed a gory accident, bringing traffic to a standstill. It was time to move things along.

"Everyone, please go to your assigned tables. Dinner is about to be served." I helped Tanya up, draping Matt's jacket over her shoulders.

The crowd dispersing, I looked at my drenched husband. "Matt, why don't you go upstairs and get changed? And take Lance with you. I'm sure you have something that will fit him."

He nodded.

"I'll take care of Tanya. We're about the same size. One of my gowns will surely fit her."

Almost back to her charming British self, she gave me an appreciative smile. "Thank you, Natalie." She rubbed her earlobes. "And thank goodness the gorgeous diamond earrings you *gave me* didn't fall off in the water." She said this loud enough so that Paige could hear her. Without another word, my daughter stalked off.

While I walked our exchange student back to the house, an unsettling feeling fell over me. I thought back to the conversation I'd had with my mother-in-law when she was here a few weeks ago. About Tanya's unusual English accent and mispronunciation of her exclusive London neighborhood. I, like Paige, found it odd she couldn't swim. But maybe she'd had some traumatic childhood experience?

And maybe tonight's American accent could be attributed to being a little inebriated. Plus, she'd been here for almost two months and was sounding more and more like an American every day.

As I helped her change into one of my Versace gowns, a slinky cobalt-blue one, I let go of all my doubts. I told her it looked perfect on her and she hugged me, telling me how much she loved me.

Silently, I thanked God she hadn't drowned tonight. I couldn't bear to lose this beautiful, beguiling girl, whom I was beginning to love like a daughter.

Heaven knows, I'd had enough loss to last a lifetime.

EIGHTEEN

PAIGE

My studio in the far corner of the backyard was my refuge. The special place where I could be alone and de-stress. Sculpting was my salvation. I loved putting my hands into the cold, wet, gray clay and molding it into anything I wanted, be it a lifelike figure, a bust, or something abstract. I loved the feel of it. The smell of it. And the transformative power of it.

It was my drug.

With basketball season in full swing, I hadn't had a chance to hang out here for a while. It was a former gardening shed that was built with the house. Since our gardeners brought their own equipment, we really didn't need it, and I'd convinced my mom to let me turn it into a studio where I could sculpt. It was the nicest thing she'd ever done for me.

From the earliest of ages, I loved to make things with clay. Real clay, not that Bazooka-pink Play-Doh my sister liked. Over the years, I'd advanced from snakes and pancakes to far more complex things. I'd taken classes and read many technique books, including some by the world's greatest sculptors. Michelangelo. Rodin. Brancusi, and more. My heroes. One day, I hoped to join them. Exhibit in galleries. Have pieces in museums as well as in Sotheby's auctions. Become the next Louise Bourgeois, another one of my idols.

My studio was small but functional. Well lit, my workplace consisted of a drafting table and stool, and shelves where I kept my tools, supplies, and reference books. It also had a sink, which I used to wet down my clay and wash my grubby hands. The walls were covered with inspirational posters of works and quotes by my favorite sculptors, and in the far corner, there was a portable kiln, which I used to fire my clay creations and transform them into ceramic sculptures.

Tonight, I really needed this escape. My father had taken Tanya to the Lakers game, and I didn't want to think about how much fun they were having in their VIP floor seats. I needed to let go of my jealousy and anger. Channel it into my clay.

Wearing AirPods and listening to some symphonic metal, I was totally zoned out and in the moment. I was working on a bust of my mother, which I planned to surprise her with on her upcoming fortieth birthday. She'd coveted one after seeing the bust I'd made of my grandma, the one person in my family other than my brother who supported my dream of becoming a sculptor. The kiln had been a gift from her and cost twice as much as my MacBook Pro.

The bust was coming along and I was pleased with the likeness, though it still needed quite a bit of tweaking. Sculpting required a lot of patience, but the end result—and the fulfillment I got—was worth the time and effort. Kobe Bryant once said that amazing things come from hard work and perseverance, and I believed him. I'd been lucky enough to see him play many times. To watch him move across the court, with his agility, grace, and speed, was pure magic. He shoots; he scores. His tragic death as well as that of his daughter Gianna had shattered me. Why did bad things happen to good people? As a tribute, I'd made a sculpture of him, jumping with a basketball in his hand. It had helped me work through my grief. One day, I hoped to give it to his family. Maybe my father's new client could put us in touch.

Perched on the table and illuminated by a clip-on lamp, the statue gave me strength and determination as I chiseled my mother's nose and cheekbones. Working away, I lost sense of time. I deliberately didn't bring my phone with me because I didn't want any distractions. And I didn't keep any type of time-piece here because I never wanted to feel pressured.

I guess because I was wearing AirPods and was so focused on my mother's bust, I didn't hear the door open. A sudden tap on my shoulder gave me a start. My heart jumped; my pulse raced. I whipped my head around, and standing behind me was Tanya. She was wearing pink-and-white-striped pajama bottoms and a Lakers sweatshirt. With the blink of an eye, my initial shock morphed into pure, unadulterated hatred.

"What are you doing in here?" I seethed, plucking the AirPods out of my ears.

"I saw a light on from my room and decided to check it out. It was keeping me up, getting in the way of my beauty sleep." She twirled her braided hair. "Oh, and by the way, the Lakers game was amazing. They won by one point and I got to meet LeBron James, who scored the winning point. A slam dunk!"

Fury pulsed through every cell of my body. I thought I might stab her with my sculpting knife.

"Get out of here. This is my private space."

She pretended like she didn't hear me and moved to the right of me so she could better see the bust. "That kind of looks like your mother."

"It *is*."

She studied the sculpture. "No offense, but her nose is narrower and she has much higher cheekbones. More like mine."

My nerves were buzzing. I felt my blood sizzling. "Get out, Tanya!"

"Not yet." She didn't budge a millimeter, her eyes landing on my Kobe statue. She inched closer to it.

"Is this like some famous basketball player?" She ran her manicured fingers along his backside.

"Get your hands off it! *Now!*"

Ignoring me, she defiantly lifted the statue off the table and examined it, flipping it around and on its sides. I wanted to grab it from her but feared there would be a tug-of-war. The fragile statue could get caught in the crossfire and be destroyed.

"Please, Tanya. Put it down!"

She fired me a smug smirk. "No worries."

To my utter horror, she let go of the statue. With an ear-splitting crash, it fell to the cement floor and shattered into smithereens.

"Oh my God! What did you just do?"

"Duh! You told me to let go of the statue and put it down. So I did."

Tears choking my throat, I jumped off my stool and crouched down on the floor. I looked up at Tanya. "Go. Please go!"

"No problemo. Night-night. And sweet dreams!"

So distraught, I didn't watch her leave. My eyes flooding, I stared at the scattered fragments of my Kobe masterpiece. It was as shattered as my heart had been when he'd left our planet.

Ashes to ashes. Dust to dust.

Beyond repair.

Holding a jagged piece between my fingers, I collapsed onto the floor and lost it. Sobbing uncontrollably. My shoulders heaving, my nose running, I was totally, utterly, positively defeated. Tanya was destroying my life and now she had destroyed my precious statue.

Remarkably, the only part that wasn't destroyed was Kobe's head. Detached from his body, it was miraculously intact and in one piece. Carefully, I picked it up and held it in the palm of my hand. I stared at it, tears blurring my vision and coating the clay.

Then suddenly, I remembered Kobe's credo: The very moment you give up is the very moment you let someone else win. More or less his words, I absorbed them like osmosis. They sank under my skin and flooded my being. Like a sad drooping flower perked up by water, I stood up.

My sobs subsided. I placed a damp cloth over my mother's bust, put my materials away, and turned off the lights. With resolve, I strode out of my studio. Each step stronger. More determined.

I wasn't going to give up.

I wasn't going to let Tanya win.

NINETEEN

PAIGE

Taking down Tanya was proving harder than I'd thought. Each day, she grew more popular at school and ingratiated herself further with my parents. I swear, if my mother had to pick a favorite, she'd pick Tanya and she wasn't even her child.

Tanya had gotten involved with all Mom's charities; they went shopping together, often coming home with matching outfits; they got their nails done together; they tried out new recipes together, and I'd more than once caught them sharing a bottle of wine. *Natanya*, my new nickname for them, was also planning our annual holiday trip to Hawaii, a place I had no interest in going back to. Been there; done that. I wasn't someone who liked to veg out on a beach, sunbathe, or catch waves. Though I must say the possibility of a tsunami wave taking out our bikini-clad exchange student was quite enticing.

I really wanted to go to Mexico—specifically to Mexico City to see Frida Kahlo's Blue House and the outlying pyramids and then to nearby San Miguel de Allende, an artists' colony that was supposed to be as beautiful as it was inspirational. Will thought that would be cool too, but no one listened to what we wanted. My father berated us, saying how stupid it would be to go to a dangerous country where we could get kidnapped by a Mexican cartel. That only fueled a new evil fantasy—a Mexican drug lord kidnapping Tanya, torturing her, and threatening to cut off her pretty little head if my father didn't pay the ransom.

Too bad the latter wasn't likely because Tanya had my father wrapped around her pretty little finger. She was a total kiss-up, always complimenting him on everything, from his attire to his cologne. She took up jogging and went running with him in the mornings before school (which made her already enviably long, toned legs even more toned), and took an extreme interest in his business dealings. One weekday when we had no school, she'd accompanied him to his office and spent the entire day there.

That night, my dad came home with boundless energy. At the dinner table, he couldn't stop raving about how helpful Tanya had been. How smart she was! She had a huge career in finance ahead of her and was half-serious when he said he was going to make her his business partner after she graduated Stanford. I swear he was treating her like she was his flesh and blood.

If you asked me, the only talent she had with numbers was gaining new Instagram followers, now close to ten thousand. It was seriously hard to believe she was so smart. For over a month, she'd begged me to help her with her Stanford application. Especially her personal statement essay with the prompt: "What Will Make You Stand Out at Stanford?" I'd practically spat in her face and told her if she was Stanford material, she could do it herself.

To appease my father, I applied to his alma mater early action, which, unlike early decision, allowed me to apply to other colleges and hold off until May to commit if I was accepted. My heart set on RISD, it took me forever to write the last personal statement essay. I must have tossed a hundred different versions into the garbage. Finally, I settled on one and submitted it just before the deadline. Tanya had submitted hers a few weeks before me. Part of me wanted to see what she'd written and have a good laugh. *I will stand out at Stanford because I'll be the dumbest blonde on campus.* That's what I would have written.

The time I spent on my Stanford application paled compared to the time I spent putting together a portfolio of my work for RISD. I poured everything I had into it because I wanted it to be outstanding. RISD was as hard as Stanford to get into, with only twelve percent of applicants accepted. My father was still adamantly opposed to me becoming a sculptor. He felt it was not only a waste of time, but a waste of my life and a waste of his money. He continued to threaten that he wouldn't pay a dime of my tuition if I went there. Maybe I'd get a scholarship.

"Have either of you heard from Stanford?" my dad asked, after a bite of his veal medallions, *Natanya*'s latest gourmet dinner. I'd stuck to my vegan diet and was devouring a tasty Indian curry with lentils and cauliflower. I'd found several online sites that delivered frozen gourmet vegan meals. While my mom offered to prepare fresh vegan entrées nightly, I couldn't trust her little helper Tanya. I wouldn't put it past her to poison me.

"I think it's too soon to hear," I responded, the rumor at school being that early decision and early action applicants would hear right before Thanksgiving. To be honest, I hoped they'd lost my application.

My mom interjected. "Actually, Paige, something came in the mail for you today."

I felt a kernel of dread unfurl in my stomach. Hearing so quickly usually meant they either loved you or hated you. Fingers crossed it was the latter and I could have the last laugh with my grandma.

"Where is it?" asked my father, eagerness in his voice.

"In the kitchen." My mom rose from her chair. "I'll go get it."

A few moments later, she returned with a letter-size white envelope in her hand.

"Give it to me," demanded my father.

"But it's addressed to Paige," she countered.

My father's face hardened. "Natalie, just do as I ask and give it to me." The only time he called my mother by her full name was when he was frustrated or angry with her. "Now!"

The color draining from her face, my mom padded over to him and handed him the envelope. With a mix of anticipation and apprehension, I watched him tear it open. His eyes flickered with excitement as I held my breath, waiting for him to remove the contents. He unfolded the single sheet of paper and silently began to read it. The expression that came over his face was one I'd never seen. It was dark and menacing, his nostrils flaring, his lips snarled. His eyes, two burning embers, met mine.

"What the *hell*, Paige!?"

"Matt, your language. The children!" my mom chided.

"Shut up, Natalie!"

My mother cowered as if he might jump up and slap her. My father's fiery eyes stayed on me.

"Paige, how in the world could you do this? You're a total embarrassment."

I scrunched my face so hard it hurt. "I don't understand. What are you talking about?"

His face grew so flaming red I thought his head would rocket off his neck. His voice grew louder by decibels. "You plagiarized someone else's essay almost word for word."

"What!? I did not!" I felt myself shaking.

"They ran your essay through a foolproof program that shows your essay is almost identical to another student's who submitted theirs three weeks before yours." His heated face looked demonic. "Let me read you portions of it."

My heart was beating so hard I thought it would burst out of my ribcage and crash-land on the table. I sat paralyzed as he began.

"Theirs: *We must live every day to the fullest because life can change in a snap. Here today, gone tomorrow. Look at Michael Jackson!*

"Yours: *We must live every minute to the fullest because life can change in an instant. You can be here today, gone tomorrow. Look at Kobe Bryant and his daughter!*

"Theirs: *I want to live my life to the max. Every morning when I get up, I want to be stoked by the surprise of another day.*

"Yours: *I want to live my life to the best I can. Each morning when I wake up, I want to be excited by the gift of a new day.*

"Theirs: *Mostly, I want to live my life with no regrets. I am sure if I get to go to Stanford, I will never regret attending this awesome university.*

"Yours: *Most of all, I want to live my life with no regrets. I know if Stanford admits me, I will never regret my decision to attend this great institution of higher learning.*"

My father paused. He looked at me pointedly, contempt scorched in his eyes. "Are you satisfied, Paige? Or do I need to read more?"

My mouth went dry. I was at a loss for words. Suddenly, an unusually quiet Tanya burst out. "Oh my God! She stole *my* personal statement essay."

"What?" I cried out before my father could say another word.

"I can prove it! I'll go print it out."

Tanya leaped up from the table and sprinted out of the dining room. In less than a minute, she was back with the one-page essay dangling from her fingers. She handed it to my father and returned to her seat, her eyes on him as he read it.

"My God, I can't believe it!" He palm-slapped his forehead, horror written all over his face. "It's identical!"

She gave him a smug smile. "Mr. Merritt, I mean Matt, Paige must have stolen it off my desk or seen it on my computer. She can get into my bedroom from the hallway door."

I stared at her. "I did no such thing! You stole the essay from *me*!"

"I did not! I can't even get into your room. It's locked from both sides."

"Paige, dear," interrupted my mom, now seated, "can you prove you wrote it?"

"No! I didn't save a copy on my laptop because I seriously didn't care about it."

My head began to spin. How the hell did Tanya get access to my essay? My mind did somersaults and then it came to me. The drafts I threw out. I'd even accidentally printed out a dozen copies of a close-to-final one and tossed them in the trash without shredding them. She must have found them.

"Dad, Tanya found my essay and copied it." Tears pricked the backs of my eyes. "You have to believe me!"

My furious father continued to breathe in and out of his nose. I honestly thought red-hot flames would fly out of his nostrils like a dragon's.

"Paige, you are an utter embarrassment to me. And to our family. All the Merritt men and women have gone to Stanford." He went back to reading the letter. *"We understand that your family is legacy and are major contributors to the university, but we have a no-tolerance policy for plagiarism. It is with great regret that we cannot admit you to our institution and wish you much success elsewhere. Sincerely, Richard H. Shaw, Dean of Admissions."*

Rage burning on his cheeks, my father tore up the letter into a million tiny pieces and then banged his fist on the table so forcefully the plates shook.

"Paige," he hissed, "go up to your room. I am cutting off your phone and taking away your car keys for an indefinite amount of time."

There was a hushed silence around the table. Tanya shot me a smug, triumphant look as I rose to my feet and slumped out of the room.

"Can I please be excused too?" I heard my little brother say as I turned a corner.

Five minutes later we were sitting on my bed. I was crying. Tanya had done it again.

"Willster, do you believe me?"

"Do you seriously have to ask me that question?" He looked at me earnestly. "That girl is so dumb she needs a headband to hold onto her thoughts."

I couldn't help but laugh through my tears. "But she gets away with it. Now, I don't have a phone or car."

"Hey, Pudge, look at the bright side. Now, you don't have to go to Stanford."

For the first time all night, I smiled. "You're right!"

We high-fived.

Screw my father. Screw Tanya. I wouldn't be surprised if she'd bribed someone to falsify her grades. She was the ultimate con artist.

I spent the rest of the night working on my RISD portfolio. Asking Will to safeguard it in his room lest the psycho find it and destroy it. Or make it hers.

I knew now that nothing was beneath her in her quest to destroy me.

TWENTY

NATALIE

"Happy birthday to you..."

Two years ago, as I lay in bed contemplating ending my life, I never thought I'd hear that refrain again. Nor the harmonious voices of my family belting it out.

With a tingly smile on my face, I sauntered into our breakfast room where we ate breakfast on special occasions. I loved this room. Located off our kitchen, it was octagon-shaped, with built-in robin-blue cabinets and a hand-painted coffered ceiling. All original to the house. To keep with the airy spirit of the room, I'd furnished it with a round glass-top table and vintage moss-green wicker chairs with delightful chinoiserie-print cushions. It was pretty enough to be in an interior design magazine.

This year my birthday fell on the first Sunday in November. Matt, Paige, and Will, clad in their pajamas like me, were standing around the table. It was beautifully arranged, placemats set up with my Herend floral china, a housewarming gift from my mother-in-law, and a Lalique crystal vase filled with vibrant pink peonies in the center. My favorites. On the antique sideboard, neatly wrapped presents were grouped together next to my silver coffee service, pitchers of orange juice and milk, a fresh fruit platter, and a tray of assorted pastries—croissants, muffins, and palmiers from my favorite patisserie. One of them —a shimmering sugarcoated blueberry muffin—was already on my plate on the table. A single pink birthday candle was anchored in the middle.

I laughed. "You guys! I'm not turning one, I'm forty. The big four-oh."

Matt chuckled. I don't think my kids appreciated my sense of humor. They both rolled their eyes.

Matt stood and pecked my cheek. "Don't worry, babe. You don't look a day over thirty-nine." Something my envious friends said to my face all the time. If only they knew...

The truth: I *wasn't* a day over thirty-nine. This was actually my thirty-sixth birthday. When I met Matt at the trade show, I was only seventeen and a minor. I'd lied about my age (and a lot of other things) and told him I was twenty-one. I looked older than my years, more sophisticated, and I'd become an excellent actress out of necessity. Almost two decades later, I was still acting.

"Where's Tanya?" I asked, suddenly realizing she wasn't among us.

"She's probably still in bed, hungover," quipped Paige.

I narrowed my eyes at my daughter. "That's really presumptuous. Tanya's a lovely girl. Sometimes, I wish you were more like her."

Before we could get into a tiff, the last thing I wanted on my birthday, Matt took out his monogrammed gold lighter and lit the candle. He urged me to blow it out and make a wish.

I lowered my head, and as the flame flickered in my eyes, I contemplated a wish. There was only one—I wished that my beloved Anabel could be here with me to celebrate my birthday and the rest of my life. Fighting back tears, I extinguished the flame with one breath.

My family clapped and cheered, extinguishing my sadness.

"Let's eat!"

We all helped ourselves to the lovely continental breakfast, which included vegan poppy-seed muffins and almond milk for Paige. As I sat down at the table, with some coffee and my plate piled with deliciousness, my phone rang. I retrieved it from the pocket of my robe.

The caller ID said LAPD. A foreboding feeling fell over me as I accepted the call.

A stern, male voice on the other end greeted me. "Hello, is this the Merritt residence?"

"Yes, this is Mrs. Merritt."

"This is Officer Hamilton with the LAPD."

My heart pounded. My stomach clenched. I always knew this day would come. Trying to stay as calm as possible, I asked, "Is there something I can do for you, Officer?"

"There's been an accident involving a vehicle registered to your husband."

"What do you mean?" I was both relieved and confused that this was why the police were calling me. "All our cars are here parked in our garage."

"Do you own a 2020 white Jeep Cherokee with the license plate number 823KYZ?"

"Yes, that's my daughter's car, and she's sitting beside me."

Able to overhear the conversation, Paige shot me a quizzical look. The officer continued.

"Another girl was driving the vehicle. The only form of identification she was carrying was her school ID. It says her name is Tanya Blackstone and listed you as her emergency contact." A beat. "Mrs. Merritt, are you related to her?"

"No, but I guess you could say I'm her guardian. She's a guest of our family... a foreign exchange student who's staying with us." I took a long, shuddery breath. "Is she okay?"

"I'm unable to answer that. She crashed into a tree and was

taken by ambulance to Cedars-Sinai Medical Center. To the emergency department."

"Oh my God!" My mouth dropped open and I felt my body tremble. The phone shook in my hand.

"You should know, Mrs. Merritt, we found her unconscious."

My heart almost beat out of my chest as he continued. "The car was towed. Here's the number to call to retrieve it."

Not having a pen to jot it down, I asked him to text it to me. In a frenzy, I was barely able to get the words out.

"Natalie, what's going on?" asked Matt as I ended the call.

"Honey, we need to get to Cedars right away. Tanya's been in a terrible car accident!"

With all this madness, I hadn't noticed that Paige had slipped away. She stormed back into the breakfast room, her face red with rage.

"That psycho! She stole my car and probably totaled it."

I felt my blood pressure spike. Anger rising in me like mercury, I lashed out at my daughter. "How could you care about your car when Tanya's *life* is at stake?"

Narrowing her eyes, she gave me a look that could kill. "I *hope* she dies!"

"How dare you say that!?" Furious, I sprang from my chair and marched over to her, until we were a palm's width apart. Not flinching, she just stood there, our eyes locked in an angry stare-off. As if she was daring me to hit her. Thank goodness Matt intervened.

"Get dressed, Nat. I'll drive us to the hospital."

This was so *not* how I envisioned my birthday.

It was the birthday from hell.

TWENTY-ONE

PAIGE

Picking at some fruit salad, I was still fuming. I felt like a bomb about to explode with shrapnels of rage. Will was seated across the table, stuffing his mouth with chunks of a crumbly muffin top. My left hand fisted, I was tempted to smash the muffin. Flatten it. That's how mad I was.

"The *nerve* of her! Taking my car! It's probably in some junkyard!"

My brother took a sip of his milk, then wiped off his white mustache with the back of his hand. "Hey, Pudge, it's not like you could drive it anyway."

He was right. While I'd gotten my phone back, my dad still had my car keys. I think when he said "an indefinite amount of time," he meant forever. He could be such an asshole.

But wait! If my dad still had the keys, how had Tanya gotten hold of them? Had she found them, or had he given them to her? If it was the latter, I hated my father even more.

"Willster, I meant what I said. I hope she dies and rots in hell." This spawn of Satan had made my life a living nightmare. I stabbed a berry with my good-silver fork, and suddenly, one of my grandma's pearls of wisdom popped into my head. *Every cloud has a silver lining.*

"Hey bro, we have a window of opportunity."

"To let Bear back into the house?" Outside in the yard, he was barking.

"Yeah, that too. But also something else."

"What, Pudge?"

"You can be one of the Hardy Boys and I'll be Nancy Drew. Let's go check out her room."

The spy cam hadn't gotten us much further. It acted up, didn't work in the dark, and couldn't capture Tanya in her closet. Mostly, I saw images of Tanya texting on her phone, taking selfies, and primping in her dresser mirror. Whenever the exhibitionist paraded around her room half-naked, I had to stop watching.

Will's grin met his freckles. "Only if I can be Sherlock Holmes."

My precocious brother had read all of Sir Arthur Conan Doyle's classic detective series. Some of the books twice.

"Fine. Then, I'll be Watson."

Wow! If I'd known what hellhole we were stepping into, I'd have made us wear hazmat suits. The spy cam footage only gave a hint. The room was a total pigsty. Nothing like how my neat-as-a-pin sister had kept it when she was alive. The day I caught Lance in it, our housekeeper, Blanca, must have been here and straightened it up. I felt sorry for the poor hardworking woman for having to deal with this horrific mess. I hoped my mother was paying her extra.

The canopy bed was unmade. My sister's treasured stuffed animals were all over the floor. Clothes were strewn everywhere. Drawers were half-open. And along with discarded gum wrappers, skimpy panties in every color littered the carpet.

"Gross!" My brother made a disgusted face. "What are we looking for?"

"Anything that can give us a clue about who she really is. I'll search the drawers and closet. Do you think you can hack into her computer?"

"Elementary, my dear Watson." His English accent was perfect—as good as Tanya's—and I couldn't help chuckling.

With my brother at her desk, I began my search, starting with the chest of drawers. One by one, I went through them, each one more appalling than the one before. Scrunched-up underwear and mismatched socks were squashed between tops, jeans, and pajamas. Nothing was neatly folded or stacked. As I dug through the clutter, the scent of her perfume wafted up my nose. The same sickening floral one my sister used to wear. Ugh!

With each drawer, I was losing hope. I was hoping to find a passport, her student visa, or her British Airways boarding pass. Even a receipt from Heathrow. *Something.* Nope. *Nada.* Maybe she kept that kind of stuff in her backpack, which, unless it was in the closet or under the bed, wasn't in the room. My guess was she probably took it with her. For a second, I thought about my totaled Jeep and silently cursed her, then let it go.

Disappointed, I moved on to her night table. A half-drunk can of Diet Coke sat on top of it along with the CliffsNotes version of *Jane Eyre* and a framed photo of her with my mother and father. Oddly, not one photo of her with *her* father.

I pulled open the single, deep drawer. My eyes widened. Next to a box of Trident gum stood four oversized white plastic bottles, all labeled with batch numbers and names I struggled to pronounce.

Haloperidol... Aripiprazole... Quetiapine... Risperidone.

I twisted off the childproof caps. Inside them were different color pills, each bottle about halfway full.

"Hey, Sherlock. Come over here. You're gonna want to see this."

Will joined me and examined the bottles and their contents. "I think they're meds."

"Do you know what they're for?"

"No idea."

"Should we confiscate them?" I asked.

"No, that would be bad. Take photos of them with your phone and we'll google them later."

Once again, Will was the smart one. I agreed with him. "That's why you're Sherlock, and I'm Watson."

"Don't cut yourself short. You're a good Watson."

"Thanks. Have you gotten into her computer?"

"I just did."

"Have you found anything?"

"Yes. It's registered to a Mary C. Burton."

"That's weird."

"Indeed."

"Have you looked her up?"

"Not yet. I can do that later. First, I want to check out what's on her desktop and try to get into her email."

I gave him a noogie. "Go back to work, Sherlock!"

He scuttled back to the computer while I pulled out my phone and snapped photos of the meds. Returning the last bottle to the drawer, I spotted something under the box of Trident. I slipped out the slim yellow package and recognized it immediately. Ortho Tri-Cyclen. Birth control pills, the same ones I used. A three-month supply. Our family doctor, Dr. Lefferman, had prescribed them to me to mitigate my menstrual cramps and breakouts, though I knew they'd come in handy later in the year when I said goodbye to my virginity. I looked more closely at the Rx label. They, too, had been prescribed by Dr. Lefferman... on September 7, ten days after her arrival.

Carefully, I opened the box and slipped out the contents.

She'd gone through two of the blister sheets and only had one left. I thought back. I'd never heard Tanya complain about period cramps to either me or my mother. And her complexion was flawless. Then it hit me like a brick to my head. Maybe she was taking them for another reason. She'd stolen and demolished my car. Was the next thing on her agenda to steal my boyfriend and demolish our relationship? While I'd told her to her face to stay away from him, I couldn't trust her one bit. For all I knew, she'd already slept with him. Bile rose to my throat as I put back the pills, making sure they were exactly where I found them so she wouldn't know I'd ransacked her room.

That's if she comes back.

Maybe the boyfriend-slash-car thief was on her deathbed. *Ha!* It would serve her right! The wicked thought calmed me down and, with a fortifying breath, I ambled over to the walk-in closet. Like the rest of the room, it was a major disaster area. Like a Category 4 hurricane had blown through it. I was beginning to think her bedroom needed more than our housekeeper, Blanca. A federal disaster relief organization was more like it.

My sister organized her stuff meticulously, hanging her clothes up neatly, color-coding them, and labeling shoeboxes, which were always perfectly stacked. Now, her things, along with slobbo Tanya's, were all over the place, most of them scattered in messy piles on the closet floor. Also tossed haphazardly inside the closet were my sister's other possessions like photos, books, and trophies. Going through all this stuff would take hours. Instead, I did a big-picture search. Just as I'd suspected, Tanya's backpack wasn't in the closet, but something else was. Her big shiny red suitcase. Parked in the very back. Maybe that's where she kept all her travel documents... and her secrets?

Wasting no time, I got down on my knees and tried the zipper. Given that the bag had a combination lock, I was surprised when it began to slide smoothly. The hiss gave me goose bumps. When the bag was fully unzipped, I opened it.

Another major surprise.

Inside it were dozens of photos of my mother, father, Anabel, Will, and myself. The photos spanned a decade. I shuddered. It was so unbelievably creepy. How did she get them? The Internet? Facebook? Instagram? It was like she'd stalked us. And what was even creepier was that in all the photos I appeared, she'd X'd me out with a red marker. Like she was canceling me.

Among the photos was one other—a class photo from Indio High School. The year not specified. About five hundred casually dressed kids were lined up on bleachers, all smiling brightly for the camera except for one thin, mousy-haired girl in the third row center. Unlike her classmates, she looked sullen, like she didn't want to be part of the group photo. Oddly, her face was circled with red marker. Who was this girl and what was her significance to Tanya? Questions burning my brain, I gathered the photos and dashed out of the closet.

"Will, stop what you're doing! Come look at these." My brother joined me, and I showed him the photos. "What do you think?"

He examined the photos as if they were under a microscope. Then lifted his eyes and met mine. "Maybe Mom sent them to her before she came here?"

I hadn't thought about that. That's something my mother would do. Scan old family photos. I made a mental note to ask her. Still, my X'd-out face was making my skin crawl. "Sherlock, why do you think she crossed me out?"

My brother rolled his eyes. "Obviously, my dear Watson, she doesn't like you."

I snickered. That was an understatement. I showed him the last photo—the Indio High class picture.

He knitted his brows together and studied it.

"Do you recognize the girl in the middle who's circled?"

He squinted. "Hand me my magnifying glass."

"Ha-ha. Very funny." Truth is, I wish we had the literary detective's favorite investigative tool because the photo was grainy and it was hard to make her out. "Well, Sherlock?"

Will shook his head. "Sorry, I have no clue."

That made two of us. "How old do you think the photo is?"

He twisted his lips. "It's hard to tell. The kids look to be fifteen or sixteen, and most of them are wearing jeans, T-shirts, and hoodies. It could have been taken yesterday or several years ago. But I'd say it's not older than twenty years."

I muttered a *hmm*. "What should we do with these photos?"

"Take photos of the ones with you in them with your phone, but let's make a copy of that class photo... then put them back in her suitcase."

"Good idea. Did you get into her email account?"

"Yes. It's under TanyaBdreamer@gmail.com."

"Similar to her Instagram."

"Yes... again. And it was set up only the day before she came here."

"Weird. Did you find any revealing emails?"

"What I *didn't* find is actually more revealing. Not one email to her father, or vice versa. He's not even in her list of contacts."

"That's weird too." I wanted to ask if there were any emails to Lance, but refrained. If she did communicate with him, it would likely be via her phone. Texts. Kids of my generation rarely used email. Like Facebook, it was more for old fogies like my parents and grandparents.

"Anything else?"

He nodded. "A few desktop files, but they're mostly for her school stuff."

"Does she have one for her Stanford application?"

"Interesting you should ask that." He raised a knowing finger. "She does indeed."

I followed him back to my sister's desk, the bulletin board

above it now covered with photos of Tanya, and he clicked open the file. *Stanford.* Inside it were several Google Docs... including the personal statement essay she'd copied from me. I was tempted to hit delete, but what good would that do? It was after the fact.

"Were you able to check her browsing history?" I asked.

"Not yet. Want to do it together?"

"Sure." My voice was hesitant, fearful I'd discover "Planning the Perfect Murder" and "The Top Ten Deadly Poisons" searches in her cache after unearthing those unnerving photos, but instead her recent searches were confined to online shopping sites, British tabloids, and my parents. She had indeed googled my father on LinkedIn and explored my mom's various philanthropic activities. I shrugged off my disappointment.

There were two final things we had to do before we left her room, and that was to search her desk drawers, and under her bed. A lot smaller than me and nimbler, Will volunteered to do the latter while I searched the drawers.

My brother came up quickly from under the bed with a horrified expression. Just some more dirty underwear... and some icky bugs. And I'd found nothing but some school supplies and a few packs of gum. Until I had opened the bottom drawer.

Crumpled inside it was a handwritten draft of my Stanford essay that I'd thrown away. I felt myself brimming with anger. A part of me wanted to show my father what I'd found and prove that Tanya had plagiarized me. But that could backfire. The last thing I wanted was for my father to write a letter to the dean of admissions, asking him to reconsider me. Thanks to Tanya, I wasn't going to Stanford. Unknowingly, she'd done me a huge favor.

And now, at least, I had proof that Tanya was a freaking liar and a thief.

But, more importantly, I had a hunch she was hiding something.

Something way more sinister than her dark hair roots.

———

Now going on noon, my parents were still not home. Will and I retreated to his room and, sitting on the bed of his geek throne, we were back to being Pudge and Willster. My handy-dandy notebook in my lap and a pencil in my hand, I reviewed our findings with my brother. They mostly confirmed what we'd already suspected. That Tanya was:

1. Not necessarily from the UK.
2. A definite liar and thief, possibly unstable.
3. Possibly estranged from her father, or didn't have one.
4. Obsessed with my parents in a good way.
5. Obsessed with me in a bad way.

The only thing I hadn't shared with my brother was my discovery of her birth control pills and the possibility she was screwing Lance. A twelve-year-old boy didn't need to know those kinds of things.

Turning to a clean page in my notebook, I made, with Will's help, a To-Do List. Just like my methodical mom did for all her big events.

TO DO

WILL:

- Google Mary C. Burton/MacBook Registrant
- Research Tanya's meds

PAIGE:

- Ask Mom if she's heard from Tanya's father
- Ask Mom if she has Tanya's passport, student visa, and travel itinerary
- Ask Mom if she sent Tanya family photos

And lastly, one other task I didn't write down or mention to Will... ask Mom if she'd taken Tanya to Dr. Lefferman to get a birth control prescription. And why.

I wasn't sure if I wanted to know the answer.

TWENTY-TWO

NATALIE

Sitting next to Matt in the trauma unit waiting room, I gripped his hand. My heart was racing, my chest so tight it hurt to breathe as the worst-case scenarios possible bombarded my mind.

What if Tanya was disfigured?

Paralyzed?

In a coma?

Brain-dead?

On life support?

Or if she was already...

Oh, God. This couldn't be happening again. First my precious Anabel, now my lovely Tanya. My darkest thought was interrupted by the sound of footsteps. A doctor. Attractive and likely in her forties, she was clad in a white lab coat and blue scrubs. My heart in my throat, I jumped up from my seat. Matt leaped up too.

She introduced herself. Dr. Lawrence, a neurologist.

Despite how parched and tense I was, words tumbled out of my mouth. "Doctor, is she okay?"

"Your exchange student is a very lucky girl." She adjusted

her horn-rimmed glasses. "Thankfully, she was wearing her seat belt when she crashed. Upon impact, the air bag exploded in her face, causing some facial damage, but nothing major. Her body also suffered multiple contusions; she's all bruised up. She may also have a concussion. I'm awaiting the results of her MRI and want to keep her here overnight for observation."

With her monotone voice and my frazzled state, it was as if she'd read me a Wikipedia entry. I processed her words slowly, unable to respond. Matt beat me to it.

"So, Doctor, are you saying she's okay?"

She nodded. "So far, so good. But you can never tell with head injuries."

All the what-ifs returned, my mind flashing back again to my beloved Anabel. All the life knocked out of her. An icy sick feeling pooled in the pit of my stomach.

The door to Tanya's hospital room was ajar. Matt and I hesitantly walked in. His warm hand clasping my cold clammy one, he felt like my lifeline. At the sight of her, I felt a shock to my system. An ache in my chest. My poor darling Tanya! She looked terrible. Her hair was matted, her face splotchy and swollen, her eyes purplish and puffy, and above her right brow was a jagged stitched-up gash, covered by a butterfly bandage. All the monitors and IVs attached to her only added to my anguish.

"Hi, honey..." I said softly, my voice unsteady.

Her head slightly askance, she slowly turned it to face me, and at the sight of me, she burst into tears. My heart was cracking.

Breaking free of Matt, I jogged up to her bedside and brushed stray strands of hair off her face; she felt a little feverish. I resisted the urge to hug her. She looked so frail in the hospital bed, and I didn't want to inflict pain on her battered body.

"I—I'm so, so sorry!" she sobbed out.

Matt joined me as I dabbed her wet cheeks with a Kleenex.

"Shh," I soothed. "The important thing is that you're going to be all right. How do you feel?"

"Like I've been hit by a truck," she managed, her voice weak and hoarse, barely above a whisper.

"You poor thing!" I breathed out. Her pain was contagious and every bone in my body ached for her, as if she were my own child.

"Tell us what happened," said Matt.

"I borrowed Paige's car. I found the keys in the kitchen."

I looked at Matt with puzzlement. I thought he was keeping them hidden from Paige.

"I put them there, Nat, on the key rack. I was going to give them back to Paige after your birthday breakfast."

Tanya continued. "I know I shouldn't have taken them—or Paige's car. I'd planned to wake up early and walk over to the Larchmont farmers market to get Natalie some flowers for her birthday." A sniffle. "But I overslept and didn't have enough time."

Walking over to the local farmers market with our exchange student on Sunday mornings had become one of our weekly rituals. Something I used to do with Anabel, but hadn't since her death. Tanya and I both looked forward to it. She loved picking out beautiful fruits and vegetables with me as well as selecting fresh flowers. Sometimes we went to Starbucks or Noah's Bagels first and had breakfast. I begged Paige to come with us, but she had no interest. The closer I grew to Tanya, the further away I grew from my daughter.

I was beginning to think my exchange student experiment was a failure. The only one who seemed to be benefitting from having Tanya in our household was me, and now I was no longer sure.

"Natalie," she rasped, breaking into my thoughts, "can you please pass me the water?"

"Of course." I reached for the plastic cup on the stand next to her bed and held it to her parched lips. She took several long sips through the straw.

"Go on, Tanya," urged Matt with growing impatience. "Tell us more about what happened."

"Please, Matt. Be gentle with her. She's been through a traumatic experience."

"Natalie, I just want the facts." His voice didn't soften, but at least it didn't grow gruffer.

Tanya stopped drinking. "Everything was good. I got there in one piece and found the perfect bouquet of flowers for Natalie. A dozen gorgeous long-stemmed pink roses interlaced with baby's breath."

"They sound beautiful."

While I quirked a small smile, Tanya's eyes began to tear up again. "I'm sorry I couldn't give them to you. I guess they were towed with the car."

I set the water cup back on the stand, and then held her hand in mine. "Please don't worry... It's the thought that counts. What matters most to me right now is that you're alive."

"How did the accident happen?" asked Matt, his one-track mind still on a quest to get answers.

"As I was driving home, I saw a squirrel crossing the street. I didn't want to hit it, so I slammed down on the brake. But in my freaked-out state, I accidentally floored the gas pedal. I lost control of the car and crashed head-on into a tree."

I gave her hand a little squeeze. "Thank goodness you were wearing a seat belt. If you hadn't been, you might have gone right through the windshield and—"

A lump, the size of a golf ball, lodged in my throat. I

couldn't bring myself to finish my sentence. Tanya finished it for me.

"I know... I could have died."

My heart almost broke at the thought of losing her. Tears pricked my eyelids, but I held them back.

"Is the car totaled?" Her voice was small and hesitant.

"I don't know," replied Matt. "The police implied it wasn't in good shape, but we haven't seen it."

"Paige is going to hate me, like, forever."

"She'll get over it. The car's insured. If it's fixable, we'll fix it. If it's not, maybe we'll buy her another one, though with that crap she pulled with Stanford she frankly doesn't deserve one."

"What she did was wrong. What *I* did was wrong." Her bottom lip wobbled. "If you want to send me back to England, I understand, but please don't tell my father what happened."

Leaning over, I stroked her hair and held her tenderly in my gaze. "My sweetness, we'd never send you back. What happened is a freak thing. We love having you in our house. You're the best thing that's happened to me since we lost our Anabel."

"Oh, Natalie, thank you. I feel so lucky to have you and Matt in my life. You've been like parents to me." The waterworks broke loose again.

I couldn't take it anymore. I sat down on the edge of her bed and gently took her frail body in my arms. And hugged her. Feeling her heartbeat, her warmth, I let her cry against me until she could cry no more.

"It's okay, honey," I whispered against her neck.

After several long minutes, she broke away and I handed her a tissue so she could wipe her tears and blow her nose.

"How long do I have to stay here?"

"Your doctor wants to keep you overnight for observation."

"I want to go home! Please, Natalie!"

Her eyes were watering; my heart was breaking.

I told her that it wasn't possible and gently kissed her goodbye on her forehead.

She closed her eyes as Matt and I exited the room.

I couldn't wait to have her back home.

The sooner the better.

A shiver whipped through me. Another chilling what if.

What if she took a turn for the worse?

TWENTY-THREE

PAIGE

Tanya came home all too soon. The next day. I had to admit she looked pretty bad. Maybe the gnarly gash above her eye would leave an ugly permanent scar. It would serve her right. She didn't even apologize for stealing and wrecking my car.

We had the day off from school. It was one of those teacher conference days that intermittently took place throughout the year, but I knew they were just an excuse to give the teachers a three-day weekend, which was fine by me.

So far, Tanya hadn't left her room. My mother stayed home, canceling all her activities and meetings, and doted on her. Treating her as if she were a fragile porcelain doll. Will and I watched them on the spy cam until we couldn't take it anymore. Plus, we had far more important things to do.

While Will tried to track down Mary Burton, the registered owner of Tanya's laptop, I took it upon myself to research the drugs I'd found in her night table drawer. It was an easy task, but one that made my eyes pop. All of them were anti-psychotics, prescribed for schizophrenia, bipolar disorders, and extreme aggressive behavior. Questions whirled in my head.

How did Tanya get all these meds? Who was she really? And were we living with a sociopath?

I urgently needed to talk to my mom. Pump her for information. An opportunity finally presented itself when Tanya took a nap and she came downstairs. Leaving Will behind with Bear, I joined her in the kitchen. She was seated at the island, a glass of wine beside her, thumbing through a thick book.

I cleared my throat. "Hi, Mom."

Her back to me, she swiveled her stool around.

"Oh... hi, dear." She reached for the glass and took a sip of her white wine. "You startled me."

"Sorry." A beat. "What are you up to?"

She set the glass down and lifted the book. *The Vegan Gourmet's Soup to Nuts Cookbook.* "I'm looking for something to make for lunch that everyone will enjoy."

My heart warmed. I had to give my mom credit. At least she respected my vegan diet and was trying hard.

"Come join me and help me pick out a recipe. We can make it together."

Cooking with my mom? That was a first. Something I didn't recall doing when Mom's favorite, Anabel, was alive. Or since kiss-up Tanya had been here.

"Sure." I joined her at the island, sitting next to her. Another first. Just the two of us. A perfect opportunity to squeeze some information out of her.

"Mom, how's Tanya?"

As if I really cared, but it was a conversation starter.

Her face brightened. "Oh, honey, how sweet of you to ask. She had a really rough time yesterday, but she seems to be doing better today. In less pain."

"That's good." *That sucks.*

While I flipped through the cookbook, my mother imbibed some more wine. It was a little early in the day for it, though I'm sure she drank a glass or two daily with her friends at lunch. And, importantly, it would keep her loosened up.

"Did Dr. Lefferman come by and see her in the hospital?" I asked.

"No, but she visited him back in September. Your school wanted her to have a physical."

"Did he find anything wrong with her?" *Like she's mental? Or has a fatal disease?*

"No, she's in excellent physical health."

"Did he give her any meds?"

"Just a prescription for birth control pills. The same as yours."

"Why does she need birth control?" *So she can screw my boyfriend?*

"She told Dr. Lefferman she got bad menstrual cramps."

Liar! She'd never complained once about her period.

"Did she need anything else?" *Like risperidone, for one.*

"Actually, he also recommended CBD."

"For what?"

"She told him that being in a foreign country alone and in a brand-new school sometimes gave her anxiety attacks and she had a hard time sleeping."

I bristled. She probably just wanted to get high with Lance, then screw him. The only thing that might give her anxiety was the possibility of our dog attacking her, or me throwing her into the deep end of the pool and holding her head down. Otherwise, she was fearless. Hell, she even took my car on a joyride without asking.

As if my mom had read my mind, she said, "The poor thing feels terrible about borrowing and crashing your car."

Yeah, right. Believe me, I didn't expect an apology anytime soon.

She went on to explain the "extenuating" circumstances. I

pretended to be forgiving. But the truth was I hated Tanya more than ever. If I had a voodoo doll and some pins, I would name it Tanya and stab it a million times.

A few minutes later, we found a simple recipe for minestrone soup we both liked. I stayed seated while my mother brought everything we needed to the island. An armload of assorted vegetables plus some cutting boards, knives, and peelers.

"What do you want me to do?" I asked, unable to recall the last time I'd offered to help my mom. And, surprise, it didn't kill me to ask. In fact, it felt good.

My mom gave me an appreciative smile. "It would be great if you helped chop up the veggies. Just be careful not to cut off a finger."

I couldn't help a little laugh. "Don't worry... If I can handle a sculpting knife, I can handle a kitchen knife."

Sitting side by side, we got to work. It was the closest I'd been to my mother in ages and we were doing something together, other than bickering. It actually felt nice. And cutting up the veggies was relaxing. Both of us chopping, I felt her gaze on me.

"Oh, I forgot to tell you. I absolutely love the bust you sculpted of me."

"You found it?"

"Yes. When we got back from the hospital yesterday. I put it in my office on my desk. I'm sorry, I meant to thank you." Putting down her knife, she turned to give me a kiss on my cheek. I was surprised by how much I appreciated it. How much it warmed me. Maybe if Tanya wasn't here, there'd be a chance for me and my mom to grow closer. Really bond.

"It's okay," I said with a smile. "You had a lot on your plate."

My mom huffed out a breath. "That's an understatement. Thank goodness Tanya is okay."

Too bad she isn't, I silently retorted as I peeled an onion. It was making my sensitive blue eyes water.

"Darling, are you crying?"

Tears leaking, I nodded.

"Sweetheart, please don't be upset about Tanya. She's going to be fine."

I actually had to bite down on my bottom lip to stifle a laugh. Or a snort. My mother was so clueless. Time to fill her in.

"It's just the onion, Mom." I diced it and moved on to a celery stalk. *And* on to my agenda. "Mom... can I ask you a couple of questions?"

"Sure."

"Did you let Tanya's father know about the accident?"

"She begged me not to tell him but, of course, I tried to contact him. My email to him bounced back and the phone number I have wasn't in service."

Weird.

"Honey, remind me to get his new contact info from Tanya because he needs to pay the tuition for Coldwater. Someone from administration called me and let me know."

I found that interesting too. Her father hadn't paid the $45,000, or any part of it? Unless you were a scholarship student like my bestie, Jordan, Coldwater had a no-tolerance policy for late payments. Ha! Maybe she'd get kicked out, though I knew my parents would never let that happen and would likely front the money, expecting to be paid back.

Finished with cutting the celery into quarter-inch pieces, I reached for another stalk. "Have you ever seen a photo of her father?"

Her eyes on the potato she was peeling, my mom shook her head. "No, but then again, I've never asked."

"Don't you think it's strange that she doesn't have a photo of him in her room? At least one?"

My mom shrugged. "Maybe she didn't want to lug one in her suitcase. And keeps one on her phone. I do know she misses him terribly, especially since he travels all the time."

"Did you ever send her photos of our family?"

"Not directly to her but a few to the exchange student agency a while back."

The exchange student agency! A mental palm slap. Why hadn't Will and I thought about that earlier?

"Mom, you must have all the forms you filled out." *Jackpot!* "Plus Tanya's personal info, including her passport number, student visa, and home address."

"*Did.*"

"What do you mean?"

"The weirdest thing is that file mysteriously disappeared from my desktop. I can't even find it in my trash. Or remember the name of it."

Two things: Either my mom had OD'd on Xanax and wine, or Tanya had managed to delete it. My hunch was Tanya. Her computer skills were proving to be extraordinary. It wouldn't surprise me if she was a hacker.

"Did you send any photos of Anabel?" I continued.

At the mention of my sister's name, my mother took a swig of her wine. "Not a single one. Tanya didn't even know about your sister."

My mind spun. Then, where did she get *all* those photos? Off Facebook? Instagram? My sister's social media accounts were disabled, so I couldn't check them. But maybe Tanya knew how to get into them.

"Do you have Tanya's passport?" Kind of a non sequitur, but my mom didn't seem to mind me bombarding her with questions.

"No. I think it's in her room."

Think again.

"I should tell her to keep it in her backpack at all times in case she has another accident or emergency. The only form of identification she had with her was a school ID, but that's not enough."

"What about her student visa? Wasn't she in possession of that?"

"I guess not."

My guess: I bet she didn't have one.

The stalk of celery cut up, I moved on to a parsnip. "You should at least make a copy of her passport and keep it with ours. You know, in case she ever loses it."

"That's an excellent idea, Paige."

"What are the two of you doing?" At the sound of her voice, I spun around.

Tanya! Wearing my sister's shimmering pink robe, she swanned into the kitchen. I was surprised she wasn't walking stiffly. And she looked amazing. Her bottle-blonde hair freshly washed and blown, her face a lot less swollen. Almost back to normal.

"Tanya!" cried my alarmed mother, dropping her peeler. "What on earth are you doing out of bed?"

Coming our way, she raked her hand through her long locks. "I couldn't sleep, and I was getting bored."

My mom studied her and smiled. "Darling, you look so much better."

"Thank you. I took a long hot bath and it really helped. I feel much better too."

Doused in that rose-scented perfume and her skin as fresh as morning dew, she looked and smelled like an English rose. Like one of those girls in that Madonna picture book my sister and I both loved as kids. My sister thought she looked a lot like the beautiful blonde one. She did. And so did Tanya. I, on the other hand, identified with the bespectacled outsider one. Figures.

My mom broke into my thoughts. "Sit down, Tanya. I don't want you on your feet with your concussion."

"It's just a mild one."

"Please, sit." Our miraculously recovered exchange student took a seat across from me. "We're making soup. It'll be good for you."

"Thanks, Natalie. You're the best." She eyed my mother's half-depleted glass of wine. I was just waiting for her to ask if she could have some, but instead she surprised me by inquiring, "Have you heard anything about the car?"

"Not yet. Matt's heading over to our mechanic during his lunch break."

She gazed at me. "Sorr-y, Paige."

There was not one bit of sincerity in her singsong voice. Then something dawned on me. I mentally smirked. It was worth a shot.

"It must have been so scary for you to drive on the other side of the road. Especially making lefts."

She cocked a brow and grimaced. "Huh? What are you talking about?"

Ha! Gotcha!

"You know, how in the UK, cars have their steering wheels on the right and you have to drive on the other side of the street."

"Oh, r-right."

I stifled a wicked smile. *My arse.* Our befuddled exchange student was as much from Britain as I was.

Not picking up on Tanya's faux pas, my mom piped in. "Yes, Matt told me he had a horrible time driving in London when he went there in April on a business trip." She looked at our exchange student. "It's a miracle you didn't kill yourself yesterday."

Too bad she didn't.

I was now more convinced than ever she was no exchange student.

And no English rose.

Just a poisonous thorn in my side, which I needed to pluck out from under my skin.

If only they made mega-size tweezers so I could rid myself of her forever.

TWENTY-FOUR

PAIGE

Seated on the top of his geek throne, Will was glued to his laptop when I returned to his room. Faithful Bear was curled up in a big ball on the floor, snoring. He was getting old. I was eager to find out what my brother had learned about the person Tanya's computer was registered to.

I climbed up onto his bed, and shared everything I'd just learned. Tanya's origins were beyond a doubt dubious. She was for sure *not* the English exchange student she claimed to be.

"What about you, Sherlock?"

"My dear Watson, I've made a tad bit of progress."

"Elaborate."

"The bad news: There are thousands of Mary Burtons scattered all over the world. Most of them in the US, Canada, and the UK. It's quite a popular name. One is even a *New York Times* bestselling author. The good news: According to Intelius, there are only ninety-eight Mary C. Burtons registered across the United States."

"What's Intelius?"

"It's an online people-tracking site. It gives you their phone number, and sometimes their home address, and their email."

"Were you able to get any info about Mary C. Burtons living in the UK?"

"Intelius only gives out information for US residents."

I frowned. "That's too bad."

"Cheer up. From all the evidence we have, it is *highly* unlikely our suspect would have stolen a computer from someone in England, but I will ask Scotland Yard to do their own investigation."

I laughed again. My spirits brightened.

"Did you look up Tanya?"

With a smug smile, my little brother lifted a knowing finger. "I knew you would ask, and indeed I did. I could not find a Tanya Blackstone in their database."

"That makes me even *more* suspicious. Does it cost an arm and a leg to subscribe to this service?"

"I got a one-week trial rate for ninety-nine cents."

"Excellent. So, what's the next step?"

"Elementary, my dear Watson. We start to contact these Mary C. Burtons. Ask if they've recently had a MacBook stolen."

I sighed. "That's still a boatload of people to contact."

"We shall divvy them up." He reached for a colorful plastic folder—one of his many homework folders themed with robots, spaceships, and aliens. He opened it and pulled out two sheets of paper from the pockets. He handed one to me and kept the other.

"What's this?" I asked, eyeing the list.

"It's an Excel spreadsheet. I've listed all the Marys with their phone numbers. I'm not sure if they're mobile numbers or landlines, and I've also included their email addresses if available."

"Impressive. How did you learn to do this?"

"Dad taught me."

"Nice of him." Well, at least he spent some quality time

with my brother. Geeky Will was not exactly the Little Leaguer my dad had hoped for, though he did play soccer.

"I'll do the first half, you the other."

"Deal."

Each grabbing a pencil, we got to work, contacting all the Mary C. Burtons, mostly by calling or texting. It took us all afternoon. No luck.

Drained and despondent, and about to give up, I got a text back. One short, shouty word in response to our query: *Was your MacBook recently stolen?*

YES!!!

"Bingo!" I high-fived my equally excited brother. "What should we text back?"

"Tell her you found it and want to return it to her."

I did as my brother asked. She instantly texted back.

Thank goodness!

Where do you live? I asked.

Neither Will nor I recognized the area code. And there was no listed address. Fingers crossed she didn't live in Anchorage.

To our great relief, she lived in Redlands. About sixty miles away. She texted her address.

Two questions loomed: How were we going to get the laptop back to her?

And why did Tanya steal it in the first place?

TWENTY-FIVE

NATALIE

The following Sunday, exactly a week after Tanya's accident, I sat alone at the table in our charming breakfast room, drinking coffee and savoring a buttery croissant, once again using the beautiful china my mother-in-law had given us. She had a similar set she used daily. I, in contrast, reserved mine for special occasions... like birthdays. Today was one.

Sunshine sprinkled through the French doors and cast the room in a golden haze. While I loved rain, I was happy today was sunny. It brightened my spirits, and *she* would have wanted this day to be picture-perfect.

"Natalie, you look so dressed up to be going to the farmers market."

I looked up and saw Tanya coming my way. Unlike me, who was clad in a Prada floral dress and a delicate pashmina shawl, she was wearing ripped jeans, a cropped T-shirt, and sparkly pink flip-flops.

Fresh as the morning dew, she looked beautiful. She had recovered quickly from her dreadful car accident, and the scar above her eyebrow was healing nicely, although it was still visible. To make her feel less self-conscious about it, I'd taken her to my Beverly Hills hairdresser, who'd given her wispy bangs to camouflage it. The bangs suited her and made her look younger.

"I should have told you," I said. "I'm not going to the farmers market today."

"Oh. Why not?"

"Join me for breakfast and I'll explain."

I quickly set up another place setting and served her some coffee, fresh fruit, and one of the lovely pastries I'd picked up yesterday on the way home from Will's robotics meet-up.

"So, Natalie, where are you going so dressed up?" she asked, popping a berry into her mouth. "Oh, and by the way, you look positively beautiful."

I twitched a small smile. I could feel my emotions rising. A tightness in my chest.

"Thanks. It's Anabel's birthday. She would have been nineteen today." My voice sounded far away to me. Sad.

I took a fortifying sip of my coffee. "Anabel was the light of my life. I'm going to church shortly and afterward to her gravesite."

"Do you all go?" asked our guest. "Your entire family?"

"No. I prefer to go by myself." My grief was mine alone to bear.

Sadness welled up inside me. My eyes began to mist, and I couldn't stop a few tears from falling. I dabbed my eyes with my linen napkin while Tanya reached across the table and tenderly held my free hand in hers. Her gaze was filled with warmth and compassion.

"Natalie, if it's okay, I'd like to come with you. It would mean a lot to me."

With another smile, I squeezed her hand. "I'd really like that." I no longer wanted to be alone.

"Do I need to wear something black?"

"No, just the opposite. Wear something bright and cheery."

My smile widened. "Today, we are *celebrating* Anabel's life. Not mourning it."

Fifteen minutes later, Tanya bounced down the stairs. For a second, I did a double take. She was wearing one of Anabel's favorite dresses, an off-the-shoulder pink polka-dotted midi. With her new bangs, I thought I was seeing my daughter. I heard myself gasp, and then, with a headshake, erased the illusion from my mind.

———

Located in nearby Windsor Square, Saint Andrew's Church was walking distance from my house, but I'd chosen to drive as we'd be going to the cemetery located in The Valley right after mass.

Built about the same time as our house, the sizeable Gothic Revival church looked like one you might find in England, elegant and stately. The interior of the church was breathtaking, with its tall, vaulted ceiling and magnificent stained-glass windows, which let light into the chapel. The light felt like God's presence and always filled me with awe. Not a particularly religious person, I didn't go to mass regularly—usually just on holidays like Christmas and Easter and on special occasions, like my children's communions. And today.

The 9:45 a.m. mass, the most popular one, was packed. We found seats in the front of the sanctuary. I recognized many of the parishioners seated in the rich mahogany pews. With a nod or little wave, I acknowledged several seated nearby. There was a low rumbling among them, but it reduced to complete silence when Father Francis made his grand entrance up to the altar.

I followed along in my prayer book as the imposing, but benevolent, white-haired priest led us through the service. He had been a source of great comfort to me when Anabel died, but not enough to prevent my breakdown. Still, I was grateful to him and contributed generously to the church, as well as helped out with their annual fundraiser.

Intermittently, I stole a glance at Tanya. Her prayer book was closed on her lap, and she looked bored and fidgety, like she was eager to leave. Maybe she was sorry she'd asked to come along. At this point, there was nothing I could do about it, so I focused on the service.

Mass was always the same. The uplifting songs, the psalms, communion, and the sermon. Today's reading was from Jeremiah 14:10.

I listened intently as the voice of the priest thundered. His fiery eyes stayed locked on mine, like he had singled me out and was talking directly to me.

"He, the Lord, shall still remember their guilt and punish their sins."

The words reverberated in my head. Made me shudder. Guilt squeezed my heart and gnawed at my soul. God was never going to let me forget my sins. *Ever.*

"Are you okay?" whispered Tanya, noticing my shaken state.

Wordlessly, I nodded, thankful she didn't take hold of my hand. It was cold as ice and trembling.

Still shaken, I was glad when mass was over. Grabbing my bag, I stood and sidestepped out of the pew, Tanya following me. I moved quickly, keeping my head bowed to avoid a conversation with anyone I knew. I wasn't in the mood.

"Gosh, that was long!" groaned Tanya. "I wish you'd told me."

I was a bit taken aback by her remark and now wondered why she'd asked to come along. For sure she should have known how long Sunday mass is. "Don't you go to church services at home? Pray for your mother?"

She shrugged. "Not really." Then added, "Can't we just go? My feet hurt from having to stand so much."

Her impatience piqued me, but I let it go. "There's one thing I have to do before we leave."

She rolled her eyes. "Now what?"

"I have to light a candle." With a petulant pout, Tanya followed me to the cluster of votive candles located at the back of the church. There used to be wax ones to light, but the fire department deemed them a hazard several years ago, hence these flameless LED replacements. Tanya stood next to me, for the first time taking an interest.

"What are they for?"

"Mostly to remember the dead... to say a prayer for them. You can also pray to God and ask Him to help you with your most urgent needs."

"Cool. Can I light one?"

"Of course." I watched as she chose a candle close to mine.

Emotion again rising in my chest, my fingers quivering, I flipped the little switch that turned the candle on. As it lit up, I spoke silent words.

"My dearest, sweetest, beautiful Anabel. I miss you terribly, but you live in my heart every second of the day. Wherever you are, I hope you hear me and feel my great love."

Tears blurring my vision, I glanced at Tanya. Her candle was lit and she was staring at it. The slightest of smirks lurked on her lips.

A sudden chill ran through me. I tightened my shawl around my shoulders.

What could she be praying for?

TWENTY-SIX

NATALIE

It took us twenty minutes to get to Forest Lawn Cemetery. Actually, twenty-five because I made a quick stop to pick up flowers. Fresh, exquisite pink peonies that I'd asked to be arranged in a bouquet with a beautiful white bow. Anabel's favorite, and mine too.

The trek up the verdant, hilly lawn to Anabel's gravesite was challenging in my high heels. Stupid me. I should have worn sneakers like Tanya. Several times, I almost twisted my ankle and, midway, I held onto her arm to steady myself, cradling the flowers in my free arm. I was grateful she was with me, for both physical and moral support.

We passed numerous tombstones, many displaying bundles of multicolored flowers. Clearly, I wasn't the only one who had come to pay respects to a loved one. They say misery loves company, but the sight of other mourners did not make me feel any better. With each painful step, my heart grew heavier.

Thirty long, excruciating minutes later, we reached the gravesite. Even with all the spinning classes I took, I was breathless. And sweaty.

"Wow, I must not be in as good shape as I thought." I

heaved a deep breath while Tanya didn't seem one bit fazed by the challenging climb.

"That wasn't easy," she replied with a laugh. "You shouldn't compare yourself to an eighteen-year-old."

She was *eighteen*? I thought she was seventeen. Maybe I'd missed her birthday. I remembered her application had listed her age, but I didn't recall her birth date.

She stared at the tombstone. "Is this where Anabel's buried?"

"Y-yes." My voice was already cracking.

"It's a beautiful resting place."

I looked it over. It really was. The view was breathtaking, offering a panorama of the San Gabriel Mountains, and the secluded site had been kept immaculate. Matt and I paid one of the groundskeepers extra to make sure it never got overgrown or grungy. Anabel had been a beautiful soul who deserved to sleep in peace and beauty. Only not here. She was way too young to die. Heaven had gained an angel; I'd lost a daughter.

The bright high noon sun was glaring in my eyes as tears gathered behind my lids. I pulled out my dark sunglasses from my bag and put them on. My shades could go only so far to mask my grief and sorrow. My vision already blurred, I, too, stared at the tombstone. It was so plain and simple, it was elegant. Matt's parents had wanted us to inter her in their family crypt located outside San Francisco. Matt had agreed with them, but I'd thrown a tantrum. Several shattered plates later, he'd acquiesced, and I, on the verge of a breakdown, had gotten my way. I wanted my daughter close to me. One day, I would be buried here too, and we'd be at last reunited.

A tear escaping, I set the flowers down in front of the tombstone, hoping they wouldn't wilt in the heat, and then stepped back. Beneath the years she had lived was her epitaph. My watering eyes stayed on it:

Anabel Elizabeth Merritt
An extraordinary daughter, sister, and friend.
Let the sunshine in.

I was glad Tanya didn't ask me about the last line of her epitaph. It was the name of a song from the musical *Hair*. The last high school production Anabel had performed in. Recreating the role Diane Keaton had originated on Broadway, she'd been sensational.

I pushed the bittersweet memory away and fanned myself. The temperature was rising. It was extraordinarily warm for a mid-November day in Los Angeles. Maybe in the high eighties. I wish I'd brought along my floppy straw hat. But at least I had sunscreen on, and so did Tanya.

"So, tell me more about how she died."

A cloud of darkness fell over me. "Tanya, I don't want to go there. Remember, this is a celebration of her life."

"Sorry, then tell me a little about the day she was born."

I told our inquisitive exchange student that I'd had the easiest of pregnancies. Not a day of nausea or pain. Everything on track. And when my waters broke, Matt had excitedly driven me to the hospital—Cedars—and held my hand as I pushed out Anabel with an epidural and two sharp breaths. When I saw her, I knew I had given birth to a beautiful angel. Our tiny fair-haired Anabel, a symbol of grace and beauty. She hardly even cried. And when I held her in my arms for the first time and she latched her rosebud lips onto my breast, I felt a love like none other that couldn't be put into words.

Tanya sighed. "I bet firstborns always have a special place in their mums' hearts."

Despite the heat, I felt my blood freeze. I forced a smile. "Yes, dear, they do."

"My poor mum died in labor. She had a hemorrhage and

bled to death. You're so lucky you didn't have to experience that."

A chill spread from my head to my toes.

I'd once almost died, too, from a hemorrhage. I flashed back to one of the *many* worst days of my life, the memory as sharp and clear as a shard of glass. The tiny, unventilated room in the scorching hot desert. The lumpy metal bed. The stench. The agonizing pain and ear-piercing screams. The blood, sweat, and tears.

The blood. So much blood! As the vision of the soaked crimson sheet filled my head, a violent shudder ripped through me.

"Are you okay, Natalie?" asked Tanya, catapulting me back to the moment.

"Yes." My voice unsteady, I willed away the horrific memory. "Your mother must have suffered terribly. Thank goodness you survived."

"Papa told me I almost didn't. I was a very sickly child... maybe because I wasn't breastfed. I even got held back a year in school. I wish I'd had a mum, like you, to take care of me."

A burst of maternal love erupted inside me. I took her into my arms and hugged her. "You poor thing. I wish I could have been there to take care of you."

"Me too." Her voice grew watery. "Natalie... I wish you could be in my life forever."

"I will be," I said softly, then broke away. "Come, let's sit down for a bit. The weather is so beautiful, and my feet are killing me."

A few moments later, we were seated on the grass on my spread-out shawl in front of Anabel's tombstone. My shoes off, I had my legs folded under me. Tanya sat beside me with her knees pulled up to her chest. She tugged on the hem of her dress, then ran her fingers through her long blonde hair.

"So, tell me more about Anabel. What was she like as a child?"

Images from the past flashed through my head like a slideshow. The way she'd slept curled up, clutching one of her stuffed animals. Her first ballet recital. Her first-grade picture with her radiant smile and missing front tooth. Her first stage production, *The Wizard of Oz*, where she'd played the Wicked Witch and stolen the show. The day she'd made the cheerleading squad. Her many high school plays, which ran the gamut from Shakespeare to Broadway. While she was not without her faults, after she died I had what my therapist called "selective memory." I only remembered the good things about her.

"She was a bright star. Literally and figuratively. Wherever she went, she lit up a room. People, no matter how old or young, were attracted to her. Her shining personality. She was always the center of attention."

"That must have been hard for Paige."

"Not really. Paige was somewhat of a loner and happily marched to the beat of her own drum. Despite how close they were in age, they were never actually close."

"Did you love them the same?"

"You mean *do* I love them the same. I've *never* stopped loving Anabel." I paused for a moment, pondering my next words. "The answer is the same, but differently."

The truth: Anabel was always my favorite, but I wasn't going to admit that. Maybe that made me a bad mother.

"Was Anabel as smart as Paige in school?" continued Tanya, stopping me from going there.

"Academics were not her strong suit. She had other strengths. Charisma. A *joie de vivre*. And she was a leader. Teachers and fellow students loved her. She was extremely popular... captain of the cheerleading team, and she was going to be prom queen."

"Wow! Did she have lots of boyfriends?"

"I'd say she had lots of 'boy friends.'" I separated out the two words and put air quotes around them. "Not one in particular. Every boy in school had eyes for her and wished they could be her boyfriend, but she preferred to keep them all at bay. She was a tremendous flirt and loved the attention."

Tanya picked at a clump of grass. "What did she want to be when she grew up?"

"Something that her father wasn't one bit happy about."

"What?"

"An actress." *Always the drama queen.* "From the time she was in kindergarten."

"Seriously? That's what I want to be! The drama teacher at school says I'm a natural. And guess what? I forgot to tell you, I got the lead role in the school play. I'm going to play Eliza Doolittle in *My Fair Lady*. I guess the fact I'm British made me a shoo-in."

I clapped my hands together with excitement. "Congratulations! That's wonderful! I love that show and can't wait to see you in it."

Tanya beamed. "Thank you. I bet Anabel got her acting chops from you."

I cocked my head. "What do you mean?"

"You know, being a trade show model. Demonstrating and pitching products is a form of acting. You have to pretend you love the product though you might not. And sometimes you also have to pretend to be someone you're not."

Another shiver ran through me. I'd been pretending my whole adult life. I was the best actress I knew. Like Henry Higgins (or more like Richard Gere in *Pretty Woman*), Matt had transformed me into a stunning sophisticated socialite and through hard work I'd mastered the part. To stay in my extraordinary new life, I could never let him find out about my old one. If he did, I'd take my final bow. The show—the pretense—would be over. The curtains would come crashing down. And stay drawn forever.

Tanya broke into my unsettling thoughts. "I think I would have loved Anabel. We sound so much alike. Like... kindred spirits."

"I think the very same thing." With a wistful smile, I squeezed her hand. "She would have loved you, too."

"It's like we were separated at birth." She stared at Anabel's tombstone. "Besides being so much alike, do you know we even have the same birthday?"

"What!? Today's your birthday?"

With a sheepish grin, she nodded. "Yup, my eighteenth. Can you believe I was born on the very same day as her a year apart? Weird, right?"

Yes. No. No. Yes. How could I have not known this? Xanax brain?

No wonder she'd said she was eighteen earlier.

"Why didn't you tell me?"

"I knew this day was important to you. I didn't want to make it all about me."

"Oh, my sweet Tanya! You're making me cry again." I could feel tears welling up in my eyes. "I feel terrible. You should have told me. I don't even have a birthday present for you."

"*You* are my present. I love you so much, Natalie."

Her heartfelt words tugged at my heartstrings. Fraught with emotion, I palmed a hand to my chest. "I love you too."

An ear-to-ear smile split her face. "Thank you, Natalie, for letting me be here with you. It means a lot to me."

"*No*, I should be thanking you. You've made it so much easier getting through this very difficult day."

I hadn't even wept, I thought, as I gave her another big, grateful hug. Maybe it was more than a coincidence that she and Anabel shared the same birthday. Maybe, it was meant to be.

Finally, I let go of her. "Come. We should go." I slipped on my shoes, gathered my bag, and stood up. She followed suit, taking my pashmina shawl and her backpack with her.

"The rest of the day, my darling, is going to be about *you*."

I was going to take her shopping at The Grove. Let her pick out whatever she wanted. And tonight, I was going to throw her a surprise birthday party.

And make it the best night of her life.

TWENTY-SEVEN

PAIGE

My car was back from the shop. Fortunately, Tanya hadn't totaled it. It needed a brand-new front fender, two new front tires, a new windshield, and the airbags replaced. Apart from that, it was as good as new. Begrudgingly, my father gave me back my keys, which I kept with me at all times in case the car thief wanted to take my Jeep on another joyride.

With my mom visiting my sister's gravesite and Tanya with her for whatever reason, Will and I had the perfect opportunity to sneak into Tanya's room, steal her laptop, and then go on a road trip. To visit Mary C. Burton in Redlands. Since Tanya's MacBook was stored in her computer bag, she probably wouldn't notice it was missing until tomorrow morning when she slung the bag over her shoulder.

All hell was going to break loose at breakfast. But genius Will came up with a brilliant idea. To put one of my mom's Le Creuset casserole pans in the bag; it weighed about the same as the laptop. God, I loved my brother! I couldn't wait till first period when she zipped the bag open and discovered the switch. Tomorrow was going to be a fun, fun day! I only wished I had protective armor.

The drive was a piece of cake, once I was on the 10, heading east. It felt good to be behind the wheel again, cruising down the freeway. It also felt good to spend some time with Will. During the week, we were both busy with schoolwork and extracurricular activities, and on Saturdays, he had his robotics meets. It looked like his team was going to make it into the finals. Robotics was to Will what sculpting was to me. A passion.

With little traffic, we got to Mary Burton's house in less than an hour. She was expecting us as I'd texted her to make sure she'd be home. It would have been foolish to make the long trip if she wasn't going to be around.

We found a parking spot on the street right outside her house. It was a small one-story shingle structure with an attached single-car garage that was part of a cookie-cutter housing development likely dating to the seventies. Mary's house was neatly maintained, painted a slate blue with white shutters, and had a nicely manicured lawn with a bed of colorful flowers bordering the walkway. Armed with my back-pack and Will beside me, I rang the doorbell. It made a ding-dong sound. Wordlessly, we waited for someone to come to the front door. A few minutes passed and worry set in.

"Pudge, are you sure she said she'd be home?" asked Will.

"Yeah." I rang the bell again.

Then, from behind the door, to my relief, I heard a booming voice. "Coooming!"

On my next breath, the door unlocked and slid partway open, a safety chain still in place. A woman's face appeared in the crack. She was jowly and had a puff of white hair.

"Mrs. Burton?" I stuttered.

"Yes." Her voice was tentative. Distrustful.

"I'm Paige. And this is my brother, Will. We're here to return your laptop." *And to learn about the person who stole it.*

She regarded me suspiciously. "Prove it to me."

Removing my backpack from my shoulders, I fished inside the outside pocket for my driver's license. I put it to her face.

"Thank goodness!" Breaking into a smile, she undid the safety chain and swung the door open. "Sorry about that. You just can't be too careful these days. Plus, there's a penitentiary and loony bin a few miles away." She studied us briefly and then said, "Please, come in."

Mary's house was clean and tidy, though a little dilapidated. There was worn wall-to-wall powder-blue carpet, an array of drab brown-wood furniture with faded floral upholstery, and knickknacks everywhere.

Dressed in a blue chenille housecoat and matching fuzzy blue slippers (she obviously loved the color blue), she led us to her kitchen, a small but cheery knotty pine room with an outdated bisque fridge and range. She gestured to the Formica table and chairs by the window overlooking the small backyard.

"Have a seat," she said, and now that she was no longer suspicious, I could see warmth and kindness in her crinkly blue eyes. "Can I get you something to drink?" she asked as Will and I sat down side by side.

"Thank you, but I'm good," I said.

"The same," said Will.

"Are you sure? I just made some fresh lemonade from the lemons on my tree."

Will's face lit up. He loved lemonade.

"Okay, sure!"

"Make that two." And actually, I was thirsty.

A few minutes later, Mary was sitting across from us at the table, sharing a glass of lemonade. It was yummy and refreshing.

Pushing my almost depleted glass to the side, I reached for my backpack and retrieved Mary's laptop from inside it. Carefully, I set it on the table. Will snapped it open and showed Mary it was registered to her.

Her reaction, a cross between shock and joy, reminded me

of a woman I'd seen on *Antiques Roadshow*, who found out the painting she'd bought for five dollars at a yard sale was worth fifty thousand dollars.

"Oh my goodness gracious, I can't believe it! I never thought in a million years I'd see it again, and on my fixed income—I live off my pension, social security, and small savings—there's no way I could have afforded a new one. Thank the good Lord you found it!"

I wondered how she could afford a top-of-the-line MacBook Pro in the first place. They cost close to two thousand dollars if you added in the AppleCare protection plan. My question was answered.

"And it's very sentimental to me. The high school where I taught gave it to me as a farewell present when I retired."

"Wow! That was generous of them. I'm sorry all your desktop files have been wiped clean." I'm sure she had important documents stored on it.

"That's the least of my problems. Fortunately, I had most of my files backed up on one of those Time Machine gizmos. Where in heaven's name did you find it?"

"Believe it or not, in a trash can near our house," I lied.

"Where do you live?"

"In Los Angeles," replied Will.

"Goodness! That's a long ways away. I wonder if that horrible girl who stole it from me lives there too. I was so foolish to have trusted her."

My ears perked up. "What do you mean?"

"Well, back in August—to be exact, the afternoon of Friday, August 26—I heard the doorbell ring and went to the front door and peeked through the peephole. Standing outside was a tall, pretty girl with long dark-blonde hair. She looked to be seventeen or eighteen."

Tanya? From a sideways glance, I knew Will was wondering the same thing. I refocused my attention on Mary.

"She told me she'd had a big fight with her boyfriend and that he'd dumped her on the freeway and driven off before she could grab her purse. And that she'd walked all the way here in the over one-hundred-degree heat. She looked very flushed—rather disheveled—and sounded parched. She asked if she could come in and rest a bit. At least get some water. Then, she started crying."

It sounded a lot like Tanya, who could turn on the waterworks as well as the charm with the blink of an eye. "She didn't by chance have an English accent?" I asked.

Mary shook her head. "Not that I recall."

I twisted my lips. More reason to believe Tanya wasn't from Britain, but I still needed concrete evidence.

Pushing her half-moon glasses up her nose, Mary continued.

"Well, I'm a sucker for tears, and I couldn't let the poor, devastated girl melt in the terrible heat, so I unlocked my door and let her in. She was beyond grateful. I told her to sit on the living room couch while I went to the kitchen to get her some water and a plate full of chocolate chip cookies I'd just baked. She devoured them like she'd not eaten or drunk anything in a month, and afterward, I offered her my phone so she could call someone to pick her up. She stood and moved to the other side of the room while I remained seated and watched her punch some numbers. Then listened to her conversation with someone that appeared to be her mother. She didn't have the phone on speaker, so I couldn't hear the voice on the other end. Finishing the call, she returned to the couch.

"She told me she had bad news. That her parents couldn't pick her up until the next day. She said they lived all the way up by Fresno. Both were doctors and had patients to see. Then, I asked her what she was doing in this neck of the woods. She said she and her boyfriend went camping in Joshua Tree and were on their way back home. And then she began to pour on the tears again, telling me how she had no money or place to stay."

"What was her name?" I asked while Mary paused to take a sip of lemonade.

"Tabitha. She never gave me her last name."

"Did she have any distinguishing features?"

Mary scrunched her face, then nodded. "She had this cute little gap between her front teeth... and a dimple in her chin."

Tanya!

"My heart went out to her. I told her she could stay overnight with me. How could I not? I had a spare bedroom and she seemed innocent enough."

"Then what?" I asked, Mary's story getting better with every word.

"Well, to make a long story short, she was the perfect house-guest. Courteous and grateful. So appreciative of the fried chicken dinner I made and her lovely air-conditioned bedroom. She even gave me a hug. After a good night's sleep, I woke up, as usual, at the crack of dawn. And she was gone. And so was my computer bag with my laptop... plus the three hundred dollars I kept in my cookie jar."

Three hundred dollars. Enough to buy a one-way bus ticket to LA. And a piece of luggage and backpack. Plus some jeans, sneakers, and a hoodie at the outlet mall or Walmart we'd passed on our way down here, though I wouldn't be surprised if she had shoplifted everything. I thought about showing her photos of Tanya, but it would only raise questions. There was no doubt in my mind that Tabitha and Tanya were one and the same. Will gave me a sideways glance, confirming my hunch.

"Oh my God, that's awful!" I said.

"Oh, and she stole my cell phone too. An iPhone, but thank goodness I took out insurance when I bought it. In case it ever went missing."

Dang! I wish I could also have confiscated Tanya's phone. That would have really driven her nuts since it was her lifeline. And God only knows all the dirt we'd find on it.

Mary heaved a breath. "I only have myself to blame. My late husband, George, always told me I was too darn trusting."

"It's not your fault," I consoled. "My mom would have done the same thing."

She smiled. "You kids must come from a good family."

Chugging the rest of my lemonade, I thought about her words. Was ours a "good" family? My mother was a borderline alcoholic and had had a nervous breakdown; my father was a bona fide prick who was full of himself and obsessed with making money. Will and I had good values and a great relationship, but our bare-bones relationship with our self-centered parents was nothing to be proud of.

Dysfunctional. That's what we were.

I set the glass down on the table and told her we did. If only she knew.

"My husband, may he rest in peace, always said good things happen to good people. And that's why I believe the two of you came into my life and I got my computer back. He also believed what goes around, comes around." Her face darkened. "That lying little shrew will get her due. I'm sure of it!"

I nodded. "She will." I could already imagine a handful of payback punishments. Hundreds, if I thought harder. Like she'd grow gnarly fungus between her perfectly manicured toes. Develop some repulsive flesh-eating disease and lose all her hair. Contract an STD. That ugly scar above her eyebrow was just the beginning.

Putting aside my deliciously evil ruminations, I glanced at the wall clock. It was already two o'clock. "We'd better get going," I said. "The Sunday afternoon traffic can get nasty."

Mary looked disappointed. "It's been such a delight having

the two of you here. I wish I could give you both a reward, but I'm tight on money."

"No worries. You've actually given us so much. Thank you for the lemonade." *And all the dirt on Tanya.*

There was, however, one thing we had to do before leaving. Use the bathroom. Neither of us had peed since we'd left our house three hours ago. And with all that lemonade...

A guest bathroom was located in the hallway off the living room. Will went first and then it was my turn. My bladder exploding, I scurried down the hall. And made it just in time. On my way out, I noticed something hanging on the wall I'd not noticed before in my haste.

A blue-and-white felt pennant. *Indio High.* The very name of the school splayed across that mysterious photo in Tanya's suitcase. My heart galloping, I returned to the kitchen.

Grabbing my backpack from the floor, I asked Mary, "Were you a teacher at Indio High School? I noticed the pennant hanging in your hallway."

She smiled. "Almost my entire adult life. Despite constant budget cuts, it was a great school."

"Where's it located?"

"About an hour away, a little past Palm Springs. It was worth the commute. I miss teaching all those kids. A lot of them still keep in touch with me and let me know what they're up to. Many have thanked me for preparing them for college and their careers. Several of the kids I taught went on to become professors, scientists, and doctors."

"That's awesome," I said. "What years did you teach there?"

"From 1976 to 2015. Almost forty years."

The photo flashed in my head again. She was there! With her keen mind, I bet Mary would remember all the kids. And be able to identify the sad-looking girl whose face was circled in red.

Darn it! I so wish I had that class picture with me, but who would have known? As soon as I was back home, I was going to send Mary the photo, now that she had her laptop back.

And, fingers crossed, find out at last who the mysterious girl in the photo was.

TWENTY-EIGHT

PAIGE

The traffic going back home was worse than I'd imagined. Bumper to bumper the whole way because there were three accidents, including a big rig turning over. Will fell asleep while I navigated the freeway, cursing the whole way under my breath. Maybe one day, my brother would create flying robots that could transport us across the sky like those *Power Rangers* zords, and we could avert this kind of clusterjam.

We got home a little before six. The November sky already dark, I was surprised by how many cars were parked on our street. There wasn't a spot to be had. It was never like this on a Sunday, unless somebody was having an event, which was rare. It didn't really matter because I parked in our garage. Except I couldn't. There was a car in our driveway, blocking me.

"What the hell?" I yelled, waking up Will.

"Huh? What's going on?" asked my brother, snapping his head up.

"We're home. But do you know whose car that is?" It was a black Explorer.

Rubbing his eyes, he shrugged. "No clue."

Through the SUV's dark tinted windows, I could see

someone sitting behind the wheel. Pulling up behind it, I lowered my window, honked my horn, and shouted, "Get out of my driveway!"

No response. It took everything I had not to ram my Jeep into it, over and over, until whoever was inside got the message. I just didn't want to screw up my car again.

Rage surging inside me, I jumped out of my Jeep and stomped up to the SUV. Furiously, I banged on the driver's window. "Open up!" I repeated like a broken record. Finally, the window inched down.

"Hey, dude, what's your problem?" I recognized the obnoxious voice. It was Xavier Forman, our school's star quarterback. A total jerk. He was big and menacing, but I wasn't afraid of him.

"Get your frigging two-hundred-fifty-pound jock ass off my property!"

"Chill, nerd girl."

I swear I wanted to punch him out. "What are you doing here?"

"Duh. I'm here for the party."

"What party?"

"Tanya Blackstone's birthday party. Dude, *everyone's* invited. I'm just waiting here till the valet comes back."

Party? Valet? What was going on?

I was finally able to park my car in our garage, and as soon as I hopped out, I could hear a raucous clamor in our backyard. The side door to the yard wide open, I ventured through it with Will by my side. My eyes almost popped out of their sockets. We were in the throes of a full-blown party. On our veranda, a long L-shaped buffet table was set up with dozens of assorted pizzas, ginormous bowls of salad, and buckets of canned drinks and bottled waters. A banner that read, *Happy Birthday, Tanya*, hung from the trellis. White high-top cocktail tables were scattered on the grass, bearing bunches of soaring pink, white, and silver balloons, and votive candles.

Almost our entire senior class was there—either pigging out at the buffet or loudly stuffing their faces on the lawn while Britney Spears played on our outdoor sound system. I took in a whiff of marijuana. Many of the rich, privileged kids at Coldwater smoked weed, and it was no secret some did cocaine and ecstasy too. No wonder our school was often called Goldwater or Cokewater.

"Gross!" My brother winced, taking in the scene.

"Totally!"

"Pudge, I'm outta here. I wanna go see Bear and make sure he's okay. And finish my homework."

"Okay. I'll see you later. Thanks for coming with me today." Weirdly, our trip to see Mary Burton seemed like a century ago. As Will took off, I made my way deeper into the crowd. No one acknowledged me, as if I could care. These were not my people.

I was only looking for one person. Lance. I was sure my mother had invited him. And I was more than sure Tanya would want him here. My eyes darted left and right as I kept moving. Neither of them was in sight. A queasy feeling fell over me. My stomach rumbled. No wonder. I'd hardly eaten a thing all day. I made my way over to the food, hoping that one of the pies was vegan.

As I slogged down the buffet table, glumly taking in the now cold, half-eaten pizzas, a familiar voice came from behind me.

"Honey, where on earth have you been?"

I spun around. My mom. A glass of white wine in her hand. And I'm sure it wasn't her first.

"Will and I had a lot to do today," I replied. "We ran around all over the city looking for things he needed for one of his school projects. And I had something to return." At least the latter was true.

She took a long swig of her wine. "I was worried about you. Why didn't you call or text?"

Why didn't *you*? I suppose my mother was too busy putting together this party for her precious exchange student to care about the whereabouts of her son and daughter.

"Anyway, sweetheart, I'm so glad you're here. I only found out today Tanya's birthday is the same as Anabel's. Can you believe that?"

Actually, I couldn't. It was too much of a coincidence.

"So, I threw her a last-minute surprise birthday party. Your dad, thank goodness, whisked her away while I arranged the whole thing. He took her to the shooting range, and as much as I'm opposed to that horrible gun hobby he has, I had no choice."

My mother hated that my father owned a gun. A Magnum 45. And that he had joined a gun club. It was now a passion. He went to target practice every Sunday in the afternoon and would boast to us at dinner how well he did. My mother was repulsed and absolutely refused to let my brother or me go near the weapon they kept locked in their safe. And truthfully, I had no desire to learn how to use it, though since the arrival of our exchange student, I was having second thoughts. I'd be lying if I said I didn't have the urge to shoot her right between her eyes. Sometimes I fantasized doing that and watching her brains splatter. She was turning *me* into a sociopath!

My mom took another swig of her wine. "I wish you'd been here to see her reaction when she came home."

Thank God I wasn't.

"She was, as you kids say, 'blown away.' Practically in tears. And told me no one had ever done anything like this for her before!"

Why would they?

"I was so lucky Trattoria could whip up all these pizzas. There's even a vegan one for you—made with a cauliflower crust, soy cheese, and veggies." She scanned the buffet. "Ah, there it is!"

She pointed to the last pizza on the table. With only three pieces left, it looked pretty pathetic. Stale with all the veggies picked off. I lost my appetite and instead grabbed a sparkling water from one of the ice-filled buckets.

"Where's Will?" asked my mom.

"He's upstairs doing homework."

"Has he eaten?"

"Don't know, but I'm sure he can rustle something up if he's hungry." I screwed off the cap of my water and took a sip as the bubbles rose. "Is Lance here?"

"Of course. I knew Tanya would want him to come. But I haven't seen either of them for a while."

Suddenly, a sharp cramp stabbed me. I almost winced. Then another. It could be the onset of my period. While it wasn't exactly that time of the month, my cycle had become irregular with my vegan diet. Yet another knife-like contraction besieged me, and I grimaced.

"Honey, are you okay?" asked my mother.

"Mom, I've gotta go. I have to use the bathroom." Leaving the water bottle behind, I bolted toward the French doors to our house, hoping my period wouldn't come in front of all my class-mates. That would be utterly mortifying. It had happened to me once before—in the middle of a basketball game—and I'd had to dash off the court to change out of my blood-soaked white shorts. I could still hear the heckles and laughs as I'd charged to the locker room.

Once inside, I sprinted to the guest bathroom. The door was closed. Without knocking, I turned the brass knob, relieved it wasn't locked, and flung it open.

Oh. My. God.

Tomorrow, our housekeeper, Blanca, would be scraping my jaw from the floor.

TWENTY-NINE

PAIGE

I stopped dead in my tracks, not caring if my period assaulted me. I couldn't believe my eyes. Making out before me were half-dressed Tanya and Lance. Groping. Kissing. Moaning. Panting.

"Oh, Lancey, you're the best birthday present ever," Tanya purred as his muscular body thrusted against hers.

"Happy birthday, baby."

Baby? I thought I was going to puke. Fortifying myself with a deep breath, I folded my arms across my chest.

"Excuse me," I said in my loudest, most obnoxious voice. "I have to use the bathroom."

The twosome stopped what they were doing as if I'd said "freeze" and was about to shoot them. If I had my father's gun, I might have. Catching their breath, they turned to face me. Tanya's face was flushed, her lips wet and swollen. Lance's was snapper-red and his lips gulped for air like the half-dead blow-fish he'd posted on Instagram this summer.

"Paige—"

I immediately cut him off and sneered. A bitter mix of anger and disgust filled every atom of my being. Tears burned the backs of my eyes, but I held them back. I was determined not to let either of them see me cry. I especially didn't want to give the birthday girl that satisfaction. My gaze fierce, I looked him straight in the eye.

"The line 'it's not what it seems' is not going to work this time. It's crystal clear to me, Lance."

"W-what is?" he stuttered.

Jeez. Was he that much of a moron?

"Read my lips." I pointed to them. "We're *over*." I spelled it out. "O-V-E-R." He gawked at me, his face growing blanker. Rage surged inside me. Impulsively, I yanked off the heart necklace he'd given me, breaking the chain, and hurled it at him. It hit him in the face. I was disappointed he didn't wince. The severed necklace fell to the marble floor with the tiniest of clinks.

Perplexed, he gazed down at it. "Why'd you have to do that?"

"Seriously, Lance?" I didn't know whether to laugh or cry. "You *belong* with her."

I glimpsed Tanya shooting me a smug, triumphant smile while my eyes stayed fixed on Lance. My mouth curled into a snarl.

"And you know what, you're not even a good kisser. You're like a broken washing machine."

"W-what do you mean?"

Using my hand, I pretended like I was holding a phone to my ear. "Hello... Whirlpool repair man... saliva overload."

His jaw went slack. He looked seriously affronted. Make that mortified. And guess what—I was telling the truth. Whenever he kissed, spit leaked out of his mouth. He remained speechless as I hammered into him.

"For all I care, screw your *new* girlfriend. Give her *your* birthday present. I bet she'll be seriously disappointed. It's not a *big* deal. And who knows if it'll work." Lance gawped, his mouth agape like he was holding it open for a dentist. I paused, looking at the two of them heatedly. "Now, get the hell out of here. Both of you. This is *my* house, *my* bathroom, *my* rules."

"Whatever." Tanya shrugged before bending down to retrieve her sparkling halter top. She slipped it over her head, adjusting it over her big boobs. As she fixed her bra strap, a wicked glint lit her eyes.

"Whoops! I'm forgetting something."

My gaze stayed on her as she squatted down again and snatched the gold necklace in her hand like a bird swooping down for a breadcrumb. She stood up, dangling the broken necklace between her fingers, and fired me a smirk. "You know what they say... Finders keepers, losers weepers."

I was so close to crying I could taste tears on my tongue. "Keep the piece of junk."

She snickered. "You know what else they say... One person's junk is another one's treasure."

With that, she shoved the necklace into a back pocket of her new leather leggings before grabbing Lance's hand. "Lancey, let's get out of here. I think it's time for my birthday cake."

I watched as she led him out of the bathroom. Alone, overwhelmed with emotion, I heaved a couple of deep breaths, then locked the door before moving to the sink. I turned on the cold water and splashed some on my heated face. Reaching for one of the guest towels, I glimpsed myself in the mirror. My face was wet and wan. So much of me wanted to see a victorious warrior, but what I saw was a defeated soldier. Forlorn. Fatigued. Beaten down. I'd managed to steal Tanya's laptop, but she'd managed to steal my boyfriend. It didn't take a rocket scientist like my brother to figure out the winner.

Hot tears began to stream down my cheeks, mingling with the splatter of cool water on my face. Then, suddenly, between my legs, I felt a blast of wet heat. My period. Coming at me fast and furious. Could this night get any worse?

. . .

A few minutes later, I was in my pajamas, curled up into a ball, on my bed. I tried to cry myself to sleep, but it was futile. I'd never done that in my life, and though they say there's a first time for everything, this wasn't it. The sickening image of Lance and Tanya kept whipping around my brain. The party likely over, where were they now? And what were they doing? They'd already made it to third base—and with no one in the outfield to stop them, how hard would it be for Lance to score a home run?

At that thought, the tears fell harder. Faster. I'd foolishly saved myself for Lance. I'd probably be the only girl in my senior class to graduate with my V-card intact. I deserved my first big fat F for failing to lose my virginity. Inked in red like *The Scarlet Letter.*

I desperately needed to talk to someone. Unload. Not my brother, who wasn't ready for matters of the heart at the still tender age of twelve. Or sadly not my mother, who seemed to care more about our evil exchange student than her own daughter. There was only one person.

My best friend, Fly.

Forcing myself out of bed, I stumbled over to my backpack and retrieved my phone. Then crawled back into bed. The phone in my hand, I was tempted to click on the spy cam app to see if Lance was in Tanya's room, but with all the willpower I could muster, I refrained. I might be a loser, but I was done with being a masochist.

Snuggled under the comforter, propped up by a pile of pillows, I scrolled through my short list of contacts, passing Lance's name. I paused and deleted it—*Gone!*—and made a mental note to block him, then continued until I got to my BFF's name. With the tap of a finger, I speed-dialed her number.

Her phone rang and rang. *Pick up, Fly! Please!*

I was losing hope when she finally picked up and put the call to FaceTime. Despite how ghastly I must look, I accepted.

When my face popped up on the screen, I almost didn't recognize myself. My skin was blotchy. My hair disheveled. My eyes red and puffy.

"Sweetpea!" Her nickname for me. Just the sound of her husky, earthy voice made me feel better. She looked amazing. Sans makeup, in a Berkeley hoodie, the dark-skinned, six-foot-tall beauty could be a *Vogue* model with her high cheekbones, lush lips, and effervescent smile.

I admired her as much as I adored her. She never let her socio-economic background get her down; in fact, it propelled her. Her hardworking single mother had convinced her that with hard work, a good education, and determination, you could become anything you want. Rise above your circumstances. Rise to the top. One day she hoped to make a difference in the world. I knew that she would.

In her dorm room, she was sitting cross-legged on her bed. "I was just thinking about you. What's up?"

I stayed silent. I could see her studying me.

"Girl, you look terrible!" *Understatement.* "Is everything okay?"

My bottom lip quivered, then I burst into tears. "Lance cheated on me."

The words spilled out, running into each other.

Fly's mahogany-brown eyes grew wide. "He slept with someone?"

"I—I'm not sure. I found him making out with that exchange student I told you about. She was half-undressed in the guest bathroom... and he was all over her."

"Big yikes! I want to slap Lance and that girl. Let me at them!"

A tiny laugh broke through my tears. My bestie continued. "You know, Lance has *always* been a douche."

"What do you mean?"

"Seriously? He's so fake! Do you honestly think he took art

history to learn about Rembrandt and Picasso?" She gave me an exasperated eye roll. "Forget it. He only took it so it would look good on his high school transcript, and he could meet girls."

I never thought about that. That's where we met. The truth is, he *was* the only straight boy in the class. The other, Gavin, was gay and aspired to be a curator.

"And this past summer in the Galápagos? Get ready for this... I know this chick at Berkeley who went on that program. Mr. Future Corporate Lawyer had no interest in exploring wildlife. Other than exploring *her*. He tried to get into her bikini bottoms, but she wanted nothing to do with his Komodo dragon tongue."

At the mention of this betrayal, another rush of hurt whooshed through me. Then, I couldn't help but laugh. That lizard image topped the washing machine. And was way more hilarious.

"Why didn't you tell me?"

"I found this out only a week ago. I was trying to figure out the best time to drop the L-bomb."

"You mean Lance or Lizard?"

She laughed back. "One and the same. But honestly, with college apps, SATs, and the girls' basketball team on fire, I didn't want to distract you."

"Thanks." I loved my tell-it-like-it-is best friend and appreciated her discretion. Yeah, if I'd found out that the douchebag was cheating on me earlier, I may have fallen apart. Or done something rash.

She ran a hand through her slicked-back hair. "I'm so sorry you had to find out this way."

"It's okay."

"Hey, if the situation were reversed, would you have told me?"

I had to think about it. "Probably not."

She gave me the stink-eye. "You'd better! I don't want some two-timing a-hole in my bed."

She made me laugh again. "Okay, I promise." A beat. "Will you be coming home for Thanksgiving?"

"No. My mom and I don't want to spend the money, but I'll be home a few weeks later for almost a month at Christmas."

"Guess what! I'll be up in San Fran spending Thanksgiving with my grandparents as usual. I can take the BART to visit you at Berkeley."

"Awesome! You can even stay with me if you want; my roommate's going home and won't be around."

I was feeling better by the second. Not only could I spend time with my grandma, but I could also see my best friend. I had something to look forward to.

Jordan sighed. "Sweetpea, I gotta go. I have a twenty-page paper that's due tomorrow."

"Thanks, Fly, for being here for me. I feel a whole lot better."

"Trust me, Lance is a minus ten on the boyfriend scale. He doesn't deserve someone as amazing as you. It's so not worth shedding tears over that asshole."

"Lancehole!" I corrected.

Fly laughed her hearty laugh. "Trust me, *Lancehole* will get his."

Fly also believed in karma.

Like Mary Burton's husband. *What goes around, comes around.*

We blew each other kisses and said goodbye.

Sleep awaited me.

And hopefully sweet dreams.

Or dreams of killing the traitor and Tanya.

THIRTY

NATALIE

Another Monday. I woke up feeling great. I'd slept well, and the happiness I'd given our exchange student by throwing her a surprise birthday party last night was still tingling on my skin. As I drove into Beverly Hills for my weekly blowout, I thought about her ecstatic expression as she entered the backyard. It was worth a million bucks. I felt blessed I could give her so much joy when she'd done the same for me.

The only damper to this morning had been Paige. She woke up feeling ill with bad period cramps, and asked if she could stay home. Of course, I said yes. She hardly missed a day of school. Sparing Matt the time-consuming drive, Lance came by and picked up Tanya and Will.

I found it odd Lance didn't ask about Paige and even odder that last night at the party he didn't hang out with her for one minute. For a while I saw him chatting away with Tanya, then they both disappeared. I had a nagging feeling something was going on. I needed to have a talk with Paige. Get to the bottom of this, maybe later today.

———

Pierre Michel, the ultra-chic, ultra-expensive salon I frequented, was located on Beverly Drive right next to the hip, new Odéon Hotel. Running late, I valeted my Mercedes with one of the hotel attendants. The salon was extremely popular and being just five minutes late could cost you your appointment. With my jam-packed schedule, I couldn't afford to do that. I could, however, afford the sinfully exorbitant valet fee.

I whisked into the salon. It was bustling with clients getting haircuts, color, blowouts, or all of the above. I lit up at the symphony of sounds—the snip-snip-snip of scissors, the hum of blow-dryers, the rumble of gossipy conversation, the sexy French music. And marveled at the way stylists and colorists pranced around like ballerinas. Total theater. I loved this place. And the mega-talented owner, Pierre Michel, was my personal stylist. He charged an unheard-of amount for a haircut. But it was well worth it. Not a day went by without me feeling grateful. Thinking about how lucky I was. And how differently my life could have turned out.

Toting my monstrous new Saint Laurent bag, a thoughtful birthday gift from Matt, I strode up to the receptionist. Her name was Bev, and she sported spiky, purple-streaked hair, an armful of tattoos, and a bunch of piercings, including one in her nostril. I was glad neither of my daughters—nor my exchange student—were into piercings and tattoos. They repulsed me and reminded me of someone I hated. Someone I wanted to forget.

"Hi, Bev," I said. "I hope I'm not too late. The traffic on Wilshire was horrendous!"

She looked up at me and smiled. Her gleaming white teeth stood out against her eggplant-black lipstick.

"Mrs. Merritt, you're right on time. Giselle is waiting for you. Why don't you head back to her station?"

Giselle was my blowout girl. Pierre Michel, hairstylist to the stars, didn't do those kinds of mundane things. I thanked Bev and hurried back to Giselle's regular station, the pounding music putting a bounce into my already light, happy gait.

When I got to my station, my heart almost stopped. Sitting in the chair next to mine was the woman who had almost destroyed my life.

Alexa Roth.

THIRTY-ONE

NATALIE

In the mirror, I saw her. And she saw me, her shocked expression rivaling mine. Alexa and I hadn't seen each other since our last encounter over two years ago. An icy head-to-toe chill skated down my body as a chipper Giselle greeted me and escorted me back to the sinks to wash my hair.

Usually, I loved this part of the blowout. There are few things more heavenly or relaxing than getting your hair shampooed. Feeling the spray of hot water prickling against your head and the touch of strong fingertips massaging your scalp. Hearing the squishy, soothing sound of the lather. And inhaling the shampoo's aromatic vanilla-coconut scent. Somehow, salon shampoo and conditioner always smelled better than the ones you had at home. I always closed my eyes and let myself enjoy this weekly indulgence, sighing blissfully.

But today, after seeing Alexa, as I leaned back in the reclining chair, my head lolled against the sink basin so that Giselle could do her magic, I was anything but relaxed. A torrent of horrific memories whirled behind my closed eyes.

I remembered *that* morning as if it were yesterday...

———

It was a Tuesday... the middle of May. My family scrambling for breakfast. Will feeding Bear his chow. The kids scooting off to school in Anabel's Jeep. Matt asking me if I could drop off his navy-blue blazer at the cleaners. Pecking a kiss on my lips as he left for his office.

After my troupe was all gone, I tidied up the kitchen and put Bear outside in the yard. I always relished this time alone. I had the house to myself and could leisurely get ready for my day—take a hot shower and review my schedule. It was just another typical Tuesday. Until it wasn't.

On my way out to Pilates, I remembered Matt's jacket. Leaving my workout bag by the side door, I ran back upstairs to our bedroom. I found it easily, folded on the back of an armchair. Holding it up by the shoulders, I inspected it. Clinging to the gabardine fabric were three long curly red hairs. I plucked one off and held it between my thumb and forefinger like it was vermin. Then I put the jacket to my nose and took a whiff. And inhaled a familiar floral scent—jasmine with a hint of lavender.

Except it *wasn't* mine.

My stomach churned.

My heart lurched.

My husband was having an affair... With his twenty-one-year-old redheaded secretary! A powerful wave of nausea crashed through me. Tossing the jacket back onto the chair, I sprinted to our en suite bathroom, getting to the toilet just in time. Kneeling on the cold marble floor, I held up my hair and retched into the bowl until my stomach was twisted and my throat was raw. With a trembling hand, I flushed the toilet and stood up, my legs like Jell-O. Stumbling to the sink, I turned on the faucet and splashed cold water on my face. I stole a glance at myself in the mirror. I looked wan. Disheveled. *Old.*

After rinsing my mouth, the acidic taste of Matt's infidelity still on my tongue, I staggered back downstairs. Once in the kitchen, I trudged to the fridge and grabbed the barely touched chenin blanc left over from last night. All I had to do was pull out the cork. *Pop!* I put the lip to my mouth and guzzled it like soda. With the half-empty bottle in my hand, I retrieved my phone, which was charging on the counter, and then sat down at the kitchen island. Between gulps of the white wine, I canceled all my meetings, my lunch, as well as my private Pilates session. And popped a Xanax.

Half an hour later, the wine depleted, I still hadn't shed a tear. Not a single one. I was now too numb. Too drunk. Barely able to think straight, I weighed my options: I could be like my mother-in-law and look the other way. Or, I could confront Matt.

Option One was *not* an option. There was no way I could let this go. Especially given my past. I'd looked the other way until it almost destroyed me. So it boiled down to Option Two: confronting my husband.

What were the possible outcomes? A) Matt could deny it and tell me I'm crazy. *Or* B) Matt could fess up... but then what? Could I forgive him and stay in this marriage? Or could I *never* forgive—or forget—and leave him? Destroy my family and everything I'd worked so hard for.

And then, there was this possibility... *he'd* want to leave me. Move on to his secretary *or* someone else. The consequences were no less devastating. Maybe tenfold worse.

I had no answers. Only fear. An all-consuming, viselike fear of my life, as I knew it, unraveling. It was gripping me so fiercely I could barely breathe. I wanted to scream, but what I needed was someone who could help me see the sun through the clouds. Give me honest advice. There was only one person. My no-holds-barred best friend, Alexa Roth. The wife of one of Matt's best friends, Noah.

My hand shaking, I speed-dialed her number, relieved her name was at the beginning of my long list of contacts. She picked up on the first ring.

"Well, hello, *dahling!*"

"Alexa, I need to see you." The words tumbled out of my mouth like they were stuck together.

"Nat, you sound weird."

Drunk by 9 a.m.

"Is everything okay?"

"No!"

"What's wrong?"

"I don't want to talk about it over the phone. Can we meet for lunch?"

"How about the restaurant at Neiman's? That way I can do a little shopping afterward and return the pair of shoes I bought last week."

"Fine. What time?" I rushed the words in case she changed her mind.

"Why don't we say at one."

"That works. See you then."

That's if I didn't overdose on Xanax. I reached again for the bottle.

———

The Neiman Marcus café in Beverly Hills had long been a destination for "Ladies Who Lunch." While the old-fashioned décor had been updated, now contemporary and chic, the clientele was still the same. Just a little younger. Well-dressed, perfectly coiffed women with the latest designer handbags and usually at least one Neiman's shopping bag in tow.

The hostess showed me to our table. It was in the middle of the busy restaurant. Alexa preferred to be seated in the open rather than secluded in a corner because, as she put it, she liked to see and be seen. She loved to be the center of attention. Sometimes I wondered why she was my best friend. Except for serving on many of the same committees, having husbands who were best friends, and sending our kids to the same school, we weren't much alike. She was loud and brazen; I was more inner and reserved. My fashion sense was conservative, hers ostentatious, never letting age or wealth dictate her choices. Maybe I simply liked her because she was a lot of fun and spoke her mind. And you could always count on her to know the latest gossip and, most importantly, get the job done.

I glanced down at my phone. I was fifteen minutes early. I ordered a stiff drink—a whiskey straight up—something I never drank—but with what I had to tell her, I needed one.

Liquid courage.

Alexa was fifteen minutes late. By the time she arrived, I was on my second drink. Given that I'd drunk almost an entire bottle of wine earlier, it's a good thing I'd Ubered here because in my inebriated state, there was no way I was going to be able to drive home. Let alone make it out of this place without falling on my ass.

Alexa made eye contact with me. She gave me her big toothy smile and waved. She looked chic as always in a stunning Chanel suit, accented with lots of chunky gold jewelry, and breezed over to me in her six-inch-high pumps. I was convinced she was born wearing stilettos. It took me several blistering months to learn how to walk in them, the cheap, faux-leather kind from Payless, which were all I could afford before I met Matt.

Matt the philanderer.

As she neared the table, I stood and she hugged me, giving me one of those pretentious double-cheek kisses. "*Dahling,* I'm sorry I'm so late."

She reeled off a lame excuse. But it wasn't her lateness that was disquieting. She was always late. It was something else. Something that was heating me like a fever.

Her honey-blonde hair was now a vibrant shade of red and she was wearing it loose, letting it go naturally curly past her shoulders. As she hugged me, a familiar scent wafted up my nose. An unmistakable combination of jasmine and lavender. A sickening feeling pooled in the pit of my stomach. Weak in the knees, dizzy from the alcohol, I wobbled on my feet and thought I would vomit again. The world was tilted on its axis and spinning around me.

Stop the world! I want to get off!

She kept her feline-green eyes on me. "What's wrong, *dahling?* You look like you just lost your best friend."

In truth, I had. I was fraught with raw emotion. Shock. Anger. Disbelief. Hatred. Indignation. Disgust. How could Alexa do this to me? Unable to control my impulses, nor form words, I raised my hand and slapped her face so hard my palm stung.

She let out a gasp and flinched, jerking her head so I could see the five-finger red welt I left on her cheek.

"You slut!" I seethed.

Without another word and without paying for my drinks, I grabbed my bag and zigzagged out of the restaurant, not caring if every eye was on me.

No, Matt wasn't having an affair with his secretary.

He was fucking my best friend.

White-hot tears finally exploded.

THIRTY-TWO

NATALIE

The rest of *that* day is a total blur.

Another one of the *many* worst days of my life.

When I got home, I popped a Xanax, then opened another bottle of wine and drank it until I passed out on one of the couches in our living room. It was five o'clock in the afternoon when I woke up with a major hangover. My head throbbing, my mouth parched, I sat up slowly, the pain of Matt's betrayal—and Alexa's—robbing me of any rationality. Propelling me to confront him no matter what the consequences.

Butterflies swarmed my stomach at the thought of the ugly confrontation ahead. I couldn't let Matt have the upper hand. I needed to fortify myself. Make myself look presentable. Dragging myself off the couch, I crept up the flight of marble stairs like an old lady, hoping I wouldn't miss a step and fall down it. And kill myself. I made it to the landing and staggered to our bedroom at the end of the long hallway. *Our* bedroom. I wondered how long that would be the case as I stripped off my wrinkled clothes and stumbled to our adjacent bathroom.

Stepping inside the shower, I adjusted the lever and let the scalding hot needles of water recharge every cell of my body. I must have stayed under the steamy spray for at least a half hour. When I'd finally had enough, I turned off the water and stepped out of the stall. After towel-drying myself, I put on my fluffy terrycloth robe that hung next to *his*. I couldn't even say his name to myself.

Wiping off the fogged-up mirror with my elbow, I stared at myself. The shower had revitalized me. My skin was aglow, my eyes no longer glazed. Rather than blow-drying my hair, I ran a comb through it and gathered it up into a ponytail. Then reapplied my makeup, lipstick the color of blood and mascara so thick my lashes were spikes.

Feeling stronger, I returned to the bedroom and pondered what to put on. A power suit? Jeans? A sexy dress? None of the above. Instead, I opted for a pair of black silk pajamas I'd bought in Paris. Complete with my tallest, spikiest heels, I felt like a knight in shining black armor. Empowered. I mentally donned a sword and then marched out of the bedroom. Patiently, I stood at the top of the stairs waiting for him to come home. I was ready for combat. Ready for revenge.

Ticktock. Ticktock.

The passing minutes ticked in my head. Matt should be home at six. Sure enough, on the dot, I heard his car pull into the driveway. I knew his routine. He'd come in through the side door. Go to the bar. Pour himself a shot. Come upstairs to take his jacket off and wash up. My heart racing with anticipation, I did a countdown in my head. Silently singing "Ninety-Nine Bottles of Beer on the Wall." A song I used to sing with the kids on long road trips. Except I tweaked it slightly: "Ninety-Nine Bottles of Beer on the Stairs."

And if one of them happens to fall off the stairs… ninety-eight bottles of beer on the stairs.

In my head, I envisioned the bottles on the stairs.

Surrounding me on the landing. Imagining that, one by one, I would hurl them at Matt like a circus knife thrower until one struck him and sent him careening down the steep steps. A wicked smile lifted my lips at my sinfully evil fantasy. I was surprised by how much evil lurked inside me. Then again, I shouldn't be. I was born from evil, after all.

I was down to eighty-nine bottles when I heard Matt mount the stairs. A marathon runner, he climbed the steps effortlessly despite a long day at the office. Because of their serpentine nature, he didn't see me on the landing until he was almost at the top. My hands were planted on my hips and my eyes were shooting daggers. If only they were real.

His eyes met mine. "Hi, babe. Why are you standing there like that?"

I hadn't rehearsed a speech. My first words flew out of my mouth like a spray of flaming arrows. "How could you?"

He met me on the landing. "What are you talking about?"

"*Seriously?*" I punched him in the chest. Hard. It felt good. Then I kicked him in the shin.

He winced. "For God's sake, Natalie. What's wrong with you?"

"What's wrong with *me?*" I jabbed an index finger into my clavicle. "You've got to be kidding."

His eyes narrowed. "Are you drunk, Natalie?"

"*No!* I'm *not* drunk!" At least not anymore. I was as sober as a judge. Sobriety driving both my anger and actions. I stretched out my arms like a barricade as Matt grew more incensed.

"You're acting ridiculous. Please get out of my way."

He attempted to brush past me, but I grabbed him by his tie, gripping it so tightly I almost choked him.

"Jesus, Natalie. Let go of me! I can't breathe." He tried to free himself, but my strong husband was no match for my adrenaline-fueled strength. Still clutching the tie, I fisted my free hand and began to pummel him. Each punch harder, each thud louder.

"Stop it!" he choked out. "You're hurting me!"

I pounded harder. Faster. "And you think you haven't hurt *me*?"

"What the hell are you talking about?"

"Alexa!"

"Shit."

With that one word, I knew he was guilty as sin. He'd fucked my best friend! For a split second, my rage gave way to anguish, and in that brief moment of weakness, he broke free of me with a shove. Losing my footing, I landed with a thud on the hardwood floor. Smack on my ass.

He adjusted his jacket. "I'm going for a drive. I may not come back."

"Like hell you are." Before he could pivot on his heel, I grabbed one of his ankles with both hands, clasping it like a manacle.

"Let go of me!"

As he tried to shake his foot free, I bit into it. The metallic taste of blood filled my mouth.

He cursed. "You're crazy!"

"That's right!" My rage surging, I dug my teeth into him again. I'd turned into a rabid dog. I could even feel myself foaming at the mouth.

I didn't see his next move coming. My mouth latched onto his leg, he kicked me with his other foot in the face. So hard I almost saw stars. More blood flooded my palate. This time mine. We'd both become savage animals. I looked up and spat at him. A crimson spray flew out of my mouth. And a blood-coated tooth. With a plink, it landed on the floor between his feet. Tears seared my bruised cheek.

Matt met my gaze. I was expecting him to break into a

contemptuous, triumphant smile, but his expression was forlorn, his eyes weary.

"I'm sorry," he muttered.

Sor-ry. The word reverberated in my ears. *Sorry for what?* Sorry for cheating on me? Sorry for abusing me? Sorry for marrying me? The only thing he should be sorry for was being born.

"Let me help you up." He extended a hand toward me.

I scooted back, away from him. Breathing like a dragon in and out of my flaring nostrils. "Don't! You! Dare! Touch! Me!"

"Nat—"

"Don't *Nat* me."

Still breathing heavily, I anchored my hands on the floor and pushed myself up to standing. I wobbled and felt blood trickling from the corners of my mouth. Keeping our distance, we stared at each other in deadly silence. Until he broke it.

"What happened with Alexa was a mistake. I only love you."

I only love you.

His four bogus words sent me over the edge. A second wind, as strong as a hurricane, blew through me. Rage flooded every cell of my body.

"I! Hate! You!" The words were so thunderous they bounced off the walls. On my next heated breath, I tackled him, wrapping my iron-strong legs around his waist like a vise. Yanking at his hair and clawing him with my nails, I was a savage beast again. Determined to rip my prey apart.

I clung to him as he winced and swore. Blood streaked down his face, spotting the collar of his white shirt. A cacophony of shrieks, moans, and groans clogged my ears. Along with a string of expletives that ping-ponged between us.

We were dangerously close to the edge of the landing when another voice broke through the madness.

"Mom, Dad! What's going on?"

Oh my God! Anabel! Running toward us, clad in her heart-print pajamas. A mix of shock and fear was writ deep on her face. What was she doing home? I thought she had cheerleading practice until six thirty. Later I'd find out she'd texted me to tell me she'd felt ill at school and was coming home early. In my drunken stupor, I hadn't checked my messages. It was *too* late. Fate had already made up her mind.

"Go back to your room!" I ordered. But it was as if she didn't hear me.

"What are you doing, Mom?"

Trying to avert my sharp nails, Matt answered for me. "It's none of your business."

"Dad! She's hurting you!" I could hear tears in her voice. "Stop, Mom! Please stop!"

"Just go!" I pleaded.

"Please, Mom! Let go of him!" Sobbing, she tugged at my shoulders, my arms, my legs. Desperately trying to set her father free of me.

As she relentlessly kept at me, another spike of adrenaline surged inside me. I twisted my torso so I was partially facing her, and with my right elbow, gave her a shove with a She-Hulk strength I never knew I had.

Caught off guard, she let out a gasp and lost her balance. Before I could blink, the unthinkable happened. She tumbled down the stairs, step by hard step, her body thudding against the marble, her arms flailing, unable to stop herself. Her groans becoming fainter with each successive one.

Until there were none.

"Oh my God!" I cried out with wide-eyed horror.

I let go of Matt and raced down the stairs, lucky I didn't kill myself, which, in retrospect, I often wished I had. Matt followed me, cursing under his breath. Lying at the base of the stairs, unconscious, her body contorted, her eyes two glassy blue marbles, gazing at the ceiling as blood pooled on the floor, was my daughter. My beautiful daughter. Oh God! What had I done?

In a state of shock, paralyzed with horror, I glimpsed Paige and Will standing at the front door. Staring at what I was staring at.

My lifeless daughter. My precious Anabel.

She was dead.

THIRTY-THREE

NATALIE

"I'm sorry, Mrs. Merritt, I must have gotten shampoo in your eyes."

Giselle's singsong voice brought me back to the moment. I jolted.

"Um, uh, just a bit. I'm fine. It's no big deal."

The truth is, she hadn't. Tears were leaking from my eyes at the vivid memory of that fatal day.

"We're almost done. I just need to put some conditioner on your hair and we'll be out of here."

As she applied it, I inhaled the coconutty essence and sighed. A brief moment of tranquility. The second she turned off the spray and wrapped a towel around my wet hair, dread filled me. I was going to have to face Alexa again. Maybe with a little luck she'd moved to a different station. Or left the salon.

Following Giselle back to her station, I felt every muscle in my body tense. My hopes had not materialized. Alexa was still seated next to me, her stylist in the middle of blowing out her shoulder-length locks now back to a buttery shade of blonde. As our stylists worked their magic and made small talk, we stared at each other in the mirrored wall, neither of us giving as much as a sideways glance.

Dressed as chicly as ever in a pink-fringed Chanel jacket, skinny jeans, and black patent stilettos, a Birkin in her lap, she looked as uncomfortable as I did. I wondered what was going through her head. All I could keep thinking was how much I hated this woman, how much I wanted to rip off one of her thick gold-link necklaces and strangle her with it. Choke the life out of her. She'd cost me the life of my beautiful daughter.

As I faced the mirror, a sudden wave of guilt and remorse crashed over me. The horrid, irrefutable truth stared back at me. My reflection lashed out at me. *Stop the blame. You have no one to blame but yourself for Anabel's death. You pushed her. You are responsible.*

I hated myself more than I could hate anyone in the world. Including Alexa.

The tension in the air between us was so thick that even a pair of razor-edge hair shears couldn't cut through it. We finished with our blowouts at about the same time. In unison, we stood up and hugged our respective stylists. Hooking my bag over my arm, I hurried to the front desk, hoping to settle my bill, get the hell out of here, and escape her.

Once again, the cards were not stacked in my favor. There were three women ahead of me waiting to pay. In absolutely no time, Alexa was standing behind me. I could feel her warm breath on the nape of my neck. Smell her scent—it was something different from the last time I saw her. Perhaps classic Chanel N°5.

Facing forward, as rigid as a rod, I felt a light tap on my right shoulder.

"Natalie..."

Every nerve buzzing, the hairs on the back of my neck bristling, I debated whether or not to acknowledge her.

"Nat, please..."

Slowly, hesitantly, reluctantly, against my better judgment, I turned and faced her.

A forlorn expression fell over her. She gazed at me with clown eyes. "I just want to say I'm sorry."

I felt myself stiffening. The word "sorry" had no place in my vocabulary or my life. There was nothing she could say or do that would bring back my Anabel. "Please... let bygones be bygones."

At my words, her eyes began to water. "I'm so sorry about what happened to Anabel. I always thought it was partly my fault, but you need to know the whole story."

I said nothing. Matt and I were moving forward. Did I really want to revisit his affair with my former best friend?

The line moved up; we were standing side by side. "Please, Nat. Just have coffee or a glass of wine with me. I promise you we'll never have to see each other again after today."

"Fine."

It was my turn to pay.

Maybe for my sins.

THIRTY-FOUR

NATALIE

The Odéon Hotel's chic, down-lit bar was surprisingly quiet. The hostess led us to a secluded booth in the corner. I was surprised Alexa, who always preferred to be in the open, didn't object. A server in all black came by and took our drink orders. Alexa ordered a Kir Royale. My nerves on edge, I did the same. She then excused herself to use the restroom, relieving me of not having to make small talk.

The drinks, accompanied by a bowl of mixed nuts, arrived just as she returned, and an awkward stretch of silence ensued. In the past, under normal circumstances, Alexa and I would always propose a toast, be it to our friendship or to one of the galas we were co-chairing. But we were no longer friends, and she and I no longer served on the same boards. I stared at the pink-tinted champagne, watching the bubbles rise, at a loss for words.

Alexa made the first move. She lifted the flute with her perfectly manicured fingers to her lips. "Thank you, Nat, for being here. It means a lot to me." She took a quick sip of her drink. Wordlessly, I followed suit.

No toast.

Setting her flute down, she looked at me earnestly. "You know, I never come to Pierre Michel on Mondays anymore."

I'm sure she deliberately avoided me the way I avoided her. Our paths hadn't crossed in over two years. Not once.

She continued. "I have the library's annual black-tie dinner tonight. It's the first time they're holding it on a Monday... so I had to get my hair done."

I nodded. I used to love that event. But with Alexa chairing The Circle of Friends, I'd left the board.

Alexa stared down at her drink and then gazed up at me, a pained expression on her face. "I'm sorry you won't be there."

"I'm sure it will be lovely." I took another long sip of my Kir to avoid having to say more.

Another round of silence. Alexa dipped her fingers into the tub of nuts, nervously rearranging them, not eating one. She finally broke the silence.

"Nat, I've always felt terrible about that day at Neiman's."

That day, that lunch that changed my life forever. Almost ended it.

My eyes drilled into hers. "Alexa, *you* slept with my husband!"

She blinked nervously, her eyes misting. "Here's the thing... I didn't."

Anger seeped into my bloodstream. "I don't believe you!" I hissed.

A tear escaped from her eye; she brushed it away. The look on her face morphed into one of despair. "It's the honest truth. I swear on my children's lives."

The irony of her last words stung me. What about Anabel's life? Battling my own tears, I let her go on.

"Nat, please hear me out." Her normally brazen voice was small. Repentant. I resisted a sip of my Kir and nodded. She softly thanked me.

"On the Monday before *that* Tuesday, Matt came over to see Noah in the late afternoon to review his portfolio with him. Except Noah wasn't home yet from his office. He'd gotten caught in traffic. With Noah an hour away, I offered Matt a drink. It was the least I could do.

"He wanted a Campari and soda and followed me to the kitchen. While I was fixing the drink at the counter, we made small talk and then he slid up behind me. He blew on my neck. Then pressed his body against mine. It was making me very uncomfortable and I told him he should go back to the living room."

I shifted in my seat, fearful of where this story was going. I took a long sip of my Kir as Alexa persevered.

"He told me I was beautiful and wanted to know if I knew what I did to him. Before I could utter a word, he twisted my arm behind my back and placed my hand on his erection. And held it there. Pinning me against the counter, he put his other hand between my thighs. And began to rub me. I told him to stop, but he didn't. Then he flipped me around and kissed me as I tried to fight him off. I kept begging him to stop, but he wouldn't. He fondled my breasts, and wouldn't let go of my crotch. Then, he pulled down his fly. I heard the hiss of the zipper, but I was too afraid, too repulsed to look down. I begged him again to stop, but he didn't. To my utter horror, his hand slid down beneath the waistband of my jeans and into my panties. I was about to scream when I heard Noah's car pull into the driveway. Matt jumped off me and cursed under his breath. In a panic, he pulled up his fly as I fled."

She paused, tears falling from her eyes, causing her mascara to run. Inky rivulets streaked down her cheeks. I should have reached across the table to wipe them away with my cocktail napkin, but I was too stunned. Too frozen with shock. She wiped them away herself.

"When Noah met us in the kitchen, Matt acted like nothing

had happened. Shaken, I played along, but I'd never felt so violated in my entire life."

She inhaled through her nose, then expelled a loud breath.

"Not a day goes by without me thinking about what happened. Questioning my actions. My failure to say something." She paused again and held me in her watery gaze. "Natalie, can you ever forgive me?"

My heart, which had been consumed by hatred for this woman, did a flip-flop as her story unfolded. It released my deep-seated malice and swelled with compassion. I cupped a hand over hers. It was icy cold. She was telling the truth.

"Alexa, there's nothing to forgive. But why didn't you tell me this before?"

She sniffled. "I wanted to. I meant to. And then Anabel... and then you fell sick. I was at her memorial service. I sat in the back. I bawled my eyes out."

"Thank you for coming."

Hundreds turned out for the memorial (minus Matt's parents, who were away on a South Seas cruise and unable to make it back in time). The chapel was filled with all her high school friends, their parents, as well as teachers going all the way back to preschool. Additionally, numerous friends of ours, even those we'd not seen for years, came to pay their respects, along with community and business leaders we worked with. There were countless eulogies, but neither Matt nor I had the physical or emotional wherewithal to give one.

We looked terrible. I was lucky a black lace veil obscured the purple bruise on my cheek, my swollen, red-rimmed eyes, and missing tooth. Matt applied cover-up to his facial scratches and a couple of Band-Aids and told anyone who inquired about them that he'd sustained them while trying to rescue a frightened stray cat. Even the police who came to our house to inquire about Anabel's death believed that story as well as mine

—that I'd bumped into a tree while gardening. *And* our mutually agreed-upon story—that our flu-stricken daughter must have fainted and fallen down the stairs. The once perfect couple had invented the perfect set of lies. To our relief, neither Paige nor Will refuted them.

I was glad I hadn't noticed Alexa at the service as God only knows how I would have reacted. At the burial, attended by only Matt, Paige, Will, and myself, I collapsed as Anabel's casket was lowered into the ground. The pain so great I couldn't bear it. My doctor later told me I had a psychotic break. I was in bed for over six months in a delirious state with round-the-clock nurses who fed and bathed me. Ironically, the only food they could get down my throat was baby food. As if eating baby food would bring back *my* baby. My Anabel. A frightened Paige and Will came to my bedside to say goodnight to me daily, but I hardly saw Matt, who I believed was sleeping on one of the sofas downstairs. I didn't know. I didn't care. He was the last person on earth I wanted to share a bed with. The last person I ever wanted to see.

My children were my elixir. Like a magician pulling a rabbit out from a hat, I found the strength to resume my life. To be a mother for *their* sakes. It required lots of physical therapy and counseling, including couples sessions with Matt. Ultimately, with the help of Xanax, I was able to forgive and trust Matt and let go of my grief though the deep scar wedged in my heart would never disappear.

Alexa bowed her head and when she lifted it, a mixture of remorse and shame clouded her eyes. "I'm sorry I didn't give you my condolences."

I'm so sorry for your loss. How many times had I heard those meaningless words? How would they have sounded coming from the woman I thought was responsible for my daughter's death? I shook off a shudder.

"I understand. You couldn't." The guilt and pain she'd harbored over the past two years redeemed her. I squeezed her cold hand. Her eyes burned into mine.

"Nat..."

"Yes?"

"I need to tell you something else." A flicker of hesitation in her voice, she chewed the inside of her lip.

Not a muscle in my face moved. I was ready to end this conversation, unsure if I wanted to hear more.

"What?"

"You promise you won't be mad at me?" She sounded like a little girl who'd stolen her best friend's cookie and was about to confess. Her face paled. A muscle in her jaw twitched. I'd never seen her this anxious before.

"Promise." I instantly regretted agreeing and felt a prickle of apprehension.

She swallowed. Blinked. Then took a deep, shuddering breath.

"Matt and I have a history."

I felt myself flinch, my brows lift. "What do you mean?"

"I met him in college when I was spending my junior year abroad in London. At some pub. He was on a business trip."

Knowing Alexa's age, I did the calculations in my head. It must have been a couple of years before I met Matt and gave birth to Anabel.

"What happened between you?"

"I got smashed and went back with him to his hotel. We had sex and..."

"And what?" I held my breath in anticipation of what would come next. She took a long swig of her drink, then vomited the words...

"He knocked me up."

My eyes grew wide as saucers. "You got *pregnant*?"

"It was wild and impulsive. Neither of us was using protection..."

"And...?"

She picked at her thumbnail. "I had his baby." The cuticle began to bleed. "And gave it up."

I tried to swallow back my shock and the sick feeling that was rising inside me. "A boy or a girl?"

"A girl. She was quietly taken from me before I set eyes on her. Given to some wealthy, infertile British couple. A closed adoption."

Meaning she couldn't contact them and vice versa.

"Does Matt know about this?"

My kids have a half-sister... somewhere in England?

She shook her head. "No, I never told him. I didn't see him for years... not until Noah and I moved from New York to LA after our kids were born." She took another sip of her Kir. "Believe me, it was quite a shock. I've tried to avoid him, but it's hard when we travel in the same circles."

"What about your husband? Does Noah know?"

"He doesn't know a thing." She fidgeted with her diamond wedding band, twisting and turning it. "Nat, you've got to promise me not to tell them. Especially Noah. It would destroy our marriage."

I digested her words, my marriage already destroyed by my husband's actions.

"Please, Nat, can you keep a secret?" implored my former best friend.

"Yes. Don't worry." I was the best secret keeper I knew. My skin bristled.

Alexa smiled with relief. "Thanks, Nat. I owe you."

"You don't owe me anything."

The smile on Alexa's face faded. "Yes, I do. I owe you the *whole* truth. You need to know."

My heart began to pound. "Know what?"

"There are others..." Her hushed voice, now in full gossip mode, trailed off.

More bastard love children?

"I don't understand. What are you talking about?"

"The Lunch Bunch. The women who lunch with Matt at his office or the suite he maintains at the Century Hotel."

A cold wave of nausea rolled over me. I felt my throat constricting, my stomach churning. My mouth opened, but words didn't come out.

"Everyone knows about him."

Everyone except me.

As Matt's dirty secrets ate away at me, hollowing me, the server came by with lunch menus and asked if we wished to order anything. Was he kidding? I was close to throwing up. Alexa passed on behalf of both of us, but ordered another round of Kirs.

"Who else?" I at last spat out, the need to know trumping my shock.

"Nat, I can't tell you. All I will say... at least a dozen women you know. They call him Matt the Stallion."

Matt and his big dick. I thought back to my breakdown. Is that why he was rarely with me? Had he been screwing all my friends while I was practically a vegetable? And maybe all the pretty nurses? And where had he disappeared to the night of the FAFAK gala after the Tanya incident? He'd gone upstairs with Lance to change out of his wet clothes, then I never saw him until dessert came. Had he been banging one of my friends right under our roof?

"Natalie, are you okay?" asked Alexa.

One small word. One big lie. "Yes."

"I hope you don't mind me telling you."

"I'm glad you did." My voice was devoid of emotion.

Her signature wide, toothy smile spread across her Botoxed face. She polished off her sparkly pink drink.

"Nat, I've missed you terribly. Can we be friends again?"

Was she serious? Without another word, I hurtled out of the restaurant and vomited on the sidewalk while the valet got my car.

I was falling down a rabbit hole.

And wasn't sure I could get back up.

THIRTY-FIVE

PAIGE

My phone alarm.

The familiar chime played until I reached under my pillow and turned it off. I cocked an eye half-open, then the other. My heavy lids felt like they'd been cemented shut.

Despite my pep talk with Jordan, I'd hardly slept. Tossing and turning, unable to block out Lance and Tanya from my mind. My period cramps hadn't helped either. I'd finally fallen asleep at some wee hour of the morning and at best had gotten two hours of sleep.

I felt like crap. My eyes stung. My brain was in a fog. And I still had cramps. If I looked as bad as I felt (which I'm sure I did), there was no way I could go to school today. Concentrate in class. Take PE. Above all, face Lance. *Or* Tanya. Even the thrill of watching her open her computer bag, to find a cast-iron pan instead of her laptop, couldn't motivate me.

Unable to get out of bed, I texted my mom, telling her I was sick and needed to stay home from school. Mom replied with a sad-faced emoji. She told me she'd leave a tray with some hot tea and non-dairy buttered toast outside my door before she left for Pilates and have my father take Will and

Tanya to school. The mere mention of her name made me feel sicker.

I slid back under my comforter and managed to catch another few hours of shut-eye. When I re-awoke a little after ten, I actually felt a lot better. I rolled out of bed and headed to the bathroom. To my surprise, our housekeeper, Blanca, was inside with a mop and a bucket of cleaning supplies.

"*Hola!*" I said, giving her a hug.

I loved Blanca. The jovial, hardworking El Salvadorian had been with us for years. I'd helped her study to get her American citizenship. She was practically family. More of a mom to me than my own mother, who'd rather go on her merry philanthropic way.

"*Hola, mí chiquita! Tu mamá me dijo que no te sientes bien.*"

"I feel much better now."

Except Tanya's side of the bathroom could make me puke. It was a disaster as usual. Hair and toothpaste all over the sink, her grooming products in total disarray. I felt bad Blanca had to clean it up, plus tidy her pigsty of a room. I apologized for the state of the bathroom.

Blanca made a face. "*Tanya... muy sucia. Como una puerca!*"

I laughed as she told me Tanya was a filthy pig. I couldn't help making a loud snort. Blanca made an even louder one, and following a snorting match, we both laughed until we cried. After the laughter died down, I told our housekeeper that I'd clean Tanya's side of the bathroom. She protested, but I insisted. She finally gave in. Of course, I wasn't going to go anywhere near her sink. Especially without wearing a hazmat suit. Let the pig have a hissy fit. I'd just tell my mom I had to spend most of my day in the bathroom so Blanca wouldn't get in trouble.

Once Blanca left, I did my normal morning routine and

took a shower, which made me feel even better. My cramps were gone. And somehow the hot pounding water had cleansed me of Lance. For the first time as I towel-dried myself, I tried to imagine Tanya's reaction when she opened her computer bag and discovered the casserole pan. I'm sure she went ballistic and had a total meltdown. A big part of me wished I could have been there, but likely the rest of my day would have been hell. I wouldn't have put it past her to physically assault me, perhaps even bang me over the head with the heavy metal pan when I wasn't looking. Stick her posse on me. Thank God Will was away on a field trip all day and had a robotics meet-up after school or his life would be endangered too.

The hum of Blanca's vacuum in my ears, I returned to my room and put on sweats, a hoodie, and my Crocs. The toast and tea left by my mother now cold, I went downstairs to make some breakfast. Over a mug of coconut milk and a bowl of granola, I contemplated my day. There were three things I urgently needed to do.

The first took me less than a minute. I stopped following Tanya and Lance on Instagram, but decided to keep my @Spy-Girl2 handle, just in case I changed my mind. I was weirdly attached to the avatar I'd created.

With that done, I moved on to task number two and headed out the side door to my father's nearby tool shed. He was the least handy man in the world and had succumbed to asking our handyman to assemble it. He could barely change a light bulb, but he had a set of tools because it's what all guys did. I undid the latch, pulled open the door, and instantly found what I was looking for hanging from the pegboard.

An axe.

Armed with my weapon, I felt like Thor as I marched to my studio. I swung the door open and, without stopping, I charged to my worktable. On it stood the statue of Lance posed in a runner's stretch that I'd planned to give him at Christmas.

Wasting no time, I wrapped both hands around the wood handle of the heavy axe and slammed it down on the statue. *Thwack.* The sculpture I'd worked so hard on for over a month split apart in mere seconds.

I wasn't done.

With a maniacal smile, I bashed the ceramic pieces over and over until they were dust. *Ashes to ashes. Dust to dust.* Lance was *officially* dead to me. And I was *officially* an axe murderer.

On to task number three. The photo. That Indio High class photo I'd discovered in Tanya's suitcase. I needed to scan the copy I'd made, send it to Mary, and ask her if she recognized the sad-looking girl circled in red.

After taking Bear for a short walk around the block, I returned to my now very tidy room, thanks to Blanca, and grabbed my phone. As if I couldn't be in a better mood, I had dozens of shouty texts from Tanya. Most of them to the tune of:

You cretin! Where's my computer?
ANSWER ME!!
You're in big trouble!
ANSWER ME!!!
Your life is over! Just wait!
YOU BETTER ANSWER ME!!!!

I *wasn't* going to answer her. Let her fume! Shit was going to hit the fan when she came home from school, but I was actually looking forward to it. I'd simply tell my mother I was napping all day and had my phone turned off. I even had an explanation if she accused me of stealing or hiding her laptop, but let's not jump the gun.

First things first. My phone in hand, I texted Mary Burton and asked if she would be willing to help me identify someone. I explained the Indio High class photo I wanted to send her. She was more than happy to help and already had her computer hooked back up to her Wi-Fi provider. She gave me her email address.

Expecting to get a text or email back from her later in the day, I was surprised when my phone rang thirty seconds later. It was Mary. I picked up on the first ring. It was nice to hear her voice again. And see her when we agreed to FaceTime.

"Hun, I recognized the circled girl instantly and had to call you."

My heartbeat sped up. "Who is she?"

"Her name is Billie Rae Perkins." She paused. "Or should I say *was* Billie Rae Perkins. She was in my homeroom and I had her in a biology class I taught. She was quite bright but barely said a word. Kind of a loner. Always had her nose buried in a book—some fairy tale or classic. I never saw her hanging out with the other kids. Not even one. She was rather pretty but always looked so sad... like in this photo."

I dwelled on Mary's use of the past tense. "What happened to her?"

"It's a terrible story."

My curiosity piqued, I was all ears and let her continue.

"The poor thing. She lived in the Shadow Hills trailer park with her mother. The girl was skinny as a rail... always came to school with the same thing. A peanut butter and jelly sandwich in a brown paper bag. Once she came with no lunch, so I lent her a dollar so she could buy a hot one, which she wolfed down like there was no tomorrow.

"A couple of times she came to school with a black eye. Another time with a split lip. And one time she showed up with a cast on her wrist. Each time when I asked her what had happened, she said she'd bumped into something or fallen. I suspected something else. That her mother was abusing her. I contacted social services, but they didn't find any evidence of parental abuse. Plus, I met the woman and she seemed nice enough."

"What did her mother do?" I asked, reaching for a notebook

and pen from my backpack. I needed to take notes so I wouldn't forget anything.

"Based on the information we had on file, she was a homemaker. But I'm not sure. One thing, though, she was a smoker. Billie Rae's clothes, well, the few she had, always reeked of cigarette smoke and tobacco."

"What about her father?"

"According to school records, her parents were separated. His job occupation was listed as *None of Your Business*."

Wow. As much as I complained about my parents, they could be contenders for "Best Parents of the Year."

"What were their names?"

"Jolene and Roy Perkins."

"Are they still alive?"

"That's something I know for sure." She adjusted her half-moon glasses. "The answer is no. They were brutally murdered."

"Whoa!" I wasn't expecting that. "When did it happen?"

"May 2000. The end of Billie Rae's sophomore year."

She was likely fifteen or sixteen at the time, based on my mental calculations. I pressed for more details.

"Her parents were both stabbed to death in the wee hours of the morning. I guess Roy had come to visit. They found Jolene on the sleeper couch, Roy on the floor."

"What about Billie Rae? Was she okay?"

"The poor girl was missing. The police believed that whoever murdered Roy and Jolene kidnapped her."

"Did they ever find the killer?"

"No... never. I guess it's a cold case now."

"What about Billie Rae? Do you think the murderer killed her too?"

Mary's lips flattened into a thin, grim line. "I watch too many of those crime shows. They say that if they don't find the kidnapped victim within the first twenty-four hours, chances are they're dead."

But there were also those girls who were held captive for years by their abductors and managed to escape. Some like Elizabeth Smart and Jaycee Dugard had shared their harrowing stories in bestselling memoirs and gone on to do worthwhile things with their lives. Before I had a chance to mention this, Mary asked, "Hun, I forgot to ask you. Where did you find this photo?"

I bit down on my bottom lip. Why hadn't I anticipated that question? Despite being the quick thinker I was, I hedged and hawed and then... "Believe it or not, I found it in the basement of our house." Mary didn't know about our thieving exchange student and my gut told me to keep it that way. And she didn't know a thing about our house, which had no basement.

"That's very strange," she muttered.

More quick thinking.

"Maybe the people who owned our house before us were related to Billie Rae and her family?" I asked hopefully.

"Hmm. Maybe." Mary didn't seem very convinced. And I couldn't blame her. Unlike my sister and Tanya, I was not a great actress.

"But now, Mary, I'm really intrigued. You don't by chance have any newspaper clippings you can send me about the murder or investigation?"

"Sorry, hun, I don't. But I'm sure you can find some articles online. Google *The Desert Sun* and *Redlands Daily*. It was headline news: *Double Murder in Shadow Hills Trailer Park*. Perhaps come down here again and visit with the detectives who investigated the crime. I'd love to see you two kids again! And I'll have plenty of my homemade lemonade and chocolate chip cookies just waitin' for ya."

A smile bloomed on my face. To her utter delight, I told her another visit was a possibility before we exchanged goodbyes.

Waiting for me on my phone were a dozen more scathing texts from Tanya.

But I had way better things to do than read them.

I spent the rest of the afternoon curled up on my bed, investigating the murders of Jolene and Roy Perkins and the disappearance of their teenage daughter, Billie Rae. Only taking a break for lunch, a yummy vegan burrito that Blanca had prepared.

My Google search didn't yield much. A few newspaper articles and only one of them included photos of Billie Rae and her parents, Jolene and Roy. Billie Rae looked a lot like her mother, mousy-haired, solemn, and skinny, but had her father's bushy brows and sharp cheekbones. He was scary-looking, with his nose ring, full-neck tattoo, and bristly cleft chin. There was something familiar about him, but I couldn't put my finger on it. Maybe I'd watched too many episodes of *Breaking Bad*.

I did, however, glean more about the murders. The stabbings were done with kitchen knives. No outsider fingerprints were found on them; the killer must have worn gloves. There was no sign of a forced entry or a struggle, so it was likely someone they knew.

There were possible motives. Jolene was an unemployed alcoholic, who dallied with men from local bars. Roy had a felony record and a huge gambling debt, so possibly one of her local pickups had gone off the deep end or one of his debt collectors decided to make a point. The articles portrayed them as lowlifes and were mostly focused on the safe return of their missing, presumed kidnapped daughter, Billie Rae. A police call-in number was listed, including an anonymous hotline, promising that all tips would be kept confidential.

After skimming the articles, I set up a Google Alert for any new online postings that mentioned Billie Rae Perkins and/or missing girls. Maybe there would be some breakthrough in this cold case.

I glanced at the time. It was now a quarter to four. Tanya should be home any minute.

Logging out of my computer, I braced myself with a fortifying breath. I thought about barricading myself in my room but couldn't resist seeing how piss mad she'd be about her missing laptop.

I hopped off the bed and as I headed downstairs, a confident smile formed on my lips.

I was ready for all hell to break loose.

THIRTY-SIX

NATALIE

Matt the Stallion.

The words burned on my brain.

The bourbon burned on my tongue.

And each time I gulped down a glug of the bitter liquor, it burned a fiery trail from my throat to my gut.

These were not nameless, faceless women. They were women I knew. *My friends.*

Matt had a predilection for blondes and was a leg man. I thought of all the women I knew who fit the bill. Carolyn... Olivia... Gillian... The list went on. How could I face any of them again, knowing they might have slept with my husband? How could I live with the rage and humiliation?

And more insufferably, how could I live with Matt? Share the same bed as him?? I thought our marriage was on the rebound, our sex frequent and fulfilling, but now *this*. And what was more, I couldn't stop thinking about his and Alexa's daughter. What she looked like, what she did, where she lived. And *were* there others? Only one thing was for sure...

I *hated* him.

With the bourbon firing me up, I took my rage out on the

vegetables I was preparing for dinner. Chopping them with one of our razor-sharp kitchen knives. *Chop. Chop. Chop. Chop.* Each thrust of the glistening ten-inch blade harder and faster. I felt like one of those Japanese hibachi chefs who put on a dazzling knife show with their lightning-fast chopping skills and astounding juggling tricks.

Knives terrified me. I gripped the handle and stayed laser-focused, not wanting to cut off a finger. But as the bourbon seeped into my bloodstream, my lucidity ebbed and my mind began playing tricks on me. Slicing two plump vine-ripe tomatoes in half, I imagined I was chopping off Matt's balls. *Chop. Chop.* And then as I diced a large zucchini, I envisioned Matt's thick dick. *Chop. Chop. Chop...*

As I lowered the knife again to the squash, a familiar voice cut into my concentration.

"Hi, Mom. What are you making?"

Paige.

I looked up, not pausing my sinister ministrations, and a sudden sharp pain sliced through my left forefinger. Almost at once, I screamed out in agony, cursed aloud, and glanced down. I'd practically cut off my fingertip. Bright crimson blood was gushing out of the bone-deep gash and pooling on the cutting board.

Paige raced up to me, her face aghast. "Oh my God, Mom! Are you okay?"

"H-honey, get me some paper towels," I stammered.

She ran to the dispenser and returned to my side with a thick wad.

"Mom, give me your hand."

My finger throbbing, my hand trembling, she squeezed the paper towels around my digit, applying pressure. Within seconds, the blood saturated the thick white wad. I was getting queasy.

"Mom, hold the paper towel tight around your finger." With

my other hand, I squeezed hard as she dashed back to the sink, this time returning with a checkered dishtowel. Quickly, without flinching, she swapped out the red-soaked paper towel for the more absorbent cloth one.

I flashed back to her childhood and remembered how stoic she was whenever she skinned a knee while partaking in some tomboyish activity. Never shedding a single tear at the bloody mess. Just a dab of Neosporin and a Band-Aid and she was raring to go. So unlike Anabel, who was like Sarah Bernhardt at the slightest scratch. Hysterics. I, like Paige, had been a stoic child, but couldn't afford not to be. Tears were my enemy. It was better to swipe them away or hide them than have them slapped away.

The excruciating throb in my finger brought me back to the present. The blood from the cut seeped right through the cloth towel. I was growing queasier and queasier.

"Paige, sweetheart, why don't you get me some Band-Aids from upstairs?"

"Mom, Band-Aids aren't going to help. I think you need to go to the emergency room."

I weighed that option in my woozy head when another voice shook the room.

"Paige! You thief! Where the hell is my computer?"

Tanya.

THIRTY-SEVEN

PAIGE

Daggers shooting out of her eyes, Tanya stalked up to me. She tossed her computer bag on the kitchen island, unzipped it, and yanked out the cast-iron pan. Then set the heavy pan on the counter with a bang. *Better than on my head*, I thought, inwardly breathing a sigh of relief.

"Where's my laptop?" she seethed.

I shrugged a shoulder. "I have no clue what you're talking about."

Her eyebrows bunched and her nostrils flared. "Hogwash! You stole my computer and hid it."

I shot her a perplexed look. "Huh? Not guilty as charged."

"Look me straight in the eye and tell me you didn't take my computer."

I did as she asked, noticing she was wearing my necklace with the gold heart. Either she had the broken chain fixed or replaced or Lance gave her a brand-new one. It wouldn't surprise me if he kept a stockpile. Either way, I didn't give a damn. I was so done with the douchebag. She could have him. And the necklace.

Getting nowhere with me, she set her sight on my mother, oblivious to her bleeding finger.

"Natalie—"

I cut her off. "Leave my mom out of this. Can't you see she's hurt?"

"What's going on?" my mom asked, her voice small and shaky.

Tanya scrunched up her face, then shoved the pan off the counter. It crashed onto the floor with a clamor. "Your brat stole my laptop!"

My mom, her eyes glinting with pain, stole me a glance. "Paige?"

"Mom, I did no such thing."

"*Liar!*" barked Tanya, her face turning rabid.

"Prove it!" I challenged.

"I'm going to search every inch of this house!"

"Be my guest. I bet you're not going to find it."

"Tell me where it is!"

I smirked at her. "I didn't touch it. Maybe one of your jerko friends stole it last night during your little birthday party. The veranda doors were open and they had easy access to the house. And to your room."

My mother interrupted. "Please, girls, I don't feel well. Can we deal with this later?"

She looked wan from the loss of all that blood. "Mom, you should lie down and hold your finger up."

Tanya would not relent. On my next breath, she circled her hands around my neck like she was going to strangle me.

"Give it up, Paige!" She began to squeeze my neck.

My mother gasped. "Tanya, what on earth are you doing?"

"Get your hands off me!" I choked out. She tightened her grip. I began to cough, struggling for air.

"Tanya!" my horrified mother cried out again, weakly

tugging at our exchange student's arm. "Let go of Paige right now!"

"What the hell is going on here?" came a new, gruff voice.

It was my father, standing at the side door, with my little brother.

Releasing me, Tanya turned to face him. "Matt, Paige stole my laptop and won't give it back to me!"

"Dad, I didn't. Please believe me!"

Fat chance, I thought. I was still in his mind both a liar and plagiarist.

He narrowed his eyes at me, then looked to my mother for answers. She was devoid of all color and her body was swaying. It looked like she might faint.

Panic surged inside me. "Dad! Mom cut her finger really badly. She's lost a lot of blood. I think you need to take her to the emergency room."

Red with rage, Tanya stamped her foot on the floor. "Matt, *do* something! Tell your daughter to give me back my laptop!"

Ignoring her, my dad ran up to my mom. He eyed the blood-soaked towel around her finger. Gently, he unwrapped it, and upon seeing the ugly deep gash on her finger, alarm washed over him. A raging bloody river was still pouring down her digit and spreading all over her hand. His eyes wide with horror, he examined the ghastly cut.

"Jesus, Nat. You've done a number. Paige is right. You need to go to the ER."

To my shock, she pushed him away. "Leave me alone, Matt." Her voice was hoarse. Pained. She stood up slowly, then her body went limp. Just in time, my father caught her and lifted her into his arms. Effortlessly, as if she weighed nothing.

"We're going to Cedars."

"Dad, I want to come with you!"

"No, Paige. Stay here! Take care of your brother."

"What about my computer?" shrieked Tanya. "I can't do my homework without it!"

"We'll deal with it when we come back. In the meantime, look around the house. It must be here somewhere."

"Fine." Fuming, she fired the word at him.

And then she turned and gave me the most scathing of all looks. If looks could kill, this would be it.

A shiver skittered down my spine. Someone could die tonight. And it could be me.

Impulsively, I reached for the knife my mother had been using.

And as Tanya stormed out of the kitchen, I held onto it for safety.

Hurricane Tanya.

Actually, she was more like a tornado as she blew through the house, tearing up everything in her wake. Will and I were on damage control. Following her from room to room. Cleaning up after her as she recklessly tossed cushions from sofas, turned chairs upside down, removed contents from cabinets, swept up corners of rugs, and more. The two of us didn't want our poor mother to come home to this rampage. While I stayed close to Tanya, clutching the knife behind my back, I told Will to put the rest of the kitchen knives in the tool shed and to seal it with a padlock. This girl was insane. Better safe than sorry.

"So this is payback," she seethed as she continued to ransack our living room. She was now digging through the liquor cabinet, madly flinging bottles onto the floor. "I stole your boyfriend. So you stole my laptop."

"I didn't steal your computer," I said nonchalantly.

"Seriously, Paige, sometimes I think you're a better actress than I am."

I processed her words. She was practically confessing she

was a fake—an imposter—but I still didn't have the proof I needed.

"I swear on Bear's life, I didn't." I instantly regretted my words, not wanting to put our beloved dog in any jeopardy. I could hear him barking outside.

Finding nothing of interest in the liquor cabinet, she grabbed one of the bottles from the floor—an expensive Cognac —and opened it. Tilting her head back, she took several swigs and then met my gaze, her eyes glinting wickedly. "By the way, *reject*, your former boyfriend is a great lay."

A stab of hurt. Then, I took a fortifying breath and inwardly smiled. It was time to let her know she was screwing with the wrong person. *Me.*

"Oh, he *shagged* you?"

"Huh?" She contorted her face. Guess our so-called English exchange student had never seen an Austin Powers movie.

"You know..." I did some exaggerated pelvic thrusts until she got the message. "I sure hope he used a condom."

She snickered. "It doesn't matter. I'm on birth control."

"Oh, didn't he tell you he has herpes?"

She looked aghast. I had to pinch my lips together so I wouldn't burst into hysterical laughter. She took another glug of the Cognac.

"Oh, and by the way, drinking is harmful and can cause birth defects. Didn't they teach you that at your fancy boarding school?"

"*Screw you!*" she screeched, her fake British accent gone. "You're just jealous and pathetic. And ass-ugly!"

I smirked. "Don't you mean *arse*-ugly?"

The bottle in her hand, she stalked off. Feeling a little giddy, I traipsed over to the liquor cabinet and began to put the bottles back inside. Thank God she didn't fling them all over the room. Cleaning up broken glass and liquid would have taken hours. Putting the last bottle away, I heard my brother.

"Yikes!"

I turned to face him. He stared wide-eyed at the wreckage. I hadn't been able to put everything back to normal. Cushions, pillows, and books were still strewn all over the place. And one of the couches was still overturned.

I was about to ask Will to help me straighten up the room when loud, rapid footsteps sounded in my ears. An alarm bell rang inside me.

"She's heading upstairs!" My door was locked, but my brother's wasn't. "Willster, what if she tears your room apart?" At the forefront of my mind: The psycho was going to destroy the robots he'd spent weeks building.

My brother gave me a wry smile. "Don't worry, Pudge. I brought Bear inside and up to my room. The door is shut, but he'll go nuts if he hears or smells her. Trust me, she won't be going anywhere near it soon. So let's finish cleaning up this mess."

Once again, I was reminded of how much I loved my little brother. He was so smart. He would go far in life for sure.

The living room almost back in order, we heard Bear barking madly. Tanya came careening back downstairs and sneered at us. "I bet you hid my laptop in that little twerp's room. I'll find it! Meanwhile, I'm going to look outside."

"Good luck!" I said as she stomped toward the French doors that led to the backyard. Thank goodness my studio was locked and she couldn't get inside. Knowing she'd be outdoors for a while as our backyard was vast with tons of hiding places, I asked Will if he was hungry. He was starving, and I was too.

Using the veggies my mother had cut up, the knife within reach, I whipped up a pasta primavera along with a simple salad. Will wolfed down his dinner. Given how skinny he was, I didn't know where he put it.

Seated at the island, I told him about my phone call with

Mary. And the research I'd done on Jolene and Roy Perkins and their daughter, Billie Rae. Not leaving out a detail.

"Wow! That's creepy!" he said, after ingesting his last forkful of pasta. His plate was scraped clean.

"Yeah, like a ten on the creep-me-out scale." I helped myself to some of the salad. "Put your Sherlock hat back on." I laughed when he folded up a napkin into the shape of a hat and put it atop his head. "Okay, why do you think Tanya would have that old Indio High photo?"

"I've given it some thought, my dear Watson." He stole a bite of my remaining pasta. "I don't believe it's random."

I weighed his words as the sound of footsteps burst into the kitchen.

Tanya. Her face scrunched up. Her hands fisted by her sides.

"Oh, did you find your laptop?" I asked, my tone airy.

"No, I didn't. But I found *this* while I was upstairs." She extended an arm and uncoiled a fist. I recognized the small white object in her hand instantly. The spy cam. She knew what it was too.

"So, the two of you were *spying* on me?" she bit out.

I shrugged, staring at her blankly. Will followed suit. Her venomous eyes narrowed on Will.

"So, you little perv... did you enjoy watching me undress? Parade around in my knickers? Play with myself under the covers?"

Poor little Will blanched. He'd done nothing of the sort.

"Leave my brother out of this!" I hissed as I heard the jingle of keys.

I snapped my head in the direction of the side door. The knob turned and the door swung open. My parents were back home. They shuffled into the kitchen. My mom was still wan, her cut finger bandaged like an Egyptian mummy.

"How's your finger?" I asked her.

Her eyes were glassy, her face drawn, like she was drunk with weariness. "I'll live." A pause. "Ten stitches and they splinted it."

Poor Mom! "Are you hungry? I made dinner."

"Thank you, my darling, but I'm not. I just want to go upstairs and lie down."

"Does your finger hurt?"

"It does. They gave me some pain meds."

"Your mother needs to rest," said my dad, his voice tone cool.

I noticed the distance between my parents. The man who had gallantly carried her to his car was now standing a foot apart from her. No physical contact. No eye contact.

He loosened his tie.

"Natalie, I'm going to sleep downstairs in the family room."

"Fine." The word barely made it past her lips.

They parted. No kisses. No hugs.

What was going on with my parents?

THIRTY-EIGHT

NATALIE

I lay awake in our king-size bed. Alone.

Tossing and turning.

I couldn't fall asleep.

My finger throbbed. But it was nothing compared to my throbbing heart.

On the way to the emergency room, I'd smelled sex. The scent of infidelity on my husband, but I hadn't had the strength to confront him. Instead, the ride was drenched in silence. The same on the way back. He hadn't even asked how my finger felt. Silence is often louder than words. He knew I knew. Especially when I'd asked him to sleep in another room and he'd agreed without a fight. The idea of sharing the bed with him repulsed me, plus I needed space to figure things out.

Questions pounded my brain.

How was I going to work with the women on my committees without thinking they'd slept with my husband? Take Pilates with them? Spin with them at Soul Cycle?

Maybe Matt had slept with some of my instructors. Several were blonde and leggy.

When should I confront him? Make him confess to all his

transgressions? And the biggest question of all: What was I going to do? Stay with my adulterous husband? Or leave him?

Only one thing was clear: I couldn't let myself fall into a downward spiral. I couldn't fall apart like I did last time, and become a zombie.

This time I had to be strong for my children. For myself.

I had resources.

I had Xanax.

You know what they say: The first time, shame on him. The second time, shame on you.

No, I wasn't going to let him shame me. Not this time. Not ever.

Hell hath no fury like a woman scorned.

Especially one with my history.

Taking a pain pill, I closed my eyes and let sleep claim me. I was going to need every ounce of strength I had.

THIRTY-NINE

PAIGE

The next morning, I was surprised to find my mother downstairs in the kitchen, laying breakfast items out on the island counter—granola bars, blueberry muffins, fresh fruit, and OJ.

She was already clad in her Lululemon workout gear and looked much better than she did last night. Rested, the color in her face restored.

"Mom, how's your finger?" I noticed she was avoiding using her left hand. Thankfully, she was right-handed.

"It doesn't hurt as much," she replied, pouring herself a cup of coffee. "Thanks for asking."

"Where's Dad?" Usually he was the first one down here.

She took a sip of her steamy brew and shrugged. "He must have had an early morning meeting." The tone of her voice said something else.

I let it be. "What about Will?" My early-riser brother was always downstairs before me.

"He's out with Bear. Taking him for a walk since I can't." She glanced down at her bandaged finger. It took two hands to rein in our burly dog whenever he saw a squirrel and lurched.

Before I could say another word, Tanya came flying into the kitchen like debris. She shot me a contemptuous look and then turned to my mother, not asking a thing about her finger.

"Natalie, you're going to have to take me shopping after school."

"I can't today. I have an important meeting."

"Cancel it! I need a new laptop. I looked everywhere last night and couldn't find it." She gave me another dirty look and smirked. "Well, at least I'll have the latest MacBook Pro. Thanks. To. *You*."

You're welcome, I snickered silently as she snagged a granola bar.

After a quick bite, she returned her gaze to my mom. "I guess, Natalie, if you can't take me, I'll have Lance do it."

Thank goodness she didn't ask me.

"I'll just need your credit card."

"Tanya, dear, I can't give you my credit card."

She furrowed her brows. "Why not?"

"I just can't."

"Then, what am I supposed to do? I can't do my homework without a computer."

"Can't you use *your* debit card? Or one of your father's cards?"

"Um... mine just expired and I don't have access to Papa's."

I didn't believe her. Something was fishy.

My mother helped herself to a muffin. "Ask Matt. I'm sure he'll let you use *his* credit card."

Tanya's eyes narrowed. "Fine. I'll text him. Maybe he can meet us at the Apple Store in Century City since he works around there. Or better yet, I'll just show up at his office."

"I'd highly recommend you call or text him before you go to his office." A subtle sneer formed on my mom's lips. "He might be in an important meeting. *Or* an outside one. Especially if you decide to go at lunchtime."

Outside our house, a horn honked three times. I recognized it.

"Ooh, that's Lance now." Tanya's face lit up. "Gotta go. Ta-ta!"

She poured herself some coffee, took a couple of sips, and then tossed the remains in the sink. The slob didn't even put her mug into the dishwasher. My eyes stayed on her as she waltzed out of the kitchen. My heart ached as I heard the car drive off.

My mother gave me a perplexed look. "Why didn't you go with them?"

Listlessly, I unwrapped a granola bar, then after a deep breath, dropped the L-bomb. "Mom, Lance and I broke up."

She looked more upset than shocked. "Oh, honey! You poor thing, come here."

She held her arms open and I let her hug me, drawing me into her magnetic mom force.

She smoothed my hair with her good hand. "When did that happen?"

"Over the weekend."

A mix of worry and compassion washed over her. "Sweetheart, I'm so sorry. Are you okay?"

I nodded and took a bite of the crunchy bar. "I'm fine." Truth: I was still hurting. Human after all.

I wondered if my mom knew he had cheated on me with Tanya. That they were now together. Before I could tell her, Will came barreling in, holding a rambunctious Bear by his leash. Our dog jumped up on the counter and stole Tanya's leftover granola bar.

"Paige," Will said breathlessly, grabbing a muffin, "I can't be late for school. I'm the homeroom monitor this morning."

A big part of me wished I could stay home again. Not have to face Lance and Tanya together. But I had too much going on, including two exams, a presentation, and basketball practice.

With a heavy heart, I grabbed my car key and followed Will to my Jeep.

While waiting for him to buckle up, I could not stop myself from checking Tanya's Instagram.

Bile rose to my throat as I eyed a selfie of her and Lancehole lip-locked with the hashtag #*Instalove* and lots of hearts. Nauseated, I killed the app and tossed my phone into my backpack before all the obnoxious comments came pouring in, dissing me.

Maybe my mom didn't know what was going on, but the rest of the world knew.

Including everyone at Coldwater Academy.

The Instagram queen had gotten her king.

I hated him but hated her more.

So much I could kill her.

FORTY

PAIGE

The next few days were uneventful, if you didn't count me falling into a funk. Tanya got a brand-new laptop, courtesy of my father. She and Lance paraded around school holding hands while I tried to look the other way. Jealousy and sadness burned bright on my cheeks. The struggle was real. I missed having a boyfriend.

I was looking forward to Thanksgiving break, which was less than a week away. I'd have a break from seeing them all lovey-dovey, and a chance to be with my grandma, whom I knew would be a source of comfort. More than ever, I wished for Tanya to go back on her broomstick to wherever the hell she came from. The thought of spending another six months with her was unbearable. Neither Will nor I had made much progress uncovering her true identity. Or figuring out the connection between her and Billie Rae Perkins. We'd been working on the *Case of Tanya Blackstone* aka *Operation Tanya* for almost three months. So much for Sherlock and Watson.

Because my mom couldn't cook on account of her bum finger, we ordered in almost every night that week. One night Italian. Another Thai. Yet another sushi. Every order included something vegan for me. My mom was civil to my father, but she seemed altered. The spark gone. Something unspoken. Conversation was at a minimum, Tanya taking center stage. I was always happy to be done with dinner and go upstairs to my room. Will felt the same way. Neither of us knew what was going on with our parents, but whatever it was it couldn't be good.

On Sunday, the night before the start of our weeklong Thanksgiving break, we went to a chic fusion restaurant my father liked minus Tanya.

"It's a shame Tanya couldn't join us on account of her term paper," said my mom, picking at her stir-fry with her chopsticks. "She would have loved this restaurant."

I swallowed back a mouthful of my spicy vegan noodles. "Is that what she told you?"

She turned my way. It was time for headline news.

"Actually, she's out with Lance. He cheated on me with *her* and that's why I broke up with him. Now they're together."

While my father responded with indifference, Lance's infidelity struck a nerve with my mother. Her face darkened.

"I *knew* something was going on with the two of them. That's unacceptable. I'm going to have a talk with Tanya once and for all."

"Don't bother, Mom. I'm over it."

While I was past shedding tears, she gave me a hug. "My darling, you should never be with a man who cheats on you." She gave my father, who was sitting across from her, a wry smile. "Don't you agree, Matt?"

My dad paled. "Let's just get the check and split. I need to finish packing for our trip."

When we got home, something felt amiss. Usually, we could hear Bear barking in the backyard or in Will's room. The house was eerily quiet.

"Bear!" Will called out. "We're home!"

Not a yelp. Not a whimper. Not a sound. I was feeling something bad in my bones.

"Maybe he's asleep in my room," said Will, anxiousness creeping into his voice.

I followed him upstairs, both of us taking two steps at a time. I felt a flicker of relief upon seeing his bedroom door closed. Will shoved it open and we both gasped. Bear was gone!

"Will, he's got to be here!" Frantically, breathlessly, I ran after him as he raced up and down the hallway, opening every door along the way and shouting Bear's name. When we got to Tanya's room, her door was ajar. My throat constricting, I had a terrible premonition.

"Will, wait here. Let me go in first."

My heart in my stomach, I hesitantly stepped inside. The room, as usual, was a pigsty. Her bed unmade. Her dresser littered with underwear. Clothes strewn everywhere.

And there he was. Bear. On the floor. Sprawled out. Motionless. Eyes closed. His tongue lolling out of his mouth. A pool of vomit surrounded him. On the verge of tears, I clasped my hand to my mouth and breathed out, "Oh my God!"

"Bear! Bear!" came Will's hysterical voice from behind me. He sprinted over to his lifeless dog and flung himself on top of him. Sobbing. "Bear, Bear! Wake up! It's me, Will!"

Our dog didn't budge. My heart began to crack into a million pieces. Grief like I'd never known consumed me. The tears kept coming. Wiping them away, I noticed a trail of gum wrappers. Familiar silver foil ones. Trident. The kind Tanya chewed incessantly and kept in the drawer of her night table. My breath hitched. The drawer was wide open. There were several empty, chewed-up blue gum packages by the table. It was all coming together. While we were out for dinner, she must have let Bear out of Will's room and lured him into her room, the drawer deliberately left open. Our dog would eat anything. Even gum. We all knew Trident contained xylitol, a sugar substitute that was poisonous for dogs. Often lethal. Hence, we kept all xylitol products out of the house. Even the Whole Foods peanut butter we loved.

While Will continued to bawl, sprawled on top of Bear, I screamed out for my parents at the top of my lungs. I couldn't leave Will alone, not for a second.

"My God!" shrieked my mom, my dad right behind her, as she stepped into Tanya's room and saw my blubbering brother with Bear. "What's happened?"

"Bear's been poisoned," I choked out, my eyes still flooding. "I think he's dead!"

My father raced up to Will and Bear. As gently as he could, he extricated Will from our dormant dog, my brother clinging to him and resisting. "No, Dad, no!" he sobbed. "Leave me alone!"

The pain on her face almost tangible, my mother rushed over to Will and took him in her arms. He wept against her chest while my father crouched down and put a hand on Bear's back. His head spun around.

"Guys, he's breathing! He's still alive! Someone, quick! Call our vet!"

It was up to me. With not a moment to lose, I pulled out my phone. I knew better than to call our vet as it was a Sunday and after hours. So I immediately called the animal hospital where we'd once taken Bear when he'd stepped on a piece of glass. My heart racing, I had to listen to some insipid music that seemed to last an eternity until I got someone on the phone. I explained the situation, my words coming out at a hundred miles a minute. Then listened.

"Mom, Dad! We have to get him over to the West LA Animal Hospital ASAP!"

"How are we going to get him downstairs?" asked my mother, Will still clinging to her. He looked up briefly at my father.

"Dad, you need to carry him downstairs!"

Bear weighed one hundred fifty pounds. Even in as good shape as he was, my father couldn't possibly lift him. Plus, he had back problems, having slipped a disc in a game of tennis.

"Dad, pick him up!" Will cried out again.

To my wide-eyed amazement, my father knelt down and scooped our one-hundred-fifty-pound beast into his arms. *Where there's a Will, there's a way.*

"C'mon, guys. Let's go!"

Remembering what the hospital had told me, I hastily gathered up all the gum wrappers and the opened Trident packages. They needed to know how many milligrams of xylitol Bear had ingested.

Ten heart-gripping minutes later, we were in my Jeep. My dad at the wheel, my mom in the passenger seat beside him. Will, still in tears, next to me, the two of us behind our parents, with poor unconscious Bear draped across our laps.

C'mon, Bear, hang in there! I prayed as we raced to the animal hospital across town, not stopping for red lights. I'd never been so scared in my life.

Three long, grueling hours later, we were back home; it was close to midnight. Bear's prognosis wasn't good. The team of doctors who'd treated him estimated he'd ingested about twenty-five sticks of gum—close to five thousand milligrams of deadly xylitol; based on his weight, seventy-five hundred milligrams would have surely killed him. In a coma, he had hypoglycemia and possible liver damage. They did more blood work and put him on IV fluids. His life was up in the air. The next twenty-four hours were critical. We'd have to wait and see.

Tanya still wasn't home. She was probably still out with Lance. Lucky for her because the truth is if she were home, I'd probably have taken a knife to her heart or poured Clorox down her throat. Maybe found my father's gun and shown her I could use it too.

Poor Will. He hadn't stopped crying. He'd cried the entire time on the drive to the hospital, while we were there, and on our way back home. I'd never seen him like this. Quickly donning my pajamas, I jogged down the hallway and knocked on his door. I could hear his sobs through the thick wooden slab.

"Will, it's me," I said and knocked again. No answer. Ignoring his "Keep Out" sign, I turned the doorknob and let myself in.

His night-light was on, and my brother, clad in his Star Wars pajamas, was huddled in the loft bed, his knees to his chest, bawling his eyes out. Without asking, I climbed up and joined him, wrapping my arm around his heaving, slight shoulders. Sometimes, it was hard to believe that one day my little brother wouldn't be so little. That I'd be looking up at him.

As sad as I felt too, I felt something worse. Guilt. Horrible, horrible guilt. It was all my fault Bear might die. I stole Tanya's laptop, so she tried to steal our dog's life, knowing how precious he was to us. *Revenge.* A heart-wrenching, gut-wrenching mixture of guilt, sorrow, and remorse coursed through me, bringing a flood of tears to my eyes. Unable to hold them back, they poured down my face.

"I—I'm so sorry, Willster," I choked out. "Can you ever forgive me?"

"W-what do you mean?" he spluttered.

"It's all my fault."

He turned to look at me, his face a blubbering mess. His watering eyes red and puffy. His freckled cheeks wet with tears. His button nose running like a faucet.

"W-what do you mean, Pudge?"

I began to sob. "If I hadn't stolen Tanya's laptop, none of this would have happened." *I'd lied to her and sworn on our dog's life I was telling the truth.* "Bear would be here. Sleeping on the floor right below us."

He took hold of my free hand. "Pudge, it's not your fault. Stop guilt-tripping. We were partners in crime."

"Are you mad at me?"

"Go away!" He quirked a little smile.

"Oh, Will!" I gave him a hug and he hugged me back. I squeezed him harder. And felt his heart pound against mine. We'd been through so much together. Through thick and thin. Will had always been there for me and me for him. We had each other's backs. We had each other.

We finally broke away.

His tears subsided and so did mine.

"Pudge," he said, "will you stay with me tonight?"

"Sure." The truth, I couldn't fathom sleeping alone.

"One other thing. Will you pray for Bear with me?"

I gave him a noogie. "Yeah... of course."

For the second time tonight, I prayed. Up until now, I hadn't prayed in years. In fact, I don't remember the last time I did. Though we went to church on occasion, I was not a religious person. I wasn't sure if I believed in God, but tonight I did. Maybe, unbeknown to me, Will was a believer. It didn't matter. Together, we bowed our heads, steepled our hands, and prayed silently for Bear.

I also prayed hard for Tanya to get hers.

FORTY-ONE

PAIGE

Thanksgiving break. We had the week off from school.

There was good news.

And there was bad news.

The good news: Bear had survived the poisoning.

The bad news: He had to stay in the hospital for a week while we were up in San Francisco for Thanksgiving with my grandparents. The doctors said they needed to keep him on IVs and monitor him. There was still the possibility of liver damage and blood clotting, but they were optimistic he would make a full recovery.

Able to see him twice—once on Monday and again on Tuesday morning before embarking on our trip—Will and I were over-the-moon happy with the progress he'd made. On Monday, his eyes were glazed and he was very lethargic. On Tuesday, he was almost back to his old self, wagging his tail and barking at us to take him home. The staff had told us that everyone had fallen in love with our big brown, goofy dog and promised to take extra special care of him. We could even Face-Time with him. And while we were away, our housekeeper,

Blanca, promised to visit him daily. Fingers crossed we could pick him up on the way back home.

We always drove up to San Francisco. We used to take my mom's Range Rover, but once she traded it in for her Mercedes convertible, my dad rented a roomy Lincoln Navigator. I always looked forward to the trip because we took the scenic Highway 1 up the coast and stopped at Big Sur, Monterey, or Carmel. This time, due to a late start and the irritable mood my father was in, we took the boring I-5 north with little to look at but produce farms and cows. My mom sat in the front, reading fashion magazines, saying very little to my father. Will and I sat behind them, my brother playing games on his iPad, me thumbing through my sketchbook. Behind us, Tanya was sprawled on the back seat, chewing gum and complaining. The hatred Will and I felt for her was beyond words. She totally denied having anything to do with Bear's poisoning, saying it was a freak thing. That *maybe*, she'd accidentally (*on purpose!*) left her drawer open in her haste to get ready for her date with Lance.

"That stupid, vicious beast is a waste of space," she'd said to me, "and really should be put down."

If we could put *her* down, Will and I would in a New York minute.

We made it to San Fran in record time. A little under five hours. It helped that we'd missed the holiday traffic by traveling on Tuesday and likely would do the same when we drove home on Saturday. We checked into our favorite hotel in Union Square, where we always stayed. This year into a three-bedroom suite. It was magnificent except for the fact I had to share a bedroom with Tanya. That was *not* happening. And it was Tanya who threw a tantrum. One hour later, I was ensconced in my grandma's elegant, art-filled Nob Hill apartment, sharing one of the spare bedrooms with Will. There was no way I could leave him alone with the canine killer.

Thanksgiving was special to me because I got to spend time with my grandma, who I adored. On Wednesday morning, while Will went to the Exploratorium science museum with my grandpa, Grandma and I went to San Fran's Museum of Modern Art. It was one of my favorite museums in the world, and I'd been to many. I loved the architecture, natural light, the permanent collection, and to my great delight, there was a special Brancusi exhibition. Trust me, it was not a hard decision to make: Spending the day shopping with *Natanya* versus going to the museum with Grandma. *Duh.*

We got to the museum when it opened at ten and breezed through it. My grandma, a major art collector and contributor, was on the board of trustees and had donated several pieces of her collection to the museum. I loved seeing them, and the accompanying plaque—*Gift from the collection of Marjorie and Martin Merritt*—always filled me with tingly pride. One day I hoped to have one of my sculptures exhibited in this museum.

Working our way down from the top floor, we saw all my favorite pieces and then spent an hour roaming through the Brancusi exhibition.

Afterward, Grandma and I had lunch at the museum's café. Something we always did whenever we came here. We found a table for two, overlooking the breathtaking sculpture garden. It was my first opportunity to open up to my grandma. Last night had been difficult as Aunt Cecilia had come by and hogged her attention, but now Grandma was as eager to talk to me as I was to her.

"Paige," she began, unscrewing the cap of her sparkling water, "have you heard from RISD?"

A smile bloomed on my face. "I got in! Early decision!" I'd found out right after visiting Bear on Monday.

My grandma's face lit up like a firecracker, and she joyously clapped her hands together. "That's wonderful! I'm so thrilled for you!"

"You're the first one to know, other than Will." The smile fell off my face. "I haven't told my parents yet. Mom will be happy, but Dad is going to blow a gasket. He's told me over and over he's not going to pay for an arts education."

"My dear child, there is nothing to worry about. I am totally prepared to cover the tuition, whatever it is."

My eyes almost popped out of their sockets. "Seriously? You really mean that, Grandma?" An heiress to a railroad fortune, she was independently wealthy and didn't need to rely on her husband's money. Or her well-off kids.

She winked at me. "I never lie... at least to those I love."

Springing from my chair, I rounded the table and hugged her. "Oh, Grandma! I love you so much! I don't know how to thank you."

"My darling granddaughter, you just did. Now, let's eat. I'm famished."

I returned to my seat, and at once, we bit into our tofu burgers.

Grandma stabbed a forkful of her salad. "So, did that boyfriend of yours hear from Brown? Lance, right?"

"Lancehole," I corrected. "I don't know. And I don't care."

My grandma's brows rose to her forehead.

"We broke up."

Her brows rose higher. "Oh?"

"Tanya, our exchange student, stole him from me."

Anger washed over my grandma. Her face darkened, her lips pinched. "That despicable shrew! I didn't have a good feeling about her when I met her at your house. She was very off-putting and phony. Even her English accent seemed fake to me."

I proceeded to tell her everything Will and I had learned about her. That prior to coming to live with us she had no social media presence, that neither of us could find anything about her so-called diplomat father, and that she'd stolen her laptop from a lovely retiree who lived in Redlands, in the disguise of someone else. And then I told her about poor Bear, how we were positive she'd tried to poison him. Her sick revenge for us taking her computer and returning it to its rightful owner.

Grandma looked aghast. "That girl is a danger to you and your family. We must get rid of her!" A pause. "Does she have any food allergies?"

I shook my head. "Not that I know of."

"Hmm." Knitting her brows together, she looked deep in thought.

"Oh my God, Grandma! You're not thinking of *poisoning* her?" Though I had to admit I relished that deliciously wicked thought. The perfect revenge. She poisoned our dog; let's poison her.

She laughed her rich, throaty laugh. "No, darling, of course not." Then, pursing her lips, my elegant grandma toyed with the lovely pearl necklace she always wore and gave me a diabolic smile. "But we *are* going to take her down."

I listened to her plan and smiled a devilish grin.

And wondered: Had I inherited her fiendish mind?

FORTY-TWO

PAIGE

The following day was Thanksgiving. Grandma preferred to serve the meal, which she always had catered, in the late afternoon. The call time: 4 p.m.

While my grandma was in the kitchen supervising the caterers, the rest of us sat in the elegantly appointed all-beige living room, surrounded by priceless Rothkos, Pollocks, and Picassos. A fire was blazing. The bust I'd sculpted of my grandma sat proudly on the fireplace mantel, joining my grandparents' masterpieces. The tantalizing aroma of the holiday meal wafted in the air, making me hungry and second-guessing my decision to go vegan as the roasting turkey smelled so good.

Over hors d'oeuvres and beverages (assorted cocktails for the adults, sparkling apple cider for the kids), I learned that flamboyant Uncle Trevor, a renowned window dresser for department stores around the world, had just flown in from London.

"What were you doing there?" I asked, awed by his boundless energy. He didn't seem jet lagged at all.

"I had a gig with Harrods. I decorated their windows for

Christmas." He took a sip of his Manhattan. "I wish you could see them! A total winter wonderland. So *faaabulous!*"

In my periphery vision, I could see both my dad and Aunt Cecilia rolling their eyes. The shark-like businessman and high-powered divorce attorney scorned my uncle's "frivolous" occupation. Plus, they were jealous as Trevor, her youngest, was so clearly my grandma's favorite.

The three siblings, each two years apart—with Cecilia the oldest at fifty—had never gotten along growing up. They still had a contentious relationship. My father's family was as dysfunctional as our own. Yet, I had to love them. They were my only relatives—my only grandparents. My mom was an only child and her parents, who had no siblings, had perished in a terrible fire just before she met my father. Their house had burned to the ground, leaving no memories behind. Nor any online information. Clement and Dorothea Taylor had ceased to exist. And my mom didn't like to talk about them because it made her too sad.

"Trevor, how exciting!" she said, cutting into my thoughts. My mom adored my *bon vivant* uncle as much as I did. "By the way, our exchange student is from London."

I turned to Tanya, who looked bored and totally zoned out. "Tanya, do you like Harrods?"

She jolted. "Huh? I'm sorry. I wasn't paying attention."

I repeated my question.

She squirmed in her seat. "Um... yes."

"What's your favorite floor?"

"Papa and I like to stay in the penthouse whenever he's in town."

Both my mom and Trevor shot her a perplexed look. I wished my grandma could have heard that one. Every Brit in the world knew that Harrods was London's famous department store, not some five-star hotel. Before I could clue her in, my half-deaf grandpa jumped into the conversation.

"So, Tanya. My son Matthew told me you applied to Stanford early decision." He avoided eye contact with me, and I wasn't sure if my father had told him about the plagiarism scandal. Chances were he hadn't, in order to spare him the anger and humiliation on account of his heart condition. He had suffered a mild heart attack last year and had to have bypass surgery.

Tanya grinned. "Yes, I did."

"Have you heard back?"

"Yes. They're still waiting for my transcript from my school in England."

My dad expressed confidence she would get in while Will and I exchanged amused looks. England, my *arse*. This girl was as bogus as they came.

And today we were going to prove it at last.

The conversation between my father and his moved on to sports. Whether Stanford's football team would defeat longtime rival Berkeley's. At the mention of Berkeley, I felt a spark of excitement. Tomorrow, I was visiting my bestie, Jordan. She was going to show me around the campus, and I might even spend the night.

"Excuse me," said my brother, his voice cutting into my thoughts. "I have to use the bathroom." He stood up, his twinkling eyes locking with mine. The thrill of excitement tingled on my skin as I watched him skirt off.

Seated next to my mother, Tanya took a few sips of her cider, back to looking bored. She even yawned before her cell phone rang. The ringtone was distinct, Britney Spears's "Oops!... I Did It Again."

"Oh! That must be *my* boyfriend, Lance." With a smug smile, she directed the words at me. "Excuse me. I'll be back in a little bit." She sprang off the couch and dashed out of the room. All our bags were stored in one of my grandma's spare bedrooms, as she hated things like backpacks and coats strewn on the floor or over chairs. And she had a no-tolerance policy about cell phone use at family gatherings.

Perfection. Everything was going to plan.

Small talk continued. My mother asked Cecilia what she thought about a man named Jason Nussbaum.

My aunt narrowed her eyes. With her graying ash-brown hair loose, she was attractive, but with it tied back in a tight knot in a courtroom, I bet she was intimidating. A force to be reckoned with. "He's a snake... takes his clients' husbands to the cleaners. Why are you asking?"

"Just asking for a friend," said my mother. Then, she smiled.

I made a mental note: Google his name. *Jason Nussbaum.*

Tanya returned, looking a little miffed with a very smug Will trailing behind her. Both went back to their seats. I turned to Tanya.

"How's *Lancey?*" I needled. "Did you tell him I say hi?"

She scoffed at me. "That wasn't him. It was a stupid spam call."

"Oh well." Shrugging, I plucked a stuffed mushroom from the canapé tray and stuffed it in my mouth.

More small talk ensued until a shriek startled us.

Grandma! She came running into the living room, still wearing an apron and looking completely frazzled.

"Mother, what's wrong?" asked my dad.

"My pearls! They're gone! Someone stole them!"

"What!?" interjected my mom.

"They're missing from my dresser. Plain and simple."

"Marg—I mean, Mrs. Merritt—maybe one of the help stole them?" offered Tanya.

"Impossible! I've used these caterers for years. They'd *never* do such a thing!"

Will stepped in. "Grandma, when I went to use the bathroom, I saw Tanya go into your room."

Tanya leaped to her feet, splattering her apple cider on the beige carpet. She glowered at Will. "I did no such thing!"

I tutted. "Seeing is believing."

Her face grew crimson, her voice decibels louder. "He's a freaking *liar!*"

"*You're* the liar," my little brother retorted.

Cecilia, the lawyer, put in her two cents. "She's innocent until proven guilty."

"You're right." My grandma's eyes bounced between the two of them. "There's only one way to find out." She looked at my brother, my partner in crime. "Will, would you be kind enough to retrieve Tanya's backpack from the spare bedroom?"

"I'm perfectly capable of getting it myself," snapped Tanya.

"And you're perfectly capable of removing the evidence," scoffed my grandma. "Stay put!"

No one, not even Tanya, defied my grandma. Will leaped to his feet. In a jiff, he was back with Tanya's backpack.

"Give that to me, you little brat! It's mine!" Tanya tried to snatch it from him.

Too late. My brother had already handed it to Grandma, who stole a glance at the enraged Tanya.

"I hope you don't mind... I'm going to search through it."

"Be my guest. I have nothing to hide." She plopped back down on the couch, next to my mom, folding her arms across her chest.

Setting the bag on the coffee table in front of me, my grandma unlatched it and began to remove the contents, item by item. So I could clearly see them.

Lip gloss. Her cell phone. Sunglasses. A pack of Trident gum. A set of keys to our house. An emery board. Hairbrush. Mirror. Several loose tampons. A tin of CBD gummies...

And lots of scrunched-up receipts, which my grandma flattened out for my viewing. Among them, a mile-long one from a Walmart in Redlands for various beauty products, including platinum-blonde hair color, plus some clothing and luggage, dated August 27—the day she stole Mary's laptop and money. And another for a Greyhound bus ticket from Redlands to LAX dated the next day. The one on which we'd picked her up at the international terminal.

Yes! I did a mental fist pump. Still no passport, but we now had solid proof Tanya wasn't from the UK; she *hadn't* traveled from London's Heathrow. Will and I exchanged a quick look as Tanya blurted, "See, I'm innocent."

"I'm not done yet!" retorted my grandma, her hand still rifling inside the canvas bag. My gaze stayed on her as the look on her face went from furious to victorious. With a wicked glint in her eyes, she yanked out one more thing from the bag.

"My pearls!" The diamond-clasped heirloom was draped around her bony hand.

We all gasped.

Tanya's jaw fell to the floor. "What!?"

My grandma shot eye daggers at her. "You stole my pearls, young lady!"

Tanya's eyes blinked like she'd seen a mirage. "I did *not!*"

"Don't lie to me! The evidence is right here." Grandma held up her hand, the diamond clasp catching the last of the late afternoon sunlight. "And don't think I don't remember how you eyed my pearls when I first met you."

"I've been set up! Probably by that no-good granddaughter of yours." Tanya burst into tears and began to sob. I was enjoying every minute of her dramatic outburst because for once the great actress wasn't faking. Her face crumpling, she tore a look at my mother. "Natalie, please... tell her I'd never do such a thing!"

My shell-shocked mother wrapped her arms around her. She cried on my mother's shoulder, sprinkling tears on her cashmere winter-white sweater.

My mom smoothed her hair. "Shh... We all do bad things."

A red-eyed Tanya looked up at her. "You don't believe me either?"

"Tanya, just apologize to Matt's mother. I'm sure she'll forgive you."

"I will do *no* such thing!" hissed my grandma. "That girl is a down-and-out thief! I want her out of my home. Right now! You need to send her back to wherever on earth she comes from. And it's sure as hell not Great Britain. She's a phony baloney. A danger to everybody!"

My mother's face heated. She looked at my father, then at Will and me. Then shot to her feet. "Matt, children, let's go. If Tanya isn't welcome here, I don't want to stay. We'll have Thanksgiving dinner back at the hotel."

"Fine." The first word my father had uttered since the discovery of the pearls.

Will and I stayed silent.

"Natalie," said my grandma, "there's no need to ruin the children's Thanksgiving."

I looked at my parents. "Mom, Dad... Will and I want to stay with Grandma and Grandpa." Will nodded in agreement. "Plus, we're staying here, not at the hotel."

They acquiesced. My brother and I watched as my parents and the still sobbing Tanya walked out of the grand pre-war apartment.

The worst Thanksgiving ever? No, the best. My grandma even had special vegan dishes prepared for me. So delicious. And despite the Tanya incident, the conversation was lively, full of laughter thanks to Grandma and Trevor.

I helped my grandma clean up, and for the first time in my life, I gave her a high-five. Then a tight hug. Her diabolical plan of having Will use an untraceable burner phone to call Tanya after he'd planted the pearls in her backpack was a success.

The best actress in the world was Tanya Blackstone. But tonight...

The Oscar goes to... Marjorie Merritt.
And Will and I each deserved one for our supporting roles.

FORTY-THREE

NATALIE

This had to be the worst Thanksgiving ever. Well, except for the one after Anabel's death, which I'd missed because I was too ill to travel to San Francisco—sedated and bedridden with around-the-clock nurses.

When we got back to the hotel, a still tearful Tanya took to her bed, claiming she had no appetite. I couldn't blame her, and truth is, neither did I.

At his insistence, I forced myself to have dinner with Matt in the hotel's dining room. My emotions were all over the place. I felt terrible for our exchange student and was still shaken by my mother-in-law's accusation, unsure if Tanya had stolen the pearls despite the incriminating evidence.

More and more, I was having misgivings about our family guest. Her behavior of late had been erratic. Questionable. When I'd confronted her about dating Lance, she'd brushed it off and said all is fair in love and war. Then she'd accused Paige of stealing her laptop and had almost strangled her. Plus, the increasingly frequent rants and tantrums. With her extreme ups and downs, I was beginning to wonder: Was she bipolar?

On top of this unsettling thought, there was the deep-seated contempt I felt for my two-timing husband. It was going to be hard to have dinner with him without spitting at his traitorous face. My only solace: At least the kids were having a good time with their grandparents, aunt, and uncle. They didn't need to get dragged into this mess.

The dining room was surprisingly crowded. Without a reservation, we were lucky to get a small table in the corner. The two of us each ordered the turkey dinner, Matt starting out with a bourbon and me with a vodka martini. I needed something stronger than a glass of wine to calm myself and get through the next hour.

I'd decided before the drive up here I wasn't going to bring up his indiscretions until I hired a lawyer. I had a meeting this coming Monday with Jason Nussbaum. And was thrilled Cecilia had confirmed his snake-like reputation.

Little did she know she might be facing him in court... soon.

Our turkey dinners came. Everything was cold. The meat dried out. The stuffing soggy. The mashed potatoes lumpy. The green beans overcooked. We ate in silence. The coldness between us rivaled that of the lackluster meal.

I polished off my second drink, barely tasting it. I'd have to do with my husband what the farmer does with the turkey...

Co-exist with him until next Thanksgiving. And hopefully no longer.

FORTY-FOUR

PAIGE

"Wow! The view is *amazing!*" I gushed as I stood next to Jordan, staring out an observation window of Berkeley's famed landmark, the Campanile. Completed in 1916, the regal Beaux-Arts structure was the third tallest bell-and-clock tower in the world.

From my vantage point, I had a breathtaking view of San Francisco from the surrounding hills to the Golden Gate Bridge as well as of the Berkeley campus, with its majestic architecture and sprawling grounds.

Suddenly, a blast of bells filled my ears and I flinched.

"What's that, Fly?" I asked, having to shout above the thunderous toll.

"The carillon. It consists of sixty-three bells, which play at designated times during the day. These are the noon bells. Berkeley even offers a course where you can learn how to play them."

"That's so cool."

From the panoramic view and the magical bells, I felt giddy. And I was giddy with happiness to be spending time with my best friend. We hadn't seen each other since August, and, though we FaceTimed frequently, it was not the same as seeing her in person. As toned as ever, she'd let her straightened hair go *au naturel*—wearing it in a big fro—and her complexion was aglow.

After touring the rest of the campus, we went for lunch at a cool Vietnamese joint on Telegraph Avenue, Berkeley's iconic hippy-culture main drag.

Over the restaurant's specialty, a vegan noodle soup called *pho*, we talked nonstop. Fly told me about her fabulous courses and her annoying roommate. "The only Black chick who needs to go to sleep with white noise playing," which made me crack up. After my laughter died down, she asked about me.

I couldn't wait to tell her my big news. "Guess what! I got into RISD!"

"No way!"

"Way!"

"I can't even!" She leaped up and came around the table to give me a hug. "I'm just bummed I won't be able to visit you on weekends at Stanford and vice versa," she said before returning to her seat and changing the subject. "So, Sweetpea, spill the tea. What's going on with Tanya?"

Through texting and FaceTime, I'd kept her posted. She even knew about Bear's poisoning. Catching her up, I told her about our Thanksgiving and how Grandma, Will, and I had sabotaged Tanya by planting Grandma's pearls in her backpack to make her look like a thief. "And we got a chance to find out what else she was hiding in her bag."

Her wide-set brown eyes lit up. "Girl, that was so wicked! I love your grandma! Did you discover anything?"

"Hardcore proof she doesn't come from England. Redlands is more like it. My grandma told my parents to get rid of her. Send her back home."

"Whoot! Goodbye to... the exchange student from hell!"

"If I ever write a book about her, that's what I'm going to call it."

Fly laughed. "Hey, do you want to celebrate and shoot some hoops after lunch?"

"Totally!"

Shortly afterward, on a nearby outdoor basketball court, my bestie proved that she had not lost her magic touch. Air Jordan was better than ever.

"Fly, you slayed it," I said breathlessly, giving her a high five.

A moment later my phone pinged. A Google Alert.

My heart hammering, I clicked it open.

It was a news bulletin.

Charred human remains were found early this afternoon by two teens while hiking in Tahquitz Canyon in Palm Springs. Police believe the body is that of a young woman and has been there over a decade. An investigation is underway.

A chill zipped through me. Palm Springs wasn't far from Indio. They were practically adjacent.

After all these years, was it Billie Rae Perkins?

FORTY-FIVE

NATALIE

On the Monday after Thanksgiving weekend, I drove to Jason Nussbaum's office. It was located in Century City, not far from Matt's. Thankfully, they weren't in the same building, and I deliberately took a late afternoon appointment so there'd be little chance of running into my husband. Or should I say my soon-to-be *ex*-husband. The thought of that little prefix still made me feel ill.

Located on the penthouse floor, Jason's office was sleek and masculine, minimally furnished with black leather seating, chrome, and glass. A young, busty blonde sat behind the reception desk. I announced who I was. She peered at her computer screen, and then, with a small fake smile, met my gaze. "Please have a seat. Someone will be out shortly to get you, Mrs. Merritt."

The words *Mrs. Merritt* reverberated in my ears as I settled into one of the leather chairs. I'd been Mrs. Merritt for half my adult life. Everyone knew me as Natalie Merritt. After the divorce, would I go back to using my maiden name? I said it to myself. *Natalie Taylor*. In truth, I never wanted to be her again. While that name had turned my life around, it brought back too

many bad memories. Besides, it would be better for Will and
Paige if I shared their last name as much as I now despised it.
Stopping me in my thoughts, another twenty-something buxom
blonde, who could be a clone of the receptionist, came to
fetch me.

Jason Nussbaum's corner office was spacious. Offering a
panoramic view of Los Angeles from downtown to the ocean
from the wraparound windows, it was furnished a lot like the
reception area, except Jason sat behind a massive rosewood
desk. Close to him was a bookshelf filled with leather-bound
law journals.

I studied him. Despite the framed NYU law school degree,
awards, and accolades plastered on the walls, he came across as
somewhat of a sleazebag. In his mid-fifties with a swathe of
dyed, slicked-back black hair, a ruddy complexion that
screamed tanning salon, and a smarmy smile that revealed
veneers so white they were blinding. It was obvious he'd had a
lot of work done and maybe was older than he appeared.

He stood up and rounded his desk. Wearing an impeccably
tailored dark suit and a crisp open-collar white shirt, he was a
big man with broad shoulders and large hands. A gaudy pinky
ring caught my attention, but there was no gold band on his ring
finger. I wasn't sure if the divorce lawyer was married, divorced,
separated, or single. His marital status wasn't listed in any of his
five-star Yelp reviews or in his extensive bio.

Introducing himself, he extended his hand, and I shook it.
His grip was so firm it hurt. Almost bone-crunching. I guess it
came with his ruthless reputation.

"Where would you like me to sit, Mr. Nussbaum?" I sputtered, unnerved by his presence. His dark, beady eyes didn't
help. They made him look like a ferret. And the cloying cologne
he wore was making me nauseous. Though I was wearing my
red Chanel power suit, the one I often wore to board meetings, I
felt powerless.

He gave me a once-over, assessing my net worth more than my fashion sense. *Ka-ching, ka-ching,* "Anywhere you'd like. And please call me Jason. I'd prefer to call you Natalie, if that's okay by you." His gruff, Brooklyn-accented voice matched his tough, rough-around-the-edges demeanor. "It's better for the both of us if we don't refer to your married name."

"That's fine," I said, inching over to one of the club chairs flanking the coffee table. Sinking into it, I set my bag down on the dark hardwood floor and crossed my ankles while he took a seat catty-corner to me on the leather sofa. He leaned forward, sitting with his strapping legs wide apart, his hands clasped between them, a stance I always found repulsive in a man. *That's the way he sat.* So I kept my gaze on his face and away from his crotch.

"Forgive me, Natalie. I forgot to ask you, would you like something to drink? Some coffee? Tea? Perhaps a Perrier?"

"Thank you, but I'm good." While I was parched from nerves, I worried I'd spill something on myself.

His ferret eyes shot to his secretary, who was still standing by the entrance to his office. "Sweetheart, bring me some coffee. You know how I like it."

Sweetheart. I cringed at the word and how flippantly he said it.

Maybe he banged her, I thought as she disappeared. A few short minutes later she was back with a mug of coffee. She set it on a coaster on the glass table between us. I noticed how he took his coffee. Black and strong.

"Mr. Nussbaum, can I get you anything else?" asked Sweetheart, her voice sultry and laced with an accent. From her mountain-high cheekbones, I surmised she might be Slavic or Russian.

"That'll be it, Lola."

At the mention of her name, my brain started humming "Whatever Lola Wants, Lola Gets." Anabel flew into my mind.

In her sophomore year, just before she died, she'd played the part of Lola in the Coldwater Academy production of *Damn Yankees*. And knocked it out of the park.

I pushed the bittersweet memory away as Jason gave his voluptuous secretary a salacious smile; she winked back. Yup. He was banging her. Whatever Jason wants, Jason gets, I thought as I watched her sashay out of the room and close the door behind her. Maybe he'd get me a ten-million-dollar settlement and the house.

Refocusing on me, Jason took a sip of his inky brew. "So, Natalie, we both know why you're here."

I nodded.

"Good. Let's get the nitty-gritty out of the way so we're not wasting each other's time. I charge seven-fifty per hour and require a ten thousand retainer fee upfront."

I gulped. "How much do you think the divorce will cost?"

"It shouldn't cost more than a hundred grand. And the retainer will be applied. I know my fees may sound exorbitant, but I always say you get what you pay for."

Matt believed the same thing. A shiver ran down my spine.

"And the way you should look at it is as an investment in your future." He took another sip of his coffee. "Trust me, you won't be disappointed."

I felt my jaw work as I did the math in my head. I had the money—a little over a hundred thousand dollars stashed away—but I was going to have to tighten my purse strings as soon as Matt found out and cut me off from his credit cards and our joint accounts. No more Manolo Blahniks, weekly blowouts, or private Pilates. And that was for starters. The sacrifices seemed unfathomable... then Matt's sister's snide remark played in my head. *He's a snake. He always takes the husband to the cleaners.*

"It's not a problem." I hired Jason Nussbaum on the spot. "I've brought along my checkbook and can write you the retainer check."

A gloating grin flashed on his face. "Excellent. You can do that on the way out."

I was tempted to ask him if I could write the check now, get it over with, so I didn't change my mind, but refrained.

Onward.

Over the course of the next hour, we discussed the nature of my case. Matt's *alleged* infidelities. His net worth. Whether we had a prenup. The property and assets we shared. Our children, whom I didn't want involved. Or at least as little as possible. Our divorce was going to break their hearts, and I let my attorney know I was open to joint custody, whatever was the least messy and worked best for the kids. He understood, then explained to me that California was a no-fault state, and that because we had no prenup agreement, I was entitled to half of everything we had. Maybe more plus child support.

"We're going to file on the grounds of irreconcilable differences. It'll be better for the kids that way. Not knowing about your husband's indiscretions."

I agreed. My confidence level in this man was mounting. In my heart, I knew I'd made the right choice.

"How long will the whole process take?"

"More or less a year. Unless your husband contests it, in which case it'll take longer." A beat. "And cost you a lot more."

My heart sank to my stomach, and I inwardly groaned. That was a long time. And God knows how much more money. I honestly *didn't* want to know.

Instead, I asked, "Should I tell Matt I want a divorce? And have hired you?"

"No, *don't* do that." His face puckered. "We first need to get concrete evidence that he's cheating; it'll help with the alimony settlement. I'm gonna put one of my pals, a private investigator, on the case and have your husband followed. Get some photos of him with his pants down."

While I shuddered, wondering if I could stomach seeing a

photo of my husband in bed with another woman, let alone one of my friends, Jason polished off his coffee.

"By the way, that'll cost you another two hundred bucks an hour, but it shouldn't take long. He's really good."

I had a growing feeling this divorce was going to take *me* to the cleaners.

"Oh, and by the way, be prepared for some other out-of-pocket expenses. Like child custody evaluators, property appraisers, and financial analysts."

My throat constricted. I really needed some water. "How much is *that* going to cost?"

"Between twenty-five hundred and five grand. Not more than that."

I silently cursed Matt. The bastard! I was going to need every dime I could get my hands on. I toyed with my engagement ring and an idea as bright as the perfect five-carat diamond pinged in my head. I could pawn it! Make a small fortune if funds ran out. After all, I wasn't going to need it anymore. Or want it.

My spirits brightened as Jason walked me to the door. "One last thing, Natalie. I want you to continue to share a bed with your husband, as hard as that might be, until we serve him the divorce papers. It'll help deflect your intentions and not make them suspect to him or anyone in your family. There's nothing like taking them by surprise."

I nodded, a painful knot forming in the pit of my stomach. I was going to have to sleep with the enemy.

At least I was good at pretending.

FORTY-SIX

NATALIE

When I got home at a quarter past five, I was drained. It'd taken every ounce of self-restraint not to treat myself to some retail therapy at the upscale Century City mall after my meeting with Jason Nussbaum.

I immediately went to the fridge and poured myself a glass of chilled chardonnay. I took it—and the bottle—to the living room where I sank into one of our plush couches, kicked off my shoes, and stretched my legs on the coffee table, something I never did in this formal room. I needed to chill. Unwind.

I was ready for a second glass when Tanya barged into the room on the verge of tears.

"What's wrong?" I asked, setting my wineglass on the table.

"Natalie, they're going to kick me out of Coldwater!"

My brows shot up. "What do you mean?"

"My father hasn't paid the tuition. And I can't reach him."

"Why not?"

"I don't know. I've tried a gazillion times to call, text, and email him. No answer. He travels a lot to impoverished countries. Maybe I can't get through to him because there's no Wi-Fi or cell phone service, maybe he has a new mobile number, or maybe something's happened to him. What if he's being held hostage somewhere? Or been in a terrorist attack? Or got some deadly disease?"

The waterworks broke loose. I felt terrible and tried to console her.

"I'm sure he's okay." Guilt threaded through me. I hadn't gone out of my way to reach him, like contacted the British Embassy.

"I hope so," she spluttered. "In the meantime, Natalie, I have a huge favor to ask of you."

She wiped her tears with the back of her hand. I waited for her to continue.

"Can you pay the tuition? It's due before the end of the month."

I processed her words. Coldwater's annual tuition was almost fifty thousand dollars. Right now with Jason Nussbaum in the picture, I couldn't front that kind of money as much as I wanted to help her out.

"I'm sorry, honey. I can't do that right now."

"Why not?" she sniffled. "Papa will pay you back."

"I just can't. Why don't you ask Matt?"

"I did! He refused. He's mad at me and thinks I stole his mother's pearls. Which I didn't... I swear on my life. He wants me to leave. Go back home."

My heart was breaking for her, but I had to face my new harsh reality. "I'm so sorry, honey. But, honestly, right now, with what's going on, it's probably for the better."

"What do you mean? I thought you loved me like a daughter."

"I do." And then the words just tumbled out. "But Matt and I are getting divorced."

I instantly regretted them. The cat was out of the bag.

Tanya's mouth fell open. Her voice rose decibels. "How could you *do* that?"

At a loss for words, I watched as she picked up the half-full bottle of wine and flung it against a wall. *Slam.* As the bottle smashed into smithereens, she screamed, "I hate you, Natalie," and stormed out of the room, leaving behind no trace of her English accent.

I was shaking like a leaf. Maybe she was just acting out, but her act of violence totally unnerved me. Especially in my vulnerable state. This day had just gone from bad to worse.

And who knew what the rest of this year would bring.

The horrific reality of what I was doing hit me like a landslide. Something I'd vowed to never let happen. A bitter mixture of guilt, sorrow, and self-loathing burned through me.

I was breaking up my family.

FORTY-SEVEN
NATALIE

The first letter came exactly one week after I met with Jason Nussbaum. The first Monday in December.

I found it in our mailbox. It was simply marked *Merritt* on the outside. Thinking it was a notification from a neighbor who'd lost their cat, or a realtor offering to sell our house, I ripped the business-size white envelope open. Inside was a folded single sheet of paper. I unfolded it.

Written in red marker, in uppercase letters, it read:

I KNOW WHAT YOU DID.

My stomach twisted. Who could this be from? And what were they referring to? There were so many things I'd done. Things I'd tried to bury. I reread the five words and a thought popped into my head. Maybe this cryptic note was for Matt. Besides cheating on me and having an illegitimate child somewhere in England, had he done something illegal like insider trading? I wouldn't put it past the greedy bastard. Unsure, I tore it up and tossed the scraps into the trash.

I forgot about the note until another one showed up the following Monday. One word written in red uppercase letters:

BITCH!

This time I *knew* it was directed at me. A shiver ran through me. Impulsively, I speed-dialed my high-priced attorney, Jason Nussbaum. After I told him about the notes, he asked me to text a photo of the latest one.

"Does your husband know you're filing for divorce?" he asked upon receiving it.

I hesitated before replying. I'd inadvertently told our exchange student Tanya in a moment of weakness. Had she told Matt?

I vague-answered him, not telling him about Tanya. "I'm not sure. He hasn't said anything or acted differently."

"If he does know, he may be trying to mentally mess with you. Whatever you do, don't show this note or any others you get to anyone. Especially your husband. We have him under surveillance and it's going well."

A flash of trepidation flared in my chest. So he had photos. Of my husband having sex with my friends. Maybe others. I hung up the phone, not feeling one iota better. If anything, the costly fifteen-minute phone call had left me feeling worse. Way worse.

Emotionally drained, I decided to take a nap on one of the living room couches. Screw the Ladies of Hancock Park's annual Christmas luncheon at the Wiltern Theater, one of the many holiday events I had scheduled all throughout the week. Probably half "the ladies" had slept with my husband anyway. I couldn't face them... let them see the burn of shame on my cheeks while they laughed behind my back.

Just as my eyes grew heavy, my phone, which I'd left on the coffee table, rang. Groggy, I grappled for it. *Caller Unknown.*

Against my better judgment, I sat up and answered it on the third ring.

"Hello?"

Silence on the other end.

"Hello. Is someone there?"

"You... will... pay... for... what... you... did." The frightening voice sounded like it had been electronically manipulated. A hoarse whisper. I couldn't tell if it was male or female.

My breath hitched. Every nerve in my body was on edge. "Who is this?"

Click. The phone went dead. It shook in my trembling hand. I could hardly breathe. Despite Jason's warning about Matt's possible scare tactics, I felt something worse. Way worse.

I gasped for air, and as my jaw fell open, acid-hot vomit shot into my mouth, then poured out. Torrid tears seared my eyes. I was falling apart.

"Mom, are you okay?" came a concerned voice as I retched again.

Weakly, I lifted my head. It was Paige, sprinting my way, alarm written all over her.

"Mom, what's wrong?"

"Honey," I croaked, my throat burning, "get me some paper towels. And a cold wet compress."

"I'll be right back." She dashed off.

Then another familiar voice. "Natalie, are you sick or something?"

Tanya. She stood her distance.

I met her gaze. "Y-yes... I think I've come down with some kind of bug."

She made a disgusted face. "Eww! I better stay away. With the senior class Christmas party in two days and our trip to Hawaii coming up, I don't want to get it."

She darted out of the room and I heard her sprint up the

stairs. It didn't matter that she hadn't said, "Hope you feel better." Those words had no meaning for me.

Hunching over, I buried my face in my hands.

Things were only going to get worse.

And they did.

FORTY-EIGHT

NATALIE

For all I knew, I'd contracted a real bug, perhaps whatever the latest flu was. I spent the rest of the week in bed, only getting up to use the bathroom or to crawl downstairs to the kitchen to get something to eat. Usually just some tea. I barely ate a thing and was sure I'd lost several pounds. Maybe dropped a size. I looked like death. Skeletal. My cheeks hollow, my ribs protruding, and my complexion sallow.

I bowed out of all the holiday events I had scheduled, from festive luncheons to elegant cocktail parties. And all my many charitable endeavors like delivering food to the homeless and toys to children in hospitals. I fell behind on everything—including buying Christmas gifts for everyone in my family and all our help. At least I didn't feel the need to buy gifts for my close friends. They could have Matt. He'd be lucky if I gave him a bag of coal.

I had no strength. I couldn't focus or concentrate. The only upside of this ordeal was I didn't have to share my bed with Matt. The bastard was sleeping on the couch in his office, telling the kids he didn't want to get sick before we went away to Maui.

I hadn't yet finalized the trip. While I'd booked a suite at the Four Seasons, I was having a problem getting flights. And the latter was complicated by the fact that Tanya couldn't find her passport. Which also meant that I couldn't buy her a ticket back to England, having decided it would be in everyone's best interest if she went home after the holidays. I called the British Consulate and explained the situation, but unfortunately they had no appointments available and would be closed for a week beginning on Christmas Eve. Paige had been right—I should have asked for her passport and kept it with the others in our safe.

The following Monday, I felt a little stronger. I got out of bed and, for the first time in over a week, took a hot shower and got dressed. With my hair washed and blown and a tad of makeup, I looked human again. Donning a pair of skinny jeans that were now baggy on me and a cashmere turtleneck, I ate a decent breakfast and even had a cup of coffee. While I was still not up for major socializing, I was able to catch up on things.

Thank goodness for online shopping. In a matter of an hour, I was able to buy all my last-minute Christmas presents. For the kids, Tanya, Matt's family, Blanca, and even one for Bear. Using one of Matt's credit cards I still had access to, I treated myself to a new cashmere bathrobe and throw. Why not? I deserved them and was going to need all the comfort and warmth I could get in the tumultuous months ahead.

As for Matt? He had his own special present coming.

Without consulting him or the kids, I canceled the trip to Hawaii and almost put a kibosh on any kind of vacation. Fortunately, my inner voice screamed out at me to give the kids one last family vacation all together—with their dad—before we separated. Not to tell them we were divorcing until after the holidays. Yes, it would be memorable but not in a good way. And at least Matt was paying for it.

After researching several options, I decided we would go

skiing in Big Bear, only a couple hours away, something we hadn't done for a few years, but all enjoyed. We could stay at the nearby dog-friendly Lake Arrowhead Resort and Spa. Go for facials and massages, and sit in the hot tub if we didn't want to ski. Even bring along Bear, who loved the snow.

Best of all, because it didn't require air travel, it solved the Tanya problem. She could come with us. I'd barely seen her over the past week, and was more convinced than ever that the poor thing could have mental health issues. Even so, I was going to miss her terribly when she went back home to England. I'd grown to love her like a daughter, for better or worse. Fingers crossed she'd get into Stanford and I could visit her. Or she could fly down and spend some weekends with us. And I could get her some professional help.

Just as I finished booking rooms at the hotel, the doorbell rang. I jumped up from my stool at the kitchen island and hurried to the front door. Catching my breath, I peeked through the peephole. No one was there. Hesitantly, I opened the door and on the stoop was a large, white envelope. In front of my house, a helmeted man took off on his motorcycle. When he was out of sight, I bent down and retrieved the envelope.

It was weighty, with my name written on the back—Mrs. Natalie Merritt—in thick red marker, the block letters similar to those anonymous, threatening notes I'd gotten before I fell ill. It was sealed with Scotch Tape.

I felt my pulse rev up. Was it yet another attempt to intimidate and unhinge me? A shiver skittered down my spine. I was afraid to open it. As I was about to toss it in the trash, my phone rang. Prising it out of my jeans, I glanced down at the caller ID and sighed with relief. It was my attorney, Jason Nussbaum. I hit answer. His voice eclipsed mine.

"Natalie, I just had the incriminating photos dropped off."

"In a padded envelope?"

"Yeah. Have you taken a look at them?"

"N-not yet."

"Well, we've got a good case. Make that great. Are you alone?"

"Y-yes."

"Good. Open it. I think you'll be pleased."

Maneuvering the phone in my hand, I peeled off the tape and slipped out the contents.

Dozens of glossy black-and-white photographs. My fingers quivering, I flipped through them.

One after another of my husband sexually engaged with women I knew. Mariel. Heather. Christina, and more. Everything from kissing them in his office and banging them over his desk to sharing a bed in a hotel room and having wild sex.

"Hey, Natalie, are you there?" Jason's voice filtered through the phone, but words died on my lips before I could respond.

I thought my flu was gone, but it returned with a vengeance. Clutching the photos and my phone, I ran to the guest bathroom and puked in the toilet.

My illness had a name. Not swine flu. Not SARS. Not Covid.

One four-letter word.

Matt.

I recovered quickly from my initial shock. My strength and resolution surprised me. Rather than unhinging me, the sickening photos fueled me. So when Matt came storming into the living room two days later while I was putting the finishing touches on our tree, I was prepared for him.

"What the hell!" he screamed as I was about to hang another ornament on a bough. *The Wizard of Oz* Tin Man, one that Anabel had bought for me.

"Excuse me?" I didn't stop what I was doing or turn to face him.

His heavy, rapid footsteps thudded behind me, and before I could hang the ornament, he snatched it out of my hand and flipped me around.

I stared at him. His face was beet red. So red he looked as if he was having a heart attack. *If only.* Letting the Tin Man fall to the floor, he fisted his hands by his sides. So tightly his knuckles turned white.

"Are you okay, Matt?" I asked calmly.

A vein popped along his neck. "How could you do that to me?"

I batted my eyes with mock confusion. "Do what?"

"Serve me divorce papers while I was in the middle of an important meeting."

"Oh... *that.*"

"Oh... *that,*" he mock-mimicked. "Natalie, why didn't you tell me you want a divorce?"

"Why didn't you tell me you're screwing half my friends? Should I put some gift-wrapped framed photos under the tree?"

Busted. His face fell like a theater curtain. He swiped a hand across his forehead.

"Nat, let's go back to counseling. We can work things out."

"No, Matt. There's no going back."

"Please, Nat. Let's give it one more shot." His desperate expression was pathetic, but it only made me fiercer. More determined. As heartless as the Tin Man.

"*No,* Matt."

"Arrowhead will be good for us. Help us heal."

"The only reason I'm not canceling the vacation is for the children. It'll be their last family vacation with us together."

"Do they know?" His voice was small. Defeated.

"No. Only Tanya knows. I'm surprised she didn't tell you."

"She didn't." He blew out a long, resigned breath. "When are we going to tell Paige and Will?"

"I think it's best to tell them after the holidays. I don't want to ruin their Christmas."

Matt agreed. I proceeded to tell him that once we broke the news, I wanted him to move out of the house. He looked crestfallen.

"I'm going to have a drink and then I'm going to call my sister."

Without another word, he slogged over to the bar. Watching him pour some bourbon, I bent down to pick up the Tin Man. I hung the ornament on the tree right next to the hand-painted Nutcracker. And smiled.

I'd just busted my *husband's* nuts.

Score one for me.

FORTY-NINE

NATALIE

Christmas went smoothly. It was even festive.

On Christmas Eve, I made a rack of lamb with a special vegan dish for Paige, and we all went to midnight mass at Saint Andrew's. On Christmas morning, everyone woke up early and gathered in their pajamas around the tree for the opening of presents. Usually, Bear joined us, but I kept him outside with his new chew toy on account of Tanya. The good news was we hadn't lost him and maybe that was the best Christmas present ever.

To prevent a paper-tearing frenzy, we each opened our presents one at a time, beginning with Will. Then it was Paige's turn followed by Tanya's. Will and Paige were thrilled with their presents, but Tanya seemed miffed.

"Natalie, some stupid book and *only* a two-hundred-dollar gift card to Urban?"

"You better use it quickly," quipped Paige, knowing Tanya would be going home after the first of the year. There was no love lost between them. I had told my daughter about the tuition issue, leaving out the real reason I couldn't afford to let our exchange student stay.

Tanya gave Paige a dirty look, then stared at the gift card, a scowl on her face.

"You'll be surprised by how much you'll be able to buy with it as everything will be on sale tomorrow," I said to her cheerfully.

"Whatever," she huffed as she began to half-heartedly leaf through the LA fashion book I'd bought her. Looking bored, she glanced up at me. "Oh, and by the way, Natalie, I'm sorry I didn't get you or Matt anything. I didn't have the time, plus Paige wouldn't take me shopping."

She shot Paige another look. Paige smirked, their animosity in full swing. I bristled. The last thing I wanted was a fight on Christmas Day.

"No worries. We have so much." I felt a pinprick of hurt. She could have made something, even a card.

"Mom, Dad... your turn," cued Paige.

Matt and I, who were putting on a good show for the kids, started opening our presents. A pair of Lalique flutes along with a magnum of Veuve Clicquot from Matt's parents, gorgeous Burberry scarves from Trevor purchased in London, and a measly twenty-dollar Visa gift card for me from his sister, who had not one thoughtful molecule in her entire body. Mailed to me a week before Matt had called her, she probably wouldn't have sent me a thing had she known we were divorcing.

Lastly, I opened Will and Paige's present: The same as always... a beautiful leather-bound photo album to remember our annual family Christmas vacation by. I felt a stab of sadness. This would likely be the last such album.

All the presents open, I stuffed the torn paper into a trash bag.

"Mom, Dad, what did you get for each other?" asked Paige as I gathered up the last scrap of paper.

"Um... uh, we had custom things made." My voice faltered. "They didn't get here in time."

"Like what?" Paige's brows arched with curiosity, her eyes darting between me and Matt.

I noticed how gaunt my husband looked. His complexion was sallow and there were dark circles under his eyes. The divorce was taking a toll on him, which was fine by me. Paige's gaze stayed on him as a muscle in his jaw twitched.

"If we told you, that would ruin the surprise. Trust me, it's like nothing we've ever given each other."

That was true. He'd gotten the divorce papers. And I'd gotten... bupkis. I'd resigned myself to knowing I'd never receive a sparkling bauble from him again. It was a small price to pay to be rid of him.

My perceptive daughter looked at me suspiciously and then exchanged a look with her brother. She, for sure, knew something was up.

"Matthew, children, why don't you all go into the family room while I finish tidying up and make breakfast. There are some wonderful holiday movies on TV."

"Mom, do you want me to help you?" asked Paige, staying behind while the others wandered off. There was no doubt in my mind that she wanted to grill me. Find out what was going on between me and her dad. To my relief, Tanya obviously hadn't told her.

"Honey, I'm perfectly fine and would prefer if you'd join the others."

She reluctantly did as I asked. A shudder ripped through me as she retreated. I dreaded telling her and Will that their dad and I were divorcing. The family room would soon be the *broken family* room.

In the kitchen, I whipped up scrambled eggs and sausage along with a tofu and mushroom scramble for Paige. I'd learned a thousand ways to prepare tofu since she'd gone vegan. From stir-fry to lasagna, and they were all amazingly delicious.

As I transferred the eggs onto a platter, my phone rang. I

retrieved it from the new cashmere robe I was wearing, my gift to myself, and gazed at the caller ID. Unknown number. Despite the warmth of my robe, I shivered. Were the obscene Whisperer calls starting up again? I hadn't had one in over two weeks. Maybe it was my in-laws calling from Europe where they were holidaying to wish us a merry Christmas. Hesitantly, I swiped answer and put the phone to my ear.

Silence.

Then...

"Ho. Ho. Ho." The Whisperer! "*Ho!*"

"Whoever you are... leave me alone!" I breathed, keeping my voice down.

Click.

The phone rang again. Should I answer it? I did.

"Natalie..." The Whisperer again! "You weren't a very good girl for Santa this year."

This time I challenged the raspy voice. "What do you want?" Everyone was after something.

"I want you dead."

Click.

My whole body shook. Before the phone rang again, I speed-dialed the one person I could confide in. The one person who could give me advice.

My attorney. Jason Nussbaum.

Thank God he picked up on the first ring.

"Jason, it's me, Natalie. Sorry to disturb you on Christmas Day." Like everyone else in the world, his office was closed and he was off from work.

"No problemo, sweetheart. I'm Jewish. Christmas isn't my thing. And you should know, I work twenty-four-seven. Holidays included."

At $750 an hour, at least I was getting what I paid for, though this call was going to cost me an arm and a leg. *Jason's Chanukah present.*

"Hey, did Matt enjoy your Christmas present? His sister has already shot me a scathing email. But don't worry, she's chopped liver as far as I'm concerned."

"Jason, it's not about Matt. The Whisperer is calling me again. With obscenities and threats." I relayed the last two phone calls.

"Just so you know, I spoke to Dino."

Dino was the name of the private eye he'd hired to follow Matt. "What did he say? Was he able to trace the calls?"

"No. They're coming from burner phones."

"Burner phones?"

"Yes, cheap disposable phones. The user unknown. Untraceable."

"Who do you think it is?"

"I still think it's your husband. Or maybe his sister or one of her trolls. My hunch is they're trying to wear you down. Prove you're mentally unstable. If they prove mental incompetency, it's possible your husband could win full custody of your children."

I shuddered at that thought. I couldn't live without Paige and Will. Losing Anabel was painful enough. Another frightening thought jumped into my head. "Do you think my life is in jeopardy? Or that of my kids?"

A beat of silence, then, "Nah. Your husband may be a dick, but he's no murderer. I had Dino do a background check on him. He's squeaky clean. Mr. Good-In-Bed is a total Goody Two-Shoes. He doesn't even have a parking violation to his name."

"What should I do?" I asked, slightly relieved.

"You should get a new phone number."

"If I do get one, should I *not* give the number to Matt? Maybe block him?"

"As your attorney, I'd advise against that. There's no

evidence he's a physical threat. Furthermore, you have children. He needs to be able to contact you."

Unfortunately, he was right. Like what if Matt went skiing with the kids without me and something terrible happened to one of them? I'd die first, not knowing.

Another voice on the other end cut into my thoughts.

"*Zolotse*, I'm waiting for you." Lola. Jason's zaftig secretary. I was right. He *was* banging her.

"Hey, Nat, I've got company. Gotta go. Merry Christmas. Hang in there and we'll talk soon."

Arrowhead couldn't come soon enough. The first thing I was going to do was go to the spa. Soak in the Jacuzzi and then treat myself to a deep-tissue massage. Knead out the stress from every cell in my body.

On my husband's dime. Let him pay for his mistakes.

FIFTY

NATALIE

Matt and I decided on taking two cars to Lake Arrowhead in case one of us wanted to split and go back home.

With the big screaming match we'd had after all the kids had gone to sleep, that was a definite possibility. We'd fought over him moving out of the house. The knock-down, drag-out, dish-throwing fight had ended with the words "Drop dead, Natalie" and my soon-to-be ex storming out of the kitchen. And that was just half of it.

So we took Matt's BMW and Paige's four-wheel-drive Jeep, which she drove with Will, me, and Bear. Tanya went with Matt.

"Mom, why didn't you go with Dad?" Paige asked, as she followed him. I could tell from the tone of her voice she knew something was up. "And I don't understand why we need two cars. If we needed an extra one for some reason, we could rent it there."

I made up an excuse. "I didn't think you wanted to sit in a car for two hours with Tanya. Plus, we can't have Tanya anywhere near Bear." Actually, it was the truth and Paige left it at that.

With not much traffic on the 10, we got to the Arrow-head/Big Bear exit in excellent time despite a late start on account of me having to spend a long frustrating hour on the phone with a Verizon rep to change my mobile number. When Will asked me why I changed it, I told him I'd recently gotten some disturbing spam calls. Again, that was the truth. I gave out my new number to only him, Paige, Tanya, and reluctantly to Matt. And one other person, my attorney. The rest of the world would have to wait. Though I wouldn't put it past Matt to share the number with his sister and/or the person he was possibly paying to harass me. Which meant I could still get calls from The Whisperer.

The serpentine pine-lined road up the mountain added another thirty minutes to our trip. There was snow on the ground, and with another storm expected within the next twenty-four hours, Matt had to stop and get chains put on his tires by some hardworking locals. He deserved them around his neck. Or better yet, that untamed thing between his legs.

The snow became denser and denser as we made our ascent. Going from a dusting to at least three inches. By the time we reached the Lake Arrowhead Resort and Spa in the early afternoon, it was a winter wonderland. The recently reno-vated hotel looked like a deluxe alpine lodge, the picturesque setting postcard-perfect with the fresh bundle of white powder from last night's snowfall covering both the ground and the sky-high cypress trees.

We valeted the cars and the minute I stepped into the festive, pine-scented lobby, with its enormous, beautifully deco-rated tree and massive, blazing fireplace, I knew I'd made the right decision to come here. With Matt's credit card in hand, I moseyed over to check in while the others stayed behind, waiting for a porter to take care of our luggage and ski equipment.

Unable to get a suite, I'd reserved two rooms for the kids.

And one for Matt and myself. Paige and Will were sharing one room with Bear while Tanya had a single room of her own. I wished I could have booked my own room—away from Matt—but there were no more rooms available, and it would raise too much suspicion among the kids for us to be separated. Fortunately, we had a double—two queen beds. If Paige or Will questioned why we didn't have a king-size room, I'd just tell them one wasn't available. And the truth is, one wasn't. The resort was extremely popular and booked up for the Christmas holidays months in advance. I was extremely lucky I was able to make these last-minute reservations. Cancellations. Though not next to one another, the rooms were all on the same floor and afforded lovely views of the glimmering blue lake.

Once settled in, Matt and the kids took off for some fun in the snow, taking Bear with them. There was a nearby sledding hill. I stayed behind with Tanya and had lunch.

"Tanya, you should have gone with them," I said, the two of us fawning over Caesar salads and an order of fries as we dined in the resort's gourmet restaurant. "You would have had fun."

She was seated across from me, clad in an adorable all-pink *après-ski* outfit that had once belonged to Anabel. A pang of sadness stabbed me; the last time we were here was with Anabel. Over a long weekend. Four months later I lost her, and soon I would be losing Tanya, though hardly in the same way. Despite her erratic behavior, I thought more about all the good times we'd shared and was going to miss her so much. Sadly, there was no way she could stay with us.

Our exchange student shoved back her knit pom-pom hat. "Honestly, Natalie, I had no interest. I'm not a snow person. I'm still really disappointed we didn't go to Maui."

"It wasn't meant to be," I responded, not mentioning that the loss of her passport took that trip off the table.

"Whatever." She took a sip of her white wine, courtesy of our smitten young waiter who hadn't carded her. "So, Natalie..." With her pinky finger out, she plucked a French fry from the paper cone and dipped it into the small tub of mayo. "Have you rethought anything?"

I arched a brow. "What do you mean?"

She twirled the skinny fry between her fingers. "You know... About paying my tuition and letting me stay in LA with you."

I took a glug of my cabernet, then swallowed. "I'm sorry. *Les jeux sont faits.*"

She scrunched up her face. "What does that mean?"

"Oh. I thought you knew French from your British boarding school." I'd read online that three years of French was a requirement. "Anyway, it loosely means the die is cast." I took another long sip of my wine and looked her straight in the eye. My heart was aching. "My sweet girl, you know my situation. You have to go back home. I have no choice."

She rose from the table and glowered at me, her eyes fiery.

"I have no choice either."

Flinging the uneaten fry onto the table, she stormed off. Another one of her angry tantrums. Her extreme mood swings were manifesting themselves more and more. I worried she'd have a total meltdown during our vacation and spill the beans to Paige and Will that Matt and I were divorcing.

As she disappeared from the restaurant, my phone rang. The Whisperer? My stomach knotted with dread as I pulled it out of my bag. Thank goodness it was Paige. On my next breath, relief morphed into worry. My pulse sped up and I could hear my heart thudding.

Had something happened to her or Will?

FIFTY-ONE

PAIGE

"Hi, Mom!" I held my phone to my ear because there was too much noise to put the call on speaker or to FaceTime. My voice competed with the loud chatter of families at surrounding tables. Plus the endless squeals coming from kids sledding down the snow-covered hill.

"Paige, is everything okay?" Mom's voice sounded on edge.

"Yeah, we're having a blast. So is Bear. He loves running up and down the sledding hill. He even got on a sled and went sliding down it. It was hilarious."

"That's wonderful." She sounded calmer.

"We texted you some pics. Did you see the snowman we made?"

"I honestly haven't checked my messages. I'll take a look at them after I finish lunch." A pause. "Where's your father?"

Usually, she would say: *Where's Dad?* There was something off with the way she asked about his whereabouts. Her tone was frosty, no pun intended.

"He's at the food shack, getting us another round of hot dogs and hot chocolates. A veggie burger for me." All our sledding, especially climbing back up the steep hill over a dozen times, had worked up our appetites.

"Good."

"He's heading back." I squinted in his direction. "Do you want to speak to him?"

"No," she bit out. "I'll see you back at the hotel. Give Will a kiss for me and have fun."

We ended the call.

I looked at my brother. He looked adorable in his red puffer jacket and beanie. His freckles were burning brightly from the sun despite using sunblock. "Willster..."

"Yeah, Pudge." He took a big bite of his hot dog and gulped it down.

"Do you think Mom and Dad are acting all weird?"

"What do you mean?"

"I don't know... like they're keeping a distance from one another. It's even weird we took two cars up here. And Mom's always loved to go sledding with us."

Will fed the last bit of his hot dog to Bear, who was lying next to him on the snow-covered ground. Gobbling it down, our voracious dog looked up at him for more.

"Well?" I said.

"I think Mom's just stressed out. You know, with Christmas and everything."

"Have you noticed how much weight she's lost?" Over the past two weeks, it looked like she'd dropped ten pounds. All her clothes were baggy on her. I was worried. The last thing I wanted was for her to have a breakdown like she did after Anabel died. It was terrible for me and Will not to have Mom around for months on end. One day I planned to tell her how scared I'd been during that time. How much I'd missed her.

Will snagged a fry and dipped it in ketchup before chomping it. "Yeah, I have."

"Doesn't it concern you?"

"Well, she did have the flu."

"Yeah, but still."

"Hey, guys!" My dad's voice. He was stomping toward us, the crunch of his Sorel boots against the snow getting louder with each step. He set the cardboard box with our food on the outdoor table. "Will, they ran out of wieners, so I got us burgers. Another veggie one for you, Paige."

The greasy smell of the grilled patties assaulted me. After talking with my mom, I'd lost my appetite. My father plunked down on the plastic chair next to Will, across from me.

"Mom called."

"That's nice." His voice was cold as ice, his face glacial. "Dig in before everything gets cold."

We each grabbed a paper-wrapped burger and a steaming hot cocoa. I took a sip of my soy milk one to ward off the chill spreading under my jacket. It had nothing to do with the sudden drop in temperature.

My stomach twisted. I could feel it in my gut.

There was definitely something going on with my parents.

FIFTY-TWO

NATALIE

The ninety-minute deep-tissue massage was just what I needed. As I lay face down on the massage table, my masseuse's strong fingers kneading my upper back, I could actually feel and see little sparks of stress flying out from my tight, bunched-up muscles. I sighed as she dug deeper with her thumbs, the soothing music and aromatherapy oil helping me relax. I was in a Zen-like state and at some point I must have dozed off after I turned over onto my back. I was startled to hear her voice.

"That's it."

My eyes fluttered open. "It's over?"

The muscular young woman with the magic hands nodded. "I hope you enjoyed it."

Sitting up, the soft sheet gathered to my chest, I told her it was wonderful and thanked her profusely as she offered me a cup of refreshing cucumber-infused water. I gulped it down greedily.

"Drink a lot of water," she told me, helping me to my feet. "It'll help flush out the toxins."

I told her I would as she helped me into my spa robe while I slid my feet into my open-toe rubber slippers. Reaching into a pocket, I handed her two twenties. A twenty-percent tip. I could tell by her face she was thrilled by my generosity. Thank you, future ex-husband, for making this possible. I quickly shoved him out of my mind. Why let the thought of him ruin my euphoric state?

I met Tanya in the locker room. After her little tiff in the hotel restaurant, she'd returned to apologize and I'd asked if she wanted to have a spa day with me. She'd jumped at the offer, and while I was having my massage, she'd had a facial. Similarly dressed in a spa robe and slippers, her long white-gold hair gathered up in a high ponytail, she looked positively glowing. Her flawless skin radiant, her thick onyx brows, which were included in the treatment, perfectly sculpted.

"How was it?" I asked as if I didn't already know.

"*Sooo* divine!" She flung her loving arms around me. "Thank you, Natalie."

"You're so welcome. Why don't we soak in the Jacuzzi and then do the steam room? Then, after we shower and get dressed, go to the bar and have some champagne?"

A smile spread across her shining face. "Perfection."

So much for drinking water.

We returned to the restaurant and this time sat at a table for two in the bar area. A new server—equally smitten with Tanya—brought us a chilled bottle of Veuve Clicquot and filled our flutes to the brim. Some of the bubbly spilled over.

"To a happy New Year," I toasted, clinking my flute against hers. The upcoming year *was* going to be a happy one once I was divorced from Matt. It couldn't happen soon enough, especially since Jason felt I was going to make out like a bandit.

Tanya took a sip of her champagne, keeping her eyes on me. Then bit down on her lip. "Natalie, I'm worried about you."

I cocked my head to one side. "Why? I'm perfectly fine."

"It's Matt." She twirled the stem of her flute between her fingers. "I think he's dangerous."

My brows furrowed. "What do you mean?"

"You know, I spent a lot of time in the car with him on the drive up here. He said some really scary things."

"Like what?"

"For one, he said, 'If Natalie thinks she's going to take me to the cleaners, she's got it coming to her.' Then, 'I'm going to kill her if she tries anything stupid.' And this, 'She won't know what hit her when I get through with her.'"

I digested her words over a long sip of champagne and set the flute down. "He's just saying those kinds of things because he's so mad at me. He doesn't really mean them."

"That's what I thought, too, at first. Then when we had to stop so I could go to the bathroom, I opened the trunk of his car to get my backpack and saw it…"

"Saw what?" I felt a flutter of apprehension.

"His gun!"

I blinked several times. "Are you sure?"

"Of course I'm sure. And it totally freaked me out!"

I was stunned into silence. Matt had never brought his gun along on any family vacation. Tanya continued, her voice lowering to a whisper.

"Natalie, I think he's going to *kill* you!"

In a single breath, the benefits of my relaxing massage dissipated. A wave of nausea rolled through me as I thought about the blowout we'd had before coming up here. Matt had thrown things all around the kitchen, and when I'd told him I wanted him out of the house by February first, he'd picked up a knife and threatened, "I swear I'd kill you right here and now if I could get away with it," before stabbing the ten-inch blade into the butcher block. Except for the fight we'd had before Anabel's tragic fall down the stairs, which I'd initiated, I'd never seen him so violent. I was frightened to death and now I wondered: Had he really meant what he said?

Tanya broke into my turbulent thoughts. Terror swam in the depths of her eyes. "What if he's planning the perfect murder right now as we speak? He's totally deranged!"

My heart raced; my mind spun. What if he *had* figured out how to get away with it? Maybe he was planning to shoot me tonight in my sleep and bury me six feet under the snow. Because I was so thin, he'd have no problem disposing of me. Maybe he'd throw my body into the icy lake. Make it look like a suicide. I had a history of psychotic depression. The possibilities were frightening and endless.

Her lips quivering, Tanya reached across the table and squeezed my hand. "Oh, Natalie, I'd *die* if he did anything terrible to you!"

I knocked back my champagne. Then guzzled the rest of the bottle. An icy cold chill passed through me.

"He won't," I bit out. I took care of the check and rushed out of the restaurant.

I had to find Matt's gun.

FIFTY-THREE

NATALIE

My head pounding and my heart racing, I searched frantically for the gun. I tore through every drawer, checked the safe, and even under his mattress. By the time I was done, I'd searched every square inch of our room. I'd even checked the snow-covered terrace, digging through the frigid white powder until my fingers were numb.

Nada. It was nowhere to be found.

Which meant he had it with him.

Shit.

In a state of panic, I staggered to the mini bar and whipped out a nip of Johnny Walker Black. Scotch was Matt's choice of drink, never mine, but right now in my strung-out condition it was just what I needed. I twisted the cap off and drank it straight from the pint-size bottle. The bitter liquid burned a path from my throat to my gut, but it did little to calm my nerves.

As I was about to grab another, a large white envelope slid under the door. I went over to retrieve it. Only our room number in black marker was printed on it. My already rapid pulse went into overdrive. The envelope shaking in my hand, I debated whether to open it. I did and instantly regretted it.

Awaiting me was a single sheet of paper with the words boldly printed:

YOU'RE DEAD TO ME.

Again, they were in all red caps. Madly, I tore the note apart, then ran to the bathroom and flushed the pieces down the toilet. Then, I speed-dialed Jason, who I should have called right after learning about the gun. Stupid me. To my utter despair, my call went straight to his voicemail. Without leaving a message, I flung the phone on the night table.

It had to be Matt. But why was he mentally torturing me? Wasn't it enough he was going to kill me? By tomorrow, I could be dinner for a wild pack of coyotes. Or a bunch of hungry bears.

I tried Jason one more time. But again, no answer.

I cursed out loud. Every curse in the book.

What should I do? I couldn't exactly call hotel security or 911 and tell them my husband was going to shoot me. I had no proof. I didn't even have the weapon. They'd think I was a nutjob. Delusional and paranoid.

Chugging another Scotch, I paced the room like the madwoman I was, searching for answers. It was futile. Half drunk, half wound up, I couldn't think straight.

The only thing I could think about was having another drink. And I did.

I collapsed onto the bed.

Popped a Xanax.

And passed out.

FIFTY-FOUR

NATALIE

"Natalie Merritt, please rise."

Slowly, hesitantly, I stood up. My head bowed, I stared at the hideous orange jumpsuit I was wearing. It was itchy and ill-fitting, and I hated the color orange almost as much as I hated polyester. I wanted to rip it off along with the shackles on my hands and feet.

"We have a verdict." Trembling, I met the judge's fierce gaze. He was a dead ringer for the man I hated. And feared as much as the verdict.

His eyes were like knives, sharp and pointed at me. "What you did is a crime. How could you do that? The jury unanimously finds you guilty of reckless endangerment of a child. Two counts of involuntary manslaughter. And for killing your husband, one count of premeditated murder."

"No!" I recognized the voice. Paige! She and Will had come every day to my trial, sitting in the courtroom behind me. "Leave my mom alone! She's not a bad person! Please!" I heard her break out in heart-wrenching sobs. It hurt me too much to turn around and look at her.

The judge snarled. "The court is sentencing you to one hundred and thirty years in prison with no chance of parole."

"Nooo!"

———

I heard myself scream as I bolted to an upright position, bathed in a cold sweat. My breathing was shallow, my body shaking. I breathed in and out from my nose, trying to calm myself.

My heartbeat slowed; my breathing quieted. It was only a nightmare. A horrible nightmare. To make sure, I pinched myself. It hurt. I was still alive! My husband hadn't shot me. And he was still alive too. Conked out in the bed next to mine. I could hear his soft snores. What was he waiting for? Did he plan to shoot me in broad daylight?

I had no idea what time it was. The curtains were drawn, the room pitch black. I fumbled for my phone on the night table where I'd left it. It was going on midnight. I'd been passed out for hours in my now damp, perspiration-ridden clothes.

Tapping the flashlight button, I swung my legs over the side of the bed and tiptoed over to the dresser to put on some fresh pajamas. Having no idea which drawer I'd put them in, I randomly pulled one open. I reached my hand inside, rifling through it.

Beneath a folded sweater, my fingers brushed across a hard, cold metal surface. I picked up the object. My hand trembled. My heart galloped. I didn't need the flashlight to tell me what it was.

Way heavier than I imagined, it was Matt's Magnum. Tanya hadn't been making things up. He'd brought it along. She was right. A terrifying reality hit me with the speed of a bullet. Any doubts I had evaporated like water. Before I could take him to the cleaners, he was going to take *me* out!

Shoot me!

I clung to the gun, my heart thudding, my body numb. What should I do? I could toss it outside, but that would wake up Matt. And my throw sucked. He'd find it in the morning. I could hide it somewhere, but that was too risky and potentially too noisy. Again the thought of calling 911 or hotel security crossed my mind, but what would I tell them? *My husband has a gun and he's going to kill me.* But that was ridiculous. His gun was registered and legal. Plus, people hunted in these parts. And if it wasn't loaded (something I wasn't checking), what case did I have?

There was only one thing I could do for now. Keep myself safe from him.

Keep the gun in my possession.

Forgoing my pajamas, I returned to my bed and stuck the weapon under my pillow. I could feel it beneath me as I stared up at the ceiling. As if the gun was loaded with Xanax, shooting a round of oval white pills into my vessels, my mindset went from manic to tranquil.

I'd sleep on the gun. And sleep on how I'd deal with Matt tomorrow.

FIFTY-FIVE

MATT

We might have been on vacation, but my body was wired to get up at 6 a.m. Plus, I wanted to get some skiing in before another storm hit this afternoon. A few good runs might instill me with a rush of endorphins. I badly needed some. A vacation was supposed to de-stress you, but I was anything but relaxed. A ticking time bomb waiting to explode was more like it.

There was no escaping this divorce. I just wanted to get it over with. At least I'd figured out a way to deal with Natalie. She wasn't going to like what I had in store for her. But I had no choice. There was no way in hell I was going to let her take me to the cleaners. Or take away my kids.

A short ten minutes later, I was downstairs, dressed in my ski clothes, eating breakfast purchased from the hotel's snack bar. The restaurant wasn't open until seven, but I was fine with the paper cup of coffee and almond croissant, and sitting on a couch in the quiet, deserted lobby.

The first thing I did was text Will, who was also an early riser, to let him know I was heading up to Sugarloaf and that I'd be back by early afternoon. He could share my whereabouts with Paige and their mother. Natalie was the last person I wanted to talk to. Last night, to my relief, when I'd returned to the room, I'd found her conked out and this morning she was still sound asleep. Dead to the world.

And soon she'd be dead to me.

I took a few sips of my piping hot brew through the plastic lid flap and then bit into the sticky croissant. Bordering on a day old, it was hardly as good as the ones Nat bought from her favorite French pastry shop. Or the ones I'd grown up with.

I was born with a silver spoon in my mouth. I'd gotten everything I wanted and achieved everything I'd hoped for. With my good looks and bank account, I was the man every man envied. Every man wanted to be. But now, they'd be fools. Hell, I didn't even want to be me. My world was falling off its axis. Falling apart.

I'd messed up again. Big-time. While I was disciplined to a fault, my dick had a mind of its own and was insatiable. After the Alexa incident, I'd started seeing a shrink, both to deal with my grief—the loss of Anabel—and my infidelity. He said I had a personality disorder. CSBD. Compulsive sexual behavior disorder. In layman's terms, I was a sex addict. Likely caused by an overbearing mother and controlling father. My way of rebelling against them.

He was right. The impulses had started at a young age; I wasn't even an adolescent when I'd sneaked peeks at porn magazines (something you'd never find in the esteemed Merritt household) and played with myself incessantly, fantasizing about my hot sixth-grade teacher, Miss Turner. Blonde with legs up to her armpits—soon to become my type. In high school and college, I got to live out my fantasies with the most gorgeous girls on campus. Between getting laid, watching porn videos on my computer, and acing my coursework, I managed to get a stellar Stanford education. Following my graduation from the business school, I moved to LA and started my own company. Hot babes—the blonde, leggy, and smart kind—were hard to find at Stanford, but in the City of Angels, they were a dime a dozen, and with my looks, charisma, and success, I had my choice of models, starlets, and assistants.

I was one of those guys who had an agenda. A life plan. By the age of thirty, I wanted to make my first million. I did. By the age of thirty-five, I wanted to have five million in the bank, get married, and start a family. I hit the jackpot when I met Natalie Taylor. The company she literally turned me on to netted me twenty million when I sold it and she gave me three amazing kids.

Yet as much as I loved my wife and kids, I still couldn't keep my pants on. And my beautiful wife's equally beautiful friends (among others) couldn't wait for me to take them off. My life was perfect until it wasn't when Natalie found out about my transgression with her best friend. Alexa Roth. A woman with whom I'd had a fling—I'd screwed her brains out—while on a business trip to London when she was a hot twenty-year-old American exchange student. Though that part my wife didn't know.

My shrink sessions lasted a couple of months. He put me on some drugs that were supposed to suppress my sexual appetite, but they made me depressed and interfered with my concentration at work. The other alternative was group therapy, but there was no way in high holy water I was going to sit around, holding hands with a bunch of sociopaths, and talk about my sexual fantasies and escapades. So, I ditched my shrink and fell off the wagon. If you asked me, it was justified. With Natalie in a near-comatose state following the death of my oldest daughter, I wasn't getting any. There's only so much your hands can do before you want to jump out of your skin. And her sympathetic friends made it so easy. It didn't end with lunch. And it didn't stop when she recovered from her mental breakdown.

In hindsight, I wish it had. A familiar, sugarcoated voice interrupted my wishful thinking.

"Oh, hi, Matt!"

Before I could turn my head, Tanya was curled up on an overstuffed chair next to me. She was dressed in an all-pink hoodie outfit and chewing a wad of gum.

"What are you doing up so early?" I asked, not overjoyed to see her. Ever since the pearl necklace incident our relationship had grown strained. Distant. With all I had on my plate, I was glad she was going back to the UK soon.

She shrugged. "I don't know. I couldn't sleep."

"Can I get you something?"

She kept her gaze on me. "No, I'm good." Then a pause. "You screwed up, Matt."

There was a wild look in her eyes I'd never seen before. A menacing tone to her voice. I took a steeling breath.

"You mean because I didn't stand up for you when my mother accused you of stealing her pearls?"

She snickered. "That would have been nice, Matt, but that's not what I'm talking about."

"Then, what are you talking about?"

Her lips curled into a smirk. "I know about you, Matt. What *you* did."

I felt my skin bristle. "Know what?"

A diabolic smile slithered across her lips. "I caught you at your office with a friend of Natalie's, who was at her gala. The time I went to Century City to buy a new laptop."

Balls.

"You were going at it like rabbits. You didn't even know I was there." She laughed. "No wonder you were in such a good mood when you met me at the Apple Store."

I felt heat creeping up my neck and seeping into my cheeks. A sheen of sweat swept across my forehead as my chest clenched with dread. "Tanya, let's keep this between us. Please don't tell Paige or Will."

"Maybe." She cracked her gum. "Can I ask you a question?"

I hesitantly said yes.

"Have you ever noticed how much we have in common?"

"Yeah," I hedged with caution. "We like a lot of the same things."

"Yeah, that too, but have you ever noticed how much we *look* alike?"

There was a faint similarity. We both had long-lashed brown eyes, distinct brows, and dimpled chins. And her long-fingered hands were a lot like mine. *And* Paige's.

"Not really."

She cocked her head. "Did I ever tell you that I was adopted?"

This was the first time I was hearing this. Natalie had never told me. Maybe she didn't know.

"No." I could hear the edge in my voice. My skin prickled with apprehension.

"Well, I was. Some American girl gave me up..."

Where was she going with this?

"All I know is she was an exchange student, like me... spending a college year abroad in London."

The wildest thought leaped into my head. I'd screwed a lot of women, but only one stood out.

Alexa Roth.

I'd unexpectedly bumped into her in the lobby yesterday. We'd exchanged a cold, cordial hello and each walked the other way. It couldn't be. She would have told me. Or would she have? I tried to envision Alexa and Tanya side by side in my mind. Both were blondes with high cheekbones, almond-shaped eyes, and mile-high legs.

And big tits.

Oh God. It was possible. But wait! If I had a kid with

Alexa, she'd be twenty-one. Tanya was only eighteen... at least that's what she said she was. Was she lying? Had she tracked me down using one of those popular online DNA ancestry sites?

"What are you thinking, Matt?" she asked coyly while I tugged at my bottom lip.

"*Nothing.*" I needed to get off this unnerving subject and return to the far more pressing one. "Tanya, I need to know—"

"What?" She flung the word at me like a grenade.

"That I have your word you won't tell Paige or Will about my indiscretion."

Keeping her eyes on me, she folded her hands on her lap and twiddled her thumbs. "What's it worth to you, Matt?"

Christ. This girl was blackmailing me. I should have listened to my mother and gotten rid of her right after Thanksgiving. Sent her back to London.

"Well?" I heard her say as I squeezed my temples with my fingers.

I threw out a number. "A hundred grand to keep your mouth shut."

She rolled her eyes with exasperation. "That's not what I'm looking for."

"Okay. Two hundred."

She tsked. "You are *so* far off."

Rage was bubbling inside me. I could feel my blood pressure spiking. "Dammit! Stop playing games and tell me what you want!"

"I want you to reconcile with Natalie and pay my Coldwater tuition. Let me stay in your house until I start Stanford."

"I don't know if that's possible."

Glaring at me, she snarled. "*Make* it possible."

With that, she stood. Her expression softened. "Oh, and *Daddy dearest?* I hope we're still going to that new gun range later."

There was only one target I had in mind. *One person* I wanted to shoot.

The normal high I got from whipping down the challenging slopes was overpowered by everything I had on my mind. Most of all by the possibility that my kids would find out I had cheated on their mother. Who knew how far Tanya, my bat-crazy maybe daughter, would go? One thing for sure, neither Will nor Paige would want to live with me after knowing what I'd done. Let alone visit me. They would hate me for life.

To make things worse, it was frigging cold. The temperature kept dropping and dropping. Despite how layered up I was, I could feel the wind chill penetrate my ski jacket. Penetrate my bones. Moreover, the snow that had started off with light flurries when I got here was now coming down in full force. The slopes had emptied. There were only a few skiers left besides me. I was at the start of another run and told myself this was my last one. It was too risky, plus I was eager to get back to the hotel.

As soon as I got back, I was going to call my sister. Cecilia was smart. Shrewd. She'd know how to handle Tanya. Maybe she'd think of a way to get Natalie to reconsider the divorce. Lots of couples who despised each other lived under the same roof because it was easier that way. And cheaper. And that would solve the Tanya problem. Maybe give me and Nat a fresh start. Especially if I went back to therapy.

A win-win for everyone.

Halfway down the steep, narrow, tree-studded slope, I had to stop thinking about the mess I was in and focus solely on my run with every molecule of my brain. The snowstorm had morphed into a full-blown blizzard. The whoosh of the wind mingled with the whoosh of my skis grating against the accumulating white powder. Adrenaline pumped through my veins as I struggled to navigate the treacherous terrain. Literally trying to keep my head above the ground in these life-threatening conditions. Behind my goggles, I could barely see two feet ahead of me.

A whiteout.

I silently cursed.

Until I could curse no more.

Everything faded to black.

FIFTY-SIX

NATALIE

Morning came. Fully awake, I searched the bed next to mine. Matt was gone. Perhaps he'd gone for a jog around the lake— something he always did.

What wasn't gone was the gun. It was still under my pillow right where I put it. I heaved a sigh of relief. As long as it was in my possession, I was safe from my husband.

Clutching it like my life depended on it, I ambled over to the window and opened the curtains. Unlike sunshine-filled yesterday, today's sky was overcast. The lake gray. I remembered a snowstorm was expected in the early afternoon with a prediction of up to two feet of snow over the next twenty-four hours. I scanned the lake. Matt was nowhere in sight. A wicked thought flashed into my head. Maybe while he was jogging he'd drop dead of a heart attack; it was a possibility as his father had a heart condition. I smiled to myself. That would certainly put an end to my worry of Matt harming me. Furthermore, it would spare me from going through the hassle of an expensive, draining divorce. And dealing with that sleazeball lawyer. I'd inherit everything. The house. Our assets. Plus the five million from his life insurance.

And most importantly, it would spare me from doing anything rash. I may have been born from evil, but I was no Lady Macbeth. I was not going to let my bad dream become a premonition.

The chime of my phone broke into my jumble of thoughts. The gun shook in my hand. I'd never liked this gun—and in fact, I'd always been afraid of it. And still was. But as long as I had it, nothing could happen to me. Gripping it, I traipsed over to the night table and managed to get to my phone before it stopped ringing. I was relieved to see it was Tanya. I swiped answer.

"Good morning, honey." Thanks to the gun in my hand, my voice sounded confident and, in fact, cheery. "Is everything all right?"

She let out an audible sigh. "Oh, Natalie, thank God you answered. I was *so* worried."

"About what?"

"You know. About Matt. About *you*."

I curled my finger around the trigger. *Involuntarily.* I couldn't stop myself. "Sweetheart, there's absolutely nothing to worry about. I'm perfectly fine and everything's under control."

"Phew!" she breathed out. "Do you want to meet me for breakfast?"

"Sure. I'd love to!" And not having eaten dinner last night, I was starving. "Just give me a few minutes to get showered and dressed. I'll meet you downstairs in the restaurant. Grab a table if you get down there before me."

As I hung up, I noticed my phone's battery power was down to five percent. I set it back on the night table and plugged it in. I might as well leave it here and let it charge while I was at brunch. Plus, leaving it here would spare me from having my meal rudely interrupted by The Whisperer.

What I was not leaving behind was the gun. Maybe Matt wasn't really planning to kill me, but I couldn't take any chances. After all, I knew all too well what even the most innocent people were capable of. With a shiver, I put the cold metal weapon into my handbag. Along with my plastic vial of Xanax.

Fifteen minutes later, I was downstairs. Showered and dressed in a fashionable pair of ivory leggings, an Irish fisherman's sweater, and a pair of creamy fur-lined Uggs. Carrying my large luggage-brown Prada bag over my arm, which felt especially weighty on account of the gun, I breezed into the dining room and spotted Tanya seated at a table. She waved at me.

"I'm starving," I said, settling into the chair across from her. She looked anxious.

"Natalie, I hope you're not mad at me."

"For what?"

"For spilling the beans on Matt."

I gave her a reassuring smile. "Of course not. I'm glad you did."

"You're not worried?"

"Not a bit." I stifled a smirk. "Trust me, Matt's not going to do a thing. He doesn't have it in him." *Or the means.* "Let's hit the buffet before they put it away."

As I was about to rise from my chair, two effusive words filled my ears.

"Natalie, *dahling!*"

I recognized the breathy voice instantly, but when I looked up I blinked hard. It was Alexa Roth, except her wavy hair was now platinum blonde and blown straight. She'd also added a fringe of bangs. I swear with all her Botox she looked like she could be Tanya's older sister. The resemblance between them was uncanny.

Dressed in a quilted white Chanel jumpsuit, she strutted over to us, her daughter, Rachel, by her side. Rachel went to Coldwater and was a senior like Paige and Tanya. I almost didn't recognize her. She'd cut her reddish hair into a pixie and dyed it jet-black. With her father's stocky build and coloring, she'd never looked much like her mother, but now they looked like they came from different planets.

Against my better wishes, I let Alexa hug me.

"Nat, I had no idea you'd be here."

"A last-minute decision," I said flatly. "*Matt* and the kids are here too."

"Yes, I saw him briefly in the lobby yesterday."

Damn. I was hoping at the mention of Matt's name, she'd find an excuse to move on, but she lingered and turned her attention to my guest. "And you must be Tanya, Natalie's English exchange student. I've heard so much about you from my daughter."

"Hi, Rachel," mumbled Tanya. I could sense a bit of animosity between them. Rachel, like Paige, didn't seem her type.

Not looking comfortable, Rachel returned the "hi" and then tugged at Alexa's sleeve. "Mom, let's go. I don't want to be late for my snowboarding lesson."

"Raye, take a chill pill."

Her daughter pulled a face while Alexa's gaze stayed fixed on me. "*Dahling*, please forgive me. I've got to run. But maybe we can catch up later? Go to the spa or meet up on the slopes?"

In as few words as possible, I told her we should make a plan. Thrilled, Alexa and her daughter departed.

"God, I thought they'd never leave," huffed Tanya, pushing her chair away from the table.

"Tell me about it. Let's eat!"

Five minutes later, we were back at our table, our plates loaded with scrambled eggs, smoked salmon, apple sausage, and fresh fruit. We ate heartily, taking intermittent sips of our foamy lattes.

"Natalie," said Tanya, cutting into a thick sausage. "I have a little bit of a problem."

A brow shot up. "What's wrong?"

"No biggie, but I can't get my feet into those snow boots you lent me."

I'd lent her Anabel's almost brand-new ones. Her dusty-pink Ugg Adirondacks.

"They're a size seven and I wear a size ten."

"Oh. I totally forgot about that." Anabel and I had almost identical narrow, petite feet. Paige wore a size nine. Wide.

"With the big snowfall that's coming, I'd love to have boots that fit." She ingested a forkful of her eggs. "After brunch, can you take me to get a new pair?"

I took a sip of my latte and contemplated her question.

"Darling, I can't. I have other things to take care of." *Like figuring out what to do with the gun before Matt came back and discovered it was missing.* "But I'll ask Paige to take you shopping. There's a wonderful ski and snowboard store on Highway 18 that should have a big selection of snow boots. It's about twenty minutes away."

She flashed a smile. "That would be awesome."

Perfect. I'd have some time alone to work out the plan. But right now, something else was pressing. My bladder.

"Tanya, sweetheart, I need to run to the restroom." I glanced down at the monstrous purse by my feet. "Would you be a dear and watch my bag? I'll be right back."

Her smile widened. "Of course. I'll guard it with my life."

FIFTY-SEVEN

NATALIE

When I got back to the room, Matt, to my relief, still wasn't there. It was going on twelve thirty. My phone fifty percent charged, I called Paige and asked if she could take Tanya to the ski shop to buy some boots.

"Do I have to, Mom? Can't you?"

"No, I've got something important to do." *Like getting rid of your father's gun once and for all.* "It'll only take an hour and you should go soon before it begins to blizzard." Standing by the window, I could see that both the sky and lake had darkened, and flurries were already falling.

"Fine." She stabbed the word at me.

"Use your debit card, and I'll pay you back later."

Before ending the call, I asked about Will. "Is he with your father?"

"No, he's not with *our* father." I detected attitude in her voice. "Dad drove up to Big Bear—to Sugarloaf—to get in some skiing. Will's here in the room, watching a Harry Potter movie."

"Good." That meant Matt wouldn't be back for hours. I told Paige to drive safely and jabbed the red button. Just as the call disconnected, a loud rap sounded at the door. *Matt?*

I padded over to it.

"Who's there?" I asked. I couldn't be too careful.

"Thomas from the front desk. I have an envelope for you."

Cautiously, I opened the door, and standing before me was a young, uniformed valet, no older than twenty. He handed me the large white envelope that was identical to the one I'd received yesterday with our room number printed on it in black marker.

"Thank you, Thomas." I took it from him. "Do you by chance know who dropped this envelope off at the front desk?"

"Sorry, ma'am. I don't. I just started my shift."

I thanked him again and shut the door, making sure to lock it. Wasting no time, I undid the clasp and removed the single sheet of paper inside. Written on it in red caps were the words:

REVENGE IS A DISH BEST SERVED COLD.

One of Matt's favorite lines. Originating in the eighteenth-century French classic *Les Liaisons Dangereuses*, it was made famous by Marlon Brando's Don Vito Corleone in the movie *The Godfather*. Whenever Matt said it, he imitated the actor's raspy mobster accent. In my head, I could hear him. I used to think it was funny; I no longer did.

Crumpling the note, I tossed it into the wastepaper basket and returned to the window. The lacy flakes were now bigger, coming down faster. There was already a fresh coat of snow on the ground. Within an hour, the benign snowfall would morph into a blustery blizzard. I was worried about Paige and Tanya, and hoped they'd make it back to the hotel before the roads became hazardous.

Despite my concern, the snowfall was mesmerizing. An exquisite dance of nature. By tomorrow, there would be over a foot of fluffy fresh white powder on the ground with drifts rising to six feet and more. I loved going outdoors on the morning following a big snowfall. Sinking into the soft glistening white carpet, the sun blazing, making the frosted trees sparkle like Swarovski chandeliers.

The vision of a winter wonderland filled my head and suddenly, like magic, a vivid fantasy began to play out in my imagination.

Tomorrow, I'd convince Matt to go back up to Big Bear. To go snowshoeing with me in the silent, snow-covered forest. Something we enjoyed doing together. And talk "things" over. The hope of a reconciliation, the cincher.

As always, we'd forge our own path, far away from others. I'd let him lead the way, me right behind him. When he wasn't looking, I'd take out the gun and shoot him in the head at close range. He'd never hear me pull the trigger as the crunch of our snowshoes would drown out the sound. *Bang!*

No one would hear me, and even if they did hear the shot, they'd likely think it was coming from someone hunting, which was allowed in these parts. Then, as he staggered to the ground, not knowing what had hit him, I'd shoot him again, just for good measure. Wearing my ski mittens, I'd pile a ton of snow over him so he wasn't visible. Leave him behind. Then wait till the sun was almost down and run to the authorities and tell them in a panic my husband and I had gotten separated in the dark, snowy forest, and I was worried about him. Tell them I looked and looked and kept calling out his name. Maybe a bear had attacked him, I'd tell them all teary-eyed.

There was one thing I was for sure: an excellent actress. I'd been acting my entire adult life. Pretending to be someone I was not. This was just a new role for me: the poor concerned wife, soon to become the poor grieving widow. By the time they'd find his body, which could take a couple of days, especially since more snow was predicted, he'd be a frozen corpse. And probably look a lot like frightening Jack Nicholson in *The Shining*.

The police would discover he'd been shot, but they'd never

prove it was me. With no footprints thanks to the fresh layer of snow, no fingerprints thanks to my snow mitts, or any trace of my hair thanks to my ski hat, there'd be no evidence. Plus, Matt's gun would long be gone. Before I headed back to the hotel, I planned to throw it into Big Bear Lake. They'd never find it.

Plus, it was no secret weirdos hung out around here. Men and women who'd retreated from society for whatever reason and lived reclusive lives in log cabins with rifles beside them. Some were reportedly murderers.

All the better.

Yes, revenge was a dish best served cold.

The sudden trill of my phone ended my deliciously wicked fantasy and snapped me back to reality. It must be Paige, letting me know she and Tanya were back. I sprinted to the night table where it was still charging. I glanced at the caller ID. It was a blocked number—caller unknown. *Not again!*

It had to be The Whisperer, but this time I'd had enough. Fearless and furious, I answered the call.

"Okay, Matt. I know it's you or your rotten sister! You can stop—"

To my surprise, a somber male voice cut me off.

"This is Officer Axelrod with the Big Bear Sheriff's Department. Am I speaking to Natalie Merritt?"

"Yes, this is she." My voice faltered.

"I'm sorry to tell you this, but there's been an accident."

My heart pounded against my chest so hard I couldn't breathe. My greatest fear! Paige had gotten into a car accident!

"M-my daughter?"

"No, Mrs. Merritt. It involves your husband."

I heaved a breath. My heartbeat slowed, but it was still beating double time.

"What happened?"

"He was in a skiing accident. He slammed into a tree."

"Is he okay?" I was shocked by how shaky my voice was.

"He was found by a fellow skier and airlifted to Bear Valley Community Hospital."

"What's his condition?"

"Critical. Per the paramedics, he has hypothermia and may have suffered a spinal injury. Before he lost consciousness, he asked for you."

He asked for me?

At this unexpected news, I was speechless. I didn't know what to say. How to react when this was the man I hated with all I had. The man I'd just fantasized killing.

A mental reset. My chest tightened as if it were corseted. Remorse coursed through me. What madness had possessed me? Seized my overactive imagination? How could I have possibly even thought about killing my children's father? The man I'd once loved and maybe still did the teensiest bit. The man who'd given me everything after years of nothing. Years of neglect. Tears welled up in my eyes. Guilt and sorrow filled every fiber of my being.

Yes, it was just a fantasy, some whacked form of wishful thinking, but I still hated myself. I was no longer *that* person. How could I have possibly thought about murdering my husband?

The officer broke into my sorrowful, regretful, gut-wrenching thoughts.

"Your husband's car is still parked up here in Big Bear. We're going to try to have it towed to wherever you're staying..."

I was so distraught I drew a blank. Finally, it came to me.

"The Lake Arrowhead Resort and Spa."

"Just know we may not be able to do it today with the inclement weather."

"Tomorrow will be fine," I stammered.

"Here's the number of the hospital if you wish to call."

Fumbling for the pen and small pad on the night table, I managed to jot it down.

"Thank you, Officer."

"You're welcome, ma'am. I strongly suggest you don't attempt to visit him with the blizzard. The roads up here are already icy and slippery, and with the whiteout, visibility is nil. Stay safe and I hope your husband pulls through."

The call ended. I came to my senses. I immediately called the hospital. Matt had severed his spine and was in surgery. The nurse I spoke to had no idea how long it would last. She said someone would call when he was out. *If he came out.* I gave her my number in case she didn't have it.

Next, I called Matt's parents. They were away in Italy, but they needed to know. I speed- dialed Marjorie's number, hoping she'd pick up, despite my new, unrecognizable mobile number. I'd forgotten to give it to her. The phone rang several times, then went to voicemail. I left my mother-in-law an urgent message. "Marjorie, this is Natalie, calling from my new cell number. Call me as soon as you get this message. Matt's been in a skiing accident and is undergoing surgery." Given that Rome was nine hours ahead of us, making it close to midnight, it was likely they were asleep and wouldn't get the message until the morning.

I paced the room. Who else did I need to call? I bit down on my lip. Of course... the children. I had to tell them. Questions tore through my head. How was I going to break this terrible news to Will and Paige? How would they react? How would I comfort them when I was divorcing their father and couldn't comfort myself?

God, give me strength.

I sucked in a breath and speed-dialed Paige. No answer. The call went straight to her voicemail. I didn't leave a message and quickly speed-dialed Will. He picked up on the first ring.

"Hi, Mom."

"Will, is Paige with you?"

"No, she hasn't come b—"

"Have you heard from her?"

"No."

Worry pulsed through me. She should have been back a half hour ago. Maybe she was stuck in traffic on account of the weather conditions. Traffic could reduce to a crawl during a snowstorm.

"Are you okay, Mom?"

"Will, I've got to go. Call me as soon as your sister returns."

"Okie-doke."

With a jab, I ended the call, suddenly remembering I could check Paige's whereabouts with the locator app I'd installed on her phone. *Find Me.* For all I knew, she could be hanging out in the hotel lobby.

But before I could do that, another call came in.

The San Bernardino Police.

Why were they calling?

There was only one answer.

Act normal. Stay calm.

FIFTY-EIGHT

PAIGE

The snow was coming down hard and heavy. Faster than my wipers could clear it from my windshield. *Swoosh. Swoosh.* Gripping the steering wheel with my gloved hands, I kept my eyes superglued to the road and drove slowly. Thank goodness Tanya didn't distract me and sat in the passenger seat, chewing gum and occupied with her phone. Likely texting Lance, who was vacationing in Cabo with his family. The sooner we got back to the hotel, the better. Fingers crossed she wouldn't dawdle in the ski shop, trying on a gazillion pairs of boots.

"There's the shop," I said, pulling over in front of it. "Why don't you go inside while I wait here." Keeping the engine running, I reached inside my phone case. "Here's my debit card. Make it quick, and you better not use it for anything else."

With a snort, she unbuckled her seat belt and jumped out of the car. Just as she disappeared inside the store, my phone pinged with a Google Alert—a link to an article in *The Desert Sun*. With bated breath, I clicked it open. It was short and hardly front-page news.

A month since two teenagers found a charred body in

*Tahquitz Canyon, the Palm Springs Police Department
has ruled that the body is likely that of Billie Rae Perkins,
the fifteen-year-old girl who went missing after her
parents were brutally murdered in an Indio trailer park
twenty years ago. While dental records could not be
matched up, the decomposed bone matter coincides with
the time she disappeared. No other girls were reported
missing in the area at that time. The police are investigating whether she was a victim of foul play and if her
death is connected to the unsolved murders. No suspects
have been apprehended.*

I closed the alert and felt a sense of closure, though unsettling. Poor Billie Rae. A shiver shimmied down my spine as I
tried to imagine all she'd been through. If someone had set her
on fire and left her to die, I hoped he or she would be found and
get what they deserved. That they'd burn in hell. I was about to
call Will and then Mary Burton to tell them what I'd learned
when I eyed Tanya exiting the store.

Now wearing a pair of fur-trimmed tan snow boots, she
hopped back into my Jeep and threw the shopping bag with her
Docs onto the back seat. Placing her backpack between her feet,
she looked down at her new boots and huffed.

"I really wanted pink ones, but these will have to do."

I mentally rolled my eyes as I put the car in drive and pulled
away. I was ready to get back to the hotel. I'd had enough of her
for one day. At the next light, I flicked my blinker so I could
make a U-turn.

"Turn your blinker off," she ordered. "We're not going back
to the hotel yet."

"What do you mean?" I turned to face her and my eyes
gaped with shock.

She was pointing a gun at me.

"God, what are you doing, Tanya?"

"What does it look like, freak?" The fake British accent was gone and in its place was an American one. Her voice bitter and brittle. "I'm pointing a gun at you. And if you don't keep driving north, I'm afraid I'm going to have to pull the trigger."

My pulse pounded in my ears. Fear. A fear like nothing I've ever known. But I wasn't going to show her I was scared. I turned off the blinker and continued to drive north. "You're mental!"

"That's what they've told me." In my mind's eye, I could see a smirk curl on her lips.

"Where'd you get the gun?"

"It's your dad's. He brought it along. There's a new shooting range in Big Bear he promised to take me to. Thanks to him, I've become quite the marksman. An excellent shot. You should see me at target practice."

Actually, I had seen a photo on Instagram taken at the LA Gun Club with her hugging my dad and brandishing his gun. The hashtags: *#hotshot*, *#gunslinger*, and *#daddysgirl*. At the time, I was more repulsed than intimidated by it.

She let out a wicked laugh. "Guess what? You're going to be my next target. And I don't plan on missing."

A violent chill coursed through me as her words sank in. She was going to shoot *me*?

Chewing on a wad of gum, she continued. "I was going to have to figure out a way to steal the gun from your father, but your mother made things so easy for me."

"What do you mean?"

"At brunch this morning, she asked me to watch her bag while she went to the bathroom. As soon as she was gone, I snuck into her purse to steal some cash, and lo and behold, the gun was inside it."

A shard of shock. What was my mom doing with my dad's gun? She hated that gun. Wanted him to get rid of it.

Shoving those thoughts aside, I refocused on my driving.

The snow was growing heavier; it was getting harder and harder to see in front of me. "Where are we going?"

Tanya popped an obnoxious bubble. "Green Valley Lake. It's not far."

I'd never heard of it. "How do you know about it?"

"I grew up not far from here. One of the families I lived with took me camping there one time. Trust me, I'm *so* not the camping type. Seriously, do I look like someone who likes roughing it?" With an eye roll, she lifted her free hand to show off her perfect manicure. "Those lowlifes paid for that." She tsked. "Such a pity their bratty five-year-old kid had an unfortunate accident. I was watching him... well, sort of. At least the part where the little brat fell into the lake. It wasn't exactly like I could rescue him because I didn't know how to swim either."

If I didn't have to drive with two hands tight on the wheel with the slippery road and blinding snow, one of them would have gone flying to my mouth. I heard myself gasp. She'd let a little boy drown. She was responsible for his death. A new frightening reality slammed into me.

I was stuck in my car with a psychopath. A murderer! And I was going to be her next victim.

I gave her a sideways glance. A snarl lifted her lips and her eyes glinted with madness. The gun on her lap, she was still holding it firmly. Should I risk grabbing it from her? Then, she caught me looking at her and pointed it back at my head. "Don't even think about it!"

My heart pounding, I glued my eyes back on the road. "Are we almost there?"

"Another ten minutes. I'll let you know when to turn off. Oh, and by the way, the beauty of this lake is that the campsite is closed during the winter. There's no one there... well, except for a serial killer or two."

The heat was blasting in the car, but I was shivering. Questions bombarded me as fast and furiously as the falling snowflakes. Why was this happening? Why me? What was I going to do? My head spinning, my phone rang. I glanced down at the caller ID. It was my mom! Maybe she could help me.

"Tanya, that's my mom. I have to take this call."

"*No*, you don't! You can blame her. This is all *her* fault!"

What did my mother have to do with this?

Before I could ask, my Jeep began to sputter. Slipping and sliding on the icy road.

"What's going on?" asked my deranged passenger as I gripped the steering wheel, hoping not to go over the mountain road.

On my next jittery breath, the car stalled, coming to a complete halt. I glanced at the dashboard. The fuel gauge registered empty.

"We're out of gas."

"What!?" She banged the dashboard with a fist. Better than a bang of the gun. "You stupid idiot!"

Her maniacal eyes stayed on me. "Leave your phone behind and get out of the damn car! And don't try to do something stupid or you'll be roadkill. Or coyote bait. Take your pick."

Hesitantly, I did as she asked as she followed me out from the passenger side, the gun in her hand. The frigid air assaulting me, I thought about making a mad dash, but what was the point? With the icy road and blinding snow, I'd likely slip and fall, and she'd take a shot at me.

"Get in front of me so I can see you," she shouted, as she rounded my Jeep, loud enough to be heard above the howling wind. "And put your hands up."

My teeth clattering, I again did what she asked, wishing I could hug myself to keep warm. With the wind chill factor, the temperature felt like it was below zero.

"Where are we going?"

"We're going on a short scenic walk. I'm going to show you

the lake that imp fell into. You may be going for a swim too. Start walking! And remember, don't do anything stupid."

Shivering from both fear and the frigid temperature, I plowed ahead. I could hear her right behind me, her new boots crunching into the dense white powder. Maybe she'd slip and break her neck. And I'd have a chance to escape this nightmare.

Wishful thinking on my part as she bellowed...

"It sucks to be you."

FIFTY-NINE

NATALIE

First the call about Matt's accident. Now this. The phone shook in my hand. My voice shook in my throat.

"H-hello?"

"This is Detective Mendez with the San Bernardino Police Department. Is this Natalie Merritt?"

"Y-yes." My voice was so strangled I could barely get a word out. Every fiber of my being was vibrating. I felt like a tuning fork.

My life as I knew it was over.

"Do you know a Tanya Blackstone?" the caller asked.

"Yes." I was totally baffled. This was not the question I was expecting. "She's our English exchange student. She's been living with us since the end of August."

"Is she with you now?"

"No, she went out with my daughter, Paige... in Paige's car to buy some boots. I believe they're on their way back."

"Mrs. Merritt, we have evidence proving your exchange student is not who she says she is."

"What do you mean?"

"Early last month, your so-called exchange student was in an automobile accident. Correct?"

"Yes." My voice tentative, I sat down on the edge of the bed as he continued.

"According to the Los Angeles Police Department, she was not in possession of an official ID—like a passport or driver's license. So routinely, in such cases, we take a photograph of the victim and do a DNA swab..."

"And?"

"Our system is backlogged, and her DNA test got lost, but we just found out from the LAPD that both her photo and DNA match that of a missing young woman in our data bank. Her name is Bree Walker."

"That's preposterous! I know for a fact she comes from a very fine family that resides in London. She speaks with a lovely British accent and has been a delightful family guest."

"Mrs. Merritt, have you ever had contact with her father or mother?"

"No. Her mother is deceased, and her father travels a lot. He's a diplomat."

"I see. Perhaps someone else?"

"No. She's an only child. I'm not sure if she has other family. She's never mentioned any relatives." Nor did I ever ask, I added silently.

"Have you ever seen her passport?"

"No. And she recently lost it."

"Mrs. Merritt, this young woman who's been staying with you doesn't have a passport. She's never been out of the country."

"I don't believe you. I found her via a legitimate student exchange program."

"Mrs. Merritt, I know this is hard for you, but it's important you hear me out. I've texted you a photo of Bree Walker. I want you to take a look at it and then tell me if this is the young woman who's been residing with you."

"Hold on, please." I went to my messages. My eyes widened as I stared at the photo. The girl's hair was shorter and darker, her face fuller, but it was unmistakably Tanya. The same exact features. The same almond-shaped eyes, high cheekbones, full lips, and dimpled chin. And those distinct onyx eyebrows.

Shakily, I returned to the call. "It's not possible, but it is."

"Listen carefully, Mrs. Merritt, to what I'm about to tell you."

I sucked in a lungful of air. My silence a signal for him to continue.

"Bree Walker is mentally unstable. She was abandoned when she was an infant at a church outside Palm Springs."

My stomach lurched and my chest tightened as bile filled my throat. I clasped my left hand over my mouth so I wouldn't interrupt him. Or throw up.

"She was found on the doorstep by a nun and ended up being put into the system. Going from one foster home to another. From an early age, she manifested extremely aggressive behavior both with her foster families and at school—from stabbing foster parents and siblings with kitchen knives to assaulting students and teachers with scissors, pencils, and other sharp objects. She even tried to poison someone. Taken into custody, she was evaluated by a child psychiatrist and diagnosed as a sociopath with schizophrenic tendencies. And severe borderline personality disorder."

My head was spinning. My mouth was paralyzed. I couldn't get a word out if I tried so I let him go on.

"Deemed a danger to society, she was committed last year to a psychiatric hospital in Redlands, but in late August, after flinging grapefruit juice at an attendant and gouging his eye with a plastic fork, she stole his scrubs and some medications and escaped. She has been on the run ever since, squatting and using various aliases. Somehow, we're not sure how yet, she figured out a way to get to Los Angeles and worm herself into your household. Why she chose your family is not clear to us."

It was *crystal* clear to me. So crystal clear my brain pinged like a sparkling glass in a dishwasher detergent commercial.

The detective's somber voice brought me back to the moment. "Mrs. Merritt, we believe you and your family may be in grave danger. Without her medications, her behavior can be highly erratic. There's also a possibility she's armed and dangerous. Your lives are at risk. The LAPD is on their way to your house to apprehend her."

"We're not home," I faltered. "We're away. At the Lake Arrowhead Resort and Spa."

A brief silence on the other end, then... "Stay put. Due to the hazardous weather conditions in your area, we may not be able to get there until tomorrow. In the meantime, do *not* let her know of our conversation under any circumstances. Keep your family close to you. Understood?"

"Y-yes, Detective, thank you. I've got to go." I abruptly ended the call and speed-dialed Paige.

The phone rang and rang and rang.

Please, Paige, pick up! PICK UP! I shouted silently as the call went to her voicemail. And then, to my utter horror, I heard...

The mailbox is full and cannot accept any messages at this time. Goodbye.

I slapped one hand to my heart, the other to my mouth. My daughter's life was in jeopardy! And it was all my fault.

My heart was pounding like a kettledrum. I had to warn her! Find her!

Frantic, I called the ski shop. Thank God someone picked up. I described Paige and Tanya, but she'd only seen "the rude girl in the pink ski outfit." I immediately speed-dialed Tanya's number. Several rings, then it went to voicemail. I knew she was deliberately not picking up. But even if she did, what would I say?

I know who YOU are...

And then, in my distraught state, I remembered the Find Me location-sharing app on my phone. I clicked it open. Hoping, praying Paige was back at the hotel or close to it. My heart plummeted. Rather than heading toward the hotel, the GPS tracker showed she was heading away from it. My only solace was the car was moving; fingers crossed they'd not been in an accident. And weren't en route to the hospital Matt was taken to. I still hadn't heard a word about his condition, but right now, it was the furthest thing from my mind.

My mind in a tailspin, I leaped up from the bed and paced the room, every frantic step driven by panic. Paige's life was at stake! Every minute, every second counted. I was drowning in a sea of helplessness and hopelessness. Guilt and despair.

You're going to pay for what you did.

One breath away from hyperventilating, I grabbed my bag and dug inside it in search of my Xanax. My heart almost stopped. The prescription bottle was there. But the gun was gone!

Only one person could have taken it.

Oh my God! Tanya! I'd foolishly left my bag with her at brunch.

Detective Mendez's words spun in my head. *There's also a possibility she's armed and dangerous.*

Possibility was a euphemism.

The frightening truth is that she was.

Dressed head to toe in my ski clothes, I raced down the hallway and frantically banged on the door of the room Will was sharing with Paige. I had no one to turn to other than my son.

"Will, it's Mom! Open up!" I rapped again and heard Bear bark.

My son came to the door quickly and opened it. Bear was standing beside him. He immediately saw the panic on my face.

"Mom, what's wrong?"

"Will, it's Paige. She's in her car with Tanya. Her life's in jeopardy!" Spewing the words, I went on to tell him how I'd learned our exchange student was a dangerous sociopath, leaving out what else I knew about her.

Alarm filled my son's eyes. "Mom, we have to go after her! Let's find Dad. We'll go with him in his car."

"He's not back from skiing," I said, skipping over his life-and-death situation.

"What about the car rental place?"

"It's closed because of the blizzard." I told him calling for an Uber or Lyft was not an option either.

"Mom, I have an idea!"

My stomach a mass of knots, I listened intently and then hugged my brainiac son.

"Stay here! I'll keep you posted!"

"No, Mom, I'm coming with you!" Before I could protest, he donned his cold-weather clothes. "And Bear's coming too. He has a bone to pick with Tanya." Without wasting a second, he slipped off the dog's long red-leather leash from the door-knob and clipped it to his collar, then grabbed the scarf his sister had worn yesterday. "Plus, Bear can pick up Paige's scent if she's left her car." Gripping the leash, he gave the dog a pat. "C'mon, boy. Let's go!"

"*No*, Will!" I pleaded. "It's too dangerous. Tanya has your father's gun!"

"Mom, don't worry. Bear *has* a bone to pick with Tanya." He looked down at the eager-to-leave dog. "Right, boy?"

Bear gazed up at him with his big brown eyes and gave an affirmative bark. Before I could stop them, they were out the door. And on my next ragged breath, I was too.

The air outside was bitter cold. The biting wind stung my cheeks as quarter-size snowflakes danced madly around us. Shivering, with our arms folded around us, our breaths coming out in puffs of steam, Will and I stood at the entrance to the hotel with Bear, who didn't seem to mind the brutal weather one tiny bit.

In less than one freezing minute, Will spotted a candidate.

"Mom, go for it!" he shouted.

With him and Bear close behind me, I loped up to a middle-aged woman who'd just gotten out of her white Highlander. The driver's side door open, she was waiting for someone to valet her SUV. I had other plans.

"Ma'am, I have a dire emergency. I need to borrow your car."

"Excuse me?" She shot me a perplexed look. Bear barked at her, but she wasn't intimidated.

"You heard me," I said.

"Don't you dare touch my car." Her face as rabid as Bear's, she yanked me away from her vehicle by my elbow.

I shook myself free of her, and with all the muscle power I had, I gave her a forceful shove. With something between a groan and a shriek, she landed on her big butt on the icy gravel. Rage burning on her cheeks, she snagged her phone from her purse and snapped a photo of me.

"I'm going to report you to the management! File an assault charge! Plus another for grand theft! My husband's a lawyer. You won't get away with this!"

With not a moment to lose, Will, Bear, and I clambered into the vehicle. Will in the front seat next to me, Bear behind us. Clamping my seat belt, I shifted into drive and stepped hard on the gas pedal.

"Mom, that was so badass!" blurted Will as I peeled out of the driveway. "Just like Wonder Woman!"

Thanking him, I couldn't help a smile, but it faded quickly. Wonder Woman me had a much bigger mission ahead of her. To save his sister's life! Turning onto the 18, I tossed him my phone.

"Will, I need you to help me. Click on the Find Me app and let me know where Paige is."

A breath later... "Mom, it looks like she just got off the 18 and is heading toward Green Valley Lake."

In retrospect, I was so glad Will had come along; I couldn't have done this without him. He was the yin to my yang. My *Top Gun* wingman. While I kept my eyes straight ahead, he programmed Green Valley Lake into the GPS. Normally, it was a half hour drive away, but with the blizzard it could take well over an hour to get there, driving at only ten miles an hour. I checked the gas gauge. Thank goodness the tank was full as I sure wouldn't want to run out of fuel in the middle of nowhere in a raging blizzard. I then glanced at my son, who was still holding my phone.

"Will, try calling her."

"Okay."

Again, no answer and her message box was still full. I swallowed back my despair, and with my heart ticking like a time bomb, I powered through the storm as fast as I could. I was the only car on the dangerously slippery, snowy road. Even with the windshield wipers swishing like hypersonic metronomes, my lights and defroster on, I could barely see two feet ahead of me. We were in the middle of a whiteout. A life-threatening blizzard. I prayed we wouldn't get into an accident. Skid off the road, hit a tree, or fall off a cliff.

And I prayed I would get to Paige in time.

"Will, where is she now?"

"She's still on Green Valley Lake Road. The same spot. Not far from the lake."

"That means she hasn't moved, right?"

"Yeah. Maybe she escaped and left her phone behind."

I felt a glimmer of hope. It was quickly washed away by a tidal wave of fear. Paige could be in the car or out of it. In either case, injured. Or worse, dead! Oh God, had Tanya shot her? Was I too late? I'd lost one child; I couldn't bear to lose another.

And if something terrible did happen to her, it would be all my fault for bringing Tanya into our lives. How could I live with myself? I hated myself more than I ever had before.

A horrible, sick feeling gathered in the pit of my stomach. My eyes prickled with tears. Not wanting to freak Will out, I kept my deepest, darkest fears to myself and prayed again. *Please, God. Let her be okay!*

My heart hammering, I turned off the 18 onto Green Valley Lake Road, and five minutes later we came upon an abandoned, snow-covered vehicle. A Jeep Cherokee. Will saw it the moment I did. "Look, Mom! Paige's car!"

I came to a stop. From my vantage point, it didn't appear that anyone was inside the Jeep. Though I wasn't sure because it was hard to see through the dark, tinted windows and layer of snow.

"Will, what should we do?"

"We have to check it out."

I shuddered. What if Paige's body was slumped over the steering wheel? Or stuffed in the trunk?

"Will, stay in the car with Bear while I look inside it."

"No way, Mom. We're coming with you."

By this point I knew there was no holding Will back. In unison, we jumped out of the SUV, Will holding Bear by his leash with one hand, the other clutching Paige's scarf.

Scraping off some snow, we peered inside the Jeep windows. To my great relief, no one was inside. *Thank God! There's still hope.* I sighed as Will squeezed the handle of the front passenger door.

"Mom, the car isn't locked." He swung the door open before I could utter a word. "Hold onto Bear." Too late for me to protest, he handed me the leash and crawled inside the vehicle.

"Mom, Paige's backpack is in here. So is her phone."

"Will, do you see the gun anywhere?"

I watched with my heart in my throat as he searched the car.

"I can't find it."

My teeth chattered. That meant Tanya still had it in her possession. "Will, open the trunk. Do you know which button it is?"

"Seriously, Mom?" His eyes said "duh" as he popped it open. Holding my breath, I lifted up the hatch and then blew out the air stuck in my lungs. Paige wasn't there. And neither was the gun. I hurried back to Will, who was now crouched down, examining the snow.

"Look, Mom! Fresh footprints."

He pointed at them. With the snow still falling, it was hard to make them out, but he was right. There were two sets of them. The ones in front slightly wider. For sure, they belonged to Paige and Tanya (I still couldn't think of her as Bree). Tanya was trailing my daughter, but at least I knew she was alive. Make that surmised.

You will pay for what you did.

The words swirled around my head as the snow whirled around us. Wait! Maybe Tanya was after money! I could offer her anything she wanted—even a million dollars—if she let Paige go safely. It was worth a shot.

Shivering, I removed a glove, slipped my phone out of my ski jacket, and began to text her number. Except I had no signal, be it due to the inclement weather, remote location, or both. That meant Will had no signal either. We were stuck in a dead zone! Another wave of fear hit me like an avalanche. Without cell service in this completely desolate hellhole, we could freeze to death and die!

Will cut my tumultuous thoughts short. "Mom, for sure, they're headed toward the lake. The footprints go on for a while. And Bear went all crazy, picking up Paige's scent."

"Willikins, what should we do?" I hadn't called him by his baby name in ages, but at this moment, it felt good on my tongue.

In a few words, he explained what he was thinking.

With painfully mixed thoughts of love and hate, guilt and sorrow, hope and dread, I got back into the Highlander with Will and our dog. Shifting into drive, I stepped on the gas and slowly forged ahead. Watching the snowflakes on the heated windshield melt like teardrops.

Having no wits of my own, I had to trust my genius son's plan.

It all boiled down to a matter of life or death.

SIXTY-ONE

PAIGE

Green Valley Lake was unlike Big Bear or Lake Arrowhead. It was significantly smaller with no sign of civilization anywhere. Surrounded by towering pine trees now dressed in ghost-like white gowns, the campground was deserted, with just some snow-filled rowboats moored at the shore.

The snow bombarding us, the wind gusting, we stood face to face on the edge of a long, snow-covered dock overlooking the deep, partially frozen body of water. Less than three feet away, her back to the lake, Tanya held the gun aimed at me. With the sky darkening, she was a pink blur in a sea of white. I was beyond freezing cold, almost numb, and, with the 7,000-foot altitude, light-headed. *Focus, Paige, focus!* I had to stall her. Foil her. My life was at stake. At such close range, she wouldn't miss if she took a shot. I'd be X'd like in those photos I'd found. Except permanently.

"Tanya, why are you doing this to me?" I shivered, trying to ignore my stinging fingers and toes.

"You should ask your mother." She kept the gun pointed at me. "But unfortunately, you won't have a chance."

My breaths came out in steamy puffs. Hot tears, part from

the cold, part from fear, leaked from my eyes, each one freezing as they fell to my cheeks. I was about to be dinner for a pack of hungry wolves. They'd fight over me tonight...

Then, suddenly, a voice called out.

"Tanya! Put the gun down! Let's talk."

My mom!

I pivoted in her direction, and as I did, Tanya grabbed me from behind. One arm gripping my neck, choking me. The hand of the other holding the ice-cold gun to my head.

I was as good as dead.

SIXTY-TWO

NATALIE

Paige was still alive!

I wanted to get down on my knees and thank God, but knew I had to stay focused. In the moment. One step ahead of Tanya. I was dealing with a sociopath. She was holding my daughter prisoner, my husband's gun digging into her temple. One click away from shooting her.

"Tanya," I yelled, about twenty feet away from her. "Let Paige go."

"*No!* Only if you tell her the truth."

The awful truth. The lies I lived. The lies I hid. An icy, violent shudder ran through me as she ranted in her venom-filled voice, her British accent gone.

"Tell her, Natalie, who you *really* are! What you did or I'll blow her brains out!"

I *never* wanted to be *her* again. *Ever!* But with Paige's life at stake, I had no choice.

"Paige—"

Tanya cut me off. "Move closer so we can hear you better. I don't want your precious Paige to miss one word."

Hesitantly, I took ten baby steps closer, my boots digging

into the thick blanket of snow. As I neared them, I lost my footing but saved myself from falling.

"*Closer!*"

I took a few more cautious steps. Now on the dock, standing directly in front of them, I was so close I could see the fear in Paige's eyes, the madness in Tanya's despite the blinding snow.

"Continue!" barked Tanya.

"Paige..." I looked my daughter straight in the eye. "My real name is Billie Rae Perkins..."

Paige blinked with confusion. "That can't be... Billie Rae is dead!"

Tanya snickered. "Wishful thinking. Confirm it, Natalie!"

"Paige, it's true." Her jaw went slack. "Please, you *have* to believe me."

Tanya smirked. "Now, tell her who I *really* am."

I was shivering so much I could barely get words out. "P-Paige, Tanya is my daughter... my *other* daughter... my firstborn child."

I'd dropped the bomb. Revealed the horrific secret I'd kept my entire adult life.

One of the many.

Paige's eyes grew round as saucers. "What? You've known this and never told us?"

"No. I just found out."

"Go on!" roared Tanya, not interested in how I'd pieced it together. "Tell her everything."

Despite the blazing cold, I felt my face flame with shame as Paige's gaze stayed on me. My mouth dry, I found my voice. "I abandoned her shortly after she was born. Left her on the steps of a church."

Tanya spat her gum at me. "Billie, that was the *biggest* mistake of your life. You ruined my life! Do you know what it's like to be in the system? Foster care? To go from one shitty family to the next? And then be sent to the loony bin because people think you're crazy when you're only angry? Pissed off by people abusing you? Neglecting you? Not giving a damn?"

The truth was, I did. I had lived my entire childhood physically and mentally abused. Memories of my childhood painfully flashed in my head like a film on high speed. I wasn't sure, however, how much Tanya knew about my past other than the little I'd told her that day she'd helped with the FAFAK gala.

"I—I'm sorry. You're right. I did make a mistake. I was a teenager... not even sixteen... a single mother with not a penny to my name. And suffering from postpartum depression. I wasn't in my right mind."

Pausing, I flashed back to that life-changing day. From the moment she was born, she'd not stopped crying. In my mind's eye, I could so clearly see her scrunched-up crimson face, her tiny balled-up fists, her matted black hair. All the darkness that veiled her. She had inherited the genes of the ogre who had raped me.

No, I didn't make a mistake.

Maybe I did.

I sucked in a ragged breath and returned to the moment. "Tanya—"

She cut me off again. "My name is Bree. B-R-E-E. It means 'strength' or 'exalted one.' Get used to it."

Bree, I said to myself.

"*Bree*, how did you figure out I was your mother?"

"I lived with different foster families in and around the desert. Randomly, strangers would come up to me and tell me I looked a lot like this girl who had disappeared. Snatched by some wacko. So did some of my stupid-ass teachers. Her name was Billie Rae Perkins. I did some research, put two and two together, and figured out that Billie had abandoned me as a baby at the church."

There was still one major unanswered question. "How did you figure out Billie Rae and I were one and the same?"

"Luck. You hosted a benefit for the Mental Health Organization. Pictures of you—in that teal-blue Dior gown—were all over the newspaper as well as plastered on the walls of the loony bin I was stuck in. I read you were from these parts. I had some photos of Billie Rae. The poor, emaciated girl kinda looked like me with her sad, gaunt face and mousy-brown hair, but I wasn't sure until I saw that smiling, now-a-blonde photo of you and that gap between your front teeth... that's *exactly* like mine. It all clicked."

The gap inherited from my mother before she had a tooth knocked out. The gap Matt loved, so I never fixed it.

"I was positive you were my mother. We even have the same exact shape toes, but you were too busy on your phone to notice when we had mani-pedis. Just to be one hundred percent sure, I did a DNA test. I found your hairbrush and then sent this company—Genex Diagnostics—hair samples from you and me. The results came back positive. A ninety-nine-point-eight percent possibility that you were my mother. Oh, and by the way, I used your credit card."

The charge from Genex Diagnostics flashed into my head. At the time, I thought it was from the lab that had done blood work after Dr. Lefferman's physical.

"Natalie, you screwed up. All I've ever wanted was to have a real family. A mother and father who took care of me. And loved me."

I shared her anguish. I understood what she'd been through, but I had to placate her. I had to keep her from harming Paige.

"Tanya... I mean *Bree*. I want to make it up to you. I love you like a daughter. I promise I'll give you the perfect life. Everything you want. Your own convertible. A trip to Hawaii. Anything! You can even live with us."

She cackled. "Seriously, Natalie, do you think money can buy your way out of everything? You sick rich bitch. It's too late. You can *never* give me the perfect life. The perfect family. It's too bad you had to mess it up with Matt. Do you really think I want to live under your roof while the two of you are going through an ugly divorce and will hate each other forever?"

Paige's shocked eyes met mine. My heart splintered. I hated that she had to find out this way.

"By the way, I know Matt's dirty little secret. I caught him cheating on you one time when I went to his office but didn't say anything. A cheating father would have been a hell of a lot better than any of those foster ones, who liked to touch me in places. At least Matt's had the decency not to do that, though I bet by the way he's always looked at me he's been tempted."

It pained me deeply to hear she'd been sexually abused. But at the same time, I was relieved that Matt had never assaulted her. For a split second, I thought about him lying on an operating table, facing life or death. I hoped he'd pull through. But that thought was fleeting. Right now, there was only one person in the world whose life mattered. Who was everything to me.

Paige.

"Bree, put the gun down. If you shoot Paige, you'll be tried for cold-blooded murder. Spend the rest of your life in prison. Maybe get the death penalty. I can get you help."

"Oh, c'mon, *Mommy dearest!* Your promises are so lame!" She snorted. "And besides, you're not going to be around to do a thing."

I processed her words. She was going to shoot me!

Paige knew it too. But rather than terror, there was a look of fierce determination on her face. "You'll never get away with this, Tanya!"

"Puh-lease! I get away with everything. I stole your Stanford essay. I stole your boyfriend. I stole your mother's heart. And now I'm going to steal your life—"

"You're forgetting you stole the keys to my car. That didn't work out so well... Scarface!"

"Shut up!" she squawked at Paige, her eyes still pinned on

me. The gun still pressed into Paige's temple. "Natalie, say goodbye to your despicable daugh—"

Another voice cut her off. "Bear, get her!"

Will! What was he doing here? I'd told him to stay behind in the car. And he'd agreed.

My head spun around. I could barely see my precious son in the blinding blizzard. He was several feet behind a leash-free Bear, who was leaping toward Tanya. Almost flying and bearing his teeth.

Tanya's eyes grew wide with fear as our dog neared her.

She screamed. "Stop him! Get him away from me!"

Terror hijacking her wits, she let go of Paige.

"Paige, run!" I yelled.

I watched as she dashed off the dock, moving as fast as she could in the foot-deep snow.

Shrieking, Tanya began to back up, moving closer and closer to the edge of the dock. My eyes pinned on her, I didn't see Will run up to Bear.

"You little brat!" Tanya cried out. "You deserve to die too."

With fierce determination, she aimed the gun at him, and I thought I'd have a heart attack as she pulled the trigger. I darted in front of my son, ready to take the bullet. *Click.* Except to my utter shock, the gun didn't fire. Frantically, Tanya pressed the trigger again. *Click.* Again it didn't go off. Was it not loaded?

Totally flustered, she pressed the trigger one more time. Again *nada.* "What the fuck?" she muttered, oblivious to our dog's vicious growls.

"Bear, *sic* her!" Will yelled.

Everything happened so fast. Like a bolt of lightning, Bear charged at Tanya, going for one of her new boots. He sank his fangs into the deerskin, gnawing and tugging at the boot like it was a new toy or a piece of rawhide. Growling and barking. Growing more and more relentless and ferocious.

Terror washed over Tanya's face as she desperately tried to shake him off her leg. "Get him off of me!" she screamed.

Bear only grew more determined, more aggressive while Tanya grew more frantic and helpless in the tug-of-war battle. Her pink hat blew off, the fierce wind carrying it until it disappeared into the night. Her long blonde hair whipped across her face as our snow-loving dog stayed focused, ahead of the game. Tanya his prize. Shrieking, she suddenly lost her footing and fell backward. Frozen as a corpse, I gasped with a mixture of shock and horror as she careened into the swollen, half-frozen lake.

"Help me! Help me!" she wailed. "Please! I can't swim! *Pleeease!*" The word was long and drawn-out. A mournful, keening sound.

Paige, Will, and I gathered together and wordlessly, numbly watched her flounder. Her arms flapping. Her head bobbing in and out of the deep, icy water. The gun still in one hand. The wind whooshing, the snow blowing, I wrapped my arms around my children and drew them close to me. Bear snapped at his prey madly, his hackles rising like the teeth of a chainsaw. His deafening barks drowning out her desperate cries.

Then, as if he'd had enough, he stopped. Tilting up his snow-covered snout, he proudly howled into the cold, sober wilderness. *The Call of the Wild.* I'd once read that a dog howling was an omen of death. Tanya was near hers. He'd gotten his revenge.

Paige always said: *Where there's a Will, there's a way.* She was right. The gun sank. And so did she.

There was nothing we could do. For sure we'd all freeze to death in the frigid water trying to haul her to shore. I'd lost too many children and couldn't risk losing more.

Revenge was *not* a dish best served cold.

Ice-cold.

It tasted bitter.

A sudden, unexpected sadness swept over me. As mentally

ill as she was, Tanya was my daughter and much more. I had loved her and now I'd lost her. She would never know who her father was. That secret would remain mine alone until the day I died.

I hugged Paige and Will closer to me. After Anabel's death, I had lost them, too, in some way, but here they were hugging me back. My beloved children.

I was far from being the perfect mother, but at this moment, I felt like the luckiest mother in the world.

SIXTY-THREE

PAIGE

Ten months later: October

Dearest Grandma,

*I love RISD! I'm one month in and it's even more than I
expected. The student body is as extraordinary as the
faculty. For the first time, I feel like I fit in, like I've
found my tribe. And Providence is really cool too—with
its thrift stores, art galleries, and coffee shops—such an
eclectic blend of colonial and cutting-edge architecture.
Thank you, Grandma, for the BEST gift of my life!
I'm taking a big course load, a mix of art history classes
and fine arts. I have an advisor who thinks I'm a really
gifted sculptor, and he's already put me in an advanced
sculpting class. I'm working with marble! At the end of
freshman year, one of my creations will be exhibited at
the RISD Museum. I hope you will come here and see it.*

*And guess what? I have a new boyfriend. His name is
Aiden and he's from New York City. He grew up in the*

West Village (his parents are both artists) and he's really cool. Plus, he's a vegan. He wants to be a fashion photographer and can even make me look like a supermodel.

Lance (remember him?) has texted me numerous times, begging me to get in touch with him, but I've not responded. He's ancient history now. He didn't get into Brown or any of his top picks. He's going to UC Davis, and in one of his texts, he said he hates it. That's karma for you. You get what you deserve. Just like what my best friend, Jordan, always says.

I miss Will terribly and FaceTime with him daily. He's doing great despite Mom and Dad's separation, juggling weekdays with Mom and weekends with Dad. Right after Dad moved out of the house, Mom got Will another dog, a super-cute black Lab rescue, which Will named Pixel; she's a girl and loves Bear. Will says she reminds him of me because she can leap five feet in the air to catch a ball. Oh, I almost forgot to tell you... I'm starting up a girls' basketball team!

More exciting news! Will's team won a gold medal in the national high school robotics competition. Oh, and one more thing... Will has a girlfriend... an Asian girl on his team named Lisa. I'm so happy my brother is going for smart, unusual girls.

Well, that's it for now. I can't wait to see everyone and hear all about your trip over Thanksgiving break.

I love you so much!

xoPaige

A smile blooms on my face as I fold the letter and seal it in a stamped envelope. Grandma despises emails and texts; she'll be so happy to get my handwritten note, a lost art form, she says, when she and Grandpa get back next week from their three-month around-the-world cruise. Draining my latte, I gather my backpack, dash out of the campus coffee shop, and drop the letter in a mailbox en route to my favorite class.

The class takes place in a massive studio in a building known as Memorial Hall. There are only ten kids in the class and we each have our own workspace. Today Professor Fratianne, a renowned sculptor himself, is playing classical music—Vivaldi's *The Four Seasons*—a piece my mom played at her black-tie gala, which now seems like ages ago.

So much has happened since then. As I sit at my drafting table and chisel the slab of marble before me, I think about the paths my parents' lives have taken. Paralyzed from the waist down from his skiing accident, my father is now living in a one-floor apartment and gets around in his state-of-the-art power chair. Will and I are both glad he pulled through, though Mom seems ambivalent. She says things happen for a reason. She's still in the house, though likely not for long once their divorce is finalized ("irreconcilable differences," whatever that means), but seriously, who would want to live in that house with all those bad memories? Will thinks Dad has a girlfriend—his round-the-clock blonde nurse. That wouldn't surprise me.

My mother, I must say, *has* surprised me. Given all that happened, she pulled through. I think she still takes Xanax and drinks a couple of glasses of wine nightly—maybe an entire bottle—but if that's all it takes to get her through another day, that's fine by me. Her break-up with my father came as quite a shock to her highfalutin friends. It was the talk of the town, so she stopped volunteering with all those catty women and got a real, paying job as the Director of Development for Girls Like Us, a nonprofit that helps abused girls find loving families and meaningful jobs. Instead of planning galas, she now spends her time creating marketing materials and reviewing grants. I'm so proud of her.

We've refrained from talking about what happened in Big Bear. The police ruled it an accidental drowning and were glad none of us was hurt. It's something we all want to put behind us. Once, however, I asked my mom who Bree's father was. She told me it didn't matter; he was dead. She was also closed off when I asked about her childhood and the night her parents were murdered. Showing no emotion, she told me she had an uneventful childhood and couldn't remember a thing about that night. "PTSD. Post-traumatic stress disorder," she said. It must have been beyond awful for her to watch her parents get stabbed to death and then get taken by the madman. I can't even imagine.

My brother doesn't know all the sordid details. That Tanya is—or should I say *was*—our half-sister. He was too far away to overhear Mom's startling revelation with the wind gusting and Bear barking. My mom wants to keep it that way—"our little secret"—at least until he's older. Like my mom, I'm a great secret keeper, but often wish I could confide in him. And ask Sherlock if he thinks her parents' murderer held her captive and raped her. And fathered a child. I often wonder how she and the baby managed to escape him. I can't help thinking... *did she kill him?*

Grandma says some questions are better left unanswered. I guess I'll never know. For my mom, Billie Rae Perkins no longer exists. In her mind, she's dead.

Despite who Tanya-slash-Bree was and what she did, I believe my mother truly loved her.

Sometimes I've wondered what Tanya would have been like had she not been abandoned and had instead grown up with us in our house. Maybe she would have been sporty, sassy, and caring. The big sister I'd always wished for but never had.

Though her body was never found, my mother gave her a memorial that only she and I attended. She erected a resting place, right next to her half-sister, my sister, Anabel. Both tombstones are inscribed with the words:

An extraordinary daughter, sister, and friend.
Let the sunshine in.

While my mother covered the side-by-side gravesites with sprays of indigo-blue forget-me-nots and sobbed, I held her hand. It's the closest I ever felt to her.

The marble sculpture I'm working on—the one that I plan to exhibit—is called *Sisters*. It's a dark, twisted, complex abstraction.

After the exhibition, I'm going to give it to my mom.

SIXTY-FOUR

NATALIE

The following month: November

The desert wind pelts against my face as I cruise down the 10 in my Mercedes, the top down. It's unusually hot for November, maybe a hundred degrees, and though I have the air-conditioning blasting, it does little to thwart the heat. The blazing sun beats down on me, but inside my body I feel a chill.

I haven't been back here for over twenty years. It hasn't changed much. The desert looks the same, with its glistening white sand, sagebrush, and cacti. Surrounding me, the San Bernardino Mountains soar into the turquoise sky, licking the puffs of cotton-ball clouds. Trailers line the road. Murderers and serial killers lurk inside them. Bad men. Bad women. And maybe some bad kids.

After this past year, I'm more uncertain than ever if all children are born good with the events of their lives and socio-economic environment shaping them, *or* if some are hardwired to evil through genetic material handed down to them. Can our DNA predispose us to psychopathic behavior and acts of violence, as if they're an inherited disease? Even when I think about myself, the choices I've made, I can't help wondering. Nature or nurture?

I turn on the radio to distract myself from these deeply troubling thoughts to a random country music channel. Ironically, John Denver's "Take Me Home, Country Roads" is playing. I can't be far from where I grew up. Another chill. I think about turning around, but will myself to continue. To drive past the roots of my evil.

Five minutes later, I reach the location and get a jolt. The trailer park is gone. Instead, on the beige, acrid grounds where it used to be, there's a giant Walmart with a parking lot packed with cars, SUVs, and minivans in every color. They sparkle like jewels under the hot desert sun.

Relief floods me. Yet erasure, no matter how complete, isn't the same as forgetting. A Walmart, no matter how vast, can't erase my past. I can't erase my past. It's not possible. It's mine to own alone forever. The truth is, I've never totally shed that skin. We carry our past selves in tight layers as time goes by. Inside me, I've always been *that* girl, the one whose sins bind me at my core.

A few miles later, I turn off the road and head into Indio. Following my GPS, I come to a small New England-style church. Saint Ignatius. I pull into the gravel parking lot and park my car in one of the many empty spots, it being Wednesday, not Sunday. I push a button and the top of my convertible goes up as I unbuckle my seat belt. I take a deep breath and exit the car. I feel the oppressive heat. The oppressive weight of my heart.

While the architecture of the church hasn't changed much since I was here twenty years ago, it looks different. The once peeling gray clapboards have been repaired and painted with a bright coat of white. There are more succulents around the edifice and the flowering shrubs have grown. The cracked brick steps leading up to the entrance have been repaired and new hand railings have been installed. My gaze travels up to the cross that still sits on top of the gabled roof, then back down to the glass-paned front door. Now a shiny red, it, too, looks newly painted.

Slowly, carefully, I mount the three steps leading up to the entrance. I remember climbing them, exhausted from my life-and-death birthing ordeal, my torn insides so sore, and worried the decayed bricks would give out, and I'd take a tumble. I was holding a sheepskin-lined basket, a gift from the lovely Morongo women who'd taken me in, the tiny life-form inside it peeking out from under a colorful woven blanket. My nameless two-day-old baby. I couldn't bear to look down at her because she reminded me of *him*. The monster. So dark and hairy with his cleft chin. Keeping my eyes straight ahead, I crouched down and deposited the basket on the landing in front of the church door. She began to howl. Loud, sharp, ugly wails. Cries that seemed to be screaming, *please don't leave me*. I wanted to cover my ears with my hands. Or smother her. I did neither.

Instead, I gave her the softest of kisses on her wrinkled red forehead, my tears mingling with hers. She stopped crying and reached out to me, as if she wanted to take hold of my heart, and curled her tiny fingers around one of mine. I remember how forceful her grip was, like she didn't want to let go of me.

"You're strong, baby girl. Follow your dreams. Do better than me," I whispered.

Before I could change my mind, I stood and left her behind... *and* the girl I was as I knew her.

Without looking back, I hurried down the steps. Tears rained down my face as I ran to the Greyhound bus station down the street. With the money I'd found under my mother's mattress, I purchased a one-way ticket to Los Angeles. The City of Angels. The City of Dreams. Sitting alone in the back seat as the bus cruised up the 10, I couldn't stop thinking of my baby. Of the horrible thing I'd just done. Despite who her father was, she was still born from my flesh and blood. Tearfully, I prayed that she'd end up in the loving home of a childless couple. That she'd never be hungry or unloved. Or be anything like him.

I know now my prayers weren't answered. And I believe God punished me by taking away my Anabel. His own cruel game of tit for tat.

Karma.

The toll of church bells startles me and hurtles me back to the moment. I curl my fingers around the polished brass handle and pull the church door open. It's heavier than I thought. I let it close behind me. It makes a soft thud as I step inside the chapel. The air-conditioning is a welcome relief from the blistering heat.

I've never been inside this church. Though my mother was a God-fearing woman and told me God was going to strike me down if I didn't behave and do all her crap chores, we never went to church together on Sundays. She was usually too hungover. And I didn't have a means of transportation for getting here. I knew about the church because we drove past it in her dirty, beat-up Pinto every time she needed a pack of cigarettes or a bottle of booze.

Standing frozen in place, I take in the sanctuary. It's very different from Saint Andrew's, the majestic church I belong to in Los Angeles. Yet there's beauty in its simplicity. My eyes wander from the vaulted ceiling to the wood pews that can accommodate at most two hundred parishioners, and the stained-glass windows that let the sun shine in. Exalt it. To the right, I eye a pair of nuns lighting candles; they look as old as the church and I wonder if one of them found my abandoned baby. I'm not going to ask. Neither of them notices me. After they leave, I light two candles, one after the other, and say a prayer. *For them.*

Shortly afterward, I find the confessional. Sucking in a breath, I work up the courage and tread over to it. A small gold-metal cross sits on the apex of the wooden box and in front of the confessional window there's a wooden chair.

Bracing myself, I lower myself onto the chair. It is hard and uncomfortable. I tap my forehead, chest, and shoulders, and murmur, "In the name of the Father, the Son, and the Holy Spirit... Amen." And then fold my hands in prayer on my lap. Through the sheer red fabric shrouding the window, I can see a shadow of the priest behind it. His profile. He looks surprisingly young. Possibly handsome.

I clear my throat, and with a shaky breath, I begin.

"Bless me, Father, for I have sinned."

"My child, when was your last confession?"

His soothing voice is deep and melodic. A balm.

"Father, forgive me for I have never confessed before."

He nods. "There is nothing to forgive. There's a first time for everyone."

Relieved he doesn't sound angry or judgmental, I push on. My voice grows stronger.

"Father, these are my sins...

"I killed my father." *In self-defense.*

"I killed my mother." *For allowing him to rape me.*

"I abandoned a child." *Who reminded me of him.*

"Then watched her drown." *Left her for dead.*

"I shoved another child down the stairs. She fell to her death. It was an accident." *Maybe it wasn't.*

"I thought about killing my husband." *I never had the chance.*

I pause and catch my breath. "Father, I have one other confession... After I stabbed my parents, I hitched a ride with a girl from out of town, an aspiring actress, who was a few years older than me. She was heading to Los Angeles but wanted to stop and hike up Tahquitz Canyon to see the waterfall at the top. Halfway up, a brush fire broke out. As we ran down the trail to escape it, she tripped on a rock and hit her head."

I swallow back the memory, past the lump in my throat.

"In a panic, the blaze coming at us, I abandoned her and stole her identity."

Tears sear my cheeks. I cannot stop them.

Her name was Natalie Taylor.

"Father, for these sins, I am truly sorry."

I get down on my knees and beg for forgiveness.

EPILOGUE

TIFFANY

Three months earlier: August

"I'm so excited to be here, Mrs. Richmond! I've never been to Miami before."

"Please call me Catherine," she says as her Audi convertible cruises along the busy I-19. "Our family is so happy to have you as our guest."

A warm tropical breeze whips my ponytail against my cheeks while I hold onto the Miami Dolphins hat I stole at the airport so it won't fly off. I don't tell her I've never been in a convertible because it's not true. Like families, I've learned you have to choose lies wisely.

Toned and tan, my new host tucks her perfectly highlighted blonde bob behind her ears. "You're going to love it here! There's so much to do. Wait till we go to South Beach. It's such a scene! And the shopping's to die for."

Urban, here I come with my hotter than ever body. "Can't wait!" I chew my Trident gum and crack a bubble. "I'm so lucky Papa let me go to college in America. The University of Miami sounds like the bomb."

Catherine chuckles. "Funnily, my brainiac daughter, Quinn, hates it and wants to go to Oxford next year."

Ta-ta! She'll be lucky if she makes it through this year alive.

Thank goodness she doesn't have a murderous little brother. But she does have this really hot older brother, Zach, who attends the university's law school. Marriage material. *Tiffany Richmond.* In my head, the name sings on my tongue. There's a method to my madness if you haven't noticed.

Chatty Cathy cuts into my romantic fantasy. "We have an adorable little dog. A Maltipoo. Her name is Pouf. P-O-U-F." She glances in the rearview mirror. "I should warn you though. She's rather yappy and is an ankle biter."

"No worries." At least she's small. With a little luck, I'm going to make Pouf go poof. Magically disappear.

My host-slash-future mother-in-law flashes her blinker. "This is our exit. We'll be at our house in no time. Wait till you see it. It looks like a Mediterranean villa in the South of France and has a swimming pool with cabanas. I hope you love to swim."

I feel my heart hiccup. The memory of falling into that freezing lake, clinging to a piece of driftwood, and miraculously floating to safety makes me shudder. I almost drowned.

Then, the most heartsickening, gut-wrenching thought infiltrates my mind... my mother, my very own mother, left me there to die. I'll never get over that and maybe, just maybe, she'll pay the price and...

I shove that thought out of my mind and switch the subject. "Hey, can we play some music?"

"Of course, dear. What do you like to listen to?"

"I like old-school stuff."

"Me too!" She turns on the radio. Blasts it. "I already love you like a daughter!"

Britney Spears roars on. How can you not love her after all she's been through?

I sing along.
"Oops... I Did It Again."

A LETTER FROM NELLE

Dear Reader,

Thank you from the bottom of my heart for choosing to read *The Family Guest*. I plan to write more psychological suspense thrillers, and if you want to keep up to date with all my latest releases, just sign up at the following link. Your email address will never be shared and you can unsubscribe at any time.

www.bookouture.com/nelle-lamarr

I hope you loved *The Family Guest* and would be super appreciative if you could write a review. I look forward to hearing what you think, and regardless of length, please know reviews help new readers discover my books.

I know that many of you belong to thriller and suspense reader groups on Facebook. I would be forever so grateful if you would mention *The Family Guest* in one or more of those groups and include a link. I myself find new wonderful books to read in these groups. Honestly, there's nothing like word of mouth! So spread the word as well to your Goodreads friends, family members, book clubs, and other social media. And please join my Facebook reader group, Nelle's Belles, to share your love and learn more about my books.

Under the pen name Nelle L'Amour, I write romance. If you like twisty suspense with a dose of steam, you may enjoy the following books: *Jane Deyre*, *Butterfly*, *Remember Me*, and

The Bell Ringer. You can find links to them and my other books on my website.

I love hearing from my readers! You can get in touch with me via my Facebook page, Twitter, Goodreads, and my website. And you can also email me: nellelamarr@gmail.com. I especially love getting emails and personally respond to each and every one.

Thank you again for reading *The Family Guest*. I feel so honored, and I look forward to bringing you more gripping psychological thrillers in the near future.

MWAH! – Nelle

www.nellelamour.com

www.goodreads.com/author/show/40453486.Nelle_Lamarr

facebook.com/groups/194375087586301 5

 twitter.com/nellelamour1

 instagram.com/nellelamourauthor

bookbub.com/authors/nelle-lamarr

ACKNOWLEDGMENTS

First, I want to thank the entire Bookouture team for welcoming me to their amazing "family" and giving *The Family Guest* a wonderful home. A big shout-out goes to my brilliant editor, Jess Whitlum-Cooper, for passionately championing *The Family Guest* from the beginning and for working so hard to make this book the very best it could be. This was my first time working with an editor at a major publishing house, and I will admit I was scared. My fears, however, proved unfounded as Jess made the experience such a fun and mutually rewarding collaboration. Thank you for the long phone calls, your cheery sense of humor, and for always being there for me. I so enjoyed rising to your challenges to make the book tighter and "punchier." I love that word, Jess, and could not have asked for a better editor!

A collective thanks goes to my eagle-eye copy editor and proofreader, Donna Hillyer and Becca Allen, my amazing cover designer, my awesome audiobook narrators, as well as all the other hardworking members of the editorial, marketing, and publicity teams, who helped make this book happen. I also want to thank Bookouture's head of foreign rights, Richard King, and Sara Barszczowska of Harper Collins Germany for believing in my book. It's been wonderful working with all of you and I hope to do it again soon.

I also owe heartfelt gratitude to my beta readers, who read an early draft. A special thank you goes to my dear friends and fellow Bookouture authors Freida "McFab" McFadden and

Arianne Richmonde, whose brutal honesty and encouragement made me rethink one of the major plot twists and ultimately helped get the book into the world. I also want to thank authors Lorraine Evanoff and Auden Dar for their insightful suggestions, love, and support, as well as Marti Jentis, Lisa Saunders, Stephanie Burdette, and Judy Zweifel, who proof-read the draft I sent to Bookouture.

As always, I am grateful for my supportive family as well as my beloved fur babies, Pepper and Poppy, for putting up with me as I wrote and edited this book. A kiss goes to my hubby, who helped me with some troublesome scenes. I owe you big time! More than dinner!

In this social media world, I must also acknowledge the bloggers, Bookstagrammers, and BookTokkers who've read and reviewed *The Family Guest*. You're all so awesome! Thank you so much!

A hug along with a signed paperback goes to my beautiful and brilliant friend Angela Weltman, who many years ago shared stories of an evil exchange student who came to live with her family. Well, she was hardly as evil as Tanya, but she was my inspiration. Who knew at the time that her machinations would lead to this book!

Last but not least, a massive thank-you to all of my readers and listeners. You are the reason I write.

Made in the USA
Columbia, SC
24 April 2024